The Carolina Emerald

Kimberley West Gemstone Mysteries Book 3

By Lynn Franklin

Copyright

The Carolina Emerald: Kimberley West Gemstone Mystery
#3
by Lynn Franklin
© 2017 by Lynn Franklin

eBook: ISBN 978-0-9855457-5-8
Print: ISBN 978-0-9855457-6-5

Also by Lynn Franklin

Kimberley West Gemstone Mystery Series

The Blue Diamond
The Pirate's Ruby
The Carolina Emerald
The Turquoise Treasure

Novellas

The Poodle Who Picked Pockets

Readers' Specials

The Diamond Digest
Go to **LynnFranklin.com** to join

A Note from Lynn:

I've never been the greatest speller, so all of my books and stories are extensively reviewed by professional editors and proofreaders. If, however, you find an error, please email me at **Lynn@LynnFranklin.com** so I can fix it.

Actually, you can email me even if you don't find problems. I love to hear from my readers. You are the reason that I write.

LynnFranklin.com

Dedication

To Joan Rose

Sister, editor extraordinaire, so-so photographer
and all-around friend.
This book couldn't have been written without you.
Thank you for always being there.

CONTENTS

PROLOGUE

22 Years Ago
American Museum of Natural History, New York

"Did I ever tell you about the jewel theft that occurred right where we're standing?"

At the sound of her grandfather's voice, ten-year-old Kimberley West turned away from the museum's display of natural emeralds. The twinkle in Grandpa's eyes warned her this could be a trick question.

Even so, she couldn't resist showing off.

"You mean the story about Murph the Surf?" she said. "You told me about him when I was a baby."

Max Hershey tried but failed to stop his grin. His favorite granddaughter wasn't much older than a baby. Yet from the moment she could hold a book in her own hands, she'd insisted he tell her "real" bedtime stories, not those "baby, made-up things."

So he'd told her about The Great Diamond Hoax and the Black Prince Ruby imposter and the Hope Diamond curse.

And, yeah, he'd probably shared the tale of Jack Roland Murphy, Florida beach bum turned jewel thief. Murphy had broken into the American Museum of Natural History by swinging on a rope, Tarzan style, through an open window. He'd stolen a priceless collection of jewels, including the golf-ball size Star of India sapphire residing not far from where they stood.

Murphy and his cohorts had been captured and most of the stolen jewels returned to the museum.

Max grinned down at his precocious granddaughter.

"This is a different burglary," he said. "Most people don't know about it because it was never solved."

As expected, Kim's eyes widened.

"Oh, wow, a real mystery? Tell me, tell me!"

Grandpa grinned and pulled out his pocket watch. Flipping it open, he glanced at the face. "How 'bout lunch in the museum cafeteria? I can tell you the story while we eat."

Kim cast one last longing glance at the emeralds, then fell into step beside Grandpa. This was turning into the best trip ever.

Early this morning, they'd ridden a train from Baltimore to New York City. A taxi carried them from the train station to New York's Diamond District. They'd spent an hour visiting the wholesale gem and jewelry shops that Grandpa used to stock his Osprey Beach store. After completing his business, he'd hailed a taxi to take them to the American Museum of Natural History.

They'd explored the dinosaur exhibit, then strolled through the Hall of Minerals. As they walked, Grandpa described how rocks could contain minerals like emeralds, rubies and diamonds, explained the difference between metamorphic, sedimentary and igneous rocks, told stories about the California Gold Rush. Finally, he led her to the Hall of Gems to view some of the world's most famous gemstones.

First stop: the blue-gray Star of India sapphire. Unlike most of the sapphires she'd seen in Grandpa's store, this one contained no facets. Instead, the gem had been smoothed and rounded into a ball-like shape. A thin, six-sided white star spread across the sapphire's surface.

The star, Grandpa explained, was caused by a mineral called rutile. Light coming into the stone, he said, reflected off the thin fibers of the rutile to create the star shape. Jewelers called the process "asterism."

They'd studied several more gemstones with stars on them. Finally, they'd approached the emerald display that showcased the museum's famous Patricia Emerald.

At 600-some carats and stretching 3 inches long, the Patricia wasn't the largest emerald ever discovered. But its unusual shape -- 12-sided instead of the usual 6-sided -- and intense green color left no doubt that the stone belonged in a museum.

As a jeweler's granddaughter, Kim had seen her share of gems, both raw and faceted. What intrigued her most about this emerald was the gem's name -- Patricia. The man who'd discovered the stone had named it after his daughter.

Oh, how she'd love for someone to name a gemstone after her!

Problem was, no one in her family was likely to discover an important gemstone. Grandpa was too busy selling gems to go digging for them. Their occasional fossil-hunting excursions were confined to locations near her hometown of Osprey Beach. Besides, Maryland's shoreline might be a good place to hunt for fossils, but she'd never heard of an important gemstone discovery in the state.

Mom and Dad, both school teachers, showed little interest in gem hunting. And forget her aunts;

Mom's three sisters wouldn't be caught dead getting their fingernails dirty.

They reached the cafeteria to find it crowded with other tourists, school children on field trips and teachers. She smelled hamburgers, french fries and . . . Was that pizza? Yes!

She loaded her tray with two slices of pepperoni pizza and a large Coke and followed Grandpa to a small table by the windows.

Biting into the pizza, she savored the flavor of tomato sauce, basil and oregano. Grandpa chewed his slice without seeming to taste it. His eyes focused on some distant thought.

Recognizing the behavior as Grandpa's "where to start the story" expression, Kim set down her pizza.

"It's okay, Grandpa," she said. "You can start at the very beginning."

Though she was anxious to hear about the unsolved burglary, she knew Grandpa loved to add history to his stories.

Grandpa smiled, returned his pizza to its plate and reached for a napkin.

"How much have I told you about emeralds?" He wiped his fingers.

"Uh, they break easily so I should tell people to buy earrings or necklaces instead of rings and bracelets," she said.

"What else?"

When she didn't respond immediately, he added, "Didn't you write a history report about Egypt?"

"Oh, yeah!" She grinned at Grandpa. "The first emeralds were found in Egypt and Cleopatra loved them so much that she ordered her slaves to keep digging until they'd found them all. And after Cleopatra died, everyone thought there were no more emeralds anywhere in the world. But then they found emeralds in South America. And that's where all of our emeralds now come from."

Grandpa's lips spread into the biggest smile and his eyes sparkled. For a moment, Kim basked in her grandfather's approval.

"Very good." He leaned forward. "But South America isn't the only country where you can find emeralds. There are emeralds here in the U.S."

Kim felt her mouth drop open. "Where?"

"North Carolina."

"You mean, like, the state south of Virginia?"

Grandpa nodded. "Emeralds were first discovered there in the late 1800s. A North Carolina farmer found one when he was plowing his field. He poked around, found some more. Word spread and several mining companies began digging in the area.

"They found more emeralds. But they also found a totally new mineral, a yellowish green stone no one had ever seen before. They named it Hiddenite, in honor of Mr. Hidden, the mineralogist who discovered the stone."

He reached for his pizza.

"They later named a nearby town Hiddenite," he added before taking a bite.

While he chewed, Kim reflected that finding a new mineral and naming it after herself would be awesome. Even better than relying on someone else to name a gemstone after her.

Maybe she could talk Aunt Ginny, Dad's sister, into driving to North Carolina. Aunt Ginny had promised her an overnight trip "when you're older." That was a year ago; she was older now.

Even if she didn't find a totally new mineral like Hiddenite, she might uncover a huge emerald, one that would make the Patricia Emerald look puny.

She imagined digging under the hot sun, her hair pulled into a ponytail, her glasses slipping down her nose, sweat dripping off her forehead-- Yuk.

Maybe she could find her new mineral someplace cooler.

"Anyway," Grandpa said, "one of the mining companies found an emerald this big."

He held up his hands, six or eight inches apart.

"That's way bigger than the Patricia Emerald," Kim said.

Grandpa nodded. "The Patricia is a single crystal. The Carolina Emerald consisted of three crystals fused together at the base."

He reached for a clean napkin, pulled a pen from his shirt pocket and began sketching.

Kim leaned across the table, but couldn't make sense of the lines he was drawing.

Her mind drifted to the new mineral she planned to discover. What would she name it? The word Kimberlite was already taken; it referred to a rare type of rock that often contained diamonds.

Maybe she could call it Kimberleyite?

No, that didn't sound right.

The restaurant suddenly grew louder as a new group of school children tramped in and lined up at the hot-food station.

Kim idly studied them. Like the adults she'd seen, most of the kids wore dressier clothes than Kim's friends in Osprey Beach.

Grandpa had insisted she wear her new jeans today, explaining that people in cities tended to dress up and people in New York dressed up even more than most. She hated the stiffness of new jeans. But now, looking at the pressed khakis on the boys and the flounced skirts on the girls, she felt grateful she hadn't worn the jeans with the hole in the knee . . .

Wait a minute. That boy wasn't wearing fancy clothes.

He stood near the end of the line, shoulders slouched, hands stuffed into a baggy pair of worn pants that were obviously hand-me-downs. He stared at the floor, trying to ignore the obvious gap between himself and the kids in front of and behind him.

Grandpa turned the napkin around and slid the drawing toward her.

"That remind you of anything?"

She studied the three-dimensional sketch. Grandpa had drawn the classic long, six-sided bolts. A central crystal was bookended by two shorter ones. The fused crystals formed a slight V-shape, the base maybe half the size of the top.

"It looks like a castle."

"A green castle?"

"The Emerald City! Where Dorothy went."

She pictured the poster of The Wizard of Oz that hung on her bedroom wall. Whenever she looked at it, she tended to focus on the characters in the front -- Dorothy, the Scarecrow, the Tin Man, the Cowardly Lion and, of course, Toto.

But behind Dorothy's right shoulder loomed the green towers of the Emerald City. And those towers looked a lot like the emerald Grandpa had drawn.

She tapped the drawing. "Was this the model for the Emerald City?"

"No, that isn't possible. The museum didn't display the Carolina Emerald until a year after The Wizard of Oz book was published. But I'm sure the author -- Frank Baum -- must have seen other rough emeralds before writing his book."

"Can we go see this emerald next?"

Grandpa shook his head. "I'm afraid the Carolina Emerald was stolen and never recovered."

Kim's heart raced. So this was the unsolved mystery.

"Tell me," she said.

Grandpa grinned. "This happened in 1950, maybe a dozen years before Murph the Surf staged his burglary. The thief climbed a fire escape and entered through an unsecured window. The police thought the thief had visited the museum earlier in the day to unlock the window. Once inside, he broke into the case that displayed the Carolina Emerald."

"Didn't the alarm scare him away?"

"There were no alarms on the display cases. Only the doors and ground-floor windows had alarms. The Museum board members thought those alarms, coupled with the guards, would stop potential thieves."

"Couldn't they see the guy's face on the cameras?"

"They didn't have security cameras in those days."

Kim sank back into her chair. What good was a mystery if you didn't have clues to follow?

"The New York police interrogated all known jewel thieves," Grandpa added. "They all had solid alibis. The chief investigator was frustrated.

"But then he received a call from a sheriff in North Carolina."

Kim perked up. "North Carolina? Where the emerald was discovered?"

"Yep. The sheriff claimed the thieves were a couple of local men named Sawyer and Hicks."

"Why did he suspect those guys?"

"Their ancestors discovered the emerald. This was in the late 1800s. Sawyer and Hicks worked for a mining company. They were promised a bonus for every large emerald they uncovered.

"I don't remember the details, but after Sawyer and Hicks found the emerald, the foreman fired them. The mine owners refused to pay them a bonus."

Kim folded her arms. "That's so not fair."

"No, it's not. But there were no unions in those days to protect mine workers.

"Twenty years later, the millionaire J.P. Morgan purchased a collection of gems that included the Carolina Emerald and donated it to the American Museum of Natural History. Morgan paid $100,000 for the gems, which was a fortune in those days.

"When Sawyer and Hicks read about the purchase and donation, they once again confronted the mine foreman and demanded the bonus they'd been promised. The foreman told them the decision to not pay them was made by the mine owner. So the men drove to the owner's office. The mine owner refused to pay the bonus and ordered guards to throw Sawyer and Hicks from the building.

"As you can imagine, the men grew bitter. They passed the story to their sons and daughters, who passed it to their children. With each re-telling, the mine owner grew more sinister, the Sawyers and Hicks more heroic."

"Sort of like the telephone game?" Kim's teacher had used the telephone game to demonstrate the dangers of gossip. She'd whispered a sentence into a child's ear. That child whispered the sentence to the person next to her. The children continued to pass the sentence from one to another. The last person to hear the sentence then related it out loud.

It bore no resemblance to the original message.

Grandpa nodded. "Exactly like the telephone game. The North Carolina sheriff told the New York detective that the current generation of Sawyers and Hicks honestly believed the mine owner had stolen the emerald from their ancestors."

The noise in the cafeteria was steadily growing. Kim leaned forward, trying to hear Grandpa over the sound of chairs scraping and trays plopping onto a nearby table. Looked like the school kids she'd seen standing in line. They'd loaded their trays with salads, hamburgers, fries, cakes, cookies, brownies -- almost everything on the menu. How did they expect to eat all of that food?

The boy with the overlarge clothes set his almost-empty tray onto the table. As he pulled out his chair, the boys on either side of him scooted their chairs away.

Kim watched the boy reach for the ketchup bottle. But instead of shaking some onto his hotdog -- the cheapest thing on the menu -- he dumped a plop into a cup of hot water. He stirred until the concoction looked like a watery tomato soup, then took a careful sip.

Grandpa's next words dragged her focus away from the boy.

"The sheriff told the New York cops that on the night of the museum burglary, the Sawyer and Hicks families were visiting New York."

"Really?" Now here was a clue worth pursuing.

"When city police went to the hotel where the families were staying, they learned Sawyer and Hicks had already checked out-- Why do you keep looking over my shoulder?"

Kim met her grandfather's eyes.

"I'm sorry. It's just that there's this boy over there and the other kids are ignoring him. He kind of reminds me of how everyone used to treat Mary."

Mary Schultz had moved to Osprey Beach several months ago. Her owl-like glasses and hand-me-down clothes made her an obvious target for Brittany Bonnet, the wealthy classroom bully. While the other girls avoided Mary, Brittany taunted and teased her.

Grandpa had taught Kim to never back down from a bully. So when Mary revealed herself as a loyal, trustworthy friend, Kim helped her confront Brittany.

The boy at the next table didn't appear to have any supporters.

"He made soup out of ketchup," Kim added.

Grandpa turned in his chair in time to see a new boy brush past ketchup boy, "accidentally" elbowing him in the shoulder.

Grandpa frowned and scanned the room. He found the teachers at a separate table, laughing and joking and paying no attention to the children they should be guarding.

Excusing himself, he crossed the room to the teachers' table and leaned over to interrupt the conversation.

Kim's eyes darted from Grandpa to ketchup boy. He'd finished his makeshift soup and hotdog and now eyed the chocolate cake being wolfed down by the boy who'd elbowed him. The longing in ketchup boy's eyes made Kim's stomach clench.

The teachers were now frowning at Grandpa. Grandpa retained his pleasant expression, the one he used with bossy customers. One of the teachers said something Kim couldn't hear. Grandpa responded, tipped an imaginary hat and started back to their table.

Kim dug into her jeans pocket and set the contents in front of her: two pieces of Swiss chocolate, her favorite marble and a nickel.

She'd forgotten that she'd already used her allowance money to purchase a book on digging for dinosaur fossils.

Five cents wouldn't pay for a slice of cake.

Grandpa returned, but remained standing. He pulled out his pocket watch and glanced at the time.

"If we're going to visit the Metropolitan's Egyptian exhibit before taking the train home, we'd better leave. Do you want dessert first?"

Kim stuffed the money and marble back into her pocket.

"No, thanks; I have candy."

She followed Grandpa toward the exit. As they skirted the tables, however, Kim detoured toward the table of boys. She set the candy in front of ketchup boy. She felt him turn to look at her, but continued walking, not wanting to see his reaction or that of his seat mates.

She caught up with her grandfather and asked, "So what happened when the police learned the Sawyer and Hicks families weren't at the hotel?"

"They called the North Carolina sheriff and asked him to interview the men. But the men's wives claimed their husbands had disappeared the night they returned from the trip."

"Did they ever find them?"

"Found their bodies in the woods. Looked like they'd had an argument, pulled out guns and shot each other."

Kim's stomach clenched as she tried to imagine two dead guys in the woods. On television, bad guys shot each other all the time. But these had been real people with real families. Fisting her hands, she pushed the image away.

"What about the emerald?"

"The sheriff searched the men's houses but didn't find it. He decided the men must have buried the emerald. He dug up their yards and the area near the place where they'd died. He didn't find anything."

"So maybe those guys didn't steal the emerald?" Kim knew from the mystery books she read that suspects should be considered innocent until proven guilty.

"Maybe. But if not them, who? And where is the emerald today?"

They paused at the base of the outside stairs. Grandpa pulled out his map of New York. While he studied it, Kim stared up at the museum.

Above the doors, someone had engraved the words "Truth, Knowledge, Vision." Four stone pedestals held statues of men, but they were too far away to discern features.

"Grandpa? Who are those guys up there?"

Her grandfather turned to look.

"Those are a few famous explorers." He pointed at two standing side by side. "Those are Lewis and Clark. Over there is Daniel Boone. And that fellow there is John Audubon, the man who drew all those pictures of birds."

He glanced back down at the map. "The Metropolitan Museum is on the other side of Central Park. Looks like we need to take a bus or taxi."

"Taxi, please!" Kim said.

Grandpa smiled, then peered at traffic, searching for an unoccupied taxi cab.

"Grandpa? Did the stolen emerald have a name, you know, like the Patricia Emerald?"

"Not that I know of." He waved at a cab and watched it pull to the curb. "I've always called it the Carolina Emerald."

Kim grinned and bounced into the taxi's back seat. She turned to stare up at the four adventurers and the engraved words "Truth, Knowledge, Vision."

Today Grandpa had revealed what was known about the unsolved mystery. That gave her knowledge. Now she needed to use her vision to find the truth.

She promised herself that someday she'd search for and find the Carolina Emerald. Then she'd return it to the museum.

And the museum officials would be so grateful they'd name the gemstone "The Kimberley Emerald."

CHAPTER 1

Present Day
Hiddenite, North Carolina

The "no trespassing" signs were riddled with bullet holes, but Kimberley West ignored them. Staring into the North Carolina forest that swept past her car window, she searched the terrain for geological clues to the treasure hidden beneath the dense underbrush.

A cardinal's distinctive cheer-cheer drifted through the open window. The evening air tasted of autumn. The balmy night would be followed by four clear, mild days. Kim hugged her standard poodle, and smiled.

They would have perfect weather to dig for emeralds.

Rory whined and licked her glasses.

"Ewwww, dog murp."

Hearing the humor in her friend's voice, Kim grinned at the woman sitting beside her. Rachael Chan's almond eyes sparkled. Like Kim, she wore jeans and a plaid flannel shirt. Unlike Kim, diamonds sparkled from Rachael's ears and the ring finger of her left hand.

"Better get used to it." Kim pointed at Rachael's 2-carat diamond ring. "You've taken the first step to 2.5 kids, a station wagon and a dog."

"Hey, I'd never buy a station wagon." Charlie Hampton, Rachael's fiancé, grinned into the rear-view mirror. "Though kids and a dog would be nice."

The blush that spread across Rachael's face heightened her exotic beauty. Once again, Kim marveled at their unlikely friendship.

They'd met twelve years ago in a University of Maryland geology class. At first, Kim had found it hard to accept Rachael as a serious geologist. Rachael's slender frame, shiny dark hair -- compliments of her Filipino grandmother -- and stylish clothes more suited a beauty contestant than a would-be paleontologist.

Rachael, however, shared Kim's thirst for knowledge and the two had spent many glorious weekends rockhounding in Maryland and the surrounding states. They'd found garnets in Pennsylvania, Amazonite in Virginia, rubies, amethysts and moonstones in North Carolina.

But they'd never found emeralds.

Though North Carolina boasted the United States' only commercial emerald mines, most of its emerald-bearing land was privately owned and inaccessible to amateur gem hunters. The few public digging sites had long been depleted of surface gems.

So Cleopatra's favorite gemstone, the green beauties said to drive away evil spirits, protect against epilepsy and assist women at childbirth, remained beyond Kim's reach.

Until now.

Rachael's engagement to Charlie brought a surprising bonus: Access to his family's emerald mine.

The Hamptons' mine had never been as productive as its counterparts in Colombia, Russia or Brazil. But it had yielded some of the largest rough gemstones ever discovered.

Kim would be happy finding one tiny emerald.

As she reflected on the upcoming days, a thrill coursed through her. The four-day weekend would not only include digging in a real emerald mine, but also two engagement parties, a visit to the local

Gem Festival and the opportunity to explore her relationship with Scott Wilson, investigative reporter turned college professor.

As if reading her mind, Scott turned in the passenger seat. When he saw her staring, his hazel eyes softened. Kim's breath caught and the back of her neck tingled. Why did this man make her all gooey inside?

Though Kim's cousin Tiffany referred to Scott as "Professor Hotstuff," he wasn't classically handsome. At 40 years old, his brown hair was already receding and he struggled to protect his 6' frame from developing a belly paunch. But his eyes sparkled with humor and his intelligence and easy nature made him hard to resist.

And when his mouth tipped into a crooked smile, like it was doing right now, he resembled an aging Indiana Jones.

She considered surprising him with a quick kiss. She even leaned forward.

Her movement, however, attracted the attention of the sixth passenger in the car. Al, Scott's long-haired dachshund, popped up and extended a paw in her direction.

Kim dutifully shook his furry foot, removed two treats from her pocket and handed one to Al and the other to Rory.

She glanced up in time to see Scott's lips press together in amusement. With a wink, he pulled Al back onto his lap and turned to Charlie.

"I really appreciate your including me in this trip," Scott said. "Kim tells me it's next to impossible to obtain permission to dig on private land around here."

"Yeah, well, people don't understand the dangers," Charlie said. "Erosion has made small pieces of emerald accessible with a shovel. But to get to the large stuff, we have to use backhoes and dynamite. That destabilizes everything.

"Just a few years ago, one of the best -- and nicest -- emerald hunters in the business died when the walls of a mine he was working collapsed on top of him."

Sensing the collective horror, Charlie added, "Don't worry. You'll be digging in a new area where there's less soil disturbance. You shouldn't have any trouble."

Charlie slowed his black Ford Expedition and turned onto a winding dirt road. The number of "no trespassing" signs increased. To Kim's relief, no one had shot holes in these.

She leaned forward and tapped Charlie's shoulder.

"What's with the signs?" she said.

Charlie shrugged. "Just a reminder to the local rockhounding club that they don't have permission to dig in our mine."

"Why would they need reminding?" Scott shifted in the front seat so he could see both Charlie and the two women behind him. "Isn't this all private land?"

"Yeah, but a few years back, a local mine owner allowed a rock hunting club onto his land. Someone found a 50-carat emerald, the national newspapers reported it and now every treasure hunter thinks he's entitled to trespass. The insurance companies pitched a fit. Dad's agent actually called and warned him to not allow strangers to dig unless he wants to pay enormous liability rates."

He grinned into the rear-view mirror. "So if any of you get hurt, please don't tell our insurance company."

Spotting a clearing up ahead, Kim pointed. "Is that where we're going?"

"Sort of."

The car crested a hill. The trees abruptly stopped, replaced by acres of buff-colored dirt and rock. A metal gate flanked by a six-foot, chain-link fence blocked the dirt road. The fence sported "private property" and "no trespassing" signs. Beyond, Kim could see a dingy white house trailer. Weathered wooden steps led to the front door and a sign that said "Emerald Cove Mine."

Charlie stopped the car, pulled a ring of keys from his pocket and stepped out to unlock and open the gate. Kim silently urged him to hurry. Nightfall was imminent.

When she, Scott and the dogs had set out from Osprey Beach this morning, she'd known they'd arrive in Western North Carolina too late to do any digging. The GPS had predicted a seven-hour drive. Add in bathroom breaks for humans and canines and stops for food and seven hours easily turned into nine. They'd arrived at Charlie's eight-room cabin at dusk.

But Kim had waited a lifetime to view a real, working emerald mine. So before the group settled around the fireplace for a much-needed catching-up session, she'd begged Charlie for a brief tour of the mine. If he didn't hurry, she'd see nothing but shadows.

Charlie returned to the car and drove through the now-open gate. But instead of continuing on, he stopped, threw the gear shift into park and left the car to close and re-lock the gate.

What the heck was that all about? Surely, the tour wouldn't last more than ten/fifteen minutes. So why not leave the gate open?

Frustrated, she stared down the fence line. It stretched to a distant forest and abruptly stopped.

Charlie climbed into the driver's seat. Kim tapped him on the shoulder.

"Am I seeing things or does your fence stop at the forest?"

"You're not seeing things." He put the car in gear. "Dad refused to enclose the entire mine, saying fencing would make the place look like a fortress."

"So why erect a fence at all?"

Charlie shrugged. "The gate and fence discourages people from driving through the mine. But there's nothing to stop people from coming through the forest. Well, nothing but a long walk."

"Fencing is expensive," Scott said. "You have, what, a hundred acres?"

"Hundred and twenty. But money wasn't the issue." Charlie's blush deepened. "I mean, when you see my parents' house, well, you'll understand the mining business has been good to us. Dad could afford to fence the whole property or to hire guards. But he can be stubborn.

"That's why Michael Dunning, Dad's lawyer, insisted we hang 'no trespassing signs.' For all the good they do."

His tone-of-voice implied a deeper story here, but Kim was too excited to pursue it now. The SUV turned a corner. Charlie pulled the car to the side of the dirt road and aimed the headlights at the mine.

"This is the original mine," he said.

Kim gawked. A football-field-sized hole dropped maybe 100 feet into the earth. Granite boulders cluttered the bottom. Someone had parked two backhoes at the foot of the cliff. Mica embedded in the mine's craggy walls twinkled in the car's headlights.

The contrast between what Kim had envisioned and what lay before her couldn't be more pronounced.

She'd assumed the mine would appear more cave-like, that they'd have to don hardhats with headlamps and shuffle around in the dark searching for a flash of quartz.

Alternatively, she'd envisioned a smaller version of South Africa's Kimberley Diamond Mine, the mine she'd been named after. The 42-acre Kimberley Mine spread some 1,500 feet wide and 790 feet deep. But "the big hole," as she called it, progressed in steps, giving it the appearance of an inverted Aztec pyramid.

Of course, most of the Kimberley mine had been hand dug. Charlie's family had used machinery to dig.

As a result, the mine she'd yearned to see resembled nothing more than a gravel pit.

She glanced at Rachael. Her friend's dark eyes softened with pity.

"I warned you that you wouldn't be impressed," Rachael said.

Kim swallowed. "Well. Maybe they'll let us run the backhoe."

That brought a smile to Rachael's exotic face and a guffaw from Scott.

Scott turned in his seat and grinned at Kim. "That I'd like to see."

"Don't encourage them," Charlie said. "You have no idea what mischief these two can cause."

"Oh, I think I can guess," Scott said.

Before they could get into a remember-when discussion, Kim interrupted. "So are the backhoes going to be operating while we dig?"

"Yes, but you won't be anywhere near them." Charlie aimed the car toward the gate. "I've got a surprise for you. But you don't get to see it until tomorrow."

Tomorrow . . .

Kim leaned back and closed her eyes.

Tomorrow she would dig in earth that, more than 150 years ago, yielded the eight-inch Carolina Emerald stolen from the American Museum of Natural History.

No streetlights illuminated the winding road back to Charlie's cottage. Knee-high reflectors marked the edges of the long driveway to the house. The porch light barely pierced the darkness.

Charlie hurried inside to start a fire in the fireplace. After allowing the dogs to relieve themselves, Kim and Scott followed. They found Rachael standing by the front door, where they'd dropped their luggage before traveling to the mine.

"I'll show you to your rooms." Rachael eyed the pile of zippered totes, duffle bags and collapsible nylon crates, one small, one large. "Though I gotta say, I'm surprised you brought so much for a four-day weekend. You used to be a light packer."

"Still am." Kim pointed to an under-seat bag upholstered in southwestern colors. "All my stuff's in there. Scott has one of the small duffels. The rest is for the dogs."

Rachael's mouth dropped open. "Why do the dogs need so much?"

Kim exchanged an amused glance with Scott, who'd inherited his long-haired dachshund from his uncle. Like Rachael, he'd been horrified at the amount of gear dogs required.

Kim slung a tote across her shoulder. "People only need to pack clothes and toiletries. The dogs need food, water, toys, chews, collars, leashes, towels to wipe their feet, bedding, brushes, combs, dog wipes, training gear and, of course, crates to keep them safe."

She reached for her suitcase. "If you'd like, we can leave Rory's crate down here for the moment. He's pretty good about not getting into things-- Rory, when did you learn to open zippers?"

The big poodle's head was buried deep into his training bag. Hearing his name, he lifted his head. He held a red bandana clenched between his teeth.

"Good boy!" Kim dropped the suitcases and pulled a dog treat from a jeans pocket.

Rachael crossed her arms. "You reward your dog for stealing?"

"He wasn't stealing." She traded the treat for the bandana. "Well, not exactly. We're working on scent training. He's done great with finding his toys or treats or following my tracks. I thought I'd challenge him by scenting unusual objects for him to find."

She stuffed the bandana into a jeans pocket and pulled the zipper shut on the training bag.

"If you'd like," she added, "I can give you a demonstration later."

"This I gotta see." Rachael tossed a duffle over her shoulder.

Kim snagged her suitcase, the training bag and a duffle. Scott insisted on carrying the rest. They followed Rachael up a worn set of oak stairs.

At the top, Rachael turned to the right and walked down a short hall to an open door.

"Scott, we've put you in here."

Scott deposited Al's crate and most of the bags into a room outfitted with a queen-sized bed, a one-drawer bed table, a metal clothes rack and a folding suitcase stand.

With Rory's grooming bag still clenched in one hand, he removed the heaviest of Kim's bags from her shoulder and followed the women to the other end of the hallway.

"Charlie and I are in the master suite." Rachael pointed to the farthest door. "I put Kim in here because it's the only other room with an actual closet. You two will need to share a bathroom." She indicated a door on the opposite wall, then opened the door to Kim's room.

Like Scott's, this room sported a queen-sized bed, bedside table with single drawer and folding suitcase stand. The door to a tiny, empty closet stood open.

Rory leaped onto the bed. Al attempted to follow, but his short legs prevented him from reaching the top of the mattress. Kim lifted him onto the bed beside Rory.

"Well, I'll let you two get settled," Rachael said. "When you're ready, you'll find us sitting in front of the fire."

She started toward the door, then tossed Kim an impish grin. "Feel free to use only one of the rooms."

Kim reached for a pillow, but Rachael disappeared before she could toss it at her friend.

"So are you going to relegate me to the only room without a closet?" Though Scott's voice was low and husky, his eyes twinkled.

Heat spread up Kim's face. Mouth suddenly dry, she wrapped her arms around the pillow.

"Er." Her voice came out a squeak.

Scott gripped her arms, pulled her close and kissed her.

For a moment, Kim couldn't breathe. Then she felt herself responding. Leaning into him, she licked his lips. Scott moaned and deepened the kiss.

Too soon, he broke the kiss and stepped back.

"If you want to visit your friends, we'd better stop right here."

She nodded.

"You never answered my question," Scott said.

Kim smacked his shoulder with the pillow. "I'm not sharing my closet."

Laughing, Scott scooped Al from the bed. "We'll meet you downstairs."

He closed the door behind him. Grateful for a few moments alone, Kim collapsed onto the bed.

Wow, that was some kiss.

In the three months she'd known Scott, they'd shared kisses, just not as many as she'd like. They'd spent the summer dodging thieves, thugs and wannabe pirates.

The start of university classes had swept them into hectic teaching schedules. As a tenured psychology professor, Kim had some freedom in scheduling classes. But this was her first semester teaching at the University of Maryland and she needed time to adjust. She spent most weekends grading papers and helping her grandfather in his jewelry store.

Scott had been equally busy. A year before she met him, he'd been lured away from The Washington Post to teach in a new, multi-disciplinary department called "The History of Ideas." Scott and his fellow professors drew upon science, philosophy, journalism, literature and other subjects to show students how and why people's view of the world evolved.

Because they taught at the same campus, the two had managed to steal time for occasional lunches and early dinners. But she longed for more time together.

She reached over to rub Rory's belly.

"Vacation is off to a good start," she told him.

Rory snorted. She grinned, stood and called Rory to join her. He waited in the open doorway of the bathroom while she washed her hands, then accompanied her downstairs.

Voices drew her to the right and into a family room. A stone fireplace flanked by dark wood bookshelves dominated one wall. Rachael and Charlie snuggled on the couch that faced the fire. The coffee table in front of them held two glasses of wine. Scott lounged on one of the wing-back recliners with Al in his lap and a glass of wine in his hand. Seeing her, he gestured to the second recliner.

Kim headed for the chair, then squealed in delight at the sight of a mug of hot chocolate placed before it.

"See what I mean?" Scott told the others. "All I have to do is offer chocolate to make her happy."

Ignoring the laughter, Kim snuggled into the chair and reached for the mug. Rory settled onto her feet.

"Now this feels like a vacation," she said. "Thank you again for inviting all of us to your engagement parties."

In addition to Kim and Scott, Rachael had invited Kim's grandfather and Aunt Ginny, saying they seemed as much a part of her family as her own grandparents and aunts.

"Well, with Mom and Dad excavating in Florida and Grandpa too ill to travel, I need all of you here so I won't be overwhelmed by Charlie's family!"

The absence of Rachael's parents didn't surprise Kim. As field archeologists, they'd often disappeared from their only child's life.

Rachael's grandparents, however, attended every one her special occasions.

"Please tell me your grandfather's illness isn't life-threatening," Kim said.

"No, but he feels like it is. He has a painful rash caused by the chicken pox virus."

"Shingles? I thought there was a vaccine to prevent that."

"You know Grandpa. He didn't want to wait in line for the vaccine, so he never got it. Grandma is furious."

Kim smiled as she imagined Rachael's tiny, Filipino grandmother bombarding her rangy, all-American husband with I-told-you-so's.

She turned to Scott.

"I'm sorry you won't get to meet Rachael's grandparents on this trip. You'd enjoy them. They met in the Philippines right before the Japanese invaded the islands. Rachael's grandfather was a member of the U.S. Cavalry. Her grandmother was

Philippine royalty, but he wooed her with great polo playing."

"Wait a minute," Scott said. "What was the U.S. Cavalry doing in the Philippines?"

"They became part of our military presence there . . . in the 1920s?" Kim looked at Rachael for confirmation.

Her friend nodded. "Thank goodness for the Cavalry. The Japanese invaded with tanks and thousands of trained soldiers. But the sight of men charging on horseback unnerved the attackers long enough to allow the allies to retreat and organize for battle.

"My grandfather was one of a handful of Americans who escaped capture and fled into the hills to join the resistance movement. Grandma was also a member of the resistance."

"Wow. I'd sure like to interview them some time."

"That can be arranged." Rachael reached for her wine. "So when are Grandpa Max and Aunt Ginny arriving?"

"Not until Saturday night. Grandpa refused to close the shop on Saturday. Aunt Ginny offered to wait so they could drive together."

"Doesn't he have employees who could handle the store when he's away?" Rachael said. "He and Ginny would enjoy digging for emeralds."

Kim dragged fingers through her long hair. "Yeah, well, that's a sore subject. I'm the only family member he trusts to deal with customers. But when he was recovering from the armed robbery, several of Aunt Ginny's friends cared for the store while I investigated. Did a great job, too."

A vision of Grandpa laying in the hospital bed flicked through her mind. She pushed it aside.

"Believe me, if I can think of a way to entice them to come earlier, I will." Kim sipped her drink. "So what's the plan for the weekend?"

Rachael curled her legs beneath her. "Well, tomorrow we have most of the day to play in the mine." She pushed out her lips in a parody of a pout. "Charlie says he has a surprise, but won't tell me what it is."

Charlie grinned and tweaked his fiancé's nose. "It wouldn't be a surprise if I told, now would it?"

Rachael leered at him. "I have my ways to make you talk."

"Whoa, too much information," Kim said. "Let's return to the subject, okay?"

"Party pooper. Okay, tomorrow night is engagement party number one."

"Er, why are there two engagement parties?" Scott said.

"Dad thinks his business associates won't be impressed with Sunday's menu," Charlie said. "Too much quiche and non-manly tidbits. So he reserved a room at a local steak house. The restaurant's never crowded on Thursdays, so that schedule works for everyone."

"The next day -- Friday -- we'll need to help the Hamptons set up their booth for Saturday's Gem Festival," Rachael continued. "But that should only take a couple of hours and we can spend the rest of the day digging.

"Saturday, of course, is the Gem Festival. Charlie's father is giving a talk that we'll need to attend. But we can leave any time after that.

"Sunday afternoon is the official engagement party. We may not get a chance to work in the mine that day. Monday, however, is totally free."

"I'm actually looking forward to the Gem Festival," Kim said. "Most of the gem shows near us don't sell stones mined in the U.S. I can't wait to see what people have found around here. Of course, I want to spend most of my time digging. Unlike some people, I don't get to play in the dirt very often."

After their initial geology class, Rachael had pursued degrees in geology, paleontology and museum studies. Kim, however, had switched her focus to psychology.

So while Rachael spent her days searching for dinosaurs in the American West, Kim moved to Oregon to teach classes of bored undergraduates and fight for tenure. She'd not only earned tenure, but had been offered a professorship at the University of Maryland. She now taught attentive graduate students and would soon enjoy a more leisurely schedule.

Despite her professional success, she missed the carefree days of digging in the dirt, the thrill of finding raw gems. The childhood dream of discovering a new type of gemstone -- and naming it after herself -- never quite died.

"Don't worry," Charlie said. "If you don't find emeralds on this trip, you're welcome to dig whenever you visit us."

"You are planning to visit often, aren't you?" Rachael's voice pitched higher than normal.

Recognizing her friend's sudden discomfort, Kim studied Rachael's face. But Rachael refused to meet her eyes. Kim made a mental note to quiz her later.

Keeping her voice light, she said, "You're going to have a hard time keeping me away. I'd love more time to explore this area."

She smiled at Scott. "The Blue Ridge Mountains are one of the oldest ranges in the U.S., which makes them a geologist's playground. Enough time has passed for erosion to expose evidence of ancient volcanoes, colliding continents and inland seas.

"This is also a great place to hear legends and lore. Charlie, are we anywhere near Brown Mountain?"

Charlie nodded. "I'm assuming you're thinking about the 'ghost' lights?"

"Oh, no, don't let Kim tell ghost stories," Rachael said. "She told one when our geology class went overnight camping. Afterwards, no one slept."

"Then maybe I shouldn't tell you that people have actually photographed the glowing orbs that dance over Brown Mountain, right Charlie?" Kim tossed her friend a wicked grin.

Charlie slipped an arm around Rachael. "Don't worry, babe, I'll protect you. Besides, everyone knows the lights are just a lantern carried by a ghost slave looking for the owner of his plantation."

"I much prefer the Native American legend," Kim said. "This story existed before Andrew Jackson forced the Cherokee Nation to leave the East Coast and settle in Oklahoma."

"You're talking about the Trail of Tears?" Scott said.

Kim nodded. "Long before that atrocity, several tribes lived near here. They didn't always live in peace. Cherokee legend maintains that the ghost lights are the spirits of maidens searching for husbands who'd died in a great battle between the Cherokee and Catawba tribes."

"Surely there's a scientific explanation," Rachael said.

"The ones I've heard aren't satisfactory," Kim said. "Some say the orbs are caused when car headlights illuminate gas rising from swamps. But there aren't any swamps in the area and, in any event, ghost lights were recorded long before cars existed."

"Oooh, I love a good mystery," Rachael said. "Maybe after I move here, I'll investigate."

"Whatever you do," Charlie said, "please don't ask my brothers about the lights."

Everyone stared at him. Embarrassed by the sudden attention, Charlie's face flushed.

"I guess I should explain, huh? After I moved back home a few months ago, I saw lights moving through the forest."

"Flashlights?" Kim said.

"That's what I thought at first. I figured someone was digging illegally. But I haven't found evidence of that and the few times I ran into the woods to catch them in the act, well, if it is emerald poachers, they're good at hiding."

"You have more than 100 acres," Scott said. "Easy to avoid detection."

Charlie waved aside Scott's reassurance. "I played here as a child and know every inch of this forest.

"Anyway, I told my brothers about it, thinking they could help me search the woods. Instead, they've been teasing me about seeing ghost lights."

He reached for his wine glass. Rachael stared into space, frowning. Scott and Kim exchanged glances. Despite Kim's ability to tell scary ghost stories, she expected legitimate explanations for "supernatural" occurrences. She firmly believed humans created the lights Charlie saw. The only mystery here was who and why.

She opened her mouth to quiz Charlie about the local community, but Rory had other ideas.

Like a small child bored with adult conversation, Rory jumped to his feet and began racing around the room. Kim gasped when she spotted the bandana hanging from his mouth.

"How did you get that?"

"He's been slowly extracting it from your pocket." Scott struggled to hang onto Al, who clearly wanted to join in Rory's fun. "I was too fascinated to say anything." He grinned. "Besides, it's nice to see your dog acting out for a change."

"Thanks a lot." Kim softened the words with a smile. "Rory, come."

Having made his point, Rory trotted to her and dropped the bandana into her outstretched hand.

As Kim pulled a treat from her pocket, she told her dog, "I'm rewarding you for the come, not for the zoomies."

Rory cocked his head, then used his front teeth to gently remove the treat from her hand.

Rachael giggled. "You talk to him as if he understands your words."

Kim scratched behind Rory's ear. "You'd be surprised by how many words dogs can learn."

Recognizing an opportunity to steer the conversation to happier subjects, she added, "Do you still want to see how Rory finds things? He needs the intellectual stimulation."

Rachael's and Scott's enthusiastic agreement more than compensated for Charlie's lukewarm smile.

Determined to make a true believer out of Charlie, she decided to explain the science behind what she was doing.

"Unlike us, dogs view the world mostly through their noses," she said. "Human noses have 6 million olfactory receptors, but dog noses can have up to 300 million. The part of their brains that process smells is proportionately 40 times bigger than ours. C'mere, sweetie."

She positioned Rory between her and the others and lifted his muzzle toward the overhead light.

"If you look closely at a dog's nose, you'll see wing-like protrusions." She pointed. "Rory can actually rotate those wings to help him isolate a specific odor."

Releasing him, she handed him a treat. "Dogs are capable of smelling a cadaver through 80 feet of water. They can follow the trail of a specific person that's more than a week old. They can even detect cancerous tumors in human bodies and other illnesses in our breath."

Now Charlie leaned forward, finally showing interest. Time to wrap this up.

"So we know what dogs can smell. The hard part is communicating that we want them to locate a particular scent and teach them what to do when they find it."

She stood and held the bandana in front of Rory's nose.

"Wanna play find it?"

Rory's mouth pulled into a doggie grin. He sniffed the fabric.

"Rachael, could you please take my seat? Thanks. Now hang onto Rory's collar and use the other hand to cover his eyes while I hide this."

She scanned the room. She needed a spot that would challenge Rory, but not frustrate him. The sparsely furnished room offered few choices. She could tuck the bandana under a sofa cushion or beneath the throw rug or maybe behind Scott's chair.

"Why are you using a bandana?" Charlie said.

"We started out with dog treats. From there we worked on scent discrimination. I dipped cotton balls in a variety of essential oils and stuffed them into jars with holes punched into the lids. He learned to find the jar with the clove or the lavender or the lemon.

"Now that he seems to understand the find this/not that concept, I'm trying fabric scented with, well, me. Search and rescue dog trainers tend to use articles of clothing to communicate the scent to the dogs. So I thought I'd give it a try."

She frowned. If Rory tried to remove the bandana from under the rug, he might scratch the hardwood floors. And finding it behind Scott's chair would be too easy.

She crossed to the sofa and tucked the cloth beneath the cushion recently vacated by Rachael.

"How do you know he's looking for your scent and not the smell of the cotton bandana itself?" Rachael said.

Kim paused. "Huh. Good question. Keep in mind I'm an amateur. I'm only doing this as a game for Rory." She shrugged. "Let's see what he does."

She returned to Rory and instructed Rachael to release him.

"Ready, Rory? Go find it."

Rory stood, sniffed the air, then headed toward Scott and Al. He paused to touch noses with the dachshund, then sniffed Scott's pockets. Moving on, he circled the chair, then approached Charlie. As he neared the sofa, his ears perked and his tail straightened. He trotted past Charlie without slowing, stopped at the spot where Kim had hidden the handkerchief and shoved his nose under the cushion.

With the bandana dangling from his front teeth, he pranced back to Kim and waited for her to exchange bandana for treat.

Rachael applauded.

"That was so fun to watch," she said. "Can you teach him to scent for emeralds?"

Kim laughed. "I wish. I've never heard of anyone training a dog to sniff out gemstones or any kind of mineral or rock. I suspect rocks don't have a strong enough fragrance.

"However, tomorrow we might be able to put both dogs' digging ability to good use."

Rachael petted Rory. "Whatcha think, big guy? Wanna help us dig up the good stuff?"

Rory trotted to the front door and looked back at them.

Rachael's eyes widened. "Did he understand me?"

"Either that or he needs the bathroom." Kim stretched and yawned. "If I'm going to be in any shape to dig, I'd better call it a day."

The others agreed and began gathering their belongings in preparation for retiring. Kim clipped on Rory's leash and opened the front door. As Rory relieved himself, she stared up at the star-filled sky.

Though the night was beautiful, she couldn't wait until tomorrow.

CHAPTER 2

Early the next morning, the four friends and two dogs gathered in the kitchen for a quick breakfast. Kim had already loaded her rockhounding kit with the equipment she would need. Now she added the kit to a backpack containing bottles of water, collapsible dog bowl, dog treats and first aid supplies.

She dressed Rory in his harness, then clipped a 50′ light nylon line to the D ring. The long line would allow Rory to explore and play while giving her something to grab if he ignored her recall. Even though they'd be working miles from a busy road, she took no chances with the life of her dog.

"Everyone ready?" Charlie said. "Okay, follow me."

Instead of heading toward the front door and the waiting cars, he trudged through the kitchen door into the back yard.

"The mine is due east of here," Charlie said. "It's easier to walk than drive the winding road. Except, of course, after dark."

He plunged into the forest. The others followed.

Kim played out Rory's line so he could run from one side of their trail to the other. Al followed, dragging his own long line, and quickly became hopelessly covered in forest debris. The morning sun filtered through the autumn leaves, making the reds, oranges and yellows shimmer. As they passed beneath a long branch, a squirrel chittered.

"So," Charlie said, "you all want to hear about the surprise?"

"Finally!" Rachael said.

Charlie grinned. "Okay. But I have to start at the beginning because I don't think Scott and Kim know about my new emerald-finding software."

Kim glanced at Rachael, but her friend was staring at her fiancé with anticipation.

"Uh, Rachael never mentioned your new software," Kim said. "I'm kinda surprised."

Charlie prided himself for being the family black sheep. Despite pressure from his father and two older brothers, he'd refused to join the mining business. Instead, he'd studied computers in college, then signed on with a high-tech company in Kansas City.

The time spent away from his family not only allowed Charlie to blossom, but also to meet his future fiancé.

But, as Kim well knew, one never outgrows the need for family approval.

Charlie didn't seem to notice her discomfort.

"Well, Rachael gets most of the credit," Charlie said. "She's the one who told me about the ground-penetrating radar archeologists are using to survey potential dig sites."

"Mom and Dad use them all the time," Rachael said. "They have this machine that's shaped like a lawn mower, only it has a screen attached to the handle bars. When they push it across the dirt, the radar shows them images of what's below."

"My first thought was that the ground penetrating radar could help us find air pockets that might contain emeralds," Charlie said. "I talked Dad into renting the equipment for a day."

He shoved his hands into his jeans pocket. "That didn't go so well."

Charlie must have let his enthusiasm run away from his brain, Kim thought. Sure, miners sometimes found emeralds in underground air pockets. More often, however, those pockets contained nothing but quartz.

"I told him he needed to focus on what he does best," Rachael said. "He knows the geology of this area as well as anyone in his family. What he needed to do was take everything he knew about the locations where they'd actually found emeralds and create software that would predict the best places to search."

Kim nodded. Oil companies used computers to predict potential sources of oil.

"It took a bit of testing and tweaking," Charlie said. "A few months ago, I tried it in the old mine and found a nice pocket of gem-quality emeralds."

As they'd been talking, the sky had grown brighter. They stepped from the forest into a cleared field of clay-colored earth.

Man-made holes, maybe three feet deep, dotted the area. A recent storm had created rivulets in the hill, exposing granite rock that Kim itched to investigate.

Her heart beat faster when she spotted a 30-foot crater near the opposite tree line.

Rachael pointed at it. "Did you dig that for us?"

"My software indicated the possibility of large emerald pockets there." Charlie grinned. "I dug until I found you a quartz vein. Surprise!"

Rachael squealed and threw her arms around Charlie.

Scott turned to Kim. "So all I have to do to get a hug is dig a big hole?"

Kim grinned. "Nope. That hole better expose a vein of quartz."

Seeing Scott's confusion, she added, "In this area, emeralds tend to be found in quartz, though not every vein of quartz contains emeralds."

"This is the best engagement present!" Rachael grabbed Charlie's hand. "C'mon, let's get started."

But Charlie held his ground.

"You all go ahead," he said. "Dad wants me to go over some paperwork with him. I hope I'll be able to break free to dig with you before tonight's party."

He narrowed his eyes and presented Rachael with an exaggerated stern look. "I know how you lose track of time, so if you're not back at the cabin by 5, I'll come looking."

Rachael giggled and planted a quick kiss on his mouth.

As Charlie turned to leave, a soft woof drew Kim's attention to Rory.

The two dogs stood quietly beside her, waiting for permission to run into the dirt field.

"Okay, go play."

Rory began running zoomies around the group. Al, however, ran to one of Charlie's test holes. Dirt flew into the air as his big feet clawed at the ground.

Kim donned a dancing Snoopy baseball cap and nodded at Al. "If we find a promising spot, we might want to harness his energy."

She adjusted her backpack and stepped into the bright sun.

As much as she wanted to charge over to the designated digging area, she forced herself to move slowly. Charlie's work with the backhoe coupled with the recent rain had exposed broken metamorphic rock, granite and quartz. Chances were high she might find gemstones right on the surface.

She shuffled along, eyes on the ground, occasionally stooping to pick up a rock or run her fingers through debris. A small, round pebble significantly darker than the surrounding sandstone caught her eye. She snatched it and held it so the light could shine through. The rock glowed a deep, dark red.

"How 'bout giving me a running commentary about what you're doing?" Scott said.

"Okay. I guess you need to know that this part of North Carolina contains a surprising number of gems. Quartz is the most prevalent, which means there'll be amethyst, smoky and rose quartz."

"So amethyst is really purple quartz? Why not just call it that?"

"The ancient Greeks named it," Kim said. "They believed purple quartz could ward off drunkenness. The Greek word for 'not drunk' was 'amethystos,' which eventually became 'amethyst.' Bacchus would be so offended."

"I believe the Greeks called their god of wine Dionysus. Bacchus was Roman."

"Show off."

But she smiled as she said it, grateful that Scott not only tolerated but seemed to enjoy her passion for gemstone legends. The legends revealed much about the psychology of the people who wore the gems.

Greek legends surrounding amethyst were a perfect example. Historically, ancient Greece was known for its philosophers, its art and, in the end, its decadence. Claiming a purple gemstone would allow the owner to drink more wine without getting intoxicated somehow fit their Gestalt.

Scott gestured to the soil around him. "So I should pick up rocks that are a different color from the dirt?"

"Sort of. You also have to pay attention to the shape. Amethyst and other quartz is trigonal, sort of a long cube. Emeralds have six sides and tend to form in long bolt shapes. And then there are garnets."

She handed Scott the dark pebble she'd found and told him to hold it to the light.

Scott's mouth dropped open. "I thought it was black, but it's red."

"North Carolina garnets are usually too dark to cut into jewelry," Kim said. "You can't get enough fire from the cut stones." She accepted the garnet from Scott. "I just like finding them."

She felt Rory's presence before his curly head nudged her. He held something in his mouth.

"Whatcha got there?"

Rory dropped a dark, gray rock into her hand. She pulled a treat from her pocket, thanked him and made a fuss over what a nice rock he'd brought. She waited until he trotted off, tail wagging, before dropping the rock to the ground.

"Your dog brings you rocks?" Scott's eyes twinkled.

Kim dusted her hands. "Poodles are retrievers. When Rory was a puppy, he picked up everything --rocks, sticks, leaves, acorns, toads . . . I worried that he'd bite into or swallow something poisonous. So I taught him to bring whatever he'd picked up to trade for a treat."

"So now he's always bringing you things?"

"Oh, yeah. You wouldn't believe the weird stuff he's brought me. The strangest was when we were living in Oregon. We were walking in the woods in the Coast Range Mountains. I turned my back on him and suddenly heard a high-pitched 'weep, weep, weep,' like the sound a guinea pig makes."

"Okay, I'm not much into nature, but even I know there aren't any wild guinea pigs."

"Actually, there are wild guinea pigs in South America; they're called cavies and--" Seeing the amusement in Scott's eyes, Kim hurried on. "Anyway, the thing Rory found was a Coast Mole. They're the size of a guinea pig and create tunnels of loose soil on top of the ground. Rory must have plucked it from its tunnel. He dropped it at my feet."

"What did you do?"

"Told him to put it back where he found it."

Scott laughed.

"Seriously, we simply watched until the mole found its hole and disappeared. I'm just glad poodles don't have pockets. Can you imagine the things I'd find there?"

"Are we going to hunt emeralds or stand here yapping?" Rachael planted herself in front of Kim, legs spread, hands on hips. She reminded Kim of an exotic Barbie doll -- an impatient Barbie doll.

Kim knew better than to voice the thought aloud. Instead, she called to Rory and Al and followed her friend down the hill to the crater Charlie had dug.

"So why are there emeralds here and not in other places in the U.S.?" Scott said.

"It's got something to do with the way these mountains were formed." Kim accepted another rock from Rory, handed him a treat, then discreetly disposed of the rock. "Do you remember your elementary school science, about the three kinds of rock?"

"Sedimentary, igneous and metamorphic," Scott recited. "But don't ask me to define them. I remember sedimentary formed from beach stuff, sand, shells and things."

Kim nodded. "Igneous is the hardest; it formed when volcanic magma cooled. Granite is an example. But I find metamorphic the most interesting because it's sort of a mix of the other two. Marble is metamorphic."

She gestured to the hills surrounding them.

"When these mountains formed," she said, "the geologic forces were so intense--"

"I love it when you talk dirty."

Kim folded her arms. "Do you want to hear this or not?"

Scott pointed his index finger and rolled it in the movie industry gesture for "roll 'em."

"As I was saying," Kim said, "when these mountains formed, the heat was so intense that the metamorphic rock partially melted. When it cooled, veins of quartz formed."

"And quartz is the most abundant mineral."

Kim's shoulders relaxed. "So you do know some geology."

Scott flashed the half grin that reminded her of Indiana Jones. "When you invited me on this trip, I did some research."

Kim's fingers tingled and a smile spread across her face. She'd never met a man who'd taken the time to learn about her interests. Most of the men she'd dated had expected her to study their obsessions: football, soccer, baseball. Scott continually surprised her.

Now, however, was not the time to dwell on her growing attraction to him.

As if reading her mind, Scott leaned closer and his eyes softened.

Clearing her throat, Kim looked away. "Er, let's get back to the quartz."

She didn't have to look at him to feel his amusement.

"Ah, when all this was going on, scalding liquid carried beryllium through rocks containing chromium. The liquid somehow puddled in these subterranean cavities beneath the quartz. When the liquid cooled, the minerals crystallized to form emeralds.

"It's always amazed me that chromium -- the same element that makes rubies red -- makes emeralds green."

They arrived at the crater Charlie had dug and peered over the edge. Rachael had already started her descent, picking her way down to a vein of quartz that ran at a horizontal angle through the rock. With each step she took, clay colored dirt broke away and skittered to the hole's shadowed bottom.

Kim studied the hole's contours. At first, the sides sloped gently. Ten or fifteen feet down, however, the walls grew more vertical. Rachael, experienced at excavating, expertly found hand and foot holds. Kim was out of practice, but nothing was going to stop her from climbing down there.

But there was no way Rory and Al could accompany her into the crater.

Her shoulders slumped.

Rory wouldn't tolerate being left behind while everyone else dug in the crater. He'd try to follow her.

To keep the dogs safe, she needed to confine her emerald hunting to the surface land.

As if reading her mind, Scott said "I'll stay with the dogs."

"Oh, that wouldn't be fair. I invited you to go emerald hunting and--"

Scott raised his hand, stopping her. "And I'll get more pleasure watching you enjoy yourself."

He gestured toward the lower tree line. "From there, I can see what you're doing."

Kim thanked him with a hug and a kiss that promised much more.

"Would you mind if I leave some of my stuff with you? I'd better take only my digging equipment."

They crossed to a shady area. Setting her backpack on the ground, Kim removed a container of dog treats, dog bowl, several bottles of water and a hard hat.

"That must have been heavy," Scott said. "Why didn't you let me carry the pack?"

"Oh, I'm used to it." She poured water into a bowl and set it into the shade. Al immediately plopped his muzzle into it.

Rory, however, had other ideas. His head disappeared into Kim's backpack, emerging a few seconds later with his red bandana.

"Good find it!" She exchanged the bandana for a dog treat.

Scott chuckled.

"Hey, this scenting stuff might be useful." She donned her hard hat. "Last week Rory found my car keys. They'd dropped behind an end table."

Rory snatched the bandana from her hand and began racing around them.

"I have trouble imagining the curly one as useful." Scott's voice was dry, but Kim recognized the teasing glint in his eye.

She called Rory and exchanged the bandana for a dog cookie.

Shouldering her now lighter backpack, she said, "Wish me luck."

She crossed to the edge of the hole and began her climb down.

🐕

The top layer of sandstone, loosened by Charlie's backhoe, shifted beneath Kim's feet. Digging in her heels, she proceeded at an angle toward her friend. Ten feet down, however, the walls of the hole straightened and plunged vertically into the shade where Rachael squatted.

"Look for the foot-holds Charlie dug for us," Rachael called.

Kim's chest tightened. Her friend routinely climbed mountains and scaled cliffs searching for dinosaur bones. Kim's normal exercise consisted of walking and playing with her dog.

After receiving Rachael's invitation, Kim had switched from walking to jogging. She'd even played chase games with Rory in the Pirate's Cove sand. Now that she had to face a wall like a rock climber, she realized her preparations hadn't been enough.

She scanned the wall and found two nearby hand-holds and, beneath them, a hole for one foot. Telling herself this was no different than climbing trees, she snugged her left foot into the lower hole, grabbed the two hand-holds and swung into space.

For several long moments, she hung there, her right foot desperately punching the rock face.

"You're reaching too far," Rachael called. "The holes are closer together."

Kim pulled her leg closer. Her toe bumped rock, rock, rock, then disappeared into a hole in the wall. She shifted her weight so both legs now supported her. She allowed herself a moment to breath, then proceeded her crab walk down to her friend.

"Boy, you weren't kidding when you said you're out of shape," Rachael said. "Good thing Charlie positioned the holds to fit a woman's size."

Kim raised her eyebrows and compared Rachael's barely five-foot height with her own 5'6" frame.

"Woman sized?"

Rachael raised the screwdriver she clutched in her right hand. Kim grinned and in unison they chanted "Never tease a short woman holding a sharp object."

Kim set her backpack on the ground, squatted beside her friend and studied the rock before her.

Geologists didn't know exactly why emeralds had formed in North Carolina. Charlie, however, claimed he'd found emeralds only in the presence of four minerals: quartz, mica, pyrite and limonite.

Judging by the glitter in the rock, mica was common here. Charlie's backhoe had uncovered a wide vein of quartz running horizontally through the granite.

But there was no sign of pyrite or limonite. Both minerals were yellowish in color. Pyrite, also known as Fool's Gold, would be easy to recognize.

She wouldn't know she'd found limonite, however, until her fingers turned yellow. Unlike pyrite, mica and quartz, limonite never formed into crystals. Instead, it appeared as a powder. Prehistoric cave painters had used limonite for their yellow pigment.

Geology aside, Kim's job was clear: explore the quartz vein, looking for pyrite and limonite.

"How do you want to tackle this?" Kim said.

Rachael pointed to the large vein of quartz.

"How 'bout I follow this to the right and you follow it left?" she said.

"Works for me."

Kim began removing supplies from her backpack: rock pick, trowel, digging knife, collection containers, collapsible shovel and large screwdriver.

"I wish we didn't have to go to that stupid dinner tonight." Rachael brushed a lock of damp hair from her forehead.

"Stupid?"

Kim pronounced it "stooooopid," the way they did when they poked fun at themselves.

Rachael offered a wry smile.

"Yeah, stooooopid. Don't get me wrong; I'm flattered Charlie's parents wanted to throw us an engagement party. I just wish we didn't have to shorten our emerald hunting day to go to the stooooopid steak house. I don't even like steak!"

"Yes, I've always thought steak is stooooopid. Much dumber than green beans."

The two friends giggled.

"So who's going to be there tonight?" Kim grasped her screwdriver and chipped at the rock beneath the quartz vein, searching for either the two missing minerals or an air pocket.

"All of the local movers and shakers: county commissioners, a mayor, wealthy businessmen, the Hampton's lawyer, the local sheriff and, of course, Charlie's brothers Jake and Diesel."

"Jake and Diesel?"

Rachael chuckled. "They played football. Their real names are Jacob and Jonathan, but I guess those aren't macho enough."

"Ahhh."

The nicknames suited Rachael's descriptions of Charlie's brothers as overgrown studs who valued brawn over brain.

"I'm going to have a hard time calling a grown man 'Diesel,'" she said.

"Trust me; the name suits him. Think Mack truck barreling down a country road."

Rachael frowned. "Prepare yourself; we may be the only females at the dinner."

"Charlie's mother isn't attending?"

Rachael's expression softened. "Deb has multiple sclerosis, so it all depends on whether she's having a good or bad day. Right now we want her to rest for the real party."

"What's she like?"

"She's a southern lady through and through." Rachael rocked back onto her heels. "Gracious, loyal, protective of her family, loving and tough as nails. She's the reason Charlie's so wonderful."

"Ah, and now we come back to wonderful Charlie."

Kim couldn't resist teasing Rachael about her fiancé. Seemed like every time they talked, her friend gushed about Charlie's charm.

Rachael blushed and hurried to change the subject.

"Wait till you meet Jack, Deb's papillon. Deb trained him to open and shut doors, answer the phone, turn lights on and off, pick up dropped items and--"

"Wait a minute. I'm still trying to picture a tiny papillon reaching the light switches."

The toy spaniel with the distinctive butterfly-wing ears weighed less than ten pounds.

"On her bad days," Rachael said, "Deb uses a wheelchair. Jack can reach the switches while sitting in her lap. He also helps make the bed."

Kim smiled as she pictured a silky-haired lap dog tugging a sheet across a comparatively enormous mattress.

The two friends settled in for some serious excavating. Alternating the screwdriver and trowel, Kim tapped at the rock and dirt surrounding the quartz.

She quickly fell into a familiar rhythm and her mind began to wander.

How she wished Grandpa was here. It'd been years since he'd taken her fossil hunting. Even when they didn't find anything, the stories he told while they looked always delighted her.

One of her favorite North Carolina tales credited a 12-year-old boy with launching the first American Gold Rush. Conrad Reed had been playing in a stream when he discovered a large yellow rock. It was so pretty that he brought it home and used it for a door stop.

Three years later, a visitor identified the rock as a 17-pound gold nugget.

News that gold had been discovered in the U.S. spread throughout the country and prospectors flocked to North Carolina. Over the next 20 years, more than $100,000 in gold was mined in the state.

This all happened back in 1799, long before the California Gold Rush. But even in modern times, normal folk discovered remarkable gems. Not long ago, a North Carolina miner tripped over a rock, dislodging the stone. Beneath it, he saw a flash of icy blue. He looked closer and discovered a 1,000-carat aquamarine.

So while Kim blushed at the memory of her ten-year-old self aspiring to discover a new gemstone, her heart beat faster with every tap of her trowel.

"Rachael, do you know anything about the North Carolina Emerald that was stolen from the American Museum of Natural History?" She brushed hair from her eyes. "It was maybe eight inches long, three crystals fused together. Grandpa said it was discovered near here."

"Are you talking about the emerald with the curse?"

"Curse?" Kim's mouth fell open. "What curse?"

Rachael leaned back and reached for her water bottle. "That emerald brought bad luck to everyone who touched it. The men who discovered it were fired. The foreman fell and broke his leg. The mine owner went bankrupt."

"So what? That type of misfortune is common. Besides, we're talking about a little-known emerald from North Carolina, not the Hope Diamond."

Throughout the centuries, the Hope Diamond's beauty and rarity had sparked dozens of legends and lore, including rumors that it was cursed. Given that the diamond first appeared in the mid-1600s, it wasn't surprising that some of its owners suffered bad luck. People who owned the Hope Diamond had been murdered, committed suicide, lost their money, become drug addicts, ruined their marriages.

Such tales of woe accompanied many well-known gemstones. The Carolina Emerald, however, wasn't famous. If Grandpa hadn't told her about the emerald, she'd know nothing about it.

"How did you learn about the Carolina Emerald and this so-called curse?" she said.

"My grandfather grew up in this area," Rachael said. "There was quite a local uproar when someone stole the emerald from the museum. Many people believed the thieves were descendants of the men who originally discovered the stone. That Sawyer and Hicks shot and killed one another only added to the idea of a curse."

"I still don't see how these few events add up to a curse."

Rachael sighed. "There's more. Back in the 18th Century, before the mine went bankrupt, the owner sold the emerald to a Philadelphia gem collector.

The new owner sent a trusted employee to North Carolina to pick up the emerald and take it to his home in Philadelphia.

"This, of course, was before modern transportation. Trains connected some of the big cities, but none passed through Hiddenite, North Carolina. So the man assigned to pick up the emerald would need to travel part way on horseback. The buyer hired a Pinkerton detective to ride along for protection."

"Let me guess," Kim said. "They were ambushed along the way and someone stole the emerald."

"Not quite," Rachael said. "When they met, the so-called trusted employee tried to bribe the detective into stealing the emerald. He told the detective he already had a buyer. All they had to do was pretend they'd been robbed along the way."

"I guess the thief never read the Pinkerton Code of Ethics."

As a fan of mysteries, both modern and historical, Kim knew the Pinkerton detectives subscribed to a strict code that included the dictum to accept no bribes.

Rachael nodded. "When the detective refused to co-operate, the employee claimed he was just testing the detective's loyalty. But now the detective distrusted the employee. So he hired his own men to shadow them.

"They set off for the train station. Lo and behold, halfway there, a group of armed bandits attacked them."

"So what happened?" Despite Kim's skepticism over this whole curse thing, she loved a good story.

"The detective's men helped fight off the bandits. In the shoot-out, the trusted employee and would-be thieves were all killed. The detective rode on to deliver the emerald."

"Good story," Kim said, "but it illustrates greed not a curse."

Rachael grinned. "Ah, but you haven't heard what happened while the emerald was in the new owner's house. Almost immediately after the emerald arrived, one of the maids disappeared and was never found."

"Maybe she was in cahoots with the employee who tried to steal the emerald."

"Maybe. But a month after the gem collector displayed the emerald, lightning struck one of the estate's tree."

"Natural occurrence," Kim said.

"That's what the collector thought. Over the next few years, however, he had the most awful streak of bad luck. Loved ones were getting divorced or falling ill or moving away. Household items were broken or misplaced. He was robbed several times."

Rachael held up her hand, traffic-cop style. "And before you say this was all normal stuff, the bad luck stopped when he sold the emerald to J. P. Morgan."

"And did Mr. Morgan then have bad luck?"

"No. But only because he immediately donated the emerald to the American Museum of Natural History."

"Where it lived for 50 years before someone stole it."

"And the thieves died."

"Are you talking about Sawyer and Hicks?" Kim said. "Grandpa said no one ever found proof that they stole the emerald."

Her friend's mouth drew into a firm line.

"Rachael, do you really believe in curses?"

"Let's just say I'm not a disbeliever."

"But you're a trained scientist."

"Yeah, but my grandmother grew up in a culture that produced not one, not two, but three different vampire legends." Rachael grinned. "So I reserve the right to freak out over something I can't explain."

Kim chuckled. "Well, let's focus on something we can explain."

The two friends resumed their digging. Kim's thoughts, however, returned to the stolen emerald.

Years ago she'd found a photograph of it on the internet. The Carolina Emerald had been featured in some old magazine and the photo of a photo couldn't possibly capture the gem's beauty. But it clearly showed the emerald's large size and unusual shape. Three emerald crystals of varying heights jutted from a shared base. They had, indeed, resembled the towers of the Emerald City from the Wizard of Oz movie.

Maybe the unusual size and shape had triggered the rumors of a curse. People often attributed sinister qualities to the weird or different.

She pushed the thought aside and focused on the task in front of her. Falling into a rhythm, she embraced the joy of exploration.

They worked throughout the morning, stopping only to grab a sandwich for lunch. Though Kim urged Scott to try his hand at digging, he'd remained with the dogs. By mid-afternoon, however, her muscles screamed for a break.

Rachael showed no signs of slowing.

Kim stood and stretched. "I'm going to go check on Scott and the dogs."

Rachael answered with a wave of her hand.

Kim organized her tools, then started the climb upward. By the time she reached the surface, sweat dripped down her back. She wiped her forehead with her baseball cap and plopped it back on her head.

"Over here."

She turned to see Scott lounging beneath a shady tree. Rory and Al lay beside him, tongues hanging out, tails wagging. As she approached, Rory leaped to his feet, snatched something from the ground and trotted to her.

"Whatcha got there?" Kim dug a dog treat from a pocket. Rory dropped a rock into her extended hand and gently scooped the treat from the other hand. She plopped onto the ground beside Scott and examined the rock.

"He has more to show you." Scott pointed to the left. The clearing was dotted with new holes. "They wore themselves out excavating."

Kim looked closer at the two dogs. Sure enough, their black noses sported tan stripes and dirt clung to the nails of their front feet. Al sat up to beg, revealing a dirty chest and belly.

Laughing, she handed Al a treat. "Looks like they're having a great time. Why don't I watch the dogs while you do some digging? Rachael can show you what to do."

This time when Scott started to protest, she added, "I need to spend time with Rory."

Even as she said his name, Rory was back by her side, dropping another rock into her lap.

"Okay, talked me into it." He leaned close, his breath warm on her ear. "Behave."

Kim turned toward him, prepared for a kiss. But he'd already scrambled to his feet. Looking down at her, he gave her a half grin, pulled a hat from behind his back and, with two hands, dropped it onto his head at a cocky angle. Kim's back tingled.

"When did you get the Indiana Jones hat?"

"Had it for a while." Another half grin. "Been saving it for the right occasion." He spread his legs and raised his right arm in the classic Indiana Jones cracking a whip pose. "Do I look like I can handle the bad guys?"

Rory, interpreting Scott's motion as an invitation to play, leaped up, plunked his front feet on Scott's outstretched arm and began licking his face. Al gave an excited yip and ran circles around Scott; the long line dragging from his harness wrapped around Scott's ankles.

Scott looked from Rory to Al. "This is not the effect I was trying to create."

Laughing, Kim cued Rory "feet off" and helped untangle Scott's feet. Standing, she gave him a quick peck on the cheek. "Okay, Indie, go find me an emerald."

Smiling, Scott offered a mock salute, then disappeared into the mine.

Kim looked down at the two dogs sitting beside her. "So, wanna show me what you've been doing?"

She set off across the field. Rory and Al raced ahead and stopped by a hole they'd clearly dug. Kim knelt.

"Yes, it's a very nice hole."

She scooped loose dirt with her fingers, searching for small quartz, garnet or tourmaline. Though people occasionally found sapphires in this area, they were pretty rare.

Seeing her interest, Al launched himself into the hole and began digging. Flying dirt slapped Kim's face. She laughed and stood. As she brushed dirt from her face, hair and clothes, Rory batted her hand with his paw. He clenched a rock between his teeth.

"You've been busy." Kim exchanged a treat for the rock and examined it. It was the typical dark gray gneiss found in the area. A few flecks of mica glittered in the sun.

She praised Rory and, since the rock was too large to swallow, allowed him to remove it from her hand. She watched him trot toward a shady patch beneath a tree and drop the rock on top of . . . more rocks?

She gawked at the pile of rocks. Most were similar to the one he'd just handed her. But a few sported small chunks of quartz. She crossed to the rocks and picked up a piece of quartz. Black tourmaline swirled through it. As she returned the tourmaline-studded quartz to the pile, she spotted a flash of golden brown.

A rush of adrenaline shot through her. She knocked a few rocks out of the way and snagged a Grey Poupon-colored stone.

The rock was rough to the touch, its surface dotted with mica and small quartz crystals.

She carried the rock into the sunlight. Talcum-like powder had rubbed off the rock, staining her fingers yellow. Limonite.

As the thought formed, a ray of sun brightened the stone. Small flecks of pyrite -- Fool's Gold -- sparkled.

While she'd been slaving away in the mine, her poodle had found a rock containing the magic combination of limonite, pyrite, mica and quartz.

"Rory?"

Hearing the excitement in her voice, the big poodle abandoned the rock pile and trotted to her. As she looked closer, she could see that some of the dirt clinging to his nose was mustard colored.

"Where did you find this?"

Rory cocked his head.

Okay, that wasn't going to work. She frowned. How could she communicate to Rory that she wanted him to show her where he found this particular rock? If she told him to find rocks that smelled like this one, could he do it?

Well, there was one way to find out.

She held out the rock. "Sniff."

To her delight, Rory leaned forward, flared his nostrils and inhaled.

"Good boy. Go find it."

Rory looked at her eyes, at the rock, back at her eyes. With a soft "woof", he slapped a paw onto the hand holding the rock.

"Yeah, I know the rock is right in front of you. I need you to find another." Hiding the rock behind her back, she held out her dust-covered hand.

"Sniff. Good boy. Now find it."

To Kim's delight, Rory turned away, sniffed the air, then trotted along the tree line. Al fell into step, his little legs pumping to match Rory's stride.

Kim followed, wondering if this was a waste of time. Maybe she should just investigate every hole that the dogs had dug. But the clearing was pockmarked with holes and, now that she looked closer, she saw more holes in the forest. It was amazing the dogs hadn't wrapped their drag lines around the trees.

Rory suddenly stopped and dropped his nose to the ground. For a moment, he froze, tail up, body rigid. Before Kim could react, Rory charged into the woods, nose hovering above the ground, tail wagging, Al close to his heels. They moved so fast Kim didn't have time to step on their long lines to stop them.

They disappeared behind a bush.

"Rory come!"

She ran after the dogs. They'd probably scented a squirrel, rabbit or deer. She just hoped whatever they chased didn't have a white stripe down its back.

Al's high-pitched baying led her to a grove of trees whose thick trunks and gnarled branches indicated their old age. Al stood with his front feet planted against one tree, barking at the grey squirrel chattering above him.

Rory, however, sniffed around the exposed roots.

She stooped to grab the two dogs' drag lines. No telling when Al's sensitive nose would detect another critter to chase.

As she stood, Rory pawed the ground, then started digging. Clay colored soil flew between his legs, smacking Al on his side. Al yipped, turned and joined Rory. Kim stepped back to avoid the flying dirt.

"Hey, guys, let's not mess with this poor old tree . . ." She broke off as Rory dropped his head and pulled something from the ground.

The sides of his mouth actually turned up in a grin as he carried it to her.

She accepted the grungy offering, a black pouch with a drawstring closure. It appeared to be made of some kind of nylon. The outside was scuffed, but free of insect holes. Whatever it held -- some child's secret treasure? -- was irregularly shaped.

The bag appeared old enough that she didn't think she'd violate someone's privacy by opening it. That, however, proved harder than expected. The knotted nylon cord that held the bag closed was caked in dirt, making her fingers slip and slide. She found a sturdy twig and used it to pry the knot open.

Tossing the twig aside, she expanded the bag's opening and gently tipped the contents into her hand.

A faded bandana had been wrapped around something. The bandana itself was unusual. Unlike the standard blue or red print, this one was imprinted with words: Truth, Knowledge, Vision.

She frowned. Why did that combination of words sound so familiar?

She turned the bandana over, searching for an easy way to unwrap it without tearing the fragile threads. Finding an edge, she gently teased the bandana open.

The forest, the birds, even the dogs faded into the background as she stared at a distinctive green crystal.

No, not one crystal. Three bolt-shaped emerald crystals rose from the same base, their shape resembling the turrets of a castle. The crystals were long enough to cover her palm and weighed about as much as a small bag of dog treats. Even with the sun partially blocked by trees, the pure green color shimmered.

The bandana that had wrapped it now lay beneath, the imprinted words invisible. She didn't need to see the bandana, however, to conjure the words from memory: Truth. Knowledge. Vision.

No wonder the words had seemed so familiar. She'd first seen them as a child, carved above the doors of the American Museum of Natural History.

The bandana had been someone's souvenir. And the emerald . . .

The emerald had been stolen from the museum more than half a century ago.

CHAPTER 3

The nudge of Rory's nose startled her and she almost dropped the emerald. Glancing up, she suddenly realized that she stood in the middle of a forest, out of sight of her friends. The sun had moved lower in the sky and now the woods were full of shadows.

With trembling fingers, she re-wrapped the emerald, her ears straining for the sound of Rachael or Scott. But all she heard was the beat of her own heart. Where were the birds, the insects?

Rory suddenly turned and stared deeper into the forest, tail up, body rigid. Was he alerting to deer or a squirrel . . . or something on two legs?

Kim transferred the emerald to her left hand,

gripped the dogs' long lines with her right, and urged them back the way they'd come.

Leaves rustled and twigs snapped as they retraced their steps. The journey seemed to take forever; she hadn't realized how far she'd chased the dogs. Finally, the trees thinned and she could see light ahead.

As they neared the clearing, however, she heard voices. Slamming to a stop, she jumped behind a tree, pulling the dogs with her.

Her breath caught and the pounding in her ears drowned out the words. Then she heard Scott calling her name.

Dropping the dogs' leashes, she burst through the trees. Scott stood apart from Rachael and Charlie, scanning the forest. She ran into his arms. Al yipped a greeting as the two dogs circled them.

"Are you okay?" Scott's breath warmed her ear.

She leaned back to study his face. His brows creased with concern.

"Hey, didn't you hear us calling?"

Rachael's excited voice was followed immediately by a hand gripping her shoulder. Kim reluctantly stepped from Scott's embrace to face her friend. Rachael's dark eyes gleamed. She flashed a Cheshire Cat grin and held up a hand. Yellowish dust clung to her fingers.

"Scott found limonite," Rachael said. "We followed it and oh, Kim, wait till you see! The quartz vein widened; it's huge! There must be an emerald pocket there!"

She grabbed Kim's arm. "Come see!"

Kim opened her mouth to protest. Right now, the need to return to the cabin, secure the emerald and think through the implications overrode prospecting fever.

"Better wait until tomorrow," Charlie said. "You asked me to pick you up at 5 and it's already 5:15. Dad will be unhappy if we're late for this dinner."

Rachael's shoulders slumped. "Tell me again why we can't elope?"

"Mom wants a wedding."

Rachael sighed. "Okay. But we need to get our stuff."

In a daze, Kim followed the others to where she'd left her backpack. Charlie, Rachael and Scott trudged back to the mine to retrieve the rock hunting tools, leaving Kim with the two dogs.

She stared down at the bandana-wrapped emerald still clenched in her left hand. Looking up, she noted the dogs' relaxed stance and the presence of bird song and insect chirps. She was alone.

Her fingers trembled as she pulled back the ratty old bandana to reveal the emerald. It looked exactly like the photo she'd seen. She stroked a finger across its cool, smooth surface. Turning it upside down, she squinted at the base, searching for markings from the museum. The bottom was rough to the touch, but she was unable to discern any letters or numbers. Perhaps if she had a magnifying glass--

"Whatcha got there?"

The sound of Charlie's voice caused Kim to jump. She almost dropped the precious gemstone.

"That looks like . . ." Rachael's face paled. "Is that what I think it is?"

Kim nodded. "I think so."

Seeing the confusion on Scott's face, she told him about the Carolina Emerald, its discovery, sale and subsequent theft. She didn't mention the curse.

"At the time the emerald was stolen," she concluded, "the local sheriff believed the descendants of the original discoverers took it. But when he tried to investigate, he found the two suspects dead. It appeared that they'd gotten into an argument and shot one another. So the sheriff was never able to prove his theory."

She looked down at the emerald. "Looks like he was right."

"Where did you find it?" Charlie said.

"I didn't find it; Rory did." Kim frowned. "It was buried beneath a tree, maybe 50 feet from where I exited the forest."

"Huh. Sounds like the land my grandfather won in a poker game."

"Put it back." Rachael's voice trembled. "Hurry. Before the curse gets us all."

Kim gawked at her friend's pale face and wide eyes. "Are you serious?"

Rachael swallowed. Removing her cap, she

dragged fingers through her hair.

"I sound like my grandmother, don't I?" She offered a smile that didn't reach her eyes. "Don't mind me. I'm just a bit nervous about meeting everyone tonight."

"Speaking of which, we'd better head out," Charlie said. "I brought the car. Driving will be faster than walking."

Kim tucked the emerald into a pocket of her backpack and followed the others to Charlie's car.

On the drive to the cabin, she stared out the window and let the conversation flow around her.

She'd found it. She'd actually found the Carolina Emerald.

Okay, so Rory had found it. But still. . .

She hugged the backpack and grinned. She couldn't wait to tell Grandpa.

All those many years ago, she'd stared at the facade of The American Museum of Natural History and, inspired by the inscribed words "Truth, Knowledge, Vision," made a vow she couldn't possibly fulfill.

But, thanks to Rory, her dream had come true. Heck, maybe the museum would mount a plaque thanking her for the emerald's return. Maybe they'd even allow her to name it!

She scratched Rory's ear and made a new vow: If the museum directors allowed her to name the emerald or offered to mount a thank-you plaque, she'd insist Rory's name be included.

Of course, first she had to deliver the emerald safely to the museum.

Her first instinct was to ask Scott to drive immediately to New York. But they were both exhausted from digging in the mine and in no condition to drive safely. Better to wait until morning.

Or maybe she could bring the museum to her. Grandpa had many contacts in New York. He could call and arrange for someone to contact the museum, ask to send an armored truck or something to pick up the stone.

Charlie turned the car onto the gravel driveway that wove uphill to the cabin. As they cleared the trees, he groaned.

"That's Diesel's car." He parked beside an oversized Ford pickup. "We must be running late."

While Charlie hustled Rachael inside, Kim lifted Al from the car and handed his leash to Scott. Instead of heading inside, however, he stepped close.

"Are you okay?" he said. "You came barreling out of the forest like you were being chased by a pack of hungry dachshunds."

Kim smiled. "I'm fine. It's just, back in the forest, well, it felt like someone was watching me. I didn't want the emerald to be stolen all over again."

"You're sure no one was there?"

She thought back to the minutes after Rory uncovered the emerald. The forest had suddenly grown silent, as if the birds and insects had sensed danger. Even Rory had alerted to something, though he hadn't barked.

"Something was out there," she said, "but it could have been a cat or fox."

"Well, you're safe now." Scott slipped his arm around her. "Just promise me that if you ever do encounter a thief, you'll give him what he wants. You are more important than any precious gem."

Warmth spread through Kim's body.

"I wish we didn't have to go out tonight." She gestured to the front porch and its beckoning Adirondack chairs. "Wouldn't it be wonderful to just sit here and talk?" And other things.

Before Scott could reply, Rachael opened the front door and beckoned them inside.

The cabin's downstairs consisted of one large room bisected by an oak staircase leading to the bed- and bathrooms above. To the right, a breakfast bar separated the L-shaped country kitchen from the small dining area. Four mismatched chairs surrounded a pine table.

The others had gathered in the living room. Two men leaned against the mantel.

Charlie's brothers shared his 6' height, curly dark hair, brown eyes and square jaw. But while Charlie was slender and clean-shaven, his brothers sported goatees and muscular builds.

Unlike Charlie's off-the-rack coat and tie, Jake and Diesel wore clearly custom-made suits. One brother appeared comfortable in the business clothes. The other, however, pulled at his collar and tie.

At the sight of two strangers, Rory slammed to a halt and gave a single bark. Al flattened himself to the ground and jumped side to side, barking in a piercing, high-pitched voice.

Kim tightened her hold on Rory's leash.

"Oh, look." The tie-grabber straightened and sneered at the dogs. "A yappy wiener and a frou-frou dog. Oooh, I'm scared."

Kim sighed. This must be Diesel, the Neanderthal who'd ridiculed Charlie throughout childhood and belittled him in adulthood. The stories Rachael had told reminded Kim of the bully from her own childhood. But, unlike poor Charlie, she hadn't had to live with the bully.

Rory emitted a series of low-pitched barks. Diesel's eyes widened. He took a step back.

Allowing her own smirk to show, Kim laid a hand on Rory's head. Scott scooped Al into his arms.

"Laugh all you want," Charlie said, "but today these dogs discovered one of North Carolina's most famous emeralds."

Kim stifled a groan. The more people who knew about the emerald, the harder it would be to protect it.

Fortunately, the other brother misinterpreted Charlie's statement.

"Software program still a success, huh?" Jake clapped a hand onto Charlie's shoulder.

Charlie stepped away. "Scott found limonite, but we didn't have time to pursue it. The poodle, however, found something buried in the woods."

"Charlie--"

But it was too late. Charlie had already launched into the tale of Kim chasing the dogs into the woods to find Rory digging up the infamous Carolina Emerald.

The two brothers turned to Kim.

"So let's see it," Diesel demanded.

Given that she'd found the emerald on the Hamptons' land, she couldn't deny Diesel's request. But at least she could minimize potential damage to the stone.

Motioning to the others to follow, she walked into the kitchen. She set the stone onto the table and gently teased apart the bandana that wrapped around it. The sound of tearing cloth made her wince. She located the offending thread and used a fingernail to release it from where it had snagged on the stone. She spread the cloth wide to reveal the emerald.

Jake gasped and Diesel whistled.

"Now that's what I call an emerald." Diesel reached for the emerald. Kim batted his hand away.

"Let's minimize the amount of handling," Kim said.

"What, you think you'll find fingerprints after all

these years?" Diesel said. "Think you're Nancy Drew or something?"

"No, I think the emerald is too fragile to pass around like a football."

Diesel's eyes flashed and his hands fisted. For a moment, Kim feared she'd overstepped. Charlie's laugh, however, refocused Diesel's attention.

"She pegged you pretty fast," he said. "Mr. Football Star."

Diesel's hands relaxed and he offered Kim a wry smile.

"Sorry," he said, "it's been a rough day."

"Where did you find this?" Jake stepped closer to the emerald, but kept his hands in his pockets.

"We think it was on the property that Grandpa won in a poker game."

"The old Benning place?" Diesel frowned. "I thought the rumor was that Hicks and Sawyer stole it."

"The Hickses' property borders what was once Benning's land," Charlie said. "I bet Sawyer and Hicks buried the emerald there before shooting one another."

"Or maybe Benning masterminded the whole thing and shot the other two men," Kim said.

"Doesn't matter," Diesel said. "We own the land now so the emerald is ours."

Kim opened her mouth to protest, but Scott beat her to it.

"That belongs in a museum!" He turned to Kim

and shrugged. "Always wanted to say that."

She grinned, delighted to hear Indiana Jones's words come from Scott's mouth.

Diesel's eyes narrowed. Jake's phone rang.

"No," Jake said into the receiver, "we haven't left yet. Something's come up . . . Yeah, looks like another emerald pocket, but we won't know until we break through the quartz."

Kim stiffened. We? Was Jake planning to take the digging site away from them?

She turned to Rachael, but Charlie was already leaning toward them.

"Don't worry," he said, "the site is yours. No one's going to dig there until you're finished."

As she started to relax, however, she heard Jake say, "Remember the emerald everyone said Sawyer and Hicks stole from the American Museum of Natural History?"

Kim waved her hand, trying to interrupt Jake's next words. But it was too late; he'd already revealed the dogs' discovery.

"No, I'm not shittin' ya," Jake said. "It was wrapped in a museum bandana . . . Well, I guess we return it to the museum . . . Oh? Okay, I'll tell him. Yeah, see you soon."

Jake hung up. "Michael Dunning says something's come up and he might not be able to stay for the whole din--"

He broke off as he noticed five people glaring at him. "What?"

Diesel snorted. "Even I know we shouldn't be broadcasting the existence of this thing." He waved a hand at the emerald.

Jake shrugged. "It's just Michael. You know lawyers don't talk to anyone." He glanced at his watch. "But we really do need to hurry. Dad's waiting."

"You go ahead," Charlie said. "I'll wait for the others."

The availability of two full baths enabled the women to shower at the same time. Afterwards, Kim hurriedly donned a pair of black jeans, turquoise knit top and black blazer. Pushing the sleeves to 3/4 length, she slipped on the bracelet she'd purchased in Arizona: a sterling silver cuff studded with Sleeping Beauty turquoise. She paused to admire the robin's egg blue of the famous American turquoise, wishing she'd bought the matching pendant. Thank goodness she'd purchased the earrings. She added the dangling earrings, brushed her hair into a smooth, low ponytail and turned to survey her bedroom.

The sparse furnishings might be comfortable for weekend guests, but the room offered few options to hide the emerald. She could tuck the emerald into her suitcase, but wouldn't that be the first place a thief would look? The end-table drawer was also obvious.

For a brief moment, she considered carrying the emerald in her purse. But she didn't want to risk breaking the fragile crystal.

Rory leaped to his feet a moment before someone knocked on the bedroom door. At Kim's invitation, Rachael opened it and stepped inside.

Kim's jaw fell open. "This is your idea of dressy casual?"

Her friend had donned a striking mini-dress, gold bracelets and stiletto heels. A boyfriend-style cashmere cardigan provided the only "casual" tone to the outfit.

"This will be the first time I meet these people," Rachael said. "If I'm going to live here, I need to make a good first impression."

Hearing the catch in Rachael's voice, Kim threw an arm around her.

"They're going to love you," she said. "And the ones that don't aren't worth knowing."

She felt Rachael tremble and feared her friend would start to cry.

Ever since Rachael agreed to move to North Carolina with Charlie, her moods had swung high and low. Rachael had been both thrilled and horrified when the local museum offered her a curator position. Thrilled because the new job would bring a high salary and prestige. Horrified because she loved her current position and had only applied for the North Carolina job to placate her fiancé.

Her current job allowed her time to explore the Southwestern states, searching for dinosaurs and other prehistoric animals. The low salary barely covered food and rent and the rugged working conditions created sore muscles and burned skin. But Rachael loved the work and repeatedly told Kim she wouldn't trade places with anyone.

When Rachael accepted Charlie's marriage proposal, she'd assumed they'd continue to live in Kansas City. But the success of Charlie's emerald-hunting software coupled with his father's sudden acceptance drew Charlie back to North Carolina. He heard about the opening at the local museum and urged Rachael to apply.

She told Kim that never in her wildest dreams did she think the well-respected museum would offer a curator job to a lowly field anthropologist. But they did and she felt obligated to accept it.

In the following weeks, Kim had watched her friend grow increasingly insecure. She'd call at odd hours to blurt out new fears. What if Charlie's father had forced the museum to hire her? What if she hated the job? What if the locals wouldn't accept a half-Filipino?

Now Kim gripped Rachael's arms.

"You are going to impress everyone at the dinner." Kim stared into her friend's anxious eyes. "The museum is going to love you. Charlie loves you."

A whistle drew their attention to the open bedroom door. Charlie leaned against the doorframe. "You ladies look wonderful."

Though he'd included Kim in his compliment, his eyes remained on Rachael.

Well, time to get back to business.

"Do you have a safe?" Kim said.

Charlie finally looked at Kim. "A safe?"

"You know, locked place to secure valuables."

"There's probably one at my parents' the house. Are you concerned about leaving the emerald here? Don't worry. We've never had a break-in. It's not the sort of place where you'd expect to find valuables."

He looked back at Rachael. "We really have to leave."

"I need to hide the emerald first," Kim said. "Is there anywhere in your room that would work?"

Rachael shook her head. "All of the bedrooms are sparsely furnished." She scowled at Charlie. "A fact we'll change if you expect me to live here."

Charlie chuckled. "When you move in here permanently, you can decorate all you want."

Before the couple fell into another of their lovey-dovey sessions, Kim pushed them toward the door.

"You two go on without us; we'll follow in Scott's car."

She carried the emerald, purse and cell phone downstairs and set them on the kitchen counter. Most kitchens contained all kinds of hidey-holes. Surely she'd find something in here.

After a few minutes, however, her shoulders drooped in defeat. She'd hoped to find an open box of cereal or can of coffee -- something that belonged in a kitchen but large enough to hide the emerald.

But Charlie had stocked the cabinets and drawers with only basic supplies of utensils, pots and pans, dishes and mugs. The coffee came in a useless, clear jar. Bread, teabags, peanut butter and packets of sweetener and sugar rounded out the non-perishables.

The refrigerator held a quart of milk, a few containers of yogurt, half a dozen eggs and a hunk of cheese. The freezer was empty.

She tapped her fingers on the counter. If this were a Sherlock Holmes story, she could hide the emerald in plain sight.

Yeah, right; maybe in a showcase of other emeralds.

"You look lovely."

At the sound of Scott's voice, Kim looked up. Her breath caught. Instead of the traditional suit, he'd changed into trousers, dress shirt and tie -- all in black -- and a heathered charcoal sport coat. The look was fashionable and sexy as hell.

Maybe the best way to protect the emerald was to skip the dinner, stay here so no one could steal it.

Even as the thought formed, her cell phone rang. She checked the caller I.D. Rachael.

"Don't even think about skipping this," Rachael said. "I need you here."

Kim sighed. "Okay, okay, we're coming."

"You haven't left yet, have you?"

"Uh, we're just going out the door."

"Yeah, right." Rachael hung up without saying goodbye.

Kim smiled at Scott.

"Rachael's getting impatient. Would you mind pottying the dogs while I put the emerald in my room? I just got a brilliant idea for hiding it."

She trotted back up the stairs and into her bedroom. Crossing to her gem-hunting backpack, she pulled out the bandana she'd been using for Rory's scent training. Next, she unwrapped the emerald, trying to minimize tearing of the museum bandana.

She wrapped the emerald in her own bandana, laid it on the bedside table, then adjusted the folds so it looked like someone had used the bandana and tossed it carelessly onto the table.

Stepping back, she studied the results. After a bit of fluffing, it did, indeed, look like a used handkerchief.

Or at least it did until Rory charged in and snatched the bandana, emerald and all, from the table. She grabbed him as he turned. He readily relinquished his "find" and grinned up at her, waiting for a cookie.

"Sorry, he got away from me," Scott said from the doorway.

"No harm done. But would you mind if we put Rory in your room with Al?"

"I was going to suggest that," he said. "They can

keep each other company."

They walked the dogs into Scott's room. Scott tossed a dog biscuit into Al's sleeping crate. The incorrigible dachshund thief couldn't be trusted to roam free without supervision. Al followed the cookie into the crate and sighed as Scott closed and locked the door. Rory laid down on the floor beside his buddy.

They turned off the overhead light so the dogs could rest and shut the bedroom door. Returning to Kim's room, she once again arranged the bandana-wrapped emerald to look like a used handkerchief.

Surely no self-respecting thief would examine a snot-filled bandana.

During the 20-minute drive to the restaurant, Scott entertained Kim with descriptions of Rory's and Al's antics while she'd been digging in the mine. The silly conversation effectively eased Kim's tension and they entered the restaurant with smiles on their faces.

They found Charlie and Rachael standing near the bar beside a tall man who could only be Charlie's father. Though he had to be in his early 60s, Mark Hampton retained a full head of wavy brown hair. Like his older sons, Mark sported a designer suit and shoes that shined. Yet the hand he extended contained the calluses of a field worker.

"I hear you've solved one of our local mysteries," Mark said.

Kim returned his infectious smile. "We won't know for sure until I have a chance to study it closer. The museum should have engraved numbers or something on the bottom. But the shape is pretty distinctive."

Mark turned sparkling brown eyes to Scott and shook his hand. "And Charlie said you've uncovered a new pocket of emeralds."

"Dad, can you please lower your voice?"

Mark clamped a large hand onto Charlie's shoulders. "Why, we're all friends here."

"Not exactly." Charlie's eyes flicked to the bar crowded with couples waiting for tables. Kim followed his line of sight to three men separated from the others by some invisible barrier.

At first glance, they made an attractive group. The man on the far left resembled Robert Redford in his early movies: tousled blond hair, blue eyes, chiseled jaw. While Kim much preferred the older Redford with the character lines on his face, she could understand why several women at the bar kept glancing at Blondie.

The man on the far right wore his brown hair cropped Marine-corps short. The short-sleeved shirt he wore showed off muscular shoulders and arms. Like Blondie, this guy focused on the man standing between them, the one doing all of the talking.

Tall and muscular like the others, the third man

sported a Johnny-Depp style goatee, tight jeans and bad-boy attitude. He spoke with his hands, long fingers splayed or curled to illustrate whatever held his two listeners captive. As she watched, his right hand fisted and searing brown eyes targeted Charlie.

Spiders raced up Kim's spine. She glanced at Charlie, but he was focused on his father and missed Goatee's angry look. Rachael, however, stepped back, away from Goatee.

"Ignore the idiots at the bar," Kim said. "This is supposed to be a fun celebration for you and Charlie."

"Charlie said several of the high school bullies still lived in town," Rachael said. "What do you want to bet goatee-man is one of them?"

Before Kim could answer, Mark Hampton turned to include their entire group. "We've got the back dining area to ourselves. I think everyone's here."

"We'll be along in a minute, Dad," Charlie said.

As soon as Mark was out of hearing range, Charlie turned his back to the room. "I need to warn you that the people at this dinner--"

"So the Prodigal Son returns," a man's voice cut in.

Charlie whipped around to face Goatee and his two buddies.

"What do you want, Donny?"

"Can't an old friend welcome you home?" Goatee's sneer made the innocuous words threatening. "Or have you forgotten our unfinished business?"

"I'm not a kid anymore," Charlie said. "I suggest you grow up, too."

"C'mon, Donny," the blond said. "This isn't the time or place."

Goatee -- Donny -- frowned at Blondie. "I don't know why I put up with you. Who do you think you are, the United Nations?"

Blondie spread his hands, palms up. "Just trying to help."

"Well, don't." Donnie turned back to Charlie. "You want adult? Let's talk adult." He ogled Rachael. "Introduce me to your little brown bitch."

Kim's mouth dropped open. Rachael gasped. Charlie's fist smashed into Donny's nose.

Donny's head snapped sideways and blood splattered Blondie's shirt. A growl rumbled from Donny's throat and his lips pulled into a snarl.

Kim wrapped her hands around the strap of her shoulder bag, the only weapon at hand. Scott stepped in front of her. Kim sidled around him, bumping into Rachael who clutched her own purse like a weapon.

A short, red-headed man stepped between Charlie and Donny. Laying a hand on Donny's chest, the man said, "Don't you have something you need to do, Donny?"

Donny scowled at Redhead.

"Get out of my way, Dunning," he said. "This has

nothing to do with you."

"That so?"

Kim detected a hardness under Redhead's mild tone.

Donny must have heard it, too, because he planted his feet and glared down at the shorter man. To Kim's surprise, Redhead held his ground.

"What's going on here?"

A man dressed in a sheriff's uniform loomed into view. Arms perched on hips, he scanned the group with a practiced eye before settling on Donny.

"Looks like it's time for you to leave," the sheriff said.

Donny's eyes flashed. "I'm the one with the bloody nose." He pointed at Charlie. "Arrest him."

"Sheriff." Redhead stepped in front of Charlie. "As the Hampton's attorney, I insist--"

The sheriff held up a hand.

"Save it for the courtroom, Michael. Donny, I want you and your friends gone."

"But Sheriff--"

"Go. Or would you rather give me a tour of that hunk of junk that's parked outside?"

Donny's chin jutted forward. "You can't do that without a warrant! I know my rights."

The sheriff flashed a smile that didn't meet his eyes.

"Why, Donny, haven't you ever heard of probable cause? I might spot a lit cigarette on the console. Wouldn't be safe to wait for a warrant, now would it?"

"Okay, okay, we're leaving."

Donny jerked his head toward the door. His two friends fell into step. They disappeared through the front door.

Kim studied their rescuer. Tall and trim, his salt-and-pepper hair, receding hairline and creases around his mouth indicated a man in his early sixties -- about the same age as Charlie's father. The slight dip to the outside corners of his eyes, however, gave him an exotic, Robert Mitchum sexiness.

Right now those eyes looked more sad than angry.

"Fighting in a restaurant?" he said. "I expect more of you, Charlie."

Charlie's face flushed and he looked at his feet. "I'm sorry, Uncle Walt."

Uncle Walt?

Kim and Rachael exchanged glances. In all the years they'd known Charlie, he'd never mentioned an Uncle Walt, the sheriff.

Charlie's uncle patted his shoulder.

"Try to rein in that temper, okay? I don't want to spoil your party by arresting you."

He turned to Rachael.

"And you must be Charlie's lovely fiancé. I'm Walter Spits."

Rachael blushed as the sheriff shook her hand. Kim grinned, fascinated that her normally self-contained friend was so easily flustered. And then Kim was shaking the sheriff's hand and feeling her own face flush. There was a definite movie-star quality about Sheriff Walter Spits.

"Well, you folks have a nice dinner," Sheriff Spits said. "And, Charlie, stay out of trouble, okay?"

"Aren't you joining us?" Charlie said.

A rueful smile crossed the sheriff's face. "Wasn't invited. But don't worry, I'll be there on Sunday."

He tossed the group a smile before leaving the restaurant.

Charlie rubbed his hand. "Donny still has a hard head."

"You never told me the sheriff is your uncle." Rachael's tone was accusatory.

"He's not my real uncle," Charlie said. "He's a close friend of Mom's and, well, when we were kids, we always called him uncle."

He sighed. "It's a long story."

"Too long to discuss now." The redheaded man extended a hand to Scott. "Michael Dunning. I'm the Hampton's attorney."

Scott shook Dunning's hand and introduced himself.

"And you must be the intrepid emerald hunter."

Michael Dunning flashed a practiced smile at Kim.

"Er, I'm Kimberley West."

Dunning's handshake was surprisingly strong for a small-framed man. Kim dropped her eyes to his shoulders, but the cut of his pinstriped suit hid any evidence of weight-lifting or other muscle-building activities. A gold chain draped from a vest pocket to a button loop -- evidence of both a pocket watch and a pretentious nature. The backpack slung over his shoulder, however, ruined the effect.

Dunning's chin dipped and one side of his lips pulled up in a boyish "ya caught me" expression.

"The pack ruins the line of the suit, doesn't it?" he said. "I'm having a hell of a time adapting to local expectations. My clients like me to dress casual, but the judge insists we wear suits in court. This is my compromise."

"You're not local, then?" Kim said.

"Not hardly. I'm from Pennsylvania."

"What brought you here?"

The lawyer's intense stare made Kim suspect he was consciously hiding emotion. She glanced down in time to his feet shuffle. When she looked back at Michael's face, she caught the hint of anger in his eyes. It passed so quickly, she wondered if she'd imagined it.

"Work, what else?" he answered her question. "Isn't that what makes everyone leave home?"

He grinned and gestured toward Kim's oversized purse.

"Looks like you have as many pockets in that thing as I have in my pack. How do you organize it? I could have a grizzly bear hidden in here and not know it."

She shrugged. "It takes some practice."

"Maybe you could give me some tips during dinner."

Kim forced a polite smile.

Michael reached into his vest pocket, removed a gold watch, flipped it open and checked the time.

"Ah, I think our host is ready for us," he said.

Snapping the watch closed, he extended an elbow. "Shall we go to dinner?"

Kim snagged Scott's arm with her left hand and gestured with her right.

"After you."

The lawyer shrugged off the insult and headed toward the rear room, stopping here and there to pat someone on the back or exchange a few words.

"What's wrong?" Scott said.

"I don't like him."

"Michael Dunning?" Scott grinned. "You just met him."

"He's hiding something." Seeing the confusion on his face, she added, "He didn't want to tell me why he moved here."

"How'd you know that?"

"Body language. He knew enough to control his eyes and facial muscles. But his feet shuffled." She grinned. "Most people, even hotshot lawyers, don't realize how their feet can reflect their thoughts."

Scott laughed and slipped an arm around her shoulders. "Remind me to never lie to you."

As they made their way to the dining room, Kim

asked Charlie about the man he'd punched.

"Who were those guys?"

"Just some jerks from high school," Charlie said. "Kirk Ballas -- he's the blond -- was star quarterback and ladies' man. Rocky DiSoto, the dark-haired guy without face hair, played defensive linebacker. He was frequently fined for being too aggressive."

"And the guy you punched?"

"Donny Driver, class hood. When he wasn't smoking in the bathroom, he bullied people he didn't like, girls as well as guys. As you can imagine, computer geeks were a prime target."

Kim frowned. "So you've got two former football stars hanging out with a local hood. Doesn't that seem odd?"

"Not really," Charlie said. "Rocky and Donny lived next door to each other when they were kids. I guess they stayed friends. The one that surprises me is Kirk. I thought he'd be married with kids by now."

Charlie paused at the entry to the private dining room, giving Kim a chance to look around. A long table covered in white cloth stretched the length of the room. She counted 20 place settings. Business-suited men occupied half of the chairs while other men and a scattering of women mingled near a small bar. Waiters scurried around with trays of salad.

Charlie's father sat at the head of the table. The two chairs to either side of him were empty. Jake and Diesel lounged beside the empty chairs. They were accompanied by women wearing large diamonds set in wedding rings.

"Hey, Charlie!"

A tall, African American strode over to shake Charlie's hand. Charlie greeted him with enthusiasm.

"This is Drew McDonald," Charlie said, "the last of the honest lawyers."

Drew's laugh was infectious and Kim couldn't help smiling.

"Charlie's only saying that because we survived high school together," Drew said.

"But it's true," Charlie said. "Drew left a cushy job as a public defender because he tired of defending slime bags. So now he protects the little guy from big corporations. He--"

"Charlie!" Mark Hampton waved, then gestured toward the empty chairs beside him.

As if some magic button had been pushed, people from the bar strode to the table, everyone jockeying to sit as close to Mark Hampton as possible. There was no way Kim and Scott could sit near her friends.

Rachael tossed Kim a panicked look. Kim responded with the "it'll be okay" smile she'd given Rory when she'd taken him to the vet to be neutered.

Rachael didn't look any more reassured than Rory had.

She found two side-by-side chairs at the far end of the table. To her relief, Drew McDonald sat across from them.

"Are you a paleontologist like Rachael?" He leaned forward, clearly interested in hearing her response.

Kim couldn't help smiling. Most men didn't think to ask women about their careers. Charlie had chosen this friend wisely.

"I wish," she replied. Just the short time digging today reminded Kim of how much she enjoyed field work. "I teach psychology at the University of Maryland."

"Oh! Then you're the jeweler's granddaughter?"

Kim felt her mouth falling open. "How in the world did you know that?"

"Oh, Charlie's been regaling me with stories about you discovering rare diamonds and dodging criminals." Drew grinned. "He's afraid you're going to lead Rachael astray."

Before Kim could reply, Mark Hampton stood and waited for silence.

"I've taken the liberty of special ordering Kobe beef steak for everyone," he began. "The waiters will be coming around to find out how you'd like your steak prepared."

Kim would have preferred something a little lighter to settle her nervous stomach. She scanned the faces of the others, wondering how they'd accepted Mark's cavalier control of their dinners.

The men sitting with Charlie's brothers rubbed their bellies and otherwise indicated delight in the upcoming food. Charlie looked resigned, Rachael annoyed, Drew amused.

"While you're eating your salads," Mark continued, "please allow me a few moments to brag. I'm sure you've heard that one of our guests and her dog--" He nodded toward Kim-- "may have solved an old, local mystery today."

The diners clapped politely.

"I can't say any more right now," he continued, "until we confirm the find. But I can share the great news that Charlie's software has identified another new pocket of emeralds--"

"Dad, we've only found an enlarged quartz vein--"

"But you followed it to the end of the yellow brick road, didn't you?" Mark turned to the others. "I've told this story before, but in light of today's discoveries, I think it's appropriate to tell it again."

He paused as if waiting for objections. No one spoke.

"You've all seen the movie The Wizard of Oz or read the book? If you'll recall, Dorothy needed to reach the Emerald City. To do that, she was told to follow the yellow brick road.

"In real life, we follow the yellow-colored limonite to the pocket of emeralds. Here in North Carolina, following the yellow brick road inevitably leads to the Emerald City.

"But despite my years as an emerald miner, I've never passed through the Emerald City's most guarded door, never walked that long hallway, never stepped behind the curtain to meet the Wizard of Oz.

"Until today. Today I can pull back the curtain to reveal the wizard."

He lifted his glass of wine and turned toward Charlie.

"My son, computer genius and phenomenal emerald hunter. Now that my family is all together again, I hope to have more exciting revelations in the near future."

Charlie's face flushed as he returned his father's impromptu hug. Everyone applauded.

A waiter appeared at Kim's shoulder to ask how she wanted her steak prepared. Knowing she'd never eat a large chunk of meat, she ordered it medium well and specified no added seasoning. The leftovers would make wonderful dog-training treats.

She turned to Scott to find him discussing the plight of the newspaper industry with the man beside him.

With a mental shrug, she reached for her water glass. Drew smiled and leaned forward.

In a voice only loud enough for her ears, he said, "So tell me how your dog found the stolen museum emerald."

Kim jerked, spilling water onto the table.

"How did you . . .?"

"I overheard Michael Dunning asking Mark about it."

Kim frowned and dabbed at the wet spot with her napkin. "Michael's got a big mouth for a lawyer."

"I'm not sure anyone told Dunning to keep the discovery quiet. Besides, Mark just alluded to a long-standing local mystery. Most locals won't have trouble figuring it out."

He steepled his long fingers. "If you're concerned, I promise to not reveal details."

"I'd appreciate that. At least until we return the emerald to the museum."

Keeping her voice low, she described chasing the dogs into the forest and Rory's subsequent find.

"That is absolutely fascinating." Drew sipped his water. "But why did your poodle dig in that particular spot?"

"My guess is that he smelled the cotton bandana. I've been using a similar bandana to play scenting games with him."

"I've got an English bulldog," Drew said. "Wish I could teach him to do something useful."

The image of tall, elegant Drew walking a pudgy bulldog made Kim smile.

The waiters entered in a flurry of sizzling meat and tantalizing smells. As she studied the steaming plate before her, Kim's resentment disappeared. Mark Hampton may have been bossy when he predetermined their dinners, but he'd chosen well. She could almost cut the meat with the side of her fork.

She savored a bite of steak and baked potato, then turned back to Drew.

"Charlie said the land where we found the emerald originally belonged to someone named Benning?"

"That would be Randy Benning. My grandfather used to say Benning was the only white man worse off than us African Americans."

"I'm sorry." Kim laid down her knife and fork. "I forgot this all occurred long before Civil Rights. I hope your family didn't live in poverty."

Drew flashed his charming smile. "Well, to hear my grandfather talk, you'd think my great-grandparents were on the brink of starvation. Truth is, during World War II, most folks around here were pretty poor. Well, with the exception of Charlie's ancestors."

"You don't seem to resent that."

Drew shrugged. "I grew up middle class. Charlie may have been wealthy, but he never flaunted it. It was easy to forget we came from different social classes.

"Actually, now that I think about it, the Benning family had once been wealthy. Used to own as much land as Charlie's family. That's probably why Donalda Sawyer married Randy."

"Donalda Sawyer? Any relation to the Sawyer who helped steal the Carolina Emerald?"

"Yes, ma'am. Donalda was Dominick Sawyer's widow." He tossed her a conspiratorial grin. "Given that you discovered the emerald buried on Randy's land, makes you wonder, doesn't it?"

"Do you think Randy Benning masterminded the entire theft?"

Drew laughed. "Hardly. Randy was a compulsive gambler. His mind was always on the next game."

"So he needed money. What would he do if he saw Sawyer and Hicks burying something on his land? Was he desperate enough to kill the two men and make it look like they'd shot one another?"

"Nah. Randy Benning didn't have a sneaky or mean bone in his body. If you're looking for a mastermind, Donalda Sawyer might qualify."

"Why Donalda? Why not the other man's wife?"

"The Hickses have certainly been involved in plenty of illegal activities. But they don't tend to migrate beyond the immediate area. I can't imagine a Hicks planning a trip to New York, let alone a successful burglary.

"Donalda, however, was from some hoity-toity but recently impoverished Boston family."

Kim speared a tomato from her salad. "How'd she meet Dominick Sawyer? People didn't travel much in those days."

"Dominick placed an ad in the major Eastern newspapers, something along the lines of 'healthy, well-off male seeking genteel lady, object matrimony.' This was during the peak of the Great

Depression, so he got a lot of responses. I've heard Donalda was pretty.

"She was also uppity and never fit in with the locals." He chuckled. "Wish I could have seen her face when Dominick introduced her to his best buddy Gary Hicks."

"Why?"

"I'm sorry; I shouldn't have said that. The Hicks family has endured generations of poverty and bad luck. Most never went to school beyond eighth grade."

Kim nodded. "If Donalda was as class conscious as you describe, she wouldn't have appreciated her husband's choice of friends."

She frowned, trying to create a timeline in her head.

"So let's say Donalda planned the theft of the Carolina Emerald. The two families travel to New York and somehow steal the emerald. They return to North Carolina and . . ."

"And the men bury the emerald on Benning's land," Drew said. "Then they get into an argument and, bang-bang, both men die."

"But even though the widows know their husbands intended to bury the emerald on Randy Benning's land, they don't know the exact location."

"So Donalda seduces Randy Benning and marries him. It all fits."

"Except for why Donalda never found the emerald," Kim said.

Drew waved aside her objection. "She never got a chance to look. Shortly after they married, Randy lost everything in a poker game."

"The game Charlie's ancestor won?"

"Yes ma'am. After losing, Randy went home, shot Donalda, then turned the gun on himself."

Kim gasped. "Those poor people."

"It could have been worse. The night of the poker game, Donalda's daughter -- the one from her marriage to Dominick Sawyer -- was spending the night with a friend. So Amy was spared. Unfortunately, she's also the one who discovered Randy and her mother."

"How old was she?"

"Ten, maybe eleven." He frowned. "Now that I think about it, she was about the same age as Tommy Hicks when this all happened. He's gotta be in his early 70s now."

"Do they still live around here?"

If they did, Kim needed to avoid them. No telling how they'd react to a stranger digging up the emerald their parents had stolen.

"Tommy and his whole clan still own the property that borders what was once Randy Benning's land," Drew said. "As for Amy, she was placed in foster care and later ran away from home. I hope the poor girl found a better life."

A waiter appeared at Kim's side and asked if she wanted a box for her half-finished steak. Kim readily agreed, then began cutting the steak into small, dog-training-sized bites.

"Whoa, don't tell Buster Brown you're bringing steak to your poodle," Drew chuckled. "He'll never forgive me for not saving him some."

"Is Buster Brown your bulldog? How old is he?"

For the next few minutes, they shared funny stories about their dogs. By the time Mark Hampton stood and clinked his glass, the tension in Kim's shoulders had eased.

Mark raised his half-full wine glass.

"I promised Deb we'd save the champagne for Sunday's official engagement party. So would you all please use whatever glass is available and help me toast Charlie and his lovely bride-to-be."

He waited for everyone to raise their glasses. "To Charlie and Rachael. May you be as happy together as Deb and I."

The party quickly broke up. Rachael and Charlie disappeared first, followed by Michael Dunning and a few businessmen. Kim and Scott held hands and stepped outside. Only a few lights illuminated the dark parking lot. Kim couldn't help glancing over her shoulder.

"Something wrong?" Scott said.

"Just nervous. Too many people know that we found the Carolina Emerald."

"Yeah, Mark's reference to a local mystery was ill-advised. The guy sitting next to me asked if you'd found the emerald."

"What did you tell him?"

"I played dumb. Got him to tell me the whole story about Sawyer and Hicks discovering the emerald."

He opened the passenger side door. "We can compare notes on the way home."

As they drove, Scott shared the story he'd heard at dinner. The only new piece of information was the community's disdain for the Hicks family.

"Sounded like people blame the Hickses for everything from burglary to vandalism to tipping over cows," Scott said.

"People don't really tip over cows, do they?"

"Nah, I'm pulling your leg." Scott grinned and touched the brake. "So, what are we going to do to celebrate your finding the Carolina Emerald?"

"I haven't really thought about it. It stills seems unreal. I've dreamed about this since I was a kid."

Oops. She hadn't planned to reveal her childhood ambition. A child might "plan" to solve a decades-old mystery, recover the stolen emerald and demand the museum reward her by naming the gemstone The Kimberley Emerald.

Adults, however, dealt in reality. Setting far-reaching but attainable goals was acceptable, even admirable. Aiming for a Don Quixote impossibility, however, led to failure and despair.

Other than Grandpa, Rachael was the only

person who knew of Kim's dream. And telling her had been an accident. It happened after they'd spent several sleepless nights preparing for final exams. After the last test, they'd wandered into a coffee shop. Giddy from tension and sleep deprivation, they'd toasted their futures and confessed their dreams.

Rachael wanted to discover a new species of dinosaur -- preferably a large, impressive specimen. She intended to marry another paleontologist and spend her days with hubby and kids digging in the bright southwestern sunshine.

Kim's goals were undergoing a metamorphosis. She'd originally planned to obtain her geology degree and use it to search for gemstones that Grandpa could sell in his store. More and more, however, she'd found herself drawn to the study of human thought and behavior.

Why was one person able to claw her way out of poverty while another succumbed to despair? Why, despite so-called progress, couldn't people stop judging one another based on skin color, sexual orientation, religion and economic status? Why couldn't people simply live in harmony?

Finding the Carolina Emerald was the only childhood dream that persisted intact.

Yet even now, after Rory actually discovered the stolen emerald, her childhood hubris embarrassed her.

Scott's gentle questions, however, encouraged her

to reveal the entire tale. She told him about the trip to New York, the tour of the American Museum of Natural History, Grandpa's description of the burglary and the North Carolina sheriff's insistence the theft had been committed by two local losers. She described standing in front of the museum, gazing up at the words "Truth, Knowledge, Vision" and vowing to find the missing emerald.

"I guess that sounds crazy," she said.

"Childhood dreams are never crazy." He squeezed her hand. "After you return the emerald, the museum directors will probably display it with a plaque thanking you. I bet we could convince them to give it a proper name."

The tension in her shoulders eased. Still holding hands, they rode in companionable silence. The car rounded a sharp curve in the road.

Kim leaned forward. "Hey, isn't that Charlie's car?"

Up ahead, a black Ford expedition had been pulled off to the side of the road, the rear end jutting toward the road as if the owner had made a sudden stop. Its rear emergency lights blinked. The headlights from Scott's car illuminated a figure in the passenger seat.

Scott pulled off the road and parked in front of Charlie's car. As Kim stepped out, Rachael raced to them.

"Thank goodness you're here!" She gripped Kim's arm. "Charlie's in trouble, I just know he is."

"Where is he?"

Rachael swung her arm dramatically at the forest.

"In there somewhere. He said he saw that light again, the one his brothers teased him about. He ran into the woods with nothing to protect himself but a flashlight. Told me to stay here and--"

A popping sound came from deep in the forest.

"That was a gun!" Rachael charged toward the forest, screaming Charlie's name.

"Rachael, no!" Kim yelled.

Her friend paid less attention than Rory chasing a rabbit. Despite the ridiculous high-heeled shoes, Rachael quickly disappeared into the trees.

"Get in the car, lock the doors and call 9-1-1," Scott said before racing after Rachael.

Kim dashed to Scott's car, grabbed the heavy flashlight from under the front seat and followed the others into the forest.

CHAPTER 4

Kim's shoulder bag thumped against her hip. As she dodged a tree, her smooth-soled shoes slipped on fallen leaves and pine needles. She slowed her pace and clicked on the flashlight.

From somewhere nearby, Rachael screamed Charlie's name. Kim aimed the flashlight in the direction of her friend's voice. The beam illuminated Rachael slumped on the ground, one hand clenching a shoe with a broken heel, the other rubbing her ankle. Scott hovered above her.

"No, I didn't break anything," Rachael said to Scott. "Just this stupid shoe."

Scott looked up as Kim approached. "Your grandfather wasn't kidding when he said that no one ever told you what to do, was he?"

Hearing the humor in his voice, Kim dismissed the question.

"Any sign of Charlie?" she said.

"No. And he hasn't responded to Rachael calling his name."

Kim's throat tightened. Who had fired a gun? Was Charlie lying out here, bleeding? Or worse?

Scott pulled his cell phone from a pocket and checked the display.

"No reception."

Kim dug her phone from her purse. "Me neither."

It'd been -- What? A minute? Two? -- since they'd heard the shot. Why wasn't Charlie answering?

Whatever was going on, they needed to find him fast.

She turned in a circle, using the flashlight to illuminate the trees, bushes and weeds. To the left, a waist-high bush snagged her attention. She stepped closer and examined the branches. Several twigs had been broken. She touched a light-colored area where the branch had snapped off. It was moist. The damage must have occurred recently.

"I think he went this way," she said.

Scott helped Rachael to her feet. Tossing the shoe down, Rachael kicked off the other.

"Let's go."

When Scott hesitated, Rachael gave him a gentle shove. "I'm fine. Let's find Charlie."

Kim didn't wait for the others. She aimed the

flashlight to illuminate the forest from her waist down. Now she could see scrapes in the leaves and dirt as well as the occasional broken twig. She picked her way along the trail, hoping she was following Charlie and not a deer or other nocturnal creature.

And where were the creatures of the night? Not an owl hooted or a cricket chirped. The only sounds were her own feet shuffling the leaves or snapping a twig and Rachael's occasional curse as she stepped on something thorny.

Scott stayed close beside Kim. The heat resonating from his body provided a measure of comfort.

A low groan came from just ahead. She pointed the flashlight in that direction.

Charlie sprawled on his stomach at the base of a large oak, limbs splayed out like a rag doll. Just beyond his extended right hand lay a hand gun.

"Charlie!"

Rachael brushed past the others and dropped to her knees beside her fiancé.

Charlie groaned. Rachael ran anxious hands over him.

"Where are you shot?" she said.

"Shot? I'm not . . . Ouch."

Rachael stared at her hand. It glistened with blood. With a cry, she parted the hair at the back of Charlie's head. Kim shined the light on a growing bump surrounded by blood. But the bleeding seemed to have stopped.

Kim aimed the light at Charlie's eyes. He immediately protested and closed them. But she'd seen enough to know his pupils were a normal size.

"Can you move your arms?" she said.

Charlie opened his eyes.

"I can move everything." He struggled into a sitting position. "Rachael, please quit fussing."

"What happened?" Kim said.

"Everything went black," he said.

"Yeah, but before that."

She felt Scott move away from her.

"I . . . My head hurts."

Kim frowned. Though Charlie's pupils looked normal, she knew any knock to the brain could cause a concussion.

"How long were you unconscious?" she said.

"Couple seconds, maybe. But I was so foggy, I couldn't move or answer your calls." He frowned. "Did you all hear a shot?"

"Kim." Scott's voice sounded strained. "Can you bring the flashlight over here?"

She found him standing on the other side of the tree. At his direction, she aimed her light at a clearing in the woods. A man lay on his back, right leg bent at an unnatural angle, hands splayed, blank eyes staring at the sky. A splotch of blood over his heart marked the bullet's entry point.

Kim shined her light on the man's face and winced as she recognized the Robert Redford lookalike from the steak house bar.

"I don't think we need to check for a pulse," Scott said. "Probably best to not contaminate the scene."

"That's Kirk Ballas!"

They turned to find Charlie leaning against the side of the oak tree. His left arm wrapped around Rachael.

He gawked at the body, his mouth opening and closing like a guppy. With a groan, he sank to the ground and buried his head in his hands.

"I feel like I'm wading through cotton," he said. "Are you sure this isn't a nightmare?"

"We need to get you to a hospital," Rachael said.

"Just let me sit for a few minutes."

"Tell us what happened," Kim said.

The first part of Charlie's story repeated Rachael's. He'd seen a light flickering on property owned by his family and went to investigate.

"After I reached the forest, the light appeared a couple more times," he said. "So I kept walking in that direction. But as I got closer, I could hear voices."

"How many?"

"At least two. Anyway, I ducked behind this tree." He patted the tree trunk. "I thought I'd, you know, scope out what was happening before confronting the trespassers. But then something hit me on the back of the head. As I fell, I thought I heard a shot. I must have blacked out or something because I didn't hear anything else until Rachael called for me."

Frowning, Kim shined the flashlight around the area where Kirk lay. A foot-long yellow tape fluttered from an overhead branch. At the base of the tree, someone had dug a number of holes, maybe three feet deep.

"Those holes shouldn't be there." Anger punctuated Charlie's words. "I haven't started exploring this area yet."

Seeing the confusion on everyone's face, he added, "I used yellow tape to mark the areas my software identified as good places to look for emeralds." He snorted. "Looks like Kirk decided to do some emerald poaching. I bet Donny and Rocky have been digging here, too. Maybe one of them shot--"

"Charlie!" a new man's voice called. "Charlie, are you here?"

Branches cracked as someone approached from the road.

"Charlie! Answer me!"

"Oh, great, Michael Dunning," Charlie grumbled. "Now I'm going to get a lecture about coming out here on my own."

Raising his voice, he shouted Michael's name. A minute later, the lawyer burst into the clearing. His flashlight illuminated what must have appeared to be a guilty tableau.

"I saw your cars stopped by the road," Michael said. "I knew something was wrong and . . ."

His eyes widened as he spotted Kirk's body. "Oh, Charlie, what have you done?"

CHAPTER 5

Hearing Michael's words, Rachael planted herself in front of the lawyer.

"Charlie didn't do anything! Someone hit him on the head."

Sirens sounded in the distance.

"When I saw the abandoned cars," Michael said, "I called the police. When they arrive, let me do the talking."

Michael and Rachael helped Charlie to his feet.

"Someone needs to stay with the body." Kim didn't know if that was true, but she'd read enough mysteries to feel reluctant to abandon a body.

"I'll stay," Scott said.

"We'll both stay."

Michael just nodded and the trio headed toward the sirens.

A few minutes later a deputy from the sheriff's department relieved Kim and Scott of their vigilance over Kirk's corpse. They made their way back to the road to find two police cars and an ambulance parked behind Scott's car.

The doors to the ambulance were open. Charlie perched in back, feet dangling outside, while two paramedics examined his wound. Rachael held one hand. Nearby, Michael Dunning and a man in a deputy sheriff uniform scowled at each other.

"My client is injured and confused and is not answering any questions," Michael said.

"C'mon, Dunning." The deputy's voice stopped just short of a whine. "If he's innocent like he says, he can tell us what happened."

"Don't treat me like a fool," Michael said. "I may specialize in corporate law, but I understand the tricks you cops like to play. Charlie will not answer any questions until he's recovered."

The deputy scowled and crossed his arms.

Two new cars pulled behind the others. The deputy walked toward the car in front. It opened to reveal a blond-haired woman in uniform. The deputy joined her and started talking in a low voice.

Sheriff Walter Spits climbed from the second car and approached the two officers. The deputy turned to include Spits in his recital. Sheriff Spits said something, then approached the ambulance.

"How's he doing?" he said to the paramedics.

"He won't need stitches," the paramedic said. "But he's got a nasty bump and probably a mild concussion. He should be watched for 24 hours, but he's refusing to go to the hospital."

Sheriff Spits's eyes switched to Charlie's.

"That right, Charlie?"

Charlie shrugged. "You know how I hate hospitals."

"I'll watch over him." Rachael gestured toward Kim and Scott. "We'll all be together, so he should be fine."

"So tell me what happened," Sheriff Spits said.

Michael Dunning stepped forward. "I've advised my client to say nothing at this time."

"I'm asking as a friend of the family, not as sheriff."

"And as the Hamptons' representative, I insist my client remain silent until we've had time to confer."

Before Sheriff Spits could reply, a cell phone rang. Michael pulled his phone from a pocket and frowned at what he read on the screen.

"Excuse me, I have to take this call." He glared at Charlie. "Remember, not a word."

Michael moved away from the group and answered his phone.

"I didn't do it, Uncle Walt," Charlie said.

"Never thought you did," the sheriff replied. "Care to tell me what happened?"

Charlie quickly described seeing lights in the forest, investigating, hearing voices and the knock on the head.

"The others were with me when I came to," he concluded.

The sheriff turned to the others with raised eyebrows. Kim continued the story.

"We found Charlie unconscious," she said. "While Rachael and I tended to Charlie, Scott looked around and discovered Kirk Ballas's body."

"Ballas?" the sheriff said. "What the hell is he doing on Hampton property?"

"Illegally digging for emeralds," Charlie said. "We found a shovel and a number of newly dug holes near a spot I'd identified as a likely place to find emeralds. I'd lay odds that Donny and Rocky were also involved."

"And where was the gun?" Sheriff Spits said.

Kim hesitated. "Uh, it looked like the killer dropped it near Charlie."

Sheriff Spits frowned. "You didn't touch the gun, did you Charlie?"

"Of course not," Charlie said. "You know how I feel about guns."

"So let me see if I got this straight." Sheriff Spits began describing the sequence of events.

Kim turned away and scanned the area. The woman officer and deputy sheriff had disappeared; they'd probably returned to the crime scene. Michael Dunning stood a few feet away, phone pressed to his ear. He suddenly growled, "It's just a poodle!"

She bristled, crossed her arms and glared at Mr. Hotshot Lawyer. In the two years she'd owned Rory, she'd grown overly sensitive to the popular view of poodles as yappy frou-frou dogs.

She knew this reputation stemmed from the exaggerated haircuts used on show dogs. But underneath all that hair, poodles were intelligent, highly trainable and easy to live with. Michael Dunning's sneering "it's just a poodle" gave her one more reason to dislike him.

Dunning glanced her way. His eyes narrowed and he turned his back to her. A few seconds later, he tucked his phone into his pocket and walked toward her.

"You have a poodle, right?" he said. "My girlfriend just got this poodle and it's driving her crazy. It keeps stealing things and when she corrects it, it hunches over and acts like it's been beaten or something."

Kim's shoulders relaxed. She'd much rather talk about dogs than murder. "Sounds like a soft dog. She needs to figure out how to communicate what she wants without sounding harsh. Has she taken him to classes? The AKC Good Citizen classes focus on manners and things instead competition style obedience."

"Er." Michael shuffled his feet. "I'll pass that along."

Kim silently chastised herself. She had a bad habit of assuming all dog owners wanted to learn how to communicate with their furry friends. Far too often, they shared Dunning's need to vent without really wanting to learn how to prevent further trouble.

Michael looked over her shoulder. "I'd better get back to Charlie," he said.

As Michael moved away, Kim saw the woman officer emerge from the forest. The deputy who'd challenged Michael trudged a few steps behind, shoulders hunched like a beaten dog. As they neared, she could see the woman held a plastic evidence bag containing the gun.

She planted herself too close to Charlie.

"Did you touch this?" She held up the gun.

Before Charlie could answer, Sheriff Spits pushed between them.

"This is Lieutenant Cummings," he said. "She'll be leading the investigation. She just moved here from California and is still adjusting to our more neighborly style."

The woman stiffened and her lips thinned. Her eyes flicked from Sheriff Spits to Charlie.

After a moment, her shoulders relaxed and she extended a hand to Charlie.

"Sorry," she said. "Where I come from, we never had time for social niceties."

Charlie shook her hand.

"Did you touch the gun?" Lieutenant Cummings

said.

"Don't answer that," Michael Dunning said. "Sheriff, I insist I meet with my client before you conduct any interviews."

"I'm nobody's client because I'm innocent."

Charlie stood, then stumbled. Rachael grabbed his arm.

"Maybe you should go to the hospital," Rachael said.

"No, I'll be fine."

"In that case," the sheriff said, "I'd like you to come to the station now to give us a statement. The sooner we know what happened, the sooner we can find the killer."

"Fine, I'll take Rachael home and meet you all at the station."

Lieutenant Cummings, Michael Dunning and Rachael all spoke at once. Rachael insisted on driving to the station with Charlie. Michael wanted Charlie to ride with him. Lieutenant Cummings demanded Charlie ride in the back of her official car.

Sheriff Spits held up his hand for silence. "Let's do it this way. Charlie, you ride with me. Michael, you can follow in your car. When we get to the station, you and Charlie will have time to talk before he gives his statement to Lieutenant Cummings."

"I'm coming, too," Rachael said.

"You won't be allowed in the interview room,"

Sheriff Spits said. "And you seem a little stressed to safely operate a car. Why don't you get some rest? Charlie will be home soon."

Rachael rolled her eyes. "I'm coming."

"She can ride with me," Michael said. "When we're finished, I'll drive them both home."

"What about my car?" Charlie said.

At last, here was something Kim could do to help.

"Scott and I will take care of it," she said.

Charlie tossed Kim his car keys and followed the sheriff to his vehicle. He kissed Rachael, then climbed into the passenger seat.

"We'd better go," Michael said.

Rachael nodded. Kim took her friend's arm and walked to Michael's car.

"It's going to be okay," she said. "Charlie didn't shoot anyone and when they don't find his fingerprints on the gun, they'll let him go."

But nothing she said wiped the worry from Rachael's eyes.

Kim steered Charlie's car along the dark, winding roads. The headlights did little to illuminate the asphalt road or its worn center lines. She leaned forward, scanning the surrounding woods for deer.

Normally, the inky night wouldn't unnerve her. But after discovering Kirk Ballas's body, she was grateful for the presence of Scott's car behind her.

The appearance of a single traffic light indicated proximity to Charlie's cabin. As she passed under it, the light turned yellow. In her rear-view mirror, she saw Scott stop for the red.

With no safe place to pull over to wait, she continued on without him. She needed to check on the dogs. They'd been trapped inside for several hours and probably needed a potty break.

She turned onto the long, narrow driveway that led to Charlie's cabin and drove through the trees. As the lodge came into view, she heard Rory's deep-throated bark and Al's high-pitched baying.

She frowned. Were both dogs freaked out by staying alone in a new place?

Or was something else wrong?

Parking the car, she snagged the front-door keys from her purse and trotted up the porch stairs.

"I'm coming," she called.

But the barking continued. The poor dogs were so stressed they probably hadn't heard the car or her voice.

She pushed the door open and again called to the dogs. When they continued to bark, she dropped her purse and ran up the stairs to the second floor. Turning right, she headed toward the room where they'd left the dogs.

"It's okay, fellas, I'm here."

Before she could open the door, movement in her peripheral vision alerted her to an intruder. She whipped around to see a tall, menacing shape. Dressed in black from head to toe, his gloved right hand clenched something long. A knife?

Even as the thought formed, the man advanced on her.

Rory slam against the bedroom door, his barks now accompanied by growls. She reached behind her, searching for the door knob. Her fingers brushed the cold metal.

"Kim? Is everything okay?"

The intruder swerved toward Scott's voice.

"Watch out!" she called. "He's got a knife."

Scott's footsteps pounded on the steps. The man snarled and plunged down the stairs. Kim twisted the door knob. Rory burst through and ran toward the staircase. As he rounded the landing, she heard the sound of bodies falling.

"Scott!"

She reached the top of the staircase in time to see Rory leap over Scott's body. The poodle's paws skittered on the hardwood floor as he turned and raced toward the back of the house.

She ran down the stairs. "Scott?"

He groaned and pushed himself into a sitting position. She heard the back door open then slam shut. Rory's bark sounded from the kitchen. Al, trapped in his upstairs crate, continued to howl.

She ran anxious hands over Scott's body. "Are you hurt?"

"Just my pride. His shoulder block was worthy of

Bruce Smith"

"I assume you're talking about a football player."

"Redskins Hall of Famer, retired with 200 career sacks."

Kim shook her head.

"You guys and your foot--" Her eyes widened.

Hadn't Charlie said Kirk Ballas and his buddy Rocky DiSoto played high school football? They, along with the thug Donny Driver, had been at the restaurant when Charlie's father was hinting about Rory's discovery.

"Crap."

As she pushed to her feet, Rory returned to her side.

"What's wrong?"

"The emerald."

She ran up the stairs, Rory at her feet. She turned left instead of right and flew into her bedroom. Flipping on the light, she stared at the bare spot on the bedside table.

The bandana and the emerald it wrapped were gone.

CHAPTER 6

"I can't believe I allowed someone to steal the Carolina Emerald."

Kim accepted the mug of hot chocolate that Scott held out.

"You're not to blame."

Scott set his own mug on the coffee table, scooped Al off of the sofa and sat beside her. "Too many people knew about your discovery."

"That's just it. I should have hidden the emerald, never let anyone see it until I'd figured out how to keep it safe."

"You did the right thing showing the emerald to Charlie," Scott said. "After all, you found it on his family's land. And he had the right to show it to his brothers. It's not your fault that the Hamptons chose to disclose the discovery to other people.

"And don't forget: Before going to dinner, you asked Charlie to secure the emerald in the safe at his parents' house. It was his decision to keep the emerald here."

"Then you and I should have stayed to protect it."

She kicked off her shoes and curled her legs beneath her.

"That might have had worse consequences. We only saw one thief, but I doubt he came alone."

Kim frowned. "Why do you say that?"

"It's well past midnight. If the police hadn't detained us, we would all have been in bed asleep. That means the thief came prepared to neutralize us before searching our rooms. So we're probably talking about two, maybe three people."

He slipped his arm around her.

"I'm glad we weren't here."

"I know you're trying to make me feel better," she said. "But that emerald was one-of-a-kind. What if the thief chops it up so no one can identify it?"

She fought back tears. "If we don't find it fast, it'll be lost again, maybe even destroyed and it's all my fault."

Scott pulled her close and stroked her hair. The gesture removed all self-control. She clung to him and started to cry. Scott whispered reassurances, but she was too full of self-recrimination to listen.

Rory pushed between them and began licking her face. When she tried to push him away, he wrapped his front paws around her. Through her tear-drenched glasses, she saw his eyes widen with concern.

"I'm okay," she said.

She must have sounded convincing because Rory suddenly grinned, snagged one of her shoes and raced to the other side of the room. Dropping into a play bow, he wagged his tail, daring her to chase him. The silly look on his face made her laugh.

Scott set a box of tissues onto her lap, removed her glasses and used a clean handkerchief to clean them. She blew her nose and wiped her eyes. Rory trotted back and dropped the shoe into her lap.

"Oh, you expect a cookie after that performance?"

She couldn't resist, however. He had, after all, stopped her tears.

She handed Rory a cookie and accepted her now-clean glasses from Scott.

"Sorry about that."

"You can cry on my shoulder any time. Though I hate to see you unhappy."

She sighed. "I wish the police would get here. It's been an hour since we called!"

"I doubt Sheriff Spits has many deputies. They're probably all working the murder scene."

"Yeah, well, the sooner they start investigating

the theft, the sooner we can find this guy."

"You do realize that police seldom catch house burglars, right? The best they can do is question known fences or check out nearby pawn shops."

"Surely the thief is smart enough to not pawn something as distinctive as the Carolina Emerald. He'll need to find a lapidarist to cut it--"

Her heartbeat quickened and she grabbed Scott's arm.

"The Gem Festival! There'll be gem cutters participating. That would be the perfect place to find someone to cut the emerald for him."

"So when we're at the festival on Saturday, we'll talk to the lapidarists."

He pulled her close and whispered in her ear. "Why don't we think about something else for a while?"

"Or maybe not think at all." She leaned toward him.

Rory's head popped between them. Flashing a poodle smile, he licked first Kim, then Scott. She started giggling.

After a moment, Scott chuckled and leaned away.

"Maybe we need a vacation without the kids."

She placed her hands over Rory's ears. "Not in front of the children."

They shared a smile. Laying her head on Scott's shoulder, she stared into the flames. Her shoulders relaxed. She closed her eyes.

The barking of the dogs woke her from a sound

sleep.

Opening her eyes, she blinked at the unfamiliar room, disoriented. She lay on her side, her cheek resting on a scratchy sofa cushion. Scott lay behind her, one arm draped over her waist. He stirred and kissed the nape of her neck.

" 'morning."

Kim turned her face toward him and smiled.

"Good morning to you, too."

She kissed him lightly on the lips, then sat up and reached for the glasses she'd laid on the coffee table. Her cell phone indicated it was just past 5:30 a.m. They'd slept maybe three hours.

Rory and Al ran into the room, their floppy ears flying. Rachael followed close behind.

Kim took one look at Rachael's pale face and leaped to her feet.

"What's wrong?"

Rachael threw herself into Kim's arms and wailed, "They found Charlie's fingerprints on the gun!"

CHAPTER 7

A million questions swirled through Kim's mind, but she knew Rachael couldn't answer them until she'd calmed down.

"Where's Charlie?" she said.

"Outside with Drew, you remember, Charlie's lawyer friend you met at the party?"

Rachael dragged fingers through her hair, tangling it.

"Drew drove us home. He wanted to talk to Charlie alone."

"Well, when Charlie comes in he's going to be hungry."

Kim shared the British view of the restorative properties of tea heavily laced with sugar. As much as she wanted to ask how the heck Charlie's fingerprints ended up on the gun, she first needed to assuage her friend's shock. Rachael should find the process of preparing a light meal soothing.

She gently turned Rachael toward the kitchen.

"Charlie's going to need coffee and I know you'd love some tea."

After putting Rachael in charge of preparing toast, Kim set a pot of water onto the stove to boil and began preparing the teapot. She found butter and strawberry jam in the refrigerator and set them onto the table beside the toast. As she poured the now-hot water into the teapot, Charlie stepped inside.

Splotches of dirt covered the knees of the tailored trousers he'd worn to dinner. Sweat marks stained the open collar and underarms of his once-white shirt. Shoulders hunched, he shuffled to a chair and slumped into it.

He plopped both elbows onto the table and buried his face in his hands.

"I can't believe this is happening."

Rachael leaned over to hug him. He dropped his hands to his lap and straightened. His handsome face was puffy and splotched. Dark circles under his eyes attested to the sleepless night.

Scott set a mug of coffee in front of him. Charlie nodded his thanks.

"I didn't kill him," Charlie said.

"Of course you didn't," Kim said. "Anyone who

knows you would never believe you'd shoot someone."

Charlie snorted.

"Tell that to Lieutenant Cummings. As soon as she found my fingerprints on the gun, she wanted to arrest me. Thank goodness Drew was there."

Kim resisted the urge to question the appearance of Drew when Michael Dunning was on the scene. First she needed to find out what happened at the police station.

"Any idea why they found your fingerprints on the gun?" she said.

Charlie shook his head.

"I don't remember anything after that knock on the head. I guess I could have touched it as I was waking up. Drew argued that the killer tried to frame me by wrapping my fingers around the gun.

"The thing is, why would anyone want to frame me? I just moved back here a few months ago and I don't think I've offended people."

"What about Kirk's friends?"

"Donny and Rocky?" Charlie frowned. "I suppose framing me for murder would appeal to Donny. But that would mean Donny or Rocky killed Kirk. Why would they do that?"

"Well, if they were looking for emeralds together, maybe they got into an argument. Did any of those guys carry a gun?"

"In high school, Donny relied on his fists to intimidate us," Charlie said. "I suppose that could have changed; it's been more than ten years since I last saw him."

"Getting back to the gun," Scott said, "I assume the police tested your hand for gunpowder residue?"

"They found residue on my palm but not the back of my hand."

"Good," Scott said.

"What's good about it?"

Scott turned to Kim and grinned. "If the killer wrapped Charlie's hand around the gun, residue would have rubbed off on Charlie's palm. But if Charlie had actually fired the gun, there'd also be residue on the back of his hand."

"Good thing Drew knew that," Charlie said. "He's the one who insisted they swab both sides of my hand. They were only going to swab my palm."

He frowned. "Of course, that Lieutenant Cummings still wanted to arrest me. She said the new guns don't make much residue, so the back of my hand could be clean even if I fired it."

Rachael gripped Charlie's hand.

"What is wrong with that woman? She acted like she didn't believe me when I told her you carried a flashlight into the woods, not a gun."

"Drew says she's some hotshot detective from LA."

"Then what the heck is she doing here?" Kim said.

"Came with her husband," Charlie said. "He

works for Fish & Game studying diseases in bats. Drew says she wants to run for sheriff when Uncle Walt retires, so she's looking to make a name for herself."

"By arresting an innocent man," Rachael said.

Charlie squeezed her hand. "Don't worry; Drew won't let them do that."

Seeing her chance to learn more about Drew McDonald, Kim said, "Michael Dunning told the sheriff that he was your lawyer."

"Michael is Dad's lawyer." Charlie's voice was bitter. "He does nothing but contracts, property rights and wills. Before moving here, Drew had one of the highest dismissal rates in Charlotte's public defender's office."

"Then why come here?" Scott said. "I wouldn't think there'd be much work here for a defense attorney."

"He's doing corporate law now," Charlie said. "Said he grew tired of defending guilty people, but I think the real reason for switching is he wanted to live close to his aging parents. Still pisses me off that Dad hired Michael Dunning instead of Drew."

"Do you know why he chose Michael?"

Okay, so this was a bit off topic, but Kim was curious why anyone other than a racist would choose pushy Michael Dunning over personable Drew McDonald.

"Michael's in the rock club with my brothers," Charlie said. "They convinced Dad that having someone with a passing knowledge of the mining business would be preferable to someone whose only claim to fame was my recommendation."

Now that she'd met Charlie's father, the bitterness in Charlie's voice didn't surprise Kim.

"And speaking of Dad . . ." Charlie turned to Rachael. "Why did you call him? He stormed into the station before Drew arrived and cursed at anyone who crossed his path. Uncle Walt wouldn't let him talk with me and they almost got into a fist fight. I heard it all from the interview room."

Rachael threw her hands into the air.

"I didn't call your father. Michael called him on the way to the station. Then he spent the rest of the ride quizzing me about what happened and trying to coach me on what to tell the deputies. Like I was some kind of suspect or something."

"Sounds like Michael."

Charlie set his empty coffee cup on the table and stood. He hadn't even touched the toast.

"We'd better get some rest," he said. "Now that I'm Number One Suspect, Dad called a powwow for 9 a.m. We'll all need to be there."

Kim watched her friends climb the stairs and turn toward their room. Rachael's rigid, squared shoulders projected her intention to protect her man.

Did Charlie really need protecting?

She thought through what she'd been told. When the gun was fired, Charlie had been alone at the scene. Police found his fingerprints on the gun and gunshot residue on his palm.

In his defense, he'd clearly been hit on the head, he didn't have gun powder on the back of his hand and Rachael saw him run into the woods with a flashlight, not a gun.

But would a jury believe the defendant's fiancé? A good prosecutor could confuse a jury about gun powder residue and find a reason for the bump on Charlie's head. Heck, the prosecutor might claim Rachael helped Charlie by hitting him so he'd have an alibi.

The biggest danger, however, appeared to be the new hot-shot detective from California. Lieutenant Cummings wanted to make a quick arrest. Would she investigate people other than Charlie?

Someone needed to identify alternative suspects.

"So," Scott interrupted her thoughts, "we've got a few hours to kill. I assume we're going to do some investigating?"

Kim grinned at him. "Yeah, but first I want to call Grandpa."

After a quick shower, Kim donned clean jeans and a flannel shirt, then reached for her cell phone. Even though it was just past 7 a.m., she knew Grandpa would be awake and preparing the jewelry store for opening. Sure enough, he answered on the third ring.

"Your display is a great success," he said by way of greeting.

She smiled. Since moving back to Maryland, she had taken responsibility for designing Osprey Beach Jewelry's all-important front-window display. To celebrate autumn, she'd arranged preserved autumn leaves and gnarled twigs in the window, then scattered necklaces, earrings, bracelets and rings over the foliage. She'd selected jewelry set with stones the colors of autumn: rubies, fire opals, citrine, yellow and orange sapphires, mandarin garnets, Oregon sunstones. From the boardwalk, the window to her grandfather's store looked like a sugar maple tree draped in jewels.

Grandpa claimed her creative displays pulled in potential customers. Kim suspected her grandfather exaggerated to suit his own purposes. She'd only recently returned to Osprey Beach after almost a decade of living and teaching in Oregon. When she'd accepted a professorship at the University of Maryland, Grandpa had offered the use of his newly created guest suite. Knowing it might be months, if not years, before she could sell her Oregon house, she'd gladly accepted.

She paid Grandpa a small monthly rent and assisted in the shop when she wasn't teaching. She'd also served as a makeshift nurse after a bungled burglary in July landed Grandpa in the hospital.

But while the living arrangement benefited both of them, Kim had lived alone too long to be comfortable sharing space with another adult. She knew Grandpa longed for Kim to continue living in his guest suite and, even better, quit her teaching job to become part-owner in the store. She hated to disappoint him.

Which is why she now accepted his compliment without comment. Instead, she launched into a retelling of yesterday's events. Though she emphasized the discovery and loss of the Carolina Emerald, her grandfather focused on the murder.

"Please tell me you're not going to investigate this murder," he said.

"Someone took time to wrap Charlie's hand around the murder weapon," she said. "The lead investigator is looking for a quick arrest. Right now Charlie is the only suspect."

"But he has the sheriff on his side," Grandpa said. "And don't forget that you're not in Osprey Beach. You don't know the area or the people and the locals may resent you for poking around."

She paused, considering. Grandpa was right. Not only might she be unable to help Charlie, her lack of local knowledge might lead her to make the situation worse.

"Actually," she said, "I'm more interested in trying to find the Carolina Emerald. I didn't get a chance to confirm this, but I think the New York museum engraved identifying marks on the rock base of the gemstone. But those could be removed.

"Could the thief sell the emerald to a museum? It's been well over half a century since Sawyer and Hicks stole the emerald. You know how people don't pay much attention to history. And, unlike the Murph the Surf theft, this one wasn't well known."

"But there are photos of the emerald," Grandpa said. "And the size and three-column shape makes it pretty distinctive. Before buying something that rare, any reputable museum would demand proof that the seller owned the stone. Someone would investigate the emerald's provenance.

"Besides, with the current interest in American gemstones, the emerald may be worth more if it was faceted for jewelry."

"I was afraid you'd say that. But he'll need to find someone to cut the emerald."

She forced a dramatic sigh. "I guess I'll have to spend time at the Gem Festival interviewing lapidarists."

"They might be more inclined to talk to someone in the jewelry business," Grandpa said.

Kim grinned. Grandpa had responded as she'd hoped. Now she needed to push him to commit.

"Oh, Grandpa, that would be so wonderful if you could come to the festival with us!" she gushed. "I'm sure the Hamptons won't mind you and Aunt Ginny arriving early and I know Doris and Maureen are available to work in the store. How soon can you leave?"

As she waited for his reply, she crossed her fingers.

Her grandfather chuckled.

"Well, that was a well-placed trap," he said. "Okay, you win. I'll call the ladies and ask for their help. Ginny has been nagging to leave early, so she'll be thrilled. In the meantime, please stay out of trouble."

"Trouble? I don't get into trouble. We're just going to take the dogs for a walk."

"Uh, huh. While you're walking, try not to antagonize the police."

"Okay, Daniel Boone, now I'm completely lost." Scott removed his Indiana Jones hat and wiped his forehead. "Are you sure you know how to use that thing?"

Kim frowned down at the battered compass she always carried in her backpack. Aunt Ginny had given it to her years ago when they went on their first hike in the Blue Ridge Mountains. She'd been surprised at how easily one could become lost even in a highly traveled forest like the one growing alongside the Blue Ridge Parkway. Since then, the compass lived in whatever backpack she currently carried.

"Of course I know how," she said. "The problem

is Charlie's directions. He said we could reach our digging site if we walked due east from the cabin. That's what we've been doing."

"Maybe you should let Rory lead the way."

Kim smiled and watched the standard poodle romp ahead of them, the little dachshund frantically trying to keep up.

"I'm sure he'd lead us somewhere; I just don't know where."

"Well, he did find the emerald," Scott said.

"Yeah, and I wish I knew how he did that."

"Thought you said he smelled the bandana that wrapped the emerald."

"That's just a theory. And now that my bandana was stolen along with the emerald, I don't have a way to test it."

"So let's buy a new bandana." He grinned. "Of course, to do a proper scientific study, we'll need to wrap the bandana around an emerald and bury it beneath a tree."

Kim laughed, then pointed to the left. "East is this way."

Skirting a tree, she tramped over fallen leaves. Morning light filtered through the overhead branches and the air possessed that crisp aroma of fall. Twigs snapped underfoot and from somewhere nearby a blue jay squawked.

If nothing else, she mused, she was enjoying both the walk and her alone time with Scott and the dogs. Even as the thought formed, Al let out a long bay and charged through the underbrush. Rory paused, head cocked, and watched the dachshund's plumy tail disappear. Kim snagged Rory's long line as Scott made a lunge for Al's, missed and tripped into a blackberry bush.

"I'm okay," Scott said as he struggled to stand. "Catch Al."

She gripped Rory's line and ran after Al. Between the dachshund's baying and Rory's desire to reach his buddy, she had no trouble following him. A blackberry thicket suddenly blocked her way. She circled to the left and found herself at the edge of the forest. The clearing Charlie had made for their emerald hunting stretched in front of her. To her right, Al's feet scrambled in the light-color clay. But he couldn't move forward because his long line had tangled in the blackberry thorns.

Panting, she knelt and started detaching the line from the thorns. The slap of heavy boots warned her of Scott's approach.

"I've got him," she yelled.

Scott arrived at the same moment she freed Al. Totally unrepentant, the little dachshund lunged toward open space. The line, now securely twined in Kim's fist, stopped him from going far.

Kim straightened and stared in the direction Al pointed. On the other side of the clearing, police had attached yellow tape to the trees. She could hear voices, but no clear words.

"The dogs would probably love to walk along the

tree line, wouldn't you think?" Scott's voice was amused.

Kim smiled up at him. "Read my mind. Let's start over there in the warm sunshine." She pointed to an area just uphill from the police tape.

They exchanged the dogs' long roaming lines for regular leashes and strolled across the clearing. Skirting the pit they'd been excavating, they continued in a north-east direction toward the forest on the far side. Rory and Al bounded ahead of them, occasionally stopping to enlarge a test hole.

When they reached the tree line, they turned south and made their way toward the place where they'd discovered the body. As they neared, the voices grew more distinct. At first, they could discern only a few words here and there. One voice sounded young and excited. The second voice possessed the tired, been-there-done-that tone of the seasoned cop.

They finally drew close enough to hear whole sentences.

"Think Sheriff Spits will allow the Princess to arrest Charlie Hampton?" young cop said.

"If Charlie's guilty, he'll have no choice," old cop said.

"Know who I think did it? One of them Hicks."

Old cop snorted. "Can't blame everything that happens 'round here on the Hickses."

"Well, you gotta admit them Hicks get involved in some creepy shit. Hell, they built the first jail in

Taylorsville just to house a Hicks."

"That's urban legend and you know it."

"Maybe so," young voice said. "But I heard the old man's now gotten involved in Voodoo. Last week, not far from where we're standing, some kids found a headless chicken hanging from an oak tree. They said-- Hey! What are you doing here?"

Kim tightened her hold on Rory as a young cop came flying through the trees. He was moving so fast he barely stopped before crashing into the yellow tape.

Kim bit back a grin. In his haste to catch them, a low-hanging branch had knocked his hat askew.

Widening her eyes, she said in her best who-me voice,"Why, officer, we're just taking the dogs for a walk. Didn't even notice that yellow tape stuff until you appeared."

Young cop planted his feet and folded his arms. "Well, you just move along, missy. This here is a police investigation."

Kim bristled at the term "missy," but managed to keep her tone light. "Oooh, really? Are you one of those investigators just like the ones on CSI?"

The man's chest puffed out. "That's what we're doing here; looking for clues."

"And have you found any?"

"As a matter of fact--"

"That's enough, Officer Jennings." The cop with the tired voiced stepped into view. To Kim's surprise, he didn't appear any older than her.

Sunlight, long work hours and probably alcohol had roughened his skin, but she couldn't see a speck of gray in his brush-cut hair.

He made a shooing motion. "Please move along, folks. This is a crime scene."

The steel in his blue eyes told her not to argue.

Kim tossed him what she hoped was a pleasant smile, then started to turn away. As she did, movement in a nearby bush caught her attention. A boy, maybe nine or ten, peered out at her. She registered brown eyes, button nose and a dirty face before the boy backed farther into the underbrush.

Not wanting to draw the cops' attention to the child, she walked briskly away from his hiding place.

Scott waited until they were well out of hearing range before saying "That was informative."

"Maybe they'll investigate the Hickses and leave Charlie alone," she said.

"Well, if that fellow back there has his way, the Hicks family is in trouble," Scott said.

They continued their stroll in companionable silence, stopping only to allow the dogs to dig for a few minutes before moving on. The silence allowed Kim to let her mind wander.

At first, her thoughts centered around the murder and the potential danger to Charlie and Rachael. But the warm sun combined with the feel of Scott's hand in hers and enthusiastic romping of the dogs soothed her emotional turmoil.

She looked longingly at the emerald pit, hoping the meeting with Mark Hampton wouldn't take too long. She couldn't wait to investigate the area where Scott discovered limonite.

"Hey, you!"

The young cop's shout froze Kim in her tracks. She turned in time to see the red-faced man haul the boy from his hiding place.

"What are you doing here you little sneak?"

Gripping the boy's upper arms with beefy hands, the cop lifted him from the ground and shook him. The boy's sneakered feet peddled furiously as he struggled to get away.

"I asked you what you're doing?"

Another shake and the boy started to cry.

Kim tossed Rory's leash to Scott and charged up the hill.

"Take your hands off that child!"

She ducked under the police tape and ripped the boy from the cop's arms. The child spun around and wrapped his arms around her waist. She pulled him close and stepped away from the angry cop. Scott and the dogs quickly joined her.

Young cop pointed at the boy.

"That's not a child. That's a sneaky little Hicks and I want to know why he was spying on me."

"Wasn't spying," the child said into Kim's shirt.

"Then what do you call hiding in the bushes and watching me? Maybe you'll feel more inclined to talk after a ride in the backseat of my car."

The boy tightened his grip on Kim. She stared down, horrified to see the red imprint of the cop's fingers on both of the child's skinny upper arms.

"You've bruised him," she said. "I should report you for police brutality."

The cop's hands clenched into fists. She felt Scott's presence before Rory pushed in front of her, placing himself between the boy/Kim sandwich and the cop. Al ducked between Rory's legs and began barking.

The cop's eyes widened. Stepping back, his right hand reached for his gun holster.

Scott moved between the dogs and cop.

"Hey, let's take it easy here. No one wants to get into a fight."

The cop's eyes narrowed and for a moment Kim feared he'd pull his gun anyway.

"Cooper!"

A young woman burst through the trees and dashed toward them.

"Mom!"

Cooper turned and threw himself into his mother's arms.

Cooper's mother was thin, borderline anorexic. Perhaps in her late 20s -- the same age as the young cop -- she shared her son's button nose and full lips. But Cooper's brown eyes must have come from his father. The mother's were sea-water blue. And right now they flashed with defiance.

"Betty Hicks, what do you think you're doing?"

the cop said. "This is a crime scene and you're ruining my evidence."

"You keep your filthy hands off my son."

The cop scowled.

"You may have birthed this little bastard -- though why you'd take up with a Hicks is beyond me -- but he's Hicks trash and he's been spying on me and I want to know why and what he's seen."

During the cop's angry speech, Betty's face grew increasingly red. Her mouth narrowed and her chin lifted and a vein bulged in her neck.

"What's going on here?"

The older cop appeared. "Can't I even take a leak without you getting into trouble?"

Young cop pointed a finger a Cooper.

"This little bas-- brat's been spying. I'm just trying to find out what he saw."

The older man turned and knelt in front of Cooper.

"Do you know anything about what happened here last night?"

Cooper grew very still.

"No, sir," he mumbled, looking at the ground.

"Are you sure, son? Remember, it's a crime to lie to the police."

The lie tripped smoothly from the officer's lips without either a shift of his eyes or a twitch of a toe. Lying to a cop might be dumb, but it wasn't illegal. Kim made a mental note to not trust either of these men.

Cooper shuffled his feet, then raised his eyes to stare at the older cop.

"Don't know nothing."

The cop stared at Cooper, then nodded, stood and looked at Betty.

"Take him on home and keep him there." His tone softened the harsh words. "We can't have him disturbing a crime scene."

He turned toward Kim. "And as for you. . ."

"We're leaving," Scott assured him.

But as they hurried away, Kim couldn't resist one final look over her shoulder. Both cops stood planted behind the tape, legs spread, arms folded, watching her. So neither man noticed Cooper's furtive glance as his mother led him away.

CHAPTER 8

The encounter with the two deputies had consumed much of the morning. They hurried back to the cabin to find Rachael and Charlie awake, dressed and ready to tackle whatever Charlie's father had planned. Charlie offered to drive the mile to his parents' mansion. So after settling the dogs in Scott's room, Kim, Scott and Rachael piled into Charlie's car.

Like Charlie's cabin, the Hamptons' home had been built on top of a hill. Instead of a natural forest, however, the winding driveway traversed a carefully landscaped lawn. Kim recognized the glossy leaves of southern magnolias, the whitish bark of crape myrtles, the spreading branches of dogwoods. Dotted among them were the ever-present Southern favorites: azaleas and rhododendrons.

The carefully coiffed landscape should have prepared Kim for her first view of the mansion. But Charlie's childhood home offered charming surprises. A wrap-around porch welcomed visitors to the sprawling, two-story house. Slender white columns supported a second-story balcony while lacy white railings graced the porch, balcony and roof line. The walls had been painted soft peach. A deep, orangey peach door beckoned the visitor.

The fairy-tale feel was only slightly marred by the wheel-chair ramp jutting from the side porch.

"This is beautiful," Kim said as she followed Charlie up the front stairs. "I love the combination of colors."

Charlie shrugged. "Mom studied art in college."

Before he could knock, the door was opened by a middle-aged housekeeper. She gave them little time to gawk at the apartment-sized entryway, leading the way to what was obviously Mark Hampton's lair.

Unlike the home's exterior, this large room screamed testosterone. On one wall, bookshelves flanked a massive stone fireplace. In the far corner, a walnut bar stood in front of a shelf of alcohol, drink mixes and glasses. The rest of the walls were lined with book-filled shelves. Oriental carpets, overstuffed leather chairs and loveseats created conversation nooks throughout the large room.

Kim longed to browse the books and, perhaps, curl into one of the loveseats.

In front of her, Jake and Diesel stood beside a tea cart filled with pastries, coffee urn and -- yes! -- china tea pot.

"Pour you a cup?" Jake gestured with the coffee pot.

Charlie and Scott accepted coffee while Kim poured fragrant black tea into rose-decorated cups for her and Rachael. By the time she'd slipped a cherry Danish onto a matching plate and grabbed a napkin, the others had gathered by the fire.

"Scott just told us you've had a run-in with our fine sheriff's department," Diesel said.

Kim set her goodies on an end table and settled into a chair before relating what happened this morning.

"The boy lied to the cops," she concluded. "I'm really afraid he saw something last night."

"Wouldn't surprise me." Jake sipped his coffee. "The Hickses have always allowed their children to run wild."

"Is that why the police seemed so suspicious of them?"

Kim bit into the flaky pastry, rejoicing in the contrast between tart cherry and buttery crust. If the Hamptons ate like this every day, it was amazing no one was obese.

"Let's just say that whenever there's a crime in

the area, the police usually arrest a Hicks," Jake said.

Kim turned to Charlie.

"Did the murder victim hang around with the Hickses?"

Charlie shook his head.

"No. You have to understand that around here there's an economic hierarchy. Donny, Kirk and Rocky grew up middle class. The Hickses have always been poor."

"They've also always been thieves and worse," Diesel said. "During prohibition, they kept the locals supplied with moonshine. When liquor became legal some of them switched to marijuana. The Feds are sure the old man maintains a still around here, but they haven't found it."

"Why would they care?" Kim said. "Prohibition ended almost a century ago."

"Taxes," Jake said. "The Feds go crazy when people like Tommy Hicks sell cheap, tax-free booze."

"Tommy's peach brandy is actually pretty good," Diesel said, "though it kicks like a mule."

Jake's eyes widened. "You actually buy booze from that snake?"

Diesel grinned. "Hey, it's cheap and, as you say, bro, I don't have to pay taxes on it."

"Geez Louise, Diesel, you have no idea what goes into Tommy's rotgut. For all you know, there's enough lead in that stuff to strangle your car."

Diesel shrugged. "Tommy's been making that shit long enough to know how to keep it safe. Hell, if he wasn't such an ornery old cuss, the locals would erect him a shrine and name their kids after him."

"Well, just be careful," Jake said. "Tommy may seem harmless, but rumor says he's now into voodoo."

Kim rolled her eyes. She could understand the young cop spreading voodoo rumors. But Jake was pushing 40 and had multiple college degrees.

She folded her arms.

"Well, I gotta say, Cooper and his mother looked perfectly normal to me."

"Well, of course Betty looks normal," Diesel said. "She's a Corning."

"A Corning?"

"Middle class family with six daughters," Jake said. "Amanda Corning teaches high school chemistry. Neat lady. She really cares about the students and we all confided in her when we needed advice or help. I guess she had a lot of practice raising six girls. Betty is the oldest."

"Oh, that's right," Charlie said. "I felt so bad for Mrs. Corning when you told me Betty married Brian Hicks. She was, what? Eighteen years old?"

Jake nodded. "No one could understand what she saw in him."

Charlie frowned. "But didn't you tell me Brian was listed in the local paper for making the honor roll in high school? Or was that a different Hicks?"

"No, you're right, that was Brian." Jake grinned at the others. "First time a Hicks ever qualified for the honor roll."

"So maybe Brian is trying to break free of his family's heritage," Scott said. "That might explain why Betty was attracted to him."

Kim, who'd been thinking the same thing, smiled at Scott. Having been raised by a single mother and a bachelor uncle, Scott understood a family's struggle for economic independence. As an investigative reporter, he'd focused much of his research on the plight of what economists called the underclass -- people living in perpetual poverty because they were unable to obtain employment.

But Jake dismissed Scott's comment with a wave of his hand.

"Nah. Once a Hicks, always a Hicks."

A new voice added, "Which is why we need to point that woman detective in the right direction."

Everyone turned to Mark Hampton. The senior Hampton's dark hair was still damp from a shower. Dressed in a long-sleeved polo shirt and dark-rinse jeans, he could have stepped from a Ralph Lauren ad.

"Sorry I'm late," Mark continued as he crossed to the coffee pot. "I stopped to talk with Michael while out for my run."

He carried a mug of coffee -- black, of course -- to the fireplace, but remained standing.

"Charlie, Michael said the police found gun powder residue on your hand."

Rachael bristled. "Someone's trying to frame Charlie."

Mark acted like he hadn't heard her.

"I appreciate you protecting the mine from those thieves -- and I'm really impressed you actually picked up a gun -- but you should have shot to wound, not kill."

"I. Did. Not. Kill. A. Man." Charlie's voice was almost a growl.

The awkward silence that followed was broken by Scott.

"Sounds like Drew McDonald is a good defense attorney," he said.

Mr. Lord of the Manor straightened and glared at Scott.

"We need to stop this before my son is officially accused. Can you imagine what a murder charge would do to the family reputation? It doesn't matter if the case is thrown out. This is a small town and people would love to tear us down."

Before anyone could form an answer, Mark wheeled to face Charlie.

"And why can't you let Michael handle this?"

"Michael is not a criminal lawyer," Charlie said. "Drew is."

"Yeah, and by hiring Drew you're practically admitting you're guilty."

Through gritted teeth, Charlie said, "Let's not get

into this again. I told you Drew's the best and he's the lawyer I want."

The two men glared at one another. Then Mark's shoulders slumped.

"I just don't want you going to jail," he said. "Michael thinks one of the Hickses is trying to frame you."

"Now, Mark, you can't blame everything bad that happens on that poor family," a woman's voice said.

Kim turned to see a slender woman dressed in white guide an electric wheelchair through the door. Light brown hair fell in soft waves around a heart-shaped face. Kim registered blue eyes and a full mouth before she spotted the tiny dog sitting in the woman's lap.

The fine-boned dog sported huge, perky ears edged in long, feather-like fur. A white blaze ran from forehead to muzzle; the rest of his head was black. Large black patches interrupted the white silky body fur. As the dog's eyes met Kim's, he wagged a plumy black and white tail.

"A papillon!" Kim stood. "Is he friendly?"

The woman laughed.

"Oh, Jack's never met a stranger, have you sweetie?"

As she petted Jack, the enormous brilliant-cut diamond on her left hand caught the light filtering through the bay window and sent flashes around the room.

Rachael playfully punched Kim in the arm.

"Leave it to you to notice the dog first."

She crossed to the woman, leaned over and kissed her cheek. "How are you feeling, Mrs. Hampton?"

"Rachael, you know I've asked you to call me Deb." Her soft voice had a musical lilt. "Mrs. Hampton sounds so old and you are going to be family soon, right?"

Deb smiled up at Kim and extended a hand.

"You must be Kim. Rachael has told me so much about you."

"Don't believe a word of it," Kim said, shaking her hand.

"I see you've noticed my engagement ring."

Deb tossed a look at Mark that was supposed to be stern. "When we married, I told Mark I didn't want anything this flashy, but he didn't listen."

"It's a lovely ring," Kim said. "I'm surprised he didn't give you an emerald."

Deb Hampton laughed.

"That's exactly want I wanted. But Mark said emeralds were too fragile to wear daily." Her voice turned impish. "Is that true? If Mark lied to me, I'll make him sleep on the sofa tonight."

"Your husband is absolutely correct," Kim said. "Emeralds can easily shatter if you accidentally bang them against something. That's why I recommend emerald lovers purchase necklaces, earrings or pins instead of rings."

She grinned at Mark.

"Guess you're safe for tonight."

Deb laughed again and accepted a cup of tea from her husband. Mark smiled at his wife, his expression one of worship.

Kim could understand Rachael's reluctance to call this elegant woman by her first name. Despite the wheelchair, Deb Hampton moved with grace and dignity. It'd seem more reasonable to kneel and kiss her hand than to address her as Deb.

"Come sit by the fire," Mark said.

"Sweetie, I have MS, not the flu."

But she obediently followed him to the fireplace. As she turned the wheelchair to face the others, her napkin fell from her lap.

Before anyone could move, Jack the papillon leaped from her lap, snagged the napkin and, with the fabric clenched between his teeth, jumped back onto her knees.

"Thank you, sweetie." Deb ruffled the little dog's ears.

"Notice she calls both the dog and me sweetie."

Mark's voice was amused. Then his eyes fell on Charlie and his expression hardened.

"Let's return to the reason I asked you all here."

Kim couldn't resist. "Are you going to reveal the killer, Mr. Poirot?"

At the mention of Agatha Christie's famous detective, Scott grinned and Rachael giggled. Mark Hampton, however, sighed heavily.

"This isn't fiction, Ms. West," he said. "My son may be accused of a crime he didn't commit."

"You know Walt will do everything in his power to prove Charlie's innocence," Deb said.

At the mention of the sheriff's name, Mark stiffened.

"That may be so, but if that hot-shot new detective can build her case, your precious Walt may have no choice but to arrest Charlie."

Deb's mouth pressed into a thin line, but she remained silent.

"Since Alexandra Cummings is focusing on Charlie," Mark continued, "we need to identify alternative suspects. Once we have names, Michael said he can present them to the sheriff's department and insist Detective Cummings investigate."

"Michael Dunning is not my lawyer." Charlie's voice was tight.

Mark glared at Charlie.

"Fine, then Drew can do the work. First, however, we need to build a case against the obvious suspects."

He turned to Jake and Diesel.

"I want you two to poke around town, see if you can find out where the various Hicks were last night around--" He glanced at Charlie. "What time did you find the body?"

Charlie folded his arms.

"I wasn't looking at a clock."

"We arrived back at the cottage sometime near

midnight," Kim said. "Before that, we were with the cops maybe thirty, forty minutes? So the shot must have been fired between 9:45 and 10:30."

"Let's make it between 9:30 and 10:30," Mark said. "You two boys poke around the Hickses' hangouts, chat up their friends, see if anyone remembers seeing them between those times."

Mark's focus on the Hicks family made Kim uncomfortable. Sure, whenever a crime was committed, police officers interviewed known offenders. But they also dug into the victim's background to search for enemies.

"Kirk had obviously been digging in your mine," she said. "Did he belong to the local rock hound club?"

Jake nodded.

"Why don't Scott and I interview club members?" she said. "I know enough geology to engage them and they might know if Kirk had enemies."

"Diesel and I are already members," Jake said. "We should talk to them."

"I'd rather you focus on the Hickses," Mark said.

"Fine." Jake smiled at Kim. "John Houston, the club president, should be at The Hiddenite Center preparing for tomorrow's gem show."

"The four of us could drive there now," Charlie said. "I know John."

Jake pulled a wallet from his back pocket.

"They're closing the mansion and the grounds today to give everyone time to set up." He handed

Charlie some kind of ticket. "This will get you inside."

"What about the set up for your own booth?" Kim said. "Should we work on that while we're there?"

"Thank you for asking," Deb said, "but a couple of friends are already handling that. Since Mark wouldn't let us display any emeralds--"

Mark snorted. "Oh, yeah, let's give people something to steal."

Deb ignored her husband.

"We're using posters and photos and things instead of real gems, but I think it'll be attractive."

"Don't know why we need a booth at all," Mark grumbled. "After all, I'll be giving a talk."

"And then people will want to learn more."

Though Deb's voice was patient, the strain around her mouth indicated they'd had this discussion many times.

"I just don't want you exhausting yourself over this silly festival," Mark said.

Trying to lighten the mood by changing the subject, Kim turned to Deb.

"I just talked to my grandfather. After what happened last night, he and my aunt would like to drive down today or tomorrow. They can get a hotel room--"

"They most certainly will not," Deb said. "Their rooms have already been prepared and heaven knows we always have more than enough food.

And this way they'll get to attend the Gem Festival."

"We all have our assignments," Mark said. "Let's meet back here before dinner to compare notes."

CHAPTER 9

Rather than set off immediately to interview the president of the rockhounding club, Kim insisted they swing by the cabin to collect the dogs. After all, this was Rory's and Al's vacation, too.

The two-lane road to the Hiddenite Arts & Heritage Center wound through a neighborhood of small, box-shaped houses. Each house sported a neatly mown front lawn, a bit of space on either side and, presumably, a place in the back for children and dogs to run.

The local markets, churches and occasional dollar stores blended perfectly with the residential surroundings. Though the homes and shops lacked the exuberant flower borders found along the boardwalk back home, the tidiness spoke clearly of a community pride seldom seen in more urban settings.

"Didn't you say the Gem Festival is being held on the grounds of a mansion?" Kim asked Charlie. "How does an enormous building fit into this cozy setting?"

"Well, the original building was a small, two-story cottage built in 1900," Charlie said. "Diamond Jim Lucas bought the cottage and turned it into a 22-room mansion with its own electric and water plants. Nothing like indoor electricity and plumbing, huh?"

"Wait a minute," Kim said. "Diamond Jim Lucas? I know there was a Diamond Jim Brady, but I've never heard of this guy."

"Lucas imported diamonds for some firm in New York," Charlie said. "I'm not sure why he moved here, but he quickly became legend. He actually filled those rooms with stuff he collected. He owned 150 clocks, 400 walking sticks, Poncho Villa's sombrero, clothing from Buffalo Bill, nautical instruments from Admiral Dewey's flagship. He supposedly devoted one entire room to storing trunks of loose jewels. His favorite walking stick was studded in diamonds."

"Sounds like he had more money than brains," Kim said. "Diamonds may be hard, but they will shatter if struck by something heavy. People don't usually protect their walking sticks from drops and things.

"Besides, why would you need 400 walking sticks? If he was alive today, we'd probably call him a hoarder."

Charlie laughed. "Just don't call him a hoarder while we're here. People prefer to see him as eccentric."

He turned the car left onto a narrow, tree-lined driveway. All she could see of the mansion was a red roof towering above the trees.

Part way up the drive, a set of sawhorses blocked the road. Charlie rolled down his window as a man wearing a nametag stepped forward.

"Sorry, folks, but the Center is closed today so everyone can prepare for tomorrow's gem show."

Charlie held out the ticket Jake had given him. "We're actually here to help with the set-up."

The guard glanced at the ticket and nodded.

"Your folks are on the far side of the stage."

He moved a sawhorse and waved them through.

When the mansion finally came into view, Kim's mouth dropped open. After hearing about Diamond Jim Lucas, she'd expected a monstrosity. Instead, she saw a cheerful, white building trimmed in green and topped with the red roof. Porches, gables, columns and gingerbread created a story-book feel.

The mansion sprawled across a neatly trimmed lawn separated from the driveway by a white picket fence. A permanent pavilion roofed in red graced the front lawn. Brightly colored, temporary pavilions lined a concrete path. Men and women scurried around carrying boxes, tables and chairs.

Charlie found a parking space. After snapping leashes onto the dogs, they strolled toward the large pavilion.

Five or six men hustled around the stage, dragging extension cords, arranging oversized speakers and setting up microphones. In front of the stage, a poster listed the performers who'd be appearing on stage tomorrow. Kim noted that Mark Hampton would talk about local gemstones at 12:30.

As she started to turn away, a photo at the top caught her eye. A woman dressed in a Zorro style hat, ruffled red blouse and black trousers twirled a red cape while two black and white border collies whirled around her. The action photo captured the grace of both human and dogs. The sign identified the photo as "Jan Mayr and her Dancing Dogs" and indicated Jan would be performing on stage at 9 a.m.

Kim pointed at the photo.

"Okay, that I've got to see."

Scott grinned. "Thinking of dancing with Rory?"

Kim grimaced. "Trust me, you so don't want to see me dance."

"I could teach you a few steps," Scott said.

Kim imagined swaying in Scott's arms while music played in the background. She heard the music crescendo as they gazed into each other's eyes and their lips moved closer, closer . . .

She blinked and mentally shook herself. What the heck was happening to her? She'd never mooned over any man and here she was fantasizing about Scott while people shuffled around her.

She turned away, saying over her shoulder, "Thanks, but I think Rory would prefer faster moves."

Scott chuckled. Kim suddenly realized what she'd said and her face flushed. She walked faster.

They skirted the large stage and wandered along the path. Kim studied each booth they passed, making mental notes of intriguing displays to visit tomorrow when the festival opened. The exhibits featured a mix of educational material and items for sale.

One booth was devoted exclusively to the history of Hiddenite and the rare gem that gave the town its name. Emerald Hollow Mine, the pay-to-dig site open to the public, was represented as were several local jewelry stores. Kim couldn't help slowing to admire a jewelry artist's collection of wire-wrapped cabochons.

Charlie suddenly paused by a booth manned by a blond and a brunette, both attractive women in their fifties. The banner hanging from the front table featured the Hampton's emerald mine logo.

The brunette suddenly spotted Charlie. With a squeal, she rushed to embrace him.

"Welcome home," she said. "Deb has been so excited that you're back."

"You've made your mother very happy," the blond woman added.

Charlie blushed, introduced everyone. Kim greeted Stacy the blond and Jill the brunette before turning to examine the showcases they were assembling.

The first described the area geology, explaining how the mountains were formed and listing the types of gems and minerals found there.

The second display, titled "Follow the Yellow Brick Road" featured a poster of Judy Garland as Dorothy in The Wizard of Oz. The towers of the Emerald City rose in the background. Beside the poster hung a photo of Mark Hampton, fingers stained yellow, holding a six-inch, bolt-shaped emerald.

Kim compared the real emerald with the fictional Emerald City. Sure enough, the green towers looked exactly like real emeralds.

The exhibit also showed photos of the mining operation. Close-ups of quartz and limonite were accompanied by a description of the Hamptons "following the yellow limonite" to the source of an emerald pocket.

The final display showed a series of pictures of Charlie. In one, he pushed something that looked like a lawn mower with over-sized wheels and what appeared to be a computer tablet mounted to the handle. The caption identified it as "ground penetrating radar."

In the next photo, Charlie sat in front of a computer typing the results of the radar survey into his software program. The caption proclaimed Charlie's software as the future of emerald hunting.

Rory gave a sudden woof and lunged toward the opening of the pavilion. Kim dug in her feet, gripped the leash and gave a stern "leave it." She had no idea what prompted Rory's charge, but whatever it was couldn't be good for him.

Normally the "leave it" cue settled the young dog. This time, however, he continued pulling on his harness and making whimpering sounds. Al suddenly barked and pulled in the same direction as Rory.

"Darn you, Ted!" Stacy clapped her hands. "Scat!"

A black squirrel ran out from under the front table, crossed the path, then turned. Sitting up, it chittered at the dogs. The barking grew frenzied and Kim had difficulty hanging onto Rory's leash.

Snagging a stapler from the table, Stacy hurled it at the squirrel. It landed on the grass just in front of it. The squirrel jumped, wheeled around and charged up a nearby tree.

Stacy turned to the others, a sheepish smile on her face.

"That probably looked extreme, but I really wasn't aiming at Ted Bundy. If I hadn't thrown something, he'd have sat here all day teasing your dogs."

"Ted Bundy?" Kim said.

Stacy chuckled. "Yeah, we named him that because he looks cute, but he's actually evil. He teases dogs until they break free from their owners, then runs toward the road."

She gestured to the circular driveway that surrounded the mansion.

"We don't have high traffic, but some day that darn squirrel is going to get a dog killed."

Kim shuddered. "Well, thank you for chasing him away."

"Stacy, do you know where the local rock hound club is setting up?" Charlie said.

Stacy pointed to the right.

"See the pavilion with the yellow and black stripes?"

"The bumble bee one?" Kim couldn't resist saying.

Stacy grinned. "Yep. Except the booth is actually focused on honey bees. Anyway, the rock hounds are the next pavilion over."

"John Houston with them?"

Stacy rolled her eyes. "Are you kidding? You think he'd let anyone work without him supervising? He's been strutting around here like a Banty rooster all morning."

Charlie thanked the ladies and strode toward the yellow and black striped pavilion. Kim, Rachael and

Scott struggled to keep up.

"Why's Charlie in such a hurry?" Kim said.

Rachael shrugged. "He always gets like this when he doesn't want to do something. Says it's easier to just do whatever it is and then not think about it."

"I can understand tackling unpleasantness quickly," Scott said. "But doing it without thought can be dangerous."

They skirted the honey bee pavilion and approached a canopy-covered booth. A short, stocky man directed another man and woman as they hung posters and organized display tables.

As they neared, the stocky man glanced up and frowned.

"So you're back," he said with a disapproving tone.

Charlie hesitated only a moment before extending his hand.

"Hey, John, good to see you."

John Houston pointedly stared at Charlie's hand, then folded his arms.

"What do you want?"

"Whoa, what got into you?"

Charlie threw up both hands, palms facing the man in a placating manner.

"Kirk Ballas might have been an ass, but he was one of us," John said. "Just because your family owns that mine didn't give you the right to shoot him."

"I didn't kill Kirk!"

"That's not what I heard," John said.

"Well, whatever you heard, it's wrong," Charlie said. "I'm trying to find out who really killed him and thought you might know something helpful."

"Why, so you can accuse someone from the club?"

Scott stepped forward.

"Why don't we start this conversation over?"

He extended his hand. John reluctantly shook it. Scott introduced himself, adding "We"-- he gestured to the others -- "were with Charlie shortly after we heard the gunshot. We found Charlie knocked out from a blow to the head.

"Charlie didn't kill Kirk. We'd like to help find the real killer."

The muscles in John Houston's face softened as Scott talked. When Scott finished, John dipped his chin.

"Well, I can tell you that none of us killed him. Kirk may have been a loudmouth and a pain, but no one in the club is a killer."

"If that's the case, then you'd be wise to talk with us for a few minutes," Scott said. "We have no idea what the police are doing, but if we put our heads together, we might be able to point them in the right direction -- and away from your club."

This time John nodded.

"Okay, what do you want to know?"

Seeing the rapport Scott had established, the others allowed him to take the lead.

"There were signs near Kirk's body that indicated someone had been digging there. Kirk ever mention doing a little emerald poaching?"

John's eyes narrowed.

"You think I wouldn't have told the authorities if I knew Kirk was illegally digging somewhere?"

Scott held his ground.

"I'm not accusing you of anything. I'm just wondering if his actions surprise you."

For a moment, John Houston glowered. Then his shoulders slumped.

"You know, if you'd caught Kirk and his buddies digging on Hampton's land a few months ago, I wouldn't have been surprised. But I thought Kirk was no longer angry."

Kim and Rachael exchanged glances, but Scott kept his eyes focused on John.

"Why was Kirk angry?"

"He was pissed -- hell, we all were pissed -- that Mark Hampton denied the club permission to dig in his mine."

Scott frowned and gestured to the club's displays.

"But there are lots of places to dig around here. Why focus on the Hampton mine?"

"Do you know anything about rockhounding clubs?"

"No. But I'd like to."

That brought an actual smile to John's face.

"Rockhounding clubs wouldn't exist without the generosity of landowners," John said. "The feds won't let us dig on public land. Most of the so-called public mines have been salted with imported raw gems; they're little more than tourist traps.

"The only way to really learn about local geology is to ask permission to dig on private land. Our club has an excellent reputation for maintaining the integrity of the property, returning everything the way it was before we started digging. If we find gemstones, we alert the property owner. Usually, they allow us to take what we've found. We always notify the owners if we think an area is worth pursuing as a possible income source.

"Most people around here willingly give us permission to dig. But not Mark Hampton."

"Dad's insurance company won't allow--"

Scott's raised hand halted Charlie.

"So Mark turned down your request. What happened then?"

John's ears flushed.

"Well, we were all pissed. Kirk was the loudest objector. He was usually pretty laid back, but I think he was putting on a show for his two buddies."

"Donny and Rocky?" Charlie cut in.

John nodded. "Kirk eventually quit complaining. Just the other day I asked him about it. He shrugged and said he no longer cared that the Hampton mine was off limits."

John folded his arms and lifted his chin.

"Kirk might not care, but the rest of us are sick of

the way you people treat folks you think are beneath you."

Kim didn't bother listening to Charlie's reply. The two men would never find neutral territory. She turned to the nearest display case.

Unlike Mark Hampton, the rock club members exhibited actual specimens of raw gems found in the area: rose and smoky quartz, some light purple amethyst, a few pieces of Hiddenite. A woman bent over the case, arranging a collection of clear quartz. She met Kim's eyes, then quickly looked away.

Rory, however, had grown bored and decided to make a new friend. He trotted to the woman and leaned against her. She smiled and stroked his neck.

"I see you're a dog lover," Kim said.

"I've always wanted a dog." The woman's voice was wistful. "But my father was allergic. I thought I'd get a dog when I got my own place, but . . ."

She shrugged.

"You'll know when the time is right," Kim said. "What kind of dog do you--"

Charlie's shout interrupted her. They turned to see Charlie brandishing a sheet of paper in front of John Houston's eyes.

"What is this shit?"

"Can't you read?" John said.

Charlie's breath came in fast gasps.

"A petition? You're collecting signatures to harass my family."

John snatched the petition from Charlie's hand.

"No, we're collecting signatures demanding access to the Hamptons' emerald mine."

"That's private land," Charlie said. "You can't force us to do anything."

"Maybe not, but we can let the public know about the shitty way your family treats honest rock hounds."

Charlie clenched his hands. Rachael wrapped both hands around Charlie's bicep.

"Let's get out of here, honey," she said. "Anyone with a lick of sense will ignore the petition."

Charlie's shoulders remained tight, but he allowed Rachael to drag him into the sun. As Kim turned to follow, a hand touched her arm. She glanced over her shoulder.

The woman worker leaned close to Kim's ear.

"Tell your friend that you don't want to mess with these guys," she whispered. "They can get rough."

CHAPTER 10

"Well, that was a waste of time," Charlie said as he steered the car back toward the cabin. "I never expected such hostility from John Houston."

"The woman who was working with him said he has an explosive temper," Kim said. "How well do you know him?"

Charlie shrugged.

"Not well. In school, we traveled in different circles. But in a town this size you hear things and I've never heard anything negative about John. 'course, it's been years since I lived here and people can change."

"Let's not talk about the rock hounds anymore,"

Rachael said. "If we hurry, Kim and I can have a few hours in the mine before dinner."

"Sounds like a plan."

Charlie's phone rang. With a sigh, he punched the car's Bluetooth button.

"Hello?"

Mark Hampton's voice boomed through the car's speaker.

"Where are you?"

"Just turning onto Sulphur Springs."

"Good. Stop by the house. I have some papers for you to sign."

"Can't it wait until tonight?" Charlie said. "The girls want to go emerald hunting."

"It'll only take a few minutes."

Without waiting for a reply, Charlie's father disconnected.

"Sorry, folks," Charlie said. "When Dad gets like this, it's best to humor him. We'll be driving right past the house anyway, so it shouldn't take long. You'll still have plenty of time at the mine."

But even as he spoke the words, the car rounded a corner to reveal road construction. Charlie eased the car to a stop.

Kim peered through the front window. Three cars ahead, a worker held a stop sign. Beyond him, orange cones and workers in yellow vests blocked the right lane while a backhoe maneuvered into position. After what seemed an eternity, a line of cars began passing them on the left.

She blew out a hiss of frustration. Sleuthing could be intellectually stimulating, but she'd come here to dig for emeralds. Everything -- even the construction workers -- seemed to conspire against them.

At long last, the line of oncoming cars ended. The fellow holding the stop sign flipped it around to allow them to proceed. Charlie eased the car into the left lane.

As they crept past the backhoe, the driver glanced up. Donny Driver.

The muscles in Kim's shoulders tightened. Sensing Kim's sudden tension, Rory barked. Donny's head jerked toward the car. His eyes met Kim's and widened in recognition. Not wanting to show fear -- she'd learned the hard way that fear only encouraged bullies -- she maintained eye contact.

Donny looked away first. He scanned the car's occupants. As he spotted Charlie behind the wheel, Donny's eyes narrowed to slits. Reptile eyes. Snake eyes. She'd seen eyes like that once before in a man she thought she'd known; he'd been pointing a gun at her.

Her hands clenched into fists. A bend in the road finally blocked her view of the workers.

Kim glanced around the car, but judging by the relaxed body language, no one else had noticed Donny Driver.

"Charlie? Why does Donny Driver hold a grudge

against you?" she said.

Charlie sighed and turned his car onto his parents' driveway.

"In high school," he said, "we both liked the same girl. When he broke her heart, I was the one who comforted her. Let's just say Donny didn't like that."

His tone indicated he wouldn't provide details. Kim exchanged looks with Rachael. Rachael shrugged and addressed her fiancé.

"Okay if I show everyone Deb's secret garden?" She turned to Kim.

"Wait till you smell the roses. Some smell fruity, some spicy, some so intensely rose-like you'll think you're wearing perfume."

"Just be sure to keep the dogs on leash." Charlie parked the car.

"Remember, Deb's papillon is afraid of other dogs. When I finish with Dad, I'll find you all in the garden."

After securing the dogs to leashes, Kim and Scott followed Rachael down a wheelchair-width path lined with autumn flowers.

"Deb's favorite childhood book was The Secret Garden," Rachael said. "Did you read it or were you stuck on Nancy Drew?"

Kim mock-punched her friend.

"Hey, I didn't only read mysteries."

Her mother, an English teacher, had insisted she read some of the older childhood classics like Heidi,

The Adventures of Tom Sawyer, Winnie the Poo, Madeline, The Wind in the Willows, The Jungle Book, Little Women, Anne of Green Gables and, yes, Frances Hodgson Burnett's The Secret Garden.

"I even saw the movie," she added, "though the garden in the movie didn't match the one I'd envisioned."

Rachael grinned. "I've never seen a garden like the one described in the book. Until now."

They turned a corner and a brick wall came into view. About ten feet high, the wall stretched maybe thirty feet in either direction before angling away from them. Ivy crawled up the sides, partially obscuring the large blocks of stone.

"The walls completely enclose the garden like in the book," Rachael said, leading them to a tall, wooden door.

A rustling overhead drew Kim's eyes to the top of the wall. A male bluebird peered down at her, his head cocked to one side as if he was puzzling over their presence.

"Shouldn't you be heading South for the winter?" she said to the bird.

Rachael followed Kim's eyes.

"Oh, the bluebirds will stay. Deb raises mealworms in the basement so she has something to feed them during the cold weather."

"Mealworms?" Scott said. "As in the white things you fish with? Don't they turn into beetles?"

Kim couldn't suppress a shudder at the sudden

image of giant black beetles crawling across a basement floor.

"Yeah, but the birds eat most of them before they mature. Deb has some kind of system that involves shuffling plastic boxes around on metal shelving."

Rachael reached for the door handle.

"She feeds most of the mealworms to the bluebirds, but allows some larvae to change into beetles to repopulate the mealworms. Charlie calls the whole thing 'death row.'"

She swung the door open and Kim's nostrils were immediately assaulted with the unmistakable scent of roses. Pink, white, yellow and red roses climbed the interior walls and cast their fragrance to the wind. Wands of lavender grew at the base of the roses; though no longer in bloom, the fragrant, silver gray leaves accented the roses' colors.

Narrow flower beds extended from the lavender. Kim identified several spring-blooming plants -- violets, forget-me-nots and bearded iris -- interspersed with autumn-blooming chrysanthemums, purple salvia and hardy geraniums. The mums' brilliant shades of red and yellow gave the garden a festive ambiance.

A slate path, maybe four feet wide, wound around larger flowerbeds. The bed in front of them was so thick with plants that Kim couldn't see through them.

Rachael pointed to a flowerless bush growing in a fountain shape.

"Most of the old-fashioned roses like this one bloom only in early summer," she said. "But Deb wanted season-long color and fragrance. So she interplanted with modern climbing and bush roses, perennials and annuals. If you think this is amazing, you should come back in early summer when all of the roses are blooming."

Several nearby rose bushes were still in bloom. Kim bent to smell a multi-petaled rose that resembled the layers of a cabbage cut in half.

"Smells a little like apples," she said.

Rachael held out a pale pink bloom from a different plant.

"Try this one. It smells a little bit like brewed tea."

"Does that make it a tea rose?" Scott said.

"Actually, it does," Rachael said. "Back in the late 1800s, when breeders first produced repeat blooming roses, the fragrance of one class of rose reminded people of tea. So they called them tea roses."

"Since when did you become a rose connoisseur?" Kim said.

"Since meeting Deb. She gets to you, you know?" Rachael blinked back tears.

Knowing her friend's horror of crying in public, Kim quickly changed the subject.

"What's down the path?"

The walkway circled left and out of sight.

Rachael grinned. "More flowerbeds and paths.

Part of the fun of this garden is discovering secret nooks and flowers."

They followed the path to the left. It wove through dense, tropical-like foliage that surely must be annuals of some sort. Kim could hear a robin twittering from above her head, but couldn't see it. A tiger swallowtail butterfly bobbed above the flowers.

Up ahead, she spotted a break in the foliage. Stepping into the light, she discovered a small pond planted with waterlilies. A fountain burbled and palm-sized goldfish darted through the water.

She was so fascinated by the pond that the movement on the other side startled her. She heard the hum of an electric wheelchair. From the shadows, Deb appeared, her little dog perched on her lap.

Kim waved. Behind her, Al barked a greeting.

"Crap," Rachael said. "Jack's afraid of other dogs. Let's get out of here."

Before they could move, however, the papillon leaped to the ground and raced toward them.

Scott scooped Al into his arms. There was nothing Kim could do, however, with a dog Rory's size. Had he been in danger, she'd have stepped in front of him and attempt to ward off the charging dog. But Jack showed no signs of aggression. His feathery ears, fluttering like a butterfly as he ran, made it difficult to label him a threat.

Jack rounded the pond. Rory dropped into a play

bow, signaling his happy mood. Jack slammed to a halt. His tail wagged once, twice. Then, to everyone's surprise, Jack copied Rory's bow and charged him.

"Gentle," Kim told Rory.

Rory plunked his butt onto the ground and allowed the tiny dog to crawl all over him. Both tails wagged furiously.

"That is so amazing," Deb said, wheeling up to them. "Ever since he was attacked by a neighbor's dog, Jack has been terrified of other dogs, especially ones bigger than him."

Jack licked Rory's face, then backed away. Crouching low, he lifted one front foot after another so fast that he looked like he was tap dancing.

Deb laughed and pointed.

"He only does pappy feet when he's excited and happy."

"Sorry to intrude," Rachael said. "Charlie's doing something for Mark, so I decided to show Kim and Scott your garden."

"It's really a work of art," Scott added.

Deb beamed. "I designed it myself, though, obviously--" she gestured toward her legs -- "I didn't do the heavy work. We have a gardener to maintain it, but I still like to putter around, do some weeding and tidying."

"Well, you've done an amazing job," Kim said.

Deb waved her hand toward the far path.

"Please feel free to look around."

"Actually, would you mind if I sat with you for awhile?" Kim said. "We can let the dogs play a little longer."

And a one-on-one with Deb might provide some answers.

Rachael opened her mouth to protest, but Scott gently guided her toward the far path. He looked back and winked. Kim smiled.

Gotta love a man who supported a woman's need to snoop.

"Would you like to sit in the sun or shade?" Deb said.

"You choose. I'm happy just inhaling the gorgeous fragrance."

Deb led the way to a concrete bench in the shade. It was surprisingly comfortable. Rory laid at her feet. Jack returned to Deb's lap.

"I called your grandfather to tell him they're welcome to come early," Deb said.

"Oh, thank you," Kim said. "I hope the early arrival isn't too much of an inconvenience."

"Not at all. I'm really looking forward to meeting Max and Ginny."

She grinned. "Rachael said Ginny can give me fashion tips for wearing google eyes."

Kim laughed. Rachael must have told her future mother-in-law about Ginny's proclivity for pasting google eyes -- plastic, cartoon-like eyeballs with rolling pupils -- on greeting cards, postcards and jewelry.

"I'm sure Aunt Ginny will be delighted to share her secrets."

Kim hesitated, wondering how to steer the conversation to the people she now regarded as suspects. Was there a graceful way to shift the conversation from google eyes to murder?

Deb herself solved the problem by saying, "Your grandfather expressed concern that you might get involved in the murder investigation -- again. Was he joking or have you really helped police solve murders?"

"Uh, well, the first time someone tried to kill Grandpa and then a few months ago a close friend was the prime suspect . . ." Kim's voice trailed off.

How could she explain that, despite her love of mystery books, she hadn't set out to investigate murders? She wasn't some swooning heroine poking her nose into police work for the fun of it. Kim knew the risks. She'd gotten involved because she'd had no choice.

Or so it seemed at the time.

Deb nodded and straightened her shoulders.

"Then you're just the person we need."

She looked into Kim's eyes.

"Will you help find the person who's trying to frame my son for murder?"

CHAPTER 11

Kim's mouth dropped open.

"You want me to investigate a murder?"

"Well, not in the way you're implying," Deb said. "The police will focus on people who held a grudge against Kirk Ballas. They won't consider the ones who hate Mark's family."

"I don't understand. Why would someone who dislikes your husband's family murder Kirk?"

"Revenge."

Seeing the confusion on Kim's face, Deb added, "The Hamptons are the most powerful family in this area and they've never hesitated to exploit that fact. Mark's ancestors demanded total loyalty from their employees and anyone who stepped out of line was not only fired, but blackballed. Between the men's ruthless business practices and the women's arrogant social behavior, the Hamptons created many enemies.

"They even managed to alienate Sheriff Spits -- that would be the current sheriff's grandfather -- by inviting Randy Benning to a poker game."

"Benning's the man who owned the land where Rory found the Carolina Emerald, right? Why did inviting him to play poker offend the sheriff?"

"The Hamptons had been trying to purchase the Benning land for decades," Deb said. "But the Bennings wouldn't sell. They didn't have the money to mine their land for emeralds -- that takes an enormous infusion of cash -- but they made a decent living farming tobacco. Without their land, the Bennings would have no place to go, no source of income. So they turned down offers from first Mark's great-grandfather, then his grandfather.

"Randy Benning was the last living heir to that land. Not only was he a compulsive gambler, but he wasn't very good at it."

"So the invitation to play poker was nothing more than an attempt to win Randy's land?" Kim said.

Deb nodded. "No one, of course, predicted that after losing the land, Randy would commit murder/suicide. But a lot of people, including Sheriff Spits, blamed Mark's grandfather for the deaths.

"My point is that many locals relish the idea of a Hampton being charged with murder."

"Don't you think framing an innocent man is a bit extreme?" Kim said.

"Some of these people deal only in extremes."

A million questions swirled through Kim's mind. She understood Deb's mother-bear need to protect Charlie. But the idea that an old Hampton enemy killed Kirk Ballas and implicated Charlie seemed farfetched.

"You know," Kim said, "even if we assume the person behind all this wanted to avenge some long-ago Hampton action, there's no way he could predict that Charlie would run into the forest at the exact moment when Kirk Ballas was killed."

"I've been thinking about that," Deb said. "What if one of Mark's adversaries decided to get even by stealing emeralds from the Hampton mine? Maybe Kirk Ballas was supposed to help with the digging. But Kirk has never been reliable; I can't imagine why anyone would trust him. I can imagine an employer regretting his decision.

"Anyway, we know Kirk and his killer were digging in the mine when Charlie saw their lights. When Charlie appeared, the killer saw an opportunity to get rid of an uncooperative partner and frame a Hampton for murder."

The firm set to Deb's mouth told Kim further argument would be futile. She decided to try another tactic.

"Why don't you share your theory with Sheriff Spits and ask him to investigate? While Detective Cummings explores Kirk's background, Sheriff Spits could interview Mark's enemies."

"I do plan to tell Walt," Deb said. "But many of these people will be at Sunday's party. I don't want to do anything to ruin that for Charlie and Rachael. As it is, Mark's not going to be happy when I ask Walt to consider his business associates as potential murderers."

"Er, I noticed there seems to be a lot of tension between Mark and Walt," Kim said. "Yet Charlie called the sheriff 'Uncle Walt.' That seems incongruous. May I ask why?"

Deb's shoulders slumped. "That's a long story."

"We have time."

Deb bit her lip and stared at the ground. Her slender fingers picked a leaf from Jack's fur and began shredding it.

Kim remained silent, content to inhale the fragrance of roses and lavender. Rory stretched out on the warm stone path. A pair of bluebirds hopped nearby, totally unafraid of the two women.

"There was a time," Deb finally said, "when Mark and Walt were as close as two men can be when forced together by their wives. In hindsight, it's pretty amazing the men tolerated each other given their different backgrounds."

"How so?"

"Walt and his wife, Janine, grew up lower middle

class. Mark, of course, was raised with an emerald spoon in his mouth."

Kim giggled. "Never heard that expression before."

Deb grinned. "That's because I invented it. Thank goodness Mark thinks it's funny. Janine and I used to tease him--"

She broke off and her face clouded. "Gawd, I miss her."

For a moment, it appeared Deb would start crying. When she finally spoke, however, her voice was strong.

"Janine and I were best friends. I was maid of honor at her wedding and she was matron of honor at mine. Our husbands had few interests in common, so Janine and I didn't try to push them together. The four of us met for the occasional dinner, but for the most part, Janine and I spent our time together without husbands.

"Janine desperately wanted children, but she couldn't conceive. That broke her heart. And mine. So I asked Mark if he minded sharing our boys by making Janine and Walt an honorary aunt and uncle."

She smiled. "It was the perfect solution. It gave Janine an outlet for her mothering instincts and the boys an aunt and uncle who made time for them. Mark and Walt finally found common ground."

Deb's eyes filled with tears.

"Then everything fell apart. Janine was

diagnosed with an aggressive form of breast cancer. At the same time, doctors told me I have MS."

Kim shivered. Multiple sclerosis, or MS, was a horrible autoimmune disease in which the body attacked the protective sheath that covers brain-cell nerve endings. When that happened, communication between brain and body essentially short-circuited. A foot or leg or hand would suddenly stop working.

Sometimes the brain could rewire itself and function would return. Other times, the disconnect was permanent.

The unpredictable nature of the disease placed enormous psychological stress on the victims. As part of her graduate studies, Kim had spent a semester interning with a clinical psychologist. One of the patients, a woman suffering from MS, sought help dealing with the emotional aftermath. She'd graciously allowed Kim to observe the session.

Kim had nightmares for a week.

"It seemed like both of our diseases progressed rapidly," Deb continued. "Janine lost so much weight she looked like a skeleton. As for me, I thought I might lose my mind. When I went to sleep at night, I didn't know if I'd wake with the ability to walk or talk or even think.

"One night, when Mark was out of town on a business trip, Walt called to tell me Janine was in the hospital. The doctors didn't expect her to survive the night. I rushed to her side. Walt and I each held one of her hands, but I don't think she even knew we were there.

"After she . . . she was gone, I started to stand up. But my legs wouldn't work. I couldn't feel them at all! Walt called the doctor. They wanted me to stay the night. But all I wanted to do was get away from the hospital. I insisted on going home.

"Walt drove me home. When we got there, he had to carry me inside. We discovered Mark sitting in the living room. He'd come home from the trip early and found the house empty. I'd turned my cell phone off before we entered the hospital, so he couldn't reach me. He'd been calling friends and relatives and by the time we arrived, he'd been certain I was dead.

"Seeing me in Walt's arms, Mark jumped to the conclusion that we were having an affair. He didn't notice we were consumed by grief."

Scraping fingers through her hair, Deb stared into the distance.

"At the time, everything seemed to move in slow motion. Mark yanked me from Walt's arms, tossed me onto the sofa, then swung a fist at Walt's face. But Walt had more experience with street fighting. He dodged the punch, then hit Mark in the face. Mark tackled Walt and they fell to the floor.

"I screamed at them to stop, but they acted like they couldn't hear. So I pushed myself to my feet and tried to walk. Instead, I fell. Hard. That got their attention."

Deb shook her head. "I'll never understand why those two idiots exploded like that."

"Stress," Kim said. "Mark was worried about you and needed an outlet for all of that tension. Walt needed an outlet for his grief."

She shrugged. "Stupid, I know, but perfectly normal."

"I suppose." Deb gripped Kim's hand.

"Now you see why it's better to not involve Walt until after the engagement party. But all of Mark's colleagues are attending Sunday's party. That gives us a wonderful opportunity to gather intelligence to bolster my theory."

Deb swept a hand to indicate her wheelchair.

"I'll be poking around myself but, obviously, I'm limited. Besides, Mark's colleagues are always circumspect around me. But you're a total stranger. People might say things around you that they'd hide from me."

Remembering Grandpa's warning about becoming involved, Kim hesitated. Someone had already committed murder. If she started asking questions, she might unwittingly provoke the killer to strike again.

She opened her mouth to decline, but Deb interrupted.

"I'm not asking for you to quiz people," she said. "I'll be asking a lot of questions. But if you could please circulate and listen to conversations, you might hear something we can report to Walt on

Monday morning."

Kim dragged fingers through her hair. How could she turn down a mother trying to protect her son?

Surely mingling and eavesdropping wouldn't be dangerous.

LYNN FRANKLIN

CHAPTER 12

Saturday dawned sunny and cool. Morning light slipped under the window blinds to shine in Kim's closed eyes. She muttered and threw an arm across her face. A jab of pain brought her fully awake.

She squinted at the light. Had she overslept? Rolling over, she reached for her glasses and cell phone. The muscles in her shoulders and arms protested.

She groaned and pushed herself upright. Her back and upper thighs started throbbing.

Climbing the mine walls and digging in rock must have stressed muscles she hadn't used in months. She propped her glasses onto her nose and stared at the phone.

Six a.m.

Crap. She'd slept only four hours. She flopped back onto the bed and stared at the ceiling.

Yesterday, after leaving Charlie's parents, they'd spent several glorious hours digging for emeralds. Though they'd concentrated their efforts on the limonite and quartz seam that Scott had uncovered the day before, they'd been unable to find a pocket of emeralds.

By the time they returned to the cottage to shower and dress for dinner, Kim's shoulders ached.

She'd cheered considerably, however, when they arrived at the Hamptons' mansion to find Grandpa and Aunt Ginny sitting on the front porch.

Over dinner, they'd talked about Grandpa's jewelry store, Mark's emerald business, local geology and other non-threatening topics. Afterwards the senior Hampton gathered everyone together to discuss how they might use the Gem Festival to "uncover other suspects" in the murder of Kirk Ballas.

Charlie's brothers wanted to focus their inquiries on the Hicks family. Charlie and Rachael planned to question people about Kirk's background, searching for someone angry enough to kill the man.

Kim had listened to Mark Hampton assigning "duties" with only half an ear. No way would she put her family in danger by poking into a murder.

Instead, she planned to search for the stolen

emerald.

Grandpa would interview the lapidarists. Aunt Ginny would engage locals for relevant gossip. Kim would download and print a photo of the Carolina Emerald, then use the photo to alert vendors of the gem's theft.

If nothing else, she intended to make selling the emerald difficult.

Unfortunately, all of the planning lasted until well after midnight. Given the late hour, most people planned to sleep late. Kim, however, wanted to see the dogs who'd be dancing at 9 a.m. Scott, Grandpa and Aunt Ginny agreed to accompany her.

Now a mockingbird sang from a nearby tree, inviting her into the fresh air. A walk with Rory would clear her mind and loosen aching muscles. And if she happened to stroll past the police tape and learned something about the clues they'd found, all the better.

Swinging her legs from bed -- ouch -- she tiptoed into the bathroom. A few minutes later, she donned a pair of jeans, t-shirt and flannel shirt. Rory led the way down the stairs to the kitchen door and they quietly slipped outside.

The crisp air was cooler than she'd expected and she considered going back inside for a jacket. But she didn't want to risk waking the others. The sun felt warm on her face; her body temperature would rise as they walked.

She headed into the woods. Rory ran around her,

investigating smells but always returning to her side. For every step she took, he took ten. She appreciated the opportunity to allow him to race full out. Like a small child, the young dog needed the chance to expend energy on something totally fun.

The exercise would also make him easier to control when she took him to the Gem Festival. Strangers loved to pet the friendly poodle. Rory's presence would provide perfect opportunities to engage in chit-chat.

Up ahead, Rory skidded to a stop. They'd come to the edge of the forest. Beyond was the land Charlie had cleared for their emerald hunting. Rory's body tensed as he stared across the clearing.

Thinking he'd seen a deer, Kim stepped on the line that dragged from his harness.

"Leave it," she told him.

Rory glanced her way, then back across the field.

Kim reached down and picked up the line. Pitching her voice high and friendly, she called Rory. He twitched an ear, but continued to stare into the clearing.

Frowning, she shuffled toward him, shortening the line as she moved. As she walked, she repeated the words "stay, good stay," hoping the words would stop him from chasing after whatever held his attention.

Rory sniffed the air, but held his position. Reaching him, she gripped his harness.

She breathed deeply, then turned toward the opposite woods, trying to follow Rory's line of sight. For a moment, she saw nothing but tree trunks and underbrush. Then something moved.

A human-shaped figure, dressed in a shade of tan that blended with the trees, stood at the edge of the forest. He so resembled the evil gnomes from fairy tales that for a moment she thought her imagination had run wild. Short and wiry with a full, white beard, the man stood with arms stiff, fists clenched. From his flushed skin to his flared nostrils to his corded neck, he oozed anger. His unblinking eyes locked onto hers. She couldn't breathe.

Rory's bark broke the spell. The man's eyes narrowed and shifted to the large poodle. The hackles on Rory's back raised. The man blinked, then faded into the woods.

She didn't wait for him to reappear. Calling to Rory, she clutched his leash, turned and ran back the way they'd come.

They burst through the kitchen door to find Scott and Al waiting.

"Where's Charlie?" Maybe he knew the gnome-like man.

"He made a brief appearance when he smelled coffee."

Scott handed Kim a travel mug of already

sweetened tea.

"But he said he was returning to bed. They'll join us later at the Gem Festival."

"Crap. I wanted to ask him about something I saw."

"Tell me about it on the way. Max and Ginny are waiting for us to take them to the restaurant. It's Saturday, after all, and the breakfast places will be crowded."

"Why didn't Grandpa call me-- Oh!"

She eyed the cell phone Scott now held out. "Guess I forgot to take my phone."

He grinned. "What did you plan to do if you and the curly one solved the murder? Use smoke signals to send for help?"

Kim playfully smacked his arm.

"Let me get Rory's things and we can go."

"Already done."

Scott handed her the tote bag she used to carry dog things: spare leash, water bottle and bowl, dog treats, clicker, training toys, first-aid kit, rabies and license papers.

Kim checked the bag to make sure the water bottle was full and she had a good selection of tasty treats and toys. She frowned, remembering the scent-game bandana that had been stolen along with the Carolina Emerald. Maybe she could buy another bandana at the Festival.

She tossed her wallet, phone, keys and sun visor into the bag and zipped it shut.

"Ready when you are."

They secured the dogs in the back seat with harnesses attached to the seatbelts and drove to the Hamptons' mansion. Grandpa and Aunt Ginny were already waiting on the porch.

Kim stepped from the car and smiled as she watched them approach.

Aside from Mom and Dad, these two people had played the biggest roles in her youth. They'd cheered her when she succeeded, commiserated when she failed, encouraged her when her confidence wavered.

And yet, aside from a few more gray hairs -- caused, Grandpa said, by Kim's penchant for climbing trees -- her grandfather appeared as spry as when he'd first guided her through the American Museum of Natural History.

The years had also been kind to Aunt Ginny. The only sibling of Kim's father, Ginny Donaldson provided a much-needed antidote to Kim's other, jewelry-obsessed aunts. Yet she little resembled Kim's father. Whereas Dad dressed in earth tones, Ginny favored bright colors. Whereas Dad was slender, Ginny was plump. Whereas Dad topped six feet, Ginny barely reached five feet. The first time Ginny took eight-year-old Kim to ride a roller coaster and they approached the "are you tall enough?" sign, Kim insisted her aunt measure herself.

Now, as Kim bent to hug Ginny, she couldn't

resist saying, "Are you sure you're not shrinking?"

"Watch that," Ginny said. "I can still beat you at Scrabble."

Grinning, Kim stepped back and pointed at the plastic bag Ginny carried. "What's that?"

"A surprise."

Ginny handed the bag to Grandpa.

"Since you're sitting in the front seat, would you please keep this safe until we reach the Festival?"

Grandpa agreed. Kim and Ginny slid into the backseat. Al promptly plopped his butt onto Ginny's lap, effectively stopping Rory from doing the same. Kim pulled Rory close and they drove to the pancake house.

They found a shady parking space in front of a window. While Scott hurried inside to secure a table that would allow them a view of the car, Kim rolled down the windows to allow air to circulate and keep the dogs cool.

As predicted, the restaurant was crowded and service was slow. They ate quickly, then piled back into the car, arriving at the Gem Festival fifteen minutes before the dancing dogs were scheduled to begin.

Scott found four seats together near the front. Kim settled Rory between her legs. Al, perched on Scott's lap, sat up and used his two front paws to wave at the people searching for seats. Most stopped to point and laugh, totally disrupting what might otherwise have been an orderly process.

Kim, however, was accustomed to Al's antics. She was more interested in the plastic bag now sitting on her aunt's lap.

"When are you going to share the surprise?" she said.

"After the show," Ginny said. "Now be quiet; it's about to start."

A tall man dressed in khakis and polo shirt stepped onto the stage. He welcomed the audience to Hiddenite's first Gem Festival, gushed about the upcoming acts and -- finally! -- introduced the first performers.

"Please welcome Jan Mayr and her amazing dancing border collies, Duncan and Piper."

Latin music poured from the speakers and a tall, red-headed woman swept onto the stage. She twirled a cape over her head while a border collie weaved between her legs. A second border collie circled her.

Kim gripped the arms of her seat. If either of the dogs changed rhythm or paused, they'd trip their human partner. But the dancers reached center stage without mishap and the dogs transitioned smoothly into heel. They trotted at Jan's side as she circled the stage. At a verbal cue from Jan, Duncan and Piper spun in perfect unison.

And then the dogs were in constant motion, spinning and circling and weaving through Jan's legs. Combined with the cape work and the dramatic music, the performance held the audience enthralled.

Jan suddenly dropped to one knee and held out her cape. One after another, Duncan and Piper leaped over the cape. As they circled for a second jump, Duncan slowed his pace, allowing Piper to catch him. In unison, they soared over the cape.

A new cue from Jan sent the two dogs across the stage -- backwards -- while she gracefully rose to her feet. On the other side of the stage, Duncan and Piper dropped into synchronized bows. Jan called the dogs. They charged toward her, then rose onto their hind legs, their front paws balanced on Jan's outstretched arms. Human and canines held the pose as the music came to an abrupt end.

Kim jumped to her feet, clapping enthusiastically. Around her, others rose to give the performers a standing ovation.

On stage, Duncan and Piper faced the audience and bowed. The audience clapped louder. Jan beamed and waved.

Gripping Rory's leash, Kim turned to exit the row of seats. She just had to meet this woman. So few people trained their dogs or found interesting things for them to do. Kim would love to exchange training techniques with Jan Mayr.

By the time she reached the performers, however, Jan and her dogs were surrounded by well-wishers. Kim sighed and turned away.

She reached Scott and the others in time to see Aunt Ginny produce a wide-brimmed sun hat from the plastic bag. Ginny plunked the hat onto her head, tipping it at a cocky angle. Kim started laughing.

Her aunt had tied a wide red ribbon around the hat's crown and added a flurry of white silk roses. A red cardinal peered out from the roses. Ginny had replaced the bird's beaded eyes with a pair of googly eyes.

Ginny turned her head side to side, making the bird's eyes roll.

"What, you don't like my hat? I'll have you know this is a one-of-a-kind creation."

A woman holding hands with two little girls walked by. The girls' wide eyes were focused on Ginny's hat. Their mother tugged them along, telling them it was rude to stare.

"If you're trying to blend in," Kim said, "this isn't the way. But the hat's certainly a conversation starter."

"That's the idea," Aunt Ginny said. "And who knows, maybe people will want me to make them a hat. Could be the start of new career."

Kim grinned and turned to the men. Grandpa had donned a narrow-brimmed fedora trimmed with a small feather. Add a pair of lederhosen and he could model for postcards from his native Switzerland. Scott, of course, wore his Indiana Jones hat.

She stared down at the baseball cap she'd brought for sun protection. Compared to the others' hats, hers looked pedestrian.

With a shrug, she plunked it onto her head and pulled her ponytail through. She turned to study their surroundings.

The grounds surrounding the central pavilion and vendor tents teemed with mothers pushing baby carriages, teenagers dressed in shorts, darting children and dogs pulling at leashes. Nearby, a clown attempted to hand a yellow balloon to a screaming toddler. Behind them, a man dressed in a kilt carried an accordion onto the stage.

Did an unknown thief lurk somewhere in this melee? And if so, how would he react if he suddenly felt threatened?

"I know we'd planned to split up to work this crowd," Kim said, "but maybe we should all stick together."

"No, you youngsters will just get in the way," Grandpa said. "While I talk to the gem cutters, Ginny can engage the customers in gossip."

"I'm sure they'll all want to know where I got my hat." Ginny struck an exaggerated fashion-model pose.

Kim giggled and reached out to tweak the cardinal's beak, sending the googly eyes rolling. Insisting they stay together was being overly protective. After all, what sane person would feel threatened by an elderly man and a woman sporting a stuffed bird?

"Charlie's father is supposed to give a talk at

one," she told them. "Why don't we plan to meet back here at 11 so we can grab some lunch before Mark takes the stage?"

Everyone agreed and Grandpa and Aunt Ginny strolled toward the closest lapidary booth. Soon the silly hat disappeared into the crowd.

"So what's the plan?" Scott said.

"Let's combine your interviewing skills with my psychology knowledge and see if we can learn something."

When Scott agreed, she suggested they start at a booth selling homemade jewelry. Some of the jewelry designers faceted and polished their own gems. Though she doubted any of them could afford to buy the Carolina Emerald from the thief, she suspected the designers paid close attention to the availability of local gems.

Hand in hand, they plunged into the crowd. The vendor booths contained a mix of local information and items for sale. The booths selling rough gemstones seemed particularly crowded; Kim hoped her grandfather and aunt didn't get trampled.

Fewer people perused the local rock club's booth. As they passed, Kim couldn't resist glancing at the petition aimed at embarrassing Mark Hampton into allowing the club into his mine. The first page was almost full.

Surprised, Kim glanced up. John Houston, the club's president, glared at her. He folded his arms and lifted his chin.

Did he really expect her to challenge him?

Disgusted, she turned away and marched to the next booth. She slammed to a halt, enraptured by a display of brightly colored earrings, necklaces, hair clips, greeting cards and Christmas ornaments.

"I see you're not a fan of that silly petition."

A tall, slender woman stepped forward and extended a hand.

"I'm Rita Thompson and I made most of what you see here. Please accept a ten percent discount."

Kim shook Rita's hand, introduced herself, Scott and the two dogs. She assured the woman that a discount wasn't necessary.

"Your prices are reas-- My gosh, are these made of paper?"

She leaned closer to study a pair of dangling, flower-shaped earrings.

Rita laughed.

"Yes." She waved a hand to encompass the entire booth. "Everything here was created by paper quilling."

"May I?"

At the owner's nod, Kim removed one of the earrings from its display. Bright turquoise, purple and orange strips of paper -- maybe 1/4-inch wide -- had been rolled into shapes and glued together in a way that revealed only the paper edges. The sandwich of thin colors gave the earrings a delicate air.

"I've never heard of quilling," she said.

"Oh, quilling has been around for hundreds of years," Rita said. "History buffs think quilling started in Ancient Egypt. The designs were often used to decorate religious articles. In the 18th century, upper class ladies created beautiful designs to decorate picture frames, tea caddies and jewelry boxes."

"Why is it called quilling?" Kim said.

"The paper was originally rolled around a feather quill."

Rita reached behind the counter and pulled out something that looked like a miniature ice pick.

"Now we use something like this."

Kim accepted the offering. The metal was much thinner than an ice pick, about the diameter of a cake tester.

"I can't imagine rolling bits of paper around this." Kim returned the tool.

"Well, it does take practice."

"How long does it take to make a pair of earrings?"

"Depends on the quiller's experience and the intricacy of the design," Rita said. "But think in terms of hours, not minutes. That's why until very recently, only wealthy, upper class women -- they were called ladies of leisure -- practiced paper quilling."

Rita chuckled. "It's only recently that we commoners have begun quilling. I'm always teasing

Deb--"

She broke off and her eyes slid left toward the rock club's booth.

"Are you friends with Deb Hampton?" Kim said.

Rita's eyes narrowed. "Why do you ask?"

"Because I am a friend."

Kim paused, waiting for a reaction.

Rita folded her arms and waited.

Kim plowed ahead. "Deb is really worried that people might think Charlie killed Kirk Ballas."

Rita sighed and dropped her arms.

"She should be. You wouldn't believe the number of idiots that have walked by this booth talking about Charlie as if he's a murderer."

"Why in the world would people think that?"

"Someone said his fingerprints are on the gun," Rita said.

"That's because someone knocked Charlie unconscious and put a gun into his hand," Kim said. "Besides, I don't think they've completed ballistics yet, so the gun they found might not even be the murder weapon."

"You don't understand," Rita said. "Some people want Charlie to be the killer."

"But why? Charlie's a wonderful guy. He--"

But Rita raised her hand to stop Kim.

"I know Charlie's wonderful. The problem is he's also a Hampton."

Correctly reading Kim's and Scott's puzzled expressions, she added, "You have to understand.

This is a small town. People here have long memories. It wasn't that long ago that the town was divided into two parts: Those who lived in big mansions and those who cleaned or serviced those mansions. I warned Deb when she accepted Mark's proposal that people might treat her differently."

"But this is the 21st Century!" Kim folded her arms. "We're not living in Feudal England or a place with caste systems."

"Americans, however, have always had a love/hate relationship with the super wealthy," Rita said. "Have you read any F. Scott Fitzgerald?"

"'The rich are different from you and me,'" Kim said, quoting the 20th Century novelist. "So Charlie's fatal flaw is he was born a Hampton."

"Who moved away and came back. To many people, that makes Charlie more of an outsider than his brothers who stayed here."

Rita shrugged.

"You know how people are; it's best to blame people who aren't from here. Otherwise, they'd have to look sideways at their own friends and neighbors.

"But let's not talk about such depressing matters. I was serious about that discount. Any friend of Deb's is a friend of mine."

"Actually . . ."

As they'd talked, Kim had absently browsed the displayed jewelry.

"Do you have a pendant, something a ten-year-old would enjoy?"

A few months ago, a local tomboy's search for pirate treasure had turned deadly. In the weeks afterwards, Kim and her grandfather sought to erase the girl's nightmare experience with after-school activities at the jewelry store. Kim had noticed Liz's embarrassed attraction to the jewelry. A colorful pendant made from quilling might be the perfect gift.

Rita smiled and turned to a display at the back of the booth. When she turned around, she held out a delicate butterfly pendant.

Kim gasped and held out her hand. Rita had made the butterfly in shades of blue and purple with an occasional touch of yellow. She'd created a paper jewelry bail by gluing an open circle between the butterfly's antenna.

"I've sprayed it with a sealant so the pendant is water resistant," Rita said.

"It's perfect."

The whimsical piece of art suited Liz. Kim would add a metal bail and inexpensive chain before presenting the gift. She couldn't wait to see Liz's expression.

As Rita placed the butterfly into a protective box, Kim pulled out the photo of the Carolina Emerald.

"Have you seen or heard of anyone trying to sell an emerald that looks like this?"

She held up the photo.

Rita studied the picture.

"Is that the emerald from the museum, the one stolen from Charlie's cabin?"

Seeing Kim's surprise, Rita added, "It's a small town. And one of the dispatchers at the sheriff's office likes to gossip."

Kim made a mental note to use caution if she needed to report another crime.

"Yes, this is what we found. Have you heard any rumors about who might have stolen it?"

"Most people assume it was one of the Hickses." Rita shrugged. "I'm not from around here, so I don't know why people blame that poor family for everything bad that happens."

Kim resisted the sudden urge to defend a family she'd never met. Labeling everyone in the Hicks family as evil revealed as much prejudice as discriminating against someone based on race, religion or sex.

If people refused to accept their own neighbors as individuals, how would we ever stop more widespread bigotry?

But Rita clearly didn't agree with the local bias, so Kim simply changed the subject. They chatted a few minutes longer, but Rita had nothing else to add.

Kim tucked Liz's gift into an interior pocket of her bag and bid farewell to Rita. With the dogs trotting between them, she and Scott approached the next booth.

Fifty minutes later, they retired to the shade of a

large tree to regroup.

They'd visited half of the gem and jewelry booths and learned little about the missing emerald. Many vendors knew an emerald had been stolen from Charlie's cabin. Most assumed the emerald had been recently mined and were surprised to see the old photo Kim produced. Of those who knew the history of the Carolina Emerald, most speculated the Hicks family was responsible for the recent theft.

The only interesting comment came from an old-timer. He'd readily accused the Hicks family of stealing the emerald.

But then he'd added, "Of course, if Donalda Sawyer's daughter had stayed in the area, she'd be the one I'd suspect."

When they'd asked for details, the old man had simply turned and walked away.

Now Kim leaned against a tree, sipping her four-dollar cola. Though disappointed by their lack of progress in locating the Carolina Emerald, she'd enjoyed viewing the collections of local gems and minerals. Vendors and visitors alike readily shared stories of prospecting for gems. They seemed genuinely proud of the bounty found in North Carolina.

Throughout the morning, the number of people attending the festival had grown steadily. Like Kim and Scott, many brought their dogs. She'd seen Ted Bundy, the black squirrel, teasing one dog after another.

Right now, Ted darted back and forth just beyond the reach of a black Labrador retriever. The bushy-tailed rodent totally ignored the snarled cries of the dog's owner. Someone lobbed a small drink at the squirrel. It landed a foot away, exploded open and splashed both Ted and the feet of bystanders. With a final chitter, Ted turned and scampered away.

"Someone should catch and release that squirrel in a less populated area," Scott said.

"Wouldn't work." Kim drained the last of her drink. "I knew someone who captured a squirrel that had climbed down her chimney. She drove it three miles away and released it into a state park. It was back the next morning."

Scott grinned, then glanced at his watch.

"If we want to visit the rest of the jewelry booths before we meet the others," he said, "we should probably move on."

"Okay, I just need to use the rest room first." In her attempt to stay hydrated, she'd overdone the liquid.

But even in this she was stymied. The rest rooms were located inside the mansion. A huge sign on the door forbid dogs from entering.

"I can hold Rory," Scott said.

"Are you sure? Two dogs are a lot to handle. And Rory's strong and--"

Scott removed Rory's leash from her hand, grinned and gave her a gentle shove. "Go. I've got him."

Kim gratefully headed into the air-conditioned building. A few minutes later, refreshed, she stepped outside.

Scott stood on the edge of the crowd watching a clown juggle brightly colored balls. He held Al in his arms and Rory . . .

Oh, no. He'd looped Rory's leash over his wrist.

She hurried to Scott's side. Rory greeted her by putting his paws on her shoulders, a behavior she allowed only with special people.

"Thanks for watching him," she said, "but please don't ever loop his leash over your wrist."

Scott frowned down at the leash still dangling from his arm.

"Isn't this the best way to keep him from breaking free?"

"Think about what happens if he does decide to chase that darn squirrel," Kim said. "He takes off, the leash pulls your wrist sideways and . . ."

Scott winced. "I break my wrist. Thanks for the warning."

Shifting the dachshund to his other arm, Scott started to slip Rory's leash from his wrist. At the same time, a small blur of black charged between their legs.

Rory yipped and leaped forward. The leash flew from Scott's hand.

Kim lunged at the dragging leash. A large man, oblivious to the unfolding drama, stepped in front of her. She crashed into him, but didn't pause to apologize.

The leash was now well beyond her reach. She launched herself at it, but again was blocked by someone in the crowd.

Scott fared better. He pushed through the crowd using his bulk and a loud "excuse me." Kim called Rory's name. Standing on tiptoes, she strained to see over the crowd.

Ted the squirrel made a beeline toward the road that skirted the mansion. The nimble poodle charged after him. Scott's face was red with effort, but he was still too far away to step on the leash.

Kim cried out as the squirrel darted in front of a station wagon, Rory only a few steps behind.

CHAPTER 13

The driver of the station wagon honked. Tires squealed. The squirrel dodged the car's front bumper. Rory's front paws touched the curb.

A small woman shot from the crowd, sailing horizontal like a baseball player stealing home base. She landed on Rory's leash. The leash tightened. Rory jerked to a stop, inches from the front tires.

Kim reached Rory and scooped him into her arms. Rory wrapped his paws around her neck and slurped her glasses.

"Kisses aren't going to make things better," she told him. "You are in a world of trouble."

Rory simply grinned.

She held him for a few more minutes, the warmth

of his body calming her racing heart. Scott and a second man joined them and helped Rory's savior to her feet.

Kim set Rory onto the ground and, with the leash firmly gripped in her left hand, offered her right to the now dust-covered woman.

"I don't know how to begin to thank you for saving Rory's life," she said.

The unfamiliar man draped an arm around the woman.

"Betty hasn't played softball in years, but she still has the right moves, don't ya, honey?"

Betty smiled shyly.

"I love dogs," she said.

Her eyes suddenly widened. "Wait, I know you. You're the one who rescued Cooper yesterday!"

Now that the adrenaline was subsiding, Kim recognized the young woman as the mother of the boy who'd been spying on the police.

Kim smiled and extended her hand.

"I'm Kim and this is Scott. You've already met Rory. And the little guy is Al."

Al raised his paw. The woman bent over to shake it, then introduced herself as Betty Hicks.

"And this is my husband Brian."

Kim accepted Brian's hand. He was as tall as Scott, but slender to the point of skinny. Wire-rimmed glasses framed brown eyes. A lock of dark, wavy hair flopped onto his forehead. His smile was open and inviting.

"Thanks for defending Cooper," Brian said. "He has the typical boy's curiosity and propensity for getting into trouble, but he's a good kid."

"He's a thief," a new voice chimed in.

They all turned to see Officer Jennings, the belligerent young cop from yesterday morning, frog-march Cooper Hicks toward them.

"Cooper!"

Betty snatch her son away from Jennings and glared at the red-faced cop.

"What is wrong with you? Can't you leave us alone?"

Officer Jennings planted his feet.

"Your son stole fossils from Roger McDougal."

"Cooper!"

Betty stared at her son. "Is that true? You know better than that."

"I didn't steal fossils."

Cooper glared at Officer Jennings. "It was one trilobite. And I was gonna pay once I had money."

"Taking something before paying is stealing," Betty said. "You will return the fossil to Mr. McDougal and apologize."

"But Mom--"

"That's enough, young man," Brian said. "No television or computer games for the next week."

"But Grandpa Tommy said--"

"Cooper . . ."

Betty's quiet voice silenced her son.

Brian closed his eyes and pinched the bridge of

his nose.

"And where is your grandfather?" he said.

"He said he had to see a man about a horse," Cooper said.

Brian winced.

Trying to diffuse the situation, Kim said, "Trilobites are the best. I've always wanted to find one."

Cooper turned to Kim, eyes wide, the sullen little boy gone.

"Yes! That would be so awesome! Do you know where we can find them?"

"I'm afraid the closest sites are Ohio or western New Yo--"

"Who cares!" roared Officer Jennings. "This brat belongs in a reform school."

"What are you doing to my grandson!"

Kim felt her mouth drop open as the evil gnome from this morning stomped toward them.

Though the day was warm, the old man -- Cooper's grandfather? -- wore a flannel shirt, jeans and heavy work boots. Wiry white hair stuck out from his wizened skull. Beneath bushy white eyebrows, blue eyes blazed.

He marched up to Officer Jennings, folded his arms and glared up at the policeman.

Jennings pointed a finger at the old man.

"Don't you start, Tommy Hicks," he said. "You're not too old to grace one of our fine cells."

"That's quite enough," Brian said. "Cooper will

return the fossil and unless Mr. McDougal decides to press charges, you're done here."

Jennings' eyes narrowed and he took a step toward Brian. Brian gently pushed his son toward Betty, his eyes never leaving Jennings' face. He spread his feet into a fighter's stance and clenched his hands into fists.

Jennings's right hand slid toward his holster.

"You do realize you have witnesses, don't you officer?"

Scott's calm voice drew everyone's eyes.

Scott stood with his cell phone pointed at Jennings. The video camera was running. Jennings lift his chin. His nostrils flared. His eyes narrowed in calculation. Would he actually snatch the phone from Scott?

To Kim's relief, Jennings turned and stalked away.

Tension drained from her shoulders. She heard a collective sigh of relief. Brian Hicks stepped toward Scott and thrust out his right hand.

"Thanks, man," Brian said as they shook hands. "I won't forget this."

"No problem." Scott brandished his phone. "Video seems to be the only way to deal with bully cops these days."

"Yeah, well--" Brian shrugged. "When you grow up in a small town with a family like mine, you get used to police harassment."

Scott's eyes narrowed. "From what I've heard,

you've done nothing to deserve this kind of treatment. No one should be judged by their family, past or present."

Thinking of her own jewelry-crazed relatives, Kim agreed whole-heartedly. She linked her hand through Scott's.

Brian, however, snorted in disbelief.

"Try telling that to the folks around here. Grandpa Tommy's been persecuted ever since his father died, haven't you, Grandpa?"

He turned toward his grandfather. But the old man wasn't paying attention. He stared at something or someone in the crowd.

Kim followed his line of sight and spotted Michael Dunning standing nearby. With his red hair and stiff posture, he was hard to miss. His concession to the casual nature of the Gem Festival was to exchange his pinstriped suit for linen trousers and vest.

Oblivious to Tommy Hicks's attention, Dunning was scowling down at the pocket watch he held in his hand.

Tommy marched over to Dunning and said, "Where'd you get that watch?"

Startled, Dunning stepped back.

"Uh, it's a family heirloom."

A gnarled hand shot out and snatched the watch from Dunning's hand.

"Hey!"

Tommy ignored the lawyer. He studied the front

of the watch, then turned it over. His eyes widened, then returned to their normal scowl. He shoved the watch back at Dunning, saying "hmmph."

Kim exchanged a look with Betty. Was the old man getting senile?

Dunning accepted the odd behavior with surprising grace.

"Why the interest?" he said as he returned the watch to a vest pocket.

"Got me a watch jus' like that one."

"Yeah, well, there must have been thousands of these New York souvenir watches sold," Michael said.

Tommy flashed a set of crooked teeth.

"M'be so," he said, "but mine's also a -- whadidya call it -- a family heirloom."

Cackling, he turned to his grandson. "Ready for some grub?"

"Yeah!" Cooper said. "I'm starving."

"No food until you return that fossil and apologize to Mr. McDougal," Betty said.

"Ah, Maaa."

Hearing the universal child protest, Kim suppressed a smile.

Cooper and his grandfather stomped off, presumably to return the fossil. Betty and Brian quickly said their goodbyes before hurrying after them. With the exception of Tommy, they resembled any other family enjoying an afternoon outing.

Brian's willingness to fight an armed police officer, however, seemed excessive. Most people would have tried to placate Officer Jennings. Brian had simply prepared to fight.

Was his response merely an attempt to protect his family? Or an outward expression of his Hicks bloodline?

Perhaps he wasn't the nice guy she'd envisioned.

Beside her, Rory suddenly stiffened into attention. Kim followed his gaze. Across the street, Ted Bundy perched on the opposite sidewalk. The squirrel chittered and waggled its front paws in a Rocky Balboa victory dance.

Kim waved a liver-flavored treat in front of Rory's nose and physically turned him away from the squirrel.

"Isn't that your aunt over there?"

Kim had to stand on tiptoes to see where Scott was pointing. Sure enough, Aunt Ginny's outrageous hat bobbed in front of a booth selling homemade silk scarves and shawls. She couldn't see her grandfather, but perhaps he was hidden by the dense crowd.

Her stomach gurgled, announcing it had been far too long since breakfast. She suggested they collect Ginny and Grandpa and eat lunch before Mark's talk began.

But when they reached Aunt Ginny, Grandpa was nowhere in sight.

"He went that way."

Ginny pointed vaguely toward her left. "Said he was going to interview another gem cutter."

She held up two silk scarves, one printed with bright purple and yellow butterflies, the other with turquoise and lapis dragonflies.

"Which do you like better, the blue or the purple?"

"Ah, er, I prefer the dragonflies, but the purple and yellow color on the butterflies seems more you."

"I wonder if she has the dragonflies in purple," Ginny muttered.

Kim, however, was no longer listening. She'd spotted Grandpa hovering in front of a gem cutter's booth. The people on either side of Grandpa stared intently at something out of Kim's sight, probably a display case.

But while Grandpa's face was aimed at the case, the slight twisting of his body and tilt of his head indicated his focus was on the two men standing at the far end of the booth. They appeared to be arguing.

She looked closer and realized the gray-haired man standing behind the booth wasn't talking at all. He stood with arms crossed, a glare marring what might have been a handsome face.

All she could see of the other man was the back of his head. Feet planted, he leaned toward the booth owner, one clenched fist punching the air as he talked.

The booth owner listened a few more seconds, then shook his head, threw his hands into the air and turned to another customer.

For a moment, the angry man glared at the booth owner. Then he slammed his palms on the counter, turned and marched past Grandpa.

Kim could now see the brown goatee, flint eyes and mouth frozen in a snarl. Donny Driver, Charlie's nemesis.

Thrusting his chest out, Donny used his elbows to push through the crowd.

To her horror, Grandpa followed.

She interrupted Ginny's assessment of another bright scarf.

"Why don't you take a few minutes to decide and then we'll go to lunch," she said. "I'm going to find Grandpa."

Without waiting for a reply, she tightened her hold on Rory's leash and began weaving through the crowd.

"What's going on?" Scott fell into step beside her.

"Grandpa's following the guy that started the fight in the restaurant."

Kim slid past a family of four.

"Donny looked really mad. If he sees Grandpa behind him--"

She couldn't finish the sentence. The thought of the goateed thug hurting her grandfather sickened her.

Up ahead, Charlie's nemesis turned down a less

populated path. Grandpa hung back and Kim began to close the distance. Before she could get close enough to call out, however, a new man stepped between them.

Her breath caught as she recognized the new face: Donny's friend Rocky DiSoto.

She watched helplessly as Grandpa plunged down the now mostly deserted lane and disappeared from sight. Rocky DiSoto stomped after him.

Kim broke into a jog.

CHAPTER 14

Though Scott had longer legs, Kim's smaller size enabled her to dodge between groups of people. She reached the path where the three men had disappeared two steps ahead of Scott.

Rounding the corner, she watched in horror as Rocky grabbed her grandfather's upper arm and jerked him roughly to a stop.

"Hey, old man." Rocky towered over Grandpa. "Are you following my buddy?"

Grandpa cupped his ear.

"Eh? You'll need to speak up son. I can't hear too well these days."

There was nothing wrong with her grandfather's hearing. Kim snagged Scott's sleeve and slowed their pace. Best to wait until she understood Grandpa's ploy.

"Why. Are. You. Following. Donny?" Rocky yelled.

Hearing his name, Donny stopped and turned. Rory growled. Kim placed a hand over his muzzle so she could hear her grandfather's response.

"Following?"

Grandpa blinked his eyes and glanced around him. When his eyes met Kim's, he gave a slight head shake and continued looking around.

"Isn't this the way to the little boys' room?"

"What's going on?" Donny demanded.

He marched toward her grandfather, effectively preventing him from running away.

Time to intervene.

"Grandpa!"

Kim trotted toward the three men. Scott, still carrying Al, paced beside her.

"You're going the wrong way. The restrooms are behind us."

She linked her arm through her grandfather's.

"Let's go."

But when she turned, she found their way blocked by Rocky.

She backed against Scott. As a unit, they shuffled sideways so they could watch both men. Al started barking. Scott wrestled with the struggling dog. Rocky smirked.

"Hey, I know you!" Donny said. "You're a friend

of Charlie's."

"Actually, I'm friends with his fiancé. C'mon, Grandpa, let's find the restroom."

"Wait a minute." Rocky reached out as if he might grab her.

With a roar, Rory lunged. His front paws struck Rocky in the chest, knocking him back a step.

Rocky's face turned red. He pointed a finger at Rory.

"Keep that mutt away from me. If he bites, I'll sue."

Kim tightened her hold on her now growling poodle. Rory's action had been intended as a warning. Had he felt threatened enough to bite, he'd have kept all four feet on the ground and gone for the man's ankles or legs.

Al's barking increased into a piercing bay. Kim stared back toward freedom. People must surely hear the dogs. Why was no one coming to investigate?

"So what's going on?" Donny addressed his friend, but focused his cobra eyes on Scott.

"When you left that gem cutter," Rocky said, "this old codger followed you."

Donny glared at Grandpa. "That right, old man?"

Grandpa straightened his shoulders. "Of course I was following you."

The admission so surprised Rocky that he shuffled back a step. But there still wasn't room to run past him.

"Why were you following me?" Donny's eyes were slits.

"You rushed away so suddenly that I figured you must have prostate problems too," Grandpa said. "I thought you were heading to the restrooms."

"See?" Kim grabbed her grandfather's arm and gently turned him back the way they'd come. "Now let's find those bathrooms."

With Scott close beside her, she marched toward Rocky and the freedom beyond. A growl from Rory convinced the thug to step aside.

They reached the crowded main thoroughfare and quickened their steps. Kim didn't breathe normally until they'd placed several booths between them and the thugs.

She glanced back, but didn't see Donny or Rocky. The two men must have continued in a different direction.

With the danger past, they collected Aunt Ginny and found an empty table near the food booths. The smell of barbecue, fried dough and cinnamon made her mouth water. Leaving the dogs with Ginny and Grandpa, Kim and Scott purchased barbecue sandwiches, coleslaw and drinks and returned to the table.

"Okay," Kim said as she passed out the food, "tell us why you were following Donny Driver."

"Is that his name?" Grandpa said.

Kim quickly explained the relationship between Donny, Rocky and the dead man.

Grandpa frowned, then nodded.

"Makes a certain amount of sense, I guess." He met Kim's eyes. "Donny Driver is our emerald thief."

His statement produced the intended surprised reactions. Kim was the first to recover.

"Why are you so certain?" she said.

"He's been cruising the lapidarists, but only the ones from out of town. He's asked each one how many emeralds could be cut from a rough stone about eight inches long," Grandpa said.

Kim's stomach clenched. Though she'd suspected the emerald thief would hire someone to cut the emerald into smaller gems, confirmation made her ill.

In the years since the emerald had been stolen from the American Museum of Natural History, larger emeralds had been discovered in North Carolina. But none of them consisted of three separate crystals growing from the same foundation.

Besides, what she'd come to think of as the Carolina Emerald had held the title of "largest North Carolina emerald" for more than 80 years. If nothing else, the Carolina Emerald should be preserved, intact, for its historical significance.

She was almost afraid to ask, but . . . "Did anyone agree to cut it?"

Grandpa swallowed a bite of his sandwich.

"No one would admit to it. I didn't actually hear

the thief's spiel until I caught up with him at the last booth."

Grinning, he thrust his shoulders back and jutted his chin forward -- a competent imitation of Donny Driver. Recognizing her grandfather's intention to reenact the scene, Kim leaned back and sipped her tea.

"Hey, you," Grandpa as Donny said. "Gotta question for you. Say you find an emerald maybe this long."

He spread his fingers as wide as they'd go.

"How many emeralds can you cut from it and how much would they be worth?"

Now Grandpa crossed his arms and pulled in his shoulders to mimic the lapidarist. In a heavy, New York accident, he said, "You find an emerald that large, ya better sell it to a museum."

"But, of course," Grandpa said in his own voice, "our thief couldn't sell to a museum. Someone would surely recognize the emerald."

"So how did Donny handle the museum suggestion?" Kim said.

Grandpa again puffed out his chest. "Yeah, I hear ya, but say you really want to cut it up. Like, you have a girlfriend who's seen it and wants an emerald cut from it."

Grandpa folded his arms and assumed his New York accent.

"Then sell the emerald to a museum and use the money to buy the girlfriend an emerald."

Kim and the others burst out laughing.

Relieved to hear that the gem cutters weren't helpful to Donny, Kim reached for her sandwich. Maybe he'd realize the futility of trying to sell the emerald and . . . And what? Send it back to the museum? Unlikely.

She bit into the sandwich and, for a moment, savored the sweet spiciness. Her mind raced. She needed to tell the police that Donny might have the emerald. But who could she trust?

Detective Alexandra Cummings wouldn't be interested in the emerald theft unless she thought it pertinent to the murder of Kirk Ballas. And while the murder and theft occurred on the same night, Kim had no evidence to connect the two. So Cummings was out.

The only other police officers she'd encountered were the two men who'd been searching for clues at the mine. The older man's cynical attitude repelled her. The younger, Officer Jennings, seemed more determined to pin the murder on one of the Hickses than in learning the truth.

Which left the sheriff himself. Surely Sheriff Spits would take Grandpa's findings seriously.

Aunt Ginny interrupted her thoughts.

"What time are we meeting the others?" Ginny frowned down at her ring watch.

"I think Mark's talk starts at one o'clock," Kim said.

"It's one o'clock now," Ginny said.

"Oops. Guess we'd better amble over there." Kim stood and slipped Rory's bag over her shoulder.

As she tightened her hold on Rory's leash, a nearby crunch of gravel drew her attention. She looked up into the eyes of Officer Jennings.

Jennings stiffened. Kim sensed Scott moving beside her, slipping an arm across her shoulder.

Jennings' radio squawked.

As he raised the radio to his mouth, Jennings shifted his gaze from Scott to Kim to Grandpa to Aunt Ginny.

"This is Jennings," he said into the radio.

"We need you at the pavilion," a woman's voice said. "Demonstration is turning ugly."

Kim suddenly realized that the background sounds she'd ignored as typical crowd noise had an unusual cadence. Above the normal cacophony of children's squeals, adult conversations and shuffling feet, she heard something that sounded like a chant. She couldn't distinguish the words.

The angry tone, however, was unmistakable.

"On my way," Jennings said.

Casting one last glare at them, he turned and pushed past the nearest people.

"Isn't the pavilion where we're supposed to meet the others?" Grandpa said.

Scott, the tallest among them, peered over the crowd. "Yeah. Looks like something's happening there."

Kim turned to Grandpa and Ginny.

"Would you two please wait here with the dogs? Scott and I can move quicker if we don't have to deal with the furry ones."

Grandpa watched another police officer push toward the pavilion.

"I'm not sure any of us should go over there," he said. "If that crowd starts pushing and shoving, someone is going to get hurt."

"Rachael and Charlie are supposed to be there," Kim said.

While Rachel considered herself "tough," her small size made her vulnerable to being knocked over and trampled.

Scott met Grandpa's eyes. "I'll take care of Kim."

Grandpa nodded. Scott grabbed Kim's hand and led her through the crowd.

Scott used his shoulders to gently clear a path. As they neared the pavilion, the crowd thickened and their forward progress slowed. Up ahead, Kim saw a motley group of people waving picket signs and chanting, "Ak-SESS, Ak-SESS."

Access?

She started reading the signs. "You don't own nature." "We like to dig, too." "Say NO to Plutocrats." "Our Forefathers fought your Plutocrats." "We don't need no Emerald Kings."

She recognized the man waving the Emerald-

King sign: John Houston, president of the local rockhounding club. He seemed to be leading the chant by pumping his left fist into the air in an inciting rhythm. His furrowed brow, red face and aggressive stance seemed excessive. After all, he was demanding "Ak-SESS" to private property.

The woman who'd helped set up the rockhounding club's booth had warned Kim that Houston and company could "get rough." Was this what she had in mind?

Kim scanned the picketers' faces and finally spotted the woman standing at the back of the group. Though she chanted along with the others, the sign she held simply said "Share!"

With Scott's efforts, they worked their way toward the stage. Kim finally spotted Rachael, Charlie and his two brothers standing to the left of the stage. Charlie used his body to partially block Rachael from the press of people.

Scott tapped Kim's shoulder.

"I don't think we're going to be able to reach them until the picketers leave," he said.

Kim ground her teeth. If the crowd suddenly stampeded, they were too far away to help her friends. She'd placed Scott and herself at risk for nothing.

Sensing her frustration, Scott pulled her to stand in front of him. He wrapped his arms around her, shielding her from the surrounding people.

"Don't worry," he said. "If they need help, we'll

reach them."

Kim smiled and leaned back, breathing in Scott's Irish Spring scent. Tension drained away, replaced by warmth, comfort and a tingling awareness that this man was someone truly special.

Tapping on the microphone drew her attention to the stage. A frazzled looking woman leaned into the microphone. Behind her, Mark Hampton stood protectively next to Deb's wheelchair.

"If I could have your attention, please," the announcer said. "Please, everyone, if you could stop talking."

The audience quieted. Kim looked toward John Houston in time to see his raised fist change to an open palm. The loud chanting stopped.

"Thank you. I'd like to introduce our next guest. Many of you already know Mark Hampton and his lovely wife, Deb."

She gestured toward the couple while a handful of people applauded.

"But for those who don't, let me tell you a bit about them."

She launched into the history of North Carolina emerald mines in general, the Hampton mine in particular and Mark's civic role in the community.

As she talked, Kim studied the audience, trying to gauge people's reactions. Those who'd snagged chairs leaned forward as they tried to absorb the woman's words. A few people standing along the crowd edge drifted away. John Houston's group huddled together, their picket signs still raised, their expressions sullen.

Uniformed police officers roamed the perimeter of the crowd. Officer Jennings stood beside Detective Alexandra Cummings. As she talked, Jennings' face reddened. Judging from the scowl on the detective's face, she wasn't praising him.

"Obviously, everyone here believes in free speech," the woman on stage said. "But we ask that demonstrators refrain from chanting so that others can hear what our distinguished guest has to say. And now, please welcome Mark Hampton."

Mark waited for the polite applause to die down before flashing a killer smile.

"Do we have anyone in the audience who likes diamonds, emeralds, rubies or sapphires?"

A cheer of female voices answered.

"Well, North Carolina is one of the few states in our wondrous nation where all of what we in the trade call The Big Four gemstones have been found," Mark said. "North Carolina is also world renowned for a rare gem called Hiddenite, which was discovered not far from where we stand."

Another cheer.

"And let's not forget that long before the infamous California Gold Rush, gold was discovered in southwestern North Carolina. In fact, the first dollar gold piece was minted right here in North Carolina with North Carolina gold."

More cheering. As Mark continued his "rah-rah

North Carolina" speech, movement at the edge of the crowd drew Kim's eye. She stiffened when she recognized Donny Driver and his sidekick Rocky DiSoto slide into position not far from where Charlie and his brothers stood.

The two thugs clutched wooden handles attached to what must be signs, though at the moment the messages faced toward the men's legs. Donny's eyes scanned the crowd before focusing on John Houston's group.

A signal must have passed between them because Donny nodded, raised his sign and shouted "Ak-SESS, Ak-SESS."

Houston's group quickly joined in. But Kim paid no attention to the protestors behind her. Her eyes were riveted on the signs held by Donny and Rocky. Each contained a close-up photo of Mark Hampton. Someone had drawn a circle around Mark's head, then a red slash through his face.

She'd seen the circle/slash symbol used to indicate no smoking, drinking or whatever. Used with a person's face, however, the symbol reminded her of the crosshairs of a gun scope.

On stage, Mark tried to talk over the protestors. A few seated audience members turned to scowl at the noise makers. Officer Cummings spoke into her radio and began pushing toward Donny and Rocky. Other police officers worked their way toward John Houston's group.

The police movement seemed to spur on Donny.

Shifting position, he shoved Rachael aside and elbowed Charlie in the gut. Charlie bent over, grasping his stomach with both hands. Diesel shouted something and, fists clenched, bulled his way toward Donny.

"Stay here," Scott said before pushing through the crowd.

Kim snagged the waistband of his jeans and trotted behind him. Scott glanced back, rolled his eyes and continued forward.

They were still ten feet away when Donny swung his picket sign at Diesel's head. Diesel ducked. The sign smashed into Diesel's upper back, knocking him into the crowd.

Charlie launched himself at Donny. The two men fell to the ground and rolled around, fists flying.

Jake started toward the two men, but tripped over Rocky's outstretched foot. As Jake stumbled, Rocky kicked the back of his knees. Jake dropped to the ground. Rocky raised his picket sign above his head. Before he could bring it down on Jake, Diesel tackled him.

Kim and Scott reached the fray just as Donny pinned Charlie to the ground and wrapped his hands around his throat. Charlie swung his fists at Donny's arms and head in vain.

Kim dashed to the men.

"Stop!" she shouted. "You're killing him!"

She wrapped both hands around Donny's arm and tugged. But she couldn't break his hold on

Charlie. She watched in horror as Charlie's face turned red and his punches grew weaker.

"Kim, move away," Scott yelled.

Kim released Donny and jumped back. Scott swung his right foot, catching Donny in the side of the head.

Though she could see Scott temper the strength of his kick, the impact knocked Donny off of Charlie.

Donny's eyes blazed and he charged Scott. Scott ducked and aimed a shoulder into Donny's chest. Donny grunted but maintained his footing. His right hand disappeared behind his back, then reappeared holding a knife.

Scott jumped backward. Charlie struggled to stand, but was still having trouble breathing. Kim shrugged her dog bag from her shoulder and gripped the long handle. Donny lunged, jabbing with the knife. Scott dodged.

Kim swung her bag. It smashed into Donny's wrist. The knife went flying.

Scott plowed into Donny. The two men fell to the ground.

"Police! Step aside."

A wall of uniformed men shoved Kim aside and quickly surrounded the men, blocking her view.

She heard first Scott, then Charlie protest. Donny cursed.

Another set of police shoved handcuffed men toward the crowd's edge. Rocky DiSoto's nose bled and swelling around his left eye would soon turn dark. Blood from a cut on Diesel's forehead oozed down his face in horror-movie fashion. Jake's face appeared similarly battered.

The first set of police stepped back, allowing Kim a view of what lay beyond. Donny, Charlie and Scott had all been handcuffed.

"Wait a minute!"

Kim stomped to Scott's side and glared at the nearest cop.

"Scott was trying to stop Donny from killing Charlie. You should be rewarding him, not arresting him."

"He kicked my head," Donny said.

"That was the only way to stop you!" Kim said. She turned back to the cops. "Release Scott now."

"Calm down," a woman's voice said.

Kim whipped around to face Detective Cummings.

"Please," she said, "tell your officers to release Scott. Donny would have killed Charlie if Scott hadn't stopped him."

Detective Cummings' eyes showed no emotion. "We'll get it straightened out at the station."

"But--"

"Charlie!"

Rachael broke through the crowd and hurled herself at her fiancé.

"Are you okay? Oh, no, you're bleeding! Why are you handcuffed!"

Detective Cummings ignored Rachael and turned

to address the assembled officers.

"Take these guys downtown," she said.

Helpless, Kim and Rachael watched as the handcuffed men were marched toward the police cars.

CHAPTER 15

Kim grabbed Rachael's arm and dragged her through the crowd toward the food vendors where she'd left Grandpa and Aunt Ginny.

"Do you have the phone number for Charlie's friend Drew?" Kim said.

Rachael shook her head.

"But I know his name so I can probably find the number on the internet."

"You'll never be able to search your phone while we're moving through this crowd." Kim dodged a family of four. "Better wait until we're all in the car. We'll also need the address for the Sheriff's Department."

To her relief, she found her family and the dogs at the picnic table where they'd dined.

Kim explained the situation and led the way back to Scott's car. Thank goodness he'd shared a spare key when they'd started this trip; otherwise, they'd all be stranded.

While the others settled in -- Rachael, Aunt Ginny and the dogs in back, Grandpa in the passenger seat -- Kim located the address for the Sheriff's Department and plugged it into the GPS.

Ten minutes later, she pressed the car's accelerator to merge onto Interstate 64. The GPS indicated they'd reach the County's Sheriff's Department in eight minutes.

Kim gripped the steering wheel and tried to coral the thoughts whirring through her mind. But she couldn't erase the image of Donny Driver's corded neck, flared nostrils and bared teeth as his hands squeezed the life from Charlie.

If Scott hadn't intervened, Charlie would be dead.

Pushing down the panic, she forced her mind to analyze what she'd seen.

Before Donny and his friend Rocky appeared, the rock hunting club's demonstration had been peaceful. The atmosphere changed, however, when the two thugs displayed their picket signs -- Mark Hampton's face with a red line through it.

But though Donny had swung his sign at Diesel, he must have minimized the intensity of his swing.

The impact had knocked Diesel to the ground, but not broken bones.

By the time Donny pinned Charlie to the ground, however, he'd metamorphosed from bar brawler to psychotic killer. He'd barely felt Kim's attempts to pull him away, didn't seem to hear her frantic pleas. Despite hundreds of witnesses, Donny was fighting to the death.

Kim suddenly realized that Donny Driver exhibited signs of Intermittent Explosive Disorder.

IED was a relatively recent addition to psychology's growing list of mental disorders. It manifested as sudden violence disproportionate to the situation. A slow-moving car might trigger road rage. A wife's unguarded expression might set off physical abuse. A co-worker's promotion might spark a rampage of physical destruction.

No one seemed to know what caused IED. Kim suspected it was produced by a combination of environment and genetics. Psychologists reported IED in children as young as six years old. Treatment involved a combination of psychotherapy and mood-affecting drugs.

In the throes of blind rage, untreated sufferers like Donny Driver might well commit murder.

The voice of the GPS unit interrupted her thoughts. It was time to exit the highway. Kim turned her full attention to the road ahead.

Detective Cummings had told her officers to take Scott and the others "downtown," but their surroundings more resembled exurbia than a town. They passed open fields, a juvenile detention facility and a Super Walmart, then turned left at an auto parts store.

The sheriff's building finally came into sight. The low, angular design, sided with extra-long brick, reminded Kim a bit of Frank Lloyd Wright. Charcoal-colored brick graced the base of the walls while soft-gray brick extended above. Floor to ceiling windows reflected the surrounding countryside. All this, coupled with bright blue trim, created an unexpectedly cheerful ambiance.

Six men -- including Scott, thank goodness! -- huddled outside of the building.

Mark Hampton stood with feet planted, raised chin and clenched fists. Charlie's mouth pressed into a thin line. Diesel scowled and Jake's eyes flashed.

Scott leaned away from the others, his hands thrust into his pants pocket. Though he faced Charlie, his eyes slid toward the final man in the group: Michael Dunning.

The presence of the red-headed lawyer explained why the guys weren't still in police custody. But how had he beaten Kim to the station?

She pulled beneath a shady tree. Rachael bounded out before the car came to a complete stop and raced toward the men.

Kim turned to the others.

"This will probably go faster if you guys stay in

the air conditioning with the dogs."

Grandpa smiled. "Go. We'll be fine here."

She hurried after Rachael. Scott greeted her with one of his crooked smiles and a quick hug.

"How'd you get sprung so quickly?" she said.

Mark Hampton answered for the group. "That was Michael's doing."

He patted the lawyer on the back.

"Michael was at the fair and witnessed the fight. When he saw the police handcuff everyone, he drove straight here. Before anyone could be charged, Michael described what he'd seen. Clearly, Scott and my sons had been acting in self-defense."

"Please keep in mind," Michael said, "Charlie is still a suspect in the murder of Kirk Ballas. Public brawling is not going to endear him to Detective Cummings."

"Not a problem," Mark said. "If she can't find the killer, we'll find him."

Michael grimaced. "I advise you to not take the law into your own hands."

Mark waved a hand in dismissal.

"Oh, stop with the lawyer-speak. All we're doing is finding alternative suspects."

"And have you found any?" Michael said.

In answer, Mark looked at his sons and raised his eyebrows.

Jake nodded. "The night Kirk was killed, the Hicks clan was prowling through the woods. Tommy Hicks even chased someone with a decapitated chicken while chanting some kind of voodoo curse."

A few hours ago, Kim could have well imagined the troll-like man trying to cast an evil spell. But after witnessing the affectionate bond between Tommy Hicks and his great-grandson, she hoped the man wasn't involved in murder.

"We need to go back to the house to compare notes, make some plans," Mark said. "Michael, I'd like you to join us. I think we can fit everyone into our two cars."

"Actually, Charlie and I need to collect his car," Rachael said. "Could someone please drive us back to the festival?"

While the others coordinated seating arrangements, Kim turned to Scott.

"Did you see Sheriff Spits when you were in there?"

She gestured toward the building.

"Afraid not," Scott said. "Believe me, I'd have demanded an audience if I'd seen him."

He shrugged. "But we weren't in the station very long. The sheriff might be in his office."

"What do you want with Walt Spits?" Mark's voice was gruff, laden with suspicion.

The words "none of your business" ran through Kim's head, but for once she didn't voice them aloud. She hadn't intended to tell the others about Grandpa following Donny until after she'd talked with Sheriff Spits. But the anger in Mark's eyes warned her to tread carefully.

"Before staging that, er, protest," she said, "Donny Driver spent the morning quizzing lapidarists about cutting a large emerald."

"That punk has my emerald?"

Mark turned toward the sheriff's department.

Kim snagged his sleeve, halting him mid-stride.

"I doubt he's actually carrying it," she said. "But maybe Sheriff Spits can get a search warrant for Donny's house."

"I wouldn't advise talking to the sheriff," Michael said.

Kim gawked at him. "Why not? This may be our only opportunity to recover the emerald."

"We need Donny to remain a viable suspect," Michael said. "If Charlie actually winds up in a trial, we can use the 'some other guy did it' defense. A jury should easily believe that Donny, Rocky and Kirk were stealing emeralds, got into an argument and Kirk ended up dead.

"But if Donny planned all along to steal the museum emerald, then why would he have gone to the mine? Selling the museum emerald would generate much more money than anything he might have unearthed Thursday night. A good defense attorney would have Donny plea guilty for the burglary while maintaining no connection to the theft at the mine."

"But if I don't tell the sheriff, Donny will have time to sell or cut up the emerald. Besides, Sheriff

Spits knows darn well Charlie didn't kill anyone."

"Right now all the evidence points to Charlie," Michael said. "Charlie's fingerprints are the only ones on the weapon. He had means, motive and opportunity."

"But what about the wound on Charlie's head?" Kim said. "Doesn't that prove someone else was there?"

Michael shrugged. "A good prosecutor would say Charlie's wound could have been caused by an accomplice."

He pointed at Scott. "Maybe him."

Kim protested.

Michael raised his hands, palms toward her and talked over her.

"Hey, I'm on your side. But you need to understand Charlie's precarious position."

Rachael gripped Kim's arm.

"He's right. We can't do anything until we know Charlie is safe."

Michael looked over her shoulder and his eyes narrowed.

"Here comes trouble."

He nodded in the direction of the parking lot.

Kim turned to see John Houston, president of the rock hunting club, walking beside a balding man wearing a dark suit.

"The guy in the suit is Robinson Champion," Michael said. "He lives here but spends most of his time defending sleezeballs in Charlotte. Never loses."

As the two men swaggered by, Houston lifted his chin and sneered at Mark Hampton. Mark maintained a poker face, but his right fist clenched.

"Champion knows all the judges," Michael said. "Even though today is Saturday, Champion will find a judge to release Donny and his friends."

He met Kim's eyes.

"So you'd better make up your mind."

CHAPTER 16

"Kim, please wait to talk to Sheriff Spits," Rachael said. "What if Michael's right?"

Kim dragged fingers through her hair. "I'm sorry, but I don't see how Donny stealing the emerald removes him as a murder suspect."

Michael shrugged. "Suit yourself."

Pulling keys from his pocket, he added, "Who's riding with me?"

Diesel and Jake followed Michael to his car.

Rachael gripped Kim's hand and flashed puppy dog eyes. When Kim didn't respond, Rachael turned away.

Kim watched her friends climb into Mark Hampton's car, hoping Rachael would turn to wave.

She didn't.

"You made the right decision."

Scott squeezed Kim's hand. "Withholding information from the police is never a good idea."

"I know," Kim said. "I just hope Rachael understands that when she calms down. She's been awfully prickly lately."

She sighed. "Let's get this over with."

They entered the air-conditioned building. A receptionist sitting behind an oversized desk blocked access to the door that must lead to the sheriff. The woman frowned as they approached.

"Looks like she's having a bad day," Scott whispered. "Want me to try to charm her?"

Kim readily agreed. Despite Grandpa's repeated attempts to teach her diplomacy, she still had a tendency to blurt out whatever was on her mind.

"I wonder if you can help us." Scott flashed his Indiana Jones smile.

The woman behind the desk, however, did not smile back. Her eyes raked him head to toe before she met his eyes and scowled.

"What do you want?"

Scott continued to smile.

"Is Sheriff Spits available?"

The receptionist crossed her arms. "No."

As Scott's smile grew strained, Kim clenched her fists, silently repeating Grandpa's mantra "Be nice."

"When will he be available?" Scott said.

The woman shrugged. "Don't know."

"Sometime today?"

Another shrug.

Okay, enough with playing nice. Kim stepped closer to the desk.

"I'm sorry you're having a bad day," she said. "But we have important information for the sheriff. So please tell him we're here."

Muddy brown eyes glared at her.

"Sheriff isn't here."

"When do you expect him back?"

Surely someone as important as a sheriff maintained contact with his office.

The receptionist jiggled her shoulders like a bird fluffing its feathers.

"I have no idea. Probably won't see him until tomorrow."

"We need to talk to him sooner than that." Kim put on her most ingratiating smile. "Could you call him on his cell or--"

"If you're in such a hurry," the woman interrupted, "then talk to one of our officers. Detective Cummings is unavailable, but Officer Jennings is here."

The last thing Kim wanted to do was talk to the idiot cop who'd harassed the Hickses.

"How 'bout I leave a message for Sheriff Spits?"

"Do what you want."

The woman's tone implied that the message would hit the trashcan before they reached the front door.

Kim opened her mouth, prepared to lecture about common courtesy. But the interior door banged open and John Houston stepped into the lobby.

Kim blocked his path.

"You should be ashamed of yourself," she said. "Staging a protest was childish but allowing it to escalate was criminal."

Houston glared at her. "I didn't tell those two idiots to start a riot."

"Don't deny your involvement," Kim said. "I saw you signal them."

"They were supposed to drown out Hampton's speech, not pick a fight with his sons."

She threw her hands in the air.

"And what do you think you accomplished? People who allow rockhounders to prospect on their land already worry about liability. Do you think anyone who hears about what happened today is going to allow your club onto their property?"

As she talked, Houston's face grew increasingly red.

"You have no idea what we're up against here," he said.

"I know people like you give rockhounders a bad name," she said. "You should have been arrested along with the others."

Houston's hands fisted and, for a moment, Kim feared she'd pushed him too far. His angry eyes flicked from Kim's to Scott's to the desk sergeant's.

"Stay out of this," he growled.

Brushing past her, he stomped outside.

The sound of clapping drew Kim's attention back to the reception desk. The woman who'd thwarted their attempts to reach Sheriff Spits smacked her hands together three more times before smiling at her.

"It's about time someone pinned back John-Boy's ears," the receptionist said. "That man's been looking for trouble ever since his mama died." She nodded, then added, "Write your note to Sheriff Spits. I'll see he gets it."

Five minutes later, they returned to the car. Kim joined Aunt Ginny and the two dogs in the back. As they drove away, she updated the others.

"Donny must know we suspect he has the emerald," she concluded. "By the time the sheriff gets my message, Donny will have hidden it some place safe."

Aunt Ginny patted her hand. "You did the best you could."

"Actually, it might be better that Donny knows you talked with the sheriff," Grandpa said. "He won't be able to sell the emerald while the sheriff is watching him."

Though her grandfather made a good point, the events of the day left Kim dispirited. The last thing she wanted to do right now was attend a meeting at Mark Hampton's mansion.

Scott slowed for a traffic light, then pointed to a small shop sandwiched between a dollar store and a nail salon. Through the display window, she could see trays of caramels, truffles and fudge. A sidewalk billboard advertised homemade candy.

"Shall we stop for chocolate?" Scott said. "That always seems to cheer you."

She grinned. "You know I only eat Grandpa's Swiss choc-- Wait! Yes, please find a parking space."

Naturally, everyone started teasing her. Their words, however, fell on deaf ears. Kim was too busy congratulating herself for a brilliant idea.

Leaping from the car, she crossed the street and entered the store. She selected an assortment of milk and dark chocolates and asked the clerk to arrange them in a gold foil gift box. A bright red bow and small thank you card completed the package.

She trotted back to the car and handed the box to her grandfather.

"Hang onto this for me, please? I don't want to risk the dogs ripping it from my hand."

Chocolate -- especially the rich, dark variety Kim preferred -- was toxic to dogs.

"I know you didn't buy this for yourself," Grandpa said as the car pulled back onto the road. "Is this for Rachael?"

"Nah, Rachael's never been susceptible to bribes. I thought chocolate would be a nice way to thank

Betty Hicks for saving Rory."

Grandpa turned around and peered at her over his glasses. "And do some snooping?"

"Actually, no," Kim said. "I really do want to thank the woman."

Plus delivering the candy gave her a great excuse to miss Mark's meeting.

Pulling out her cell phone, she searched the internet for a phone number for Betty or Brian Hicks in Hiddenite. She found an address. But the phone number was unlisted.

Perfect. She could justify her need to drive to Betty's house right now.

"Scott, may I borrow your car? While you all are at Mark's meeting, I'll drop off the candy."

"No." In the rear-view mirror, Scott's eyes met hers. "If you're going to the Hickses' house, I'm going with you. Don't forget, one of those people might be a killer."

Kim crossed her arms. "Do you really think Betty or Brian killed Kirk Ballas?"

"Don't know them well enough to have an opinion," Scott said. "Betty may have saved Rory's life, but that doesn't mean she wouldn't kill someone if she felt threatened. The same goes for her husband."

"Why don't we all go?" Aunt Ginny said. "Safety in numbers and all that."

Kim scanned the car. Two dogs, a professor, a jeweler and an Auntie Mame wannabe.

"Uh, don't you think all of us together might be intimidating? I want to thank them, not scare them."

"We'll wait in the car," Grandpa said.

"That makes three against one." Scott pulled to the side of the road, then turned to face her. "I know you liked Betty. I liked her, too. But her husband's family has a long history of skirting the law. People like that can be unpredictable."

"They're not wild animals," Kim said.

"Of course not. But people who live in the Appalachian Mountains have a history of anti-social behavior. You could well be greeted by someone holding a shotgun."

Kim folded her arms. "You make them all sound like Rednecks."

Scott jerked back as if he'd been slapped.

"You know me better than that," he said quietly.

Kim dropped her arms, instantly ashamed. She reached out and touched Scott's cheek.

"I'm sorry," she said. "I know you don't judge people by their social class."

She flopped back in the seat.

"I'm just so tired of Mark Hampton and that idiot cop trying to pin a murder on the Hicks family just because they're different."

"Don't let your urge to fight for the underdog lead you to do something dangerous," Grandpa said.

Kim drew in a breath. The others were right.

Though she didn't think Betty and Brian Hicks posed a danger, she didn't know these people. Much as she valued her independence, she didn't want to do something stupid.

She read off the Hickses' address while Scott punched it into the GPS unit.

Twenty minutes later, they passed the entrance to the Hampton mine. Scott slowed the car, searching for the Hickses' driveway. It appeared on the left. The overgrown gravel drive was barely wide enough for their car. Overhanging tree branches brushed the car's sides. Gravel clinked against the undercarriage.

Finally, a turn in the road revealed Betty and Brian's homestead.

An old wooden barn perched on the left. The weathered wood had been only partially covered in red paint. The slightly faded color indicated the painter had either lost interest or run out of paint.

Someone had planted a rose garden between the barn and house, but the five bushes were spindly, the few remaining leaves light green in color.

As for the house, the wood-sided, single-story building reminded Kim of a sharecropper's hut. Double-hung windows flanked the entry door. A porch stretched across the front, but looked forlorn without even a chair to sit on.

Old tires, painted primary colors and planted with autumn flowers, lined a dirt path to the front door.

On the far right, piles of box springs, broken toys, old tires and the like marked the entrance to the forest.

If Kim had been painting the scene, she'd have titled it "Dreams Crushed."

Scott parked beneath a tree, but didn't turn off the engine. Silently, they gazed at the desolation.

Grandpa broke the silence. "Looks like her roses have an iron deficiency. But her mums look good."

Scott shook his head. "This place doesn't give me a good feeling. People who aspire to a better life, but continually hit a brick wall become desperate. I interviewed enough of them when I was a reporter."

Kim grudgingly agreed. As an undergraduate, she'd studied the psychological effects of poverty, particularly during those historical moments right before underclasses revolted. She'd been shocked to learn that peasant uprisings in France, Russia and elsewhere occurred not during the most oppressive times, but when governments eased their control and living conditions improved.

Psychologists theorized that severe poverty and oppression destroyed people's hope. Simple survival consumed every waking moment. So would-be revolutionaries had difficulty spurring people into action.

Even the most minor improvement in people's lives, however, gave people time to look beyond their every-day world. Hope renewed and, with it, a new sense of purpose. The taste of a better life often triggered deep-seated angers -- and sometimes resulted in revolution.

Kim considered Betty and Brian Hicks's reaction to the way Officer Jennings manhandled their child. Did their anger stem from the natural need to protect their child? Or was their ire a hint of repressed fury?

Gazing around the yard at the Hickses' feeble attempts to recreate a middle-class appearance, Kim's throat ached. She knew how it felt to live from paycheck to paycheck. But she'd never experienced true poverty or the universal scorn of the local community.

She reached for the candy.

"This shouldn't take too long," she told the others. "If I sense any problems, I'll leave right away."

Despite her chipper voice, however, her heart beat faster as she left the safety of the car. The short, tire-lined path seemed a mile long.

The porch floor was worn and uneven, but felt solid beneath her feet. Two steps brought her to the front door. She knocked. A scuffling sounded from inside, then silence.

She waited a minute, then noticed a narrow window edging the door. She peered through.

A handful of people huddled at the far side of a country kitchen, their faces drained of color. Betty wrapped an arm around her visibly shaking son;

her own lips and chin trembled. Brian gripped a magazine or catalog with white knuckles. Two other men stood behind him, shoulders stiff, elbows pressed to their sides. Despite the tension in their faces, she could see the resemblance to Brian.

A wiry hand pushed one of the brothers aside and the old man peered out. His narrowed eyes and flared nostrils indicated that, unlike the others, in the face of danger, he'd choose fight over flight.

Resisting the urge to run, Kim pasted a smile on her face and waved.

"It's just me," she called, feeling a bit foolish.

Betty's eyes widened. Her shoulders relaxed and a genuine smile lit her face. She said something to the others, then hurried to the front door.

As the door opened, Kim apologized.

"I'm so sorry I didn't call first," she began, "but--"

"We're unlisted," Betty said. "We were having trouble with obscene phone calls. Please, come in."

Kim moved just far enough inside the house to allow Betty to close the door, then stood awkwardly, gazing around the kitchen. On her left, a deep sink was positioned before a window that looked out toward the barn. A refrigerator was wedged on the left side of the sink while a stove with the coiled electric burners stood on the right. A worn, wooden table and chairs stood against the wall to her right. Beside it, an open bookcase served as shelves for dishes, glasses and mugs.

At the far end of the room, the male members of the family formed a barrier blocking the open door to whatever room lay beyond. Brian's eyes had softened in welcome, but his brothers loomed beside him like a pair of gargoyles. Tall and brawny with suspicious eyes, the men's glare made Kim shiver.

Brian stepped forward and extended his hand. Despite the welcoming gesture, his smile was strained.

"It's so nice to have a visitor," Betty trilled. "Let me introduce you to our family. You've already met Cooper."

Kim smiled at the boy. He blushed.

"And these are Brian's brothers," Betty said. "That's Gary on the left and--"

"Get rid of her."

Tommy Hicks marched forward and pointed a finger at Kim. "She has my emerald. She's one of Them."

Brian's face flushed. "Now Grandpa--"

"Don't you now grandpa me," the old man said. "Those mining people want to destroy us."

He shifted position so he could see all of the men while keeping an eye on Kim.

"I've warned all of you to never to trust outsiders. This woman"-- he glared at Kim--"stole our emerald!"

The vehemence in his voice sent Kim back a step. She glanced toward the door, wondering if she could escape before the others reacted.

"Stop it!"

Betty planted herself in front of the old man.

"Kim is a friend. She defended Cooper against that awful Jennings. She's a guest in our house and I won't have her insulted."

The man swung his fists onto his hips. In a less aggressive tone, he said "She stole my emerald."

"No one stole your emerald." Betty's voice softened. "It was never yours to begin with."

"My father said the museum stole it from us."

He dropped his hands to his side and scuffed the floor with a tennis-shoe clad toe. And in that gesture, the angry gnome transformed into a confused old man.

Kim's heart melted. But what could she say to comfort him?

Betty laid a hand on the man's arm.

"The mine owners treated your family poorly," she said. "But they owned the rights to the minerals the workers uncovered. Legally--"

"Legally?"

Old-man Hicks's head jerked up. His eyes blazed.

"Don't mention that word in my presence. The law has done nothing but screw us."

"Uh, Grandpa?"

Brian touched his grandfather's shoulder, drawing the man's attention away from Betty. "Weren't you planning to take Cooper prospecting?"

Cooper's face lit up. "Yeah, Grandpa. You promised."

The senior Hicks tousled his great-grandson's hair, then looked at Kim.

"Did this lady really save you from that cop?"

"Yeah! She came charging in and made him let go and told him what a jerk he was being."

Cooper beamed at Kim. "And she likes trilobites."

Kim smiled at the boy.

The old man nodded in her direction.

"I guess you're all right."

To Cooper, he added, "Where's your tools?"

"In my room."

"Let's go get them."

The old man and boy moved toward the back of the room. Brian's brothers parted to allow them through and Kim glanced a living room beyond. The two men quickly resumed their defensive position. Despite their grandfather's seeming acceptance of Kim, the men continued to scowl at her.

Were they naturally distrustful? Or had Kim interrupted some illicit discussion?

Best to conclude her business and leave.

She smiled at Betty.

"I'm really sorry I came by unannounced, but I wanted to thank you again for saving Rory this morning."

She held out the foil-wrapped candy box.

Betty's eyes widened.

"For me?"

"Yeah. I hope you like chocolate."

"I love chocolate."

Betty accepted the box and gazed down at it.

"Wow. That's so nice of you. No one's ever bought me a gift like this."

Kim shuffled her feet, unsure of how to respond.

Someone knocked on the door.

One of the brothers cursed. The second one ducked into the next room and reappeared carrying a shotgun.

Gun!

Kim opened her mouth to scream, but a hand closed over it.

"Quiet," Brian whispered.

She struggled as she felt herself being dragged backwards into a wall of bodies. The musky odor of human fear wafted over her. Brian's grip on her forearm was tight enough to bruise.

Kim clawed at the hand wrapped over her mouth.

"She can't breathe!" Betty hissed.

"Promise to keep quiet?" Brian whispered.

Kim nodded. She'd promise anything to be able to inhale deeply.

The hand fell away and she gasped for air. A gentle hand touched Kim's shoulder. Kim barely had time to register Betty's panic when the knocking changed to a pounding.

Betty whimpered. Brian released Kim to reach for his wife. Kim shuffled out of his reach. The ratchet of a shotgun froze her in place.

A face peered through the window. Scott.

Run! Even as the thought formed, Kim resisted the urge. Any sudden movement might trigger chaos.

And she couldn't outrun a bullet.

CHAPTER 17

Hoping to diffuse the situation, Kim turned toward the others, spread her arms wide -- See? I'm no threat! -- and chirped, "It's just Scott."

She met Betty's eyes. "You remember? You met him at the Gem Festival."

She glanced at Brian and took a step toward the door.

"Scott's probably trying to remind me we have an, er, appointment."

Another step.

"Don't want to miss that, right?"

No one responded, but at least they didn't rush to stop her.

Kim attempted a smile. "Ah, enjoy the candy. I

guess I'll see you around."

Turning, she strode quickly toward the door. Her back prickled. She imagined the shotgun raising, aiming.

She flung open the door. Her face must have reflected her recent fear because Scott immediately reached for her.

Before they could make a hasty exit, however, Betty appeared at her side.

"I'm sorry," she said. "We've had trouble-- Well, not your problem."

She thrust a piece of paper into Kim's hand.

"Here's my cell number. So you'll, you know, have it in case you, ah, want to do lunch or something."

She clenched the candy box to her chest. "And thank you so much for this."

Kim reached out to touch Betty's shoulder. At the same time, someone moved into her peripheral vision. She registered work boots and jeans. A work-roughened hand held something long and gray behind the man's back.

She bolted through the door. Outside, she broke into a run.

Scott reached the car two steps ahead of her and flung open the back door. She threw herself in, Scott on her heels.

"Go, go, go," he said, slamming the door behind him.

Through a blur of tears, she spotted Grandpa

behind the wheel. He pressed the gas pedal. The car exploded down the driveway. Gravel clinked against the underside. A sharp turn hurled everyone to the left and now she could see Aunt Ginny in the front passenger seat, holding Al in her lap.

Rory crawled into Kim's lap. She dug her fingers into his warm curls and closed her eyes.

And again saw the gun.

Her eyes popped open.

What was Brian's brother planning to do? Shoot the person at the door? Take Kim hostage? Kill everyone in sight before turning the gun on himself?

Stupid. Oh, she'd been so stupid to think she could waltz into the Hickses' domain without risk.

The car slowed as they joined the main road. Kim brushed the tears aside, reached for her purse and removed eyeglass cleaner. Scott watched silently as she sprayed the special cleaner onto her tear-stained glasses, then rubbed, rubbed, rubbed. She held the glasses up to check for spots. Rory slurped his tongue across the lenses.

Tension drained from her and she laughed. Scott removed the glasses from her hand and cleaned them while she let Rory lick her face. Nothing like a dog to make everything better.

"Ready to talk about it?" Scott returned her now-clean glasses.

"Sorry. The gun terrified me."

Tires screeched as Grandpa hit the brakes and pulled to the side of the road. Now three faces stared at her, their skin equal shades of white.

For a moment, silence filled the car. And then everyone spoke at once.

It was Scott's words, however, that caught Kim's attention.

"What gun?" he said.

She gaped at him.

"You didn't see the gun?

He shook his head.

"All I saw was a bunch of scared people huddled in the corner."

"But when you knocked, Brian's brother pulled out a shotgun."

"Hey, don't look so upset."

He squeezed her shoulder. "I believe he had a gun. I probably didn't see it because I was focused on you."

But Kim had been certain the gun had been pointed at the front door.

As she thought about it, however, she hadn't actually seen the brother raise the gun. Brian had covered her open, not-yet-screaming mouth and at that point all she could think about was breathing.

But why would someone grab a gun without pointing it at something?

And who had moved into view when she was saying goodbye to Betty?

"It wasn't Brian," Scott said in answer to her

question. "Must have been one of his brothers."

"Was he carrying a gun?"

Scott's mouth thinned. "Didn't see one. But he had something hidden behind his back."

Kim's cell phone rang. She ignored it. A few seconds later, she heard the beep indicating a text message.

Pulling out the phone, she retrieved the message. Rachael had written "Where are you?"

"Crap. It's Rachael. If I don't call, she'll keep texting"

"Are you feeling calm enough to deal with her?" Scott said.

Kim kissed his cheek. "I'm fine, thank you."

She dialed Rachael's number.

"Where have you been?" Rachael said.

"Hello to you, too."

"Charlie deserted me," Rachael went on as if Kim hadn't spoken. "How soon can you come back?"

"We're not far."

"Don't go to the mansion. I'm at the cabin. And Kim? I'm sorry for being a jerk. I'm just so worried."

Kim hung up and turned to the others.

"How about we join Rachael before I tell you what happened at the Hickses'? That way I won't have to repeat myself."

The others agreed and Grandpa pulled back onto the road. Less than five minutes later they arrived at the cabin to find Rachael pacing the front porch.

"Charlie's driving me nuts," Rachael said, leading the way to the living room. "He refuses to consider that he might actually be falsely arrested for that Kirk guy's murder."

Kim settled onto the floor with Rory, leaving the sofa free for Grandpa and Aunt Ginny.

"Maybe," she said, "that's just his way of coping."

Rachael threw her hands into the air.

"But he won't help his father search for evidence. When we left the police station, we were supposed to pick up Charlie's car at the Gem Festival and then join Mark at the house to discuss strategy.

"But when we reached the car, Charlie insisted I drive back to the house with the others. Said he needed to run an errand and didn't want me to ride along because 'it's a surprise.' He's still not back and--"

Rachael stopped mid-rant. Her eyes widened.

"Kim, what's wrong? You look awful. Almost like . . . Have you been crying? Oh, I'm so sorry I was mean to you. Please don't cry."

The concern in her friend's voice almost set off more tears. Kim forced them back and offered a wry smile.

"It's not you," she said. "My investigation sort of backfired."

Now that everyone was together, Kim proceeded to describe her visit with the Hicks family.

"Seeing the gun," she concluded, "pretty much

scrambled my brain."

"You could have been killed!" Rachael plopped onto the floor beside her.

Rory immediately licked her face. Ignoring him, she grasped Kim's hand.

"I couldn't live with myself if something happened to you. It's all my fault. I shouldn't have agreed to move to a place with snakes and bugs and shotgun toting hillbillies making illegal moonshine."

Trying to calm her friend, Kim kept her response light.

"I imagine if we tossed a baseball in any direction, we'd hit a still. Besides, making alcohol hasn't been illegal since Prohibition."

"Yeah, but selling it without paying taxes is illegal," Rachael said. "Mark said Tommy Hicks has organized the production and selling to the point he's practically the Walmart of moonshine. Tommy and his sons patrol the woods with shotguns and who knows what all. Mark thinks Kirk Ballas was trying to cut into their business and that's why they killed him."

"But that doesn't make sense," Kim said. "We found Kirk's body on Hampton property surrounded by prospecting equipment."

"Mark thinks the Hickses have also been illegally mining his land," Rachael said. "The police found evidence of more digging not far from where you found the body."

Kim flashed back on the image of Tommy Hicks taking his grandson prospecting. Were they heading this way?

"Sounds like the Hickses get blamed for much of what happens around here," Aunt Ginny said.

Rachael shrugged. "Mark said none of the Hickses have done an honest day's work in their lives."

"I dunno," Grandpa said. "If their moonshine business is as large as you claim, that takes a lot of work."

Rachael snorted. "Yeah, they'll work hard but only if it's against the law."

"But what about Brian Hicks?" Kim said. "Doesn't he have a real job?"

Rachael dismissed the comment with a wave.

"He's probably using it as a cover for his family's illegal activities. Once a hillbilly, always a hillbilly."

"Rachael!" Kim gawked at her friend. "You know better than to judge people based on their ancestors!"

Rachael's face flushed, but her mouth narrowed into a thin line. "It's not the same thing! My ancestors are nothing like the Hickses! You won't find thieves and murderers--"

"Just soldiers and resistance fighters," Kim said. "My point is that people do what they must to survive."

She stood. "And speaking of survival, these poor dogs haven't had a chance to play all day. I'm taking them outside."

She clipped on Rory's leash and, with Scott and Al beside her, headed for the back door.

The late afternoon sun filtered through the trees, making the autumn leaves glow orange and red and yellow. Normally, Kim would have strolled into the woods toward the emerald mine. Right now, however, she just wanted time to clear her head.

Sensing her mood, Scott turned to the right and started walking around the cabin. The dogs trotted ahead, stopping to sniff bushes, sticks and other items of canine interest.

After a moment, Kim said, "I'm sorry I dragged you into this mess."

Scott chuckled. "Being with you is always an adventure."

"You can joke, but I bet you've never been hauled into the police station for brawling."

She touched the side of his bruised face.

"Does it hurt much?"

He flashed his lopsided grin. "Gonna kiss it and make it better?"

Kim stood on tiptoe and gently brushed his cheek with her lips.

Without pulling away, she whispered "All better now?"

"Not quite."

Scott leaned toward her lips.

His arm suddenly straightened as Al jerked the

leash loose, pulling Scott off balance. Kim tried to steady him but felt Rory pull free to chase after Al. As the two adults fought for balance, the dogs raced around the side of the cabin. The little dachshund's baying pierced the silence.

Kim recovered first and ran after them, Scott on her heels. They turned the corner of the cabin and spotted the dogs barking at an overgrown rhododendron growing beneath the living room window.

Al darted back and forth issuing a constant high-pitched bark. Rory, however, plunged into the bush.

"Rory!" Images of rabid raccoons, angry foxes and knife-wielding madmen raced through Kim's mind.

She started after her dog.

Scott's arm encircled her waist, halting her.

"Lemme go!"

She struggled, trying to break free.

"Hold tight," he said. "We don't know what's in there."

"But Rory--"

The bush emitted a high peel of laughter, followed by giggling. A bushy tail appeared, then the poodle's butt and, finally, Rory's head. He clenched the bottom of a red shirt between his teeth.

"Okay, okay," a boy's voice said. "I'm coming."

Rory released the shirt. A small hand appeared, followed by a child's head.

Cooper.

A combination of relief and anger washed over Kim.

"Are you always finding ways to cause gray hair in adults?"

She took the boy's hand and helped pull him from the shrub.

Cooper pushed to his feet and dusted the dirt and leaves from his front.

"I needed to talk with you."

"You could have just knocked on the front door," Kim said.

"Yeah, but. . ."

He bit his lip. His doe-like eyes swept the area behind her and she suddenly realized the commotion had drawn Aunt Ginny, Grandpa and Rachael outside.

Recognizing the child's fear, Kim introduced him to the others.

"I thought you were going prospecting," she said.

Cooper shrugged. "Grandpa had to help Uncle Joe with something."

He stubbed his toe into the ground.

Kim studied the boy, wondering how long he'd been hiding beneath the window. Had he overheard their earlier conversation?

Before she could form a question, however, Grandpa said "Do you like chocolate?"

Cooper's eyes lit up. "Yeah!"

"Well, I happen to know where we can find

some."

The grin that spread across Cooper's face transformed him from a member of a notorious local clan into a typical ten-year-old. The boy eagerly fell into step beside Grandpa.

Kim smiled. Leave it to Grandpa to find a way to a child's heart.

Calling to Rory, she followed the others into the kitchen. Grandpa poured Cooper a glass of milk. Then, with a flourish, he produced a two-inch rectangle wrapped in bright red foil.

"Now, this is special chocolate made in Switzerland," Grandpa said. "Do you know where Switzerland is?"

"Er, someplace in Europe?"

Grandpa smiled. "That's right. Switzerland has always been known for the quality of its chocolate. Have you ever tasted Swiss chocolate?"

Eyes wide, Cooper shook his head.

Grandpa nodded at the candy. "Then let's see what you think."

Cooper lifted the candy, turned it over and reverently unwrapped it. He raised the candy to his mouth. Kim could tell he wanted to shove the whole thing in, but wasn't sure that was the proper way.

"It'll last longer if you bite it in half," she said.

Cooper did as she suggested.

"Wow!" he said, his mouth still full of chocolate. "That's really chocolaty!"

Kim grinned and pulled out a chair beside him. The others followed her example.

Rory and Al perched at Kim's side.

"Don't even think it," she told the two dogs. "Chocolate is poisonous to dogs."

Rory sighed. Al yipped, turned and, with a swish of his tail, disappeared into the living room. After a moment, Rory followed.

"So," Kim said, "what brings you here?"

"After you left," Cooper said, "Cousin Jackson called and told Dad that Officer Jennings and his partner are spying on us."

"Spying?"

Cooper nodded. "They're asking people if they saw Dad or Cousin Jackson or Grandpa Tommy in the forest the night that guy was killed."

"They're just trying to find witnesses to the murder," Aunt Ginny said gently.

"No! They're only asking about people named Hicks," Cooper said. "They don't care about anyone else. Mom won't say in front of me, but I overheard her telling Dad she's afraid they'll blame him."

"Why would they focus on your father?" Scott said.

Cooper bit his lip. "Don't know."

He squared his shoulders and looked from Scott to Grandpa, Aunt Ginny and Rachel. "But Dad would never kill someone."

Whatever he read in the others' faces caused Cooper's cheeks to flush. He turned to Kim.

"You believe Dad didn't do it, don't you?"

"I . . ."

Crap! She wanted to reassure the little boy, but she also didn't want to lie. Maybe she could reassure while telling the truth.

She touched his hand.

"Cooper, I like your dad, but I just met him and don't know--"

"You're just like the others!"

Cooper leaped to his feet and stood with his feet planted, fists clenched.

"You think everything bad that happens around here is one of us, don't you?"

"Of course not--"

"I thought you could help. You brought us candy."

Tears formed in his eyes. "I thought you were different."

Before she could respond, Cooper threw the remaining piece of chocolate at her and slammed out the kitchen door.

She ran after him. "Cooper, wait!"

But the boy disappeared into the forest without looking back.

She stared into the woods. She wanted to scream "I am different."

But was she?

When she'd seen the shotgun, hadn't her first instinct been to scream? And when Brian smashed his big hand across her mouth, hadn't she assumed he was trying to prevent her from calling for help? In her panic, she'd imagined the worst: gun firing, blood gushing, her own body used as a shield.

And yet, none of that had happened. The gun hadn't even been visible when Scott looked into the window.

Why not?

At the time, the combination of the gun and Brian's rough efforts to silence her made her feel like a hostage. If that were the case, however, wouldn't Brian's brother point the gun at the door? Why grab a gun if you weren't going to use it?

Had she misinterpreted the situation?

Okay, start from the beginning. She'd knocked on the door. Twice. When no one answered, she'd peered through a small window. She'd seen the Hicks family huddled on the far side of the room, their faces frozen with fear.

Fear of what? The police? Social workers? Tax collectors, bounty hunters, angry neighbors? Other people with guns?

Did the Hickses live in constant fear? Did they keep the gun for protection? Is that why they drew into a huddle whenever someone knocked on the door?

She thought of Betty, the woman who'd saved Rory's life. She remembered Betty's fear when Kim knocked, her delight when she recognized Kim, her awed wonder when Kim presented the chocolate.

Everything seemed perfectly normal until Scott

knocked on the door and Brian dragged her into the corner with the rest of the family and they'd closed in tight and--

The realization punched her in the stomach.

The Hickses hadn't planned to take her hostage.

They'd tried to keep her safe.

Kim closed her eyes and groaned.

She, Kimberley West -- psychology professor, dog trainer, some-time jeweler and vocal opponent to classism -- was no better than Mark Hampton or Rachael or any of the locals who'd labeled the entire Hicks clan "trash" based on prejudice, rumor and hearsay.

She pictured the half-painted barn, the struggling rose bushes, the newly planted autumn flowers -- all efforts to mimic a more genteel existence.

How could she be so blind?

And what could she do about it?

Opening her eyes, she reached into a pocket and pulled out the note Betty Hicks had given her.

She couldn't undo the mess she'd made with Cooper. But maybe she could reach out to his mother.

CHAPTER 18

Before she could change her mind, Kim dialed Betty Hicks's cell number. The delight in Betty's voice fueled Kim's guilt for doubting the woman.

"I'm so glad you called," Betty gushed. "I was afraid you wouldn't after-- Well, you called and that's what's important. Can we get together now? I need to run into town to pick up a few things for supper. There's a sandwich shop that sells the most amazing apple pie. I can be there in 30 minutes. Would that work for you?"

The eagerness in Betty's voice, coupled with the rush of words, indicated a desperate loneliness that made Kim's heart ache.

She'd called Betty to prove to herself that she

wasn't like the others, that she was capable of seeing beyond someone's social or economic standing. But it had been a long day.

"Oh, I . . . I'm sorry," Betty said. "I don't want to bother you. I mean--"

"Betty, don't apologize," Kim interrupted. "I want to see you. I was just, er, wondering what to do with my dog."

"Bring him," Betty said. "There are outside tables and it's a gorgeous day."

Kim agreed and wrote down Betty's directions to the restaurant. Returning to the cabin, she told the others of her plans.

Grandpa protested. "You look exhausted and we still need to join the Hamptons for dinner."

"Betty has to make dinner for her family," Kim said, "so she's not planning to stay long. I just need to reassure her that, well, that she's someone worth knowing."

"Why don't I drive you?" Scott said, rising. "I'd like to poke through the local newspaper archives, see if I can learn more about our various suspects. I doubt today was the first time Donny and company have seen the inside of a jail."

"That'd be great," Kim said, "but what about the dogs? I can bring Rory with me, but if I take both dogs, I won't be able to focus on Betty."

She'd trained Rory to lie quietly at her feet when she was eating or working at her computer, but the presence of his buddy Al would likely trigger play behavior. She could imagine the young dog jumping up and knocking over the restaurant table.

"I can handle Al," Grandpa said. "He can sit on my lap while I make a few calls, see if anyone has heard about the museum emerald."

"And I'll drive Max and Ginny to the house," Rachael added. "You can meet us there."

Kim nodded, collected her purse and Rory's leash and followed Scott to the car. Twenty minutes later she joined Betty at a table in front of the sandwich shop.

She'd just settled Rory beneath the table when a waitress appeared.

"Please try the apple pie," Betty said. "They make it here and it's as good as my mom makes."

Kim was particular about apple pies -- her mother made cinnamon-rich pies from the Gravenstein apples that grew in Grandpa's backyard. The flaky crust coupled with the sweet/tart apples created a melt-in-your-mouth sensation that few cooks could duplicate.

But she didn't want to offend Betty, so she ordered the pie along with a cup of tea.

As soon as the waitress moved out of hearing range, Betty leaned over the table.

"I want to apologize for Grandpa Tommy's behavior," she said. "He's been volatile ever since you found that stolen emerald."

"Word that I found it sure spread fast."

Betty shrugged. "It's a small community."

"But people have found even larger emeralds locally," Kim said. "Why is everyone so interested in this one?"

"Mystique."

Betty shifted the salt shaker a few inches to the right.

"Grandpa Tommy's ancestors never stopped complaining about the way the mining company treated them. They convinced themselves that the emerald belonged to them."

She moved the pepper shaker to join its mate.

"Tommy seems to still think that." Kim kept her voice casual, hoping Betty would expand on the thought.

Betty sighed. "It's a long story."

The waitress appeared with their food and drinks. When she left, Kim gestured toward the huge slices of pie.

"Looks like we'll be here awhile," she said. "And I love long stories."

Betty offered a weak smile, her eyes clouded with thought. She took a bite of pie, swallowed, then reached for her coffee.

"How much do you know about the emerald's history?"

"Why don't you assume I don't know anything and start at the beginning?"

"Well, the beginning goes all the way back to the late 1800s when emeralds were first discovered here," Betty said. "I think it was in 1874 when a farmer unearthed an emerald in his plowed field."

As Betty hesitated, Kim offered a reassuring smile. "I'm impressed that you know the date."

"Mom's a school teacher. She teaches chemistry, not history, but she's always been a stickler for accuracy."

She repositioned the salt and pepper shakers.

"Anyway," she continued, "a few years after finding the first emerald, the farmer leased his farm to a New York mining company. They hired local people to do the digging. Ted Hicks, Brian's great-great grandfather, was one of them."

The salt and pepper shakers clicked as she shuffled them.

"The men were grateful for the work, but it was grueling. They spent five weeks diggin' in the hot sun. But instead of emeralds, the men found a greenish gem that no one had ever seen before."

"Hiddenite," Kim said. "It's a type of spodumene."

Betty nodded. "They named our town for it. But the mine owners still wanted emeralds. So the following year, they ordered the workers to dig straight down. They dug 50 feet into the earth."

Kim winced, imagining digging into bedrock with the primitive tools available in the late 1800s.

"The owners said they'd pay the workers a bonus if they found an emerald vein," Betty continued. "But they weren't allowed to actually remove the emeralds from the rock without supervision. If they found a vein, they were supposed to notify the foreman rather than continue digging."

"That was probably their way of preventing the workers from slipping an emerald into their pockets," Kim said. "Theft can be a huge problem in gem mines. In some of the African diamond mines, employees are actually strip searched before being allowed to leave the mine."

Betty gave a mock shiver. "Tommy never mentioned anything like that, so maybe they didn't do that here.

"Anyway, one day Ted Hicks was digging alongside his buddy, Joe Sawyer. They were alone in that particular stretch of the mine shaft, working a layer of quartz. Ted hit a piece of quartz a bit too hard and a chunk fell off the wall. Behind it was a large hole. They shined a light into the hole and saw a huge emerald jutting from the wall. Said it was darn near four inches long."

Kim tried to imagine discovering a four-inch bolt of green protruding from a wall of gray and brown. The only large, nonfaceted emeralds she'd seen had been displayed in museums, solitary specimens illuminated by carefully selected lighting.

"Must have been difficult backing off and calling the foreman," Kim said.

"That's the problem," Betty said. "They didn't call the foreman. They decided to dig out the stone themselves.

"And before you ask, Ted and Joe weren't

intending to steal the emerald. They just wanted to hold it in their hands."

Kim sipped her tea but remained silent. No sense in antagonizing Betty. But, really, after slaving for weeks in a hot mine shaft, who wouldn't be tempted to tuck an emerald or two into a pocket?

Misinterpreting Kim's silence as agreement, Betty continued. "They dug around the gem, thinking it'd be easy to extract. But they had to dig deeper and deeper before finding the end. When they finally removed it, they found it was maybe eight inches long.

"They were each holding an end when the foreman walked in."

"Uh, oh."

"You're not kidding-- Hey, you haven't even tasted your pie."

Betty pointed at the untouched slice. "C'mon, I want to hear how you like it."

Kim reached for her fork, telling herself she'd rave about the pie no matter how it tasted. One bite, however, brought back memories of her mother's pies. The crust was clearly homemade, tender and flaky. The flavor of the apples, however, was the main draw: a spicy mix of cinnamon, apples and something else she couldn't quite place.

"This is amazing!" she said.

Betty looked proud and relieved. "Good stuff, huh? They use a combination of sweet and tart apples to get that deep flavor. The Arkansas Black apples are what's giving you that honey-like taste."

Kim scooped up another bite. "Well, I am truly impressed. Thanks for insisting I try this. But, please, go on with your story. I want to hear what happened after the foreman walked in."

"He fired them on the spot."

"Oh! That's awful!"

Betty nodded. "Ted and Joe tried to tell him that they just wanted to hold a large emerald, that they weren't planning to steal it. The foreman said he'd talk to the owners, but insisted they leave the mine immediately."

"So did the owners understand?"

"Nope. Not only did they fire the two men, they refused to pay the bonus they'd promised."

"Sounds like the owners were looking for an excuse to not pay the bonus." Kim took another bite of her pie.

"Yeah. It gets worse. The next day, the newspaper reported that the vein Ted and Joe uncovered contained 20 emeralds. They'd discovered a fortune in emeralds and didn't receive a penny."

"No wonder they were so bitter," Kim said.

"Bitter enough that they complained to everyone in town," Betty said. "They told the story over and over again. Their children learned to hate the mining company. The shared injustice drove the Hicks and Sawyer families together and Ted and Joe became best buddies."

"What did they do after they were fired?"

"Joe Sawyer returned to tobacco farming," Betty said. "As for Ted . . ."

She shrugged. "The Hickses have always done a bit of this and a bit of that. Ted wanted to learn emerald mining so he could prospect on his own. But the family's specialty was making and selling moonshine."

She snorted. "Tommy said his family could have been the model for the Dukes of Hazzard."

The television show about a family who made moonshine was popular before Kim was born, but she'd seen clips of the show's famous car chases.

"I still don't understand why Tommy believes the emerald belongs to his family," she said. "His ancestors were treated poorly, but they'd been hired to dig for emeralds. They accepted the job knowing any emeralds they found belonged to the mining company."

Betty's face flushed. Biting her lip, she looked away.

Kim ate her pie, silently willing Betty to reveal whatever was bothering her. When Betty looked back, Kim assumed her everything-is-okay expression, the one she used when a student appeared at her office door.

"Tommy's family actually possessed the emerald," Betty said. "At least for a few hours."

"Oh?"

Betty dragged fingers through her hair. "Since

you found the emerald, I guess you're entitled to hear the whole story."

She straightened her shoulders. "But you need to let me tell you the whole story so you'll understand why everything happened."

"I'd prefer the whole story."

Betty nodded and began.

"When Tommy was nine years old, his father came home from work in a foul mood. Tommy's father, Gary Hicks, was best buddies with Dominick Sawyer."

"Was Dominick a descendant of Joe Sawyer?"

"Yeah. Gary and Dominick used to meet at the local bar after work.

"Anyway, one day they'd been drinking their usual beers when a local woodworker began bragging about his vacation. He'd finished a huge job for one of the furniture stores in Hickory and decided to use the money on a family trip to New York.

"They'd visited the usual places -- Statue of Liberty, Central Park, Rockefeller Center -- but also spent time in the American Museum of Natural History. He told Gary and Dominick that he saw the emerald their ancestors had discovered, then whipped out photos."

"That must have been a shock," Kim said.

Betty nodded. "It triggered all of the old resentments and by the time Gary returned home, he'd decided he hated everyone including the poor man who'd taken the photo.

"Tommy's mother, however, insisted Gary invite the woodworker for dinner. She wanted to see the New York photos. All of the photos. Shortly after that, Tommy's parents announced their first ever family vacation."

Betty met Kim's eyes. "They told Tommy they'd be traveling to New York with the Sawyers."

Kim's breath quickened. "What year was this?"

"They scheduled the trip for the following year," Betty said. "Nineteen fifty."

The Carolina Emerald had been stolen from the New York museum in 1950.

Without waiting for Kim to comment, Betty hurried on. It was like she'd been waiting to tell someone Tommy's story and couldn't get it out fast enough.

"In the weeks leading up to the trip," Betty said, "Tommy and the Sawyer's daughter, Amy, played together while their parents poured over maps."

"What kind of maps?"

"Mostly street maps," Betty said. "They planned to drive, so it made sense to plan a route and familiarize themselves with the layout of New York's streets. What puzzled Tommy was the detailed map of the American Museum of Natural History. His parents said they needed the map to make their visit more efficient."

"But Tommy thinks there was another reason," Kim said.

"At the time he accepted his parents' explanation. But after they arrived in New York, he sensed something else was going on.

"After checking into their motel, they went immediately to the American Museum of Natural History."

Betty smiled. "Tommy described it as mind blowing."

"I was the same age as Tommy when I first saw the museum," Kim said. "Mind blowing is an understatement."

Tommy's experience must have been even more profound than her own. He'd grown up before computers, cell phones, Steven Spielberg. Heck, there'd been no color television, Sputnik or Disneyland.

As Betty continued telling Tommy's story, her North Carolina accent grew more pronounced. Her vowels grew longer, single syllable words expanded into liquid gold.

The change in Betty's voice somehow made the story more real, allowing Kim to see the world through Tommy's eyes.

When everyone entered the museum, Tommy wanted to run to the dinosaur exhibit. The adults, however, insisted they first visit the Carolina Emerald.

Tommy had been tempted to throw a tantrum -- after all, this vacation was supposed to be for the children -- but a look from his father silenced him.

With Amy at his side, he reluctantly followed the adults past the really interesting stuff and into the hall of gems.

As the largest emerald ever discovered in the U.S., the Carolina Emerald had been given its own display case. It sat on a velvet base, its three arms shooting skyward. Carefully angled lights illuminated the stone's rich green color.

Tommy had stared, transfixed. The emerald seemed illuminated from within, the color more intense than any shade of green he'd ever seen. He now understood his father's angry tone whenever he talked about the mining executives who'd cheated his ancestors.

For a moment, no one spoke.

Finally, Tommy's father said, "That should belong to us."

"And so it will," his mother answered before turning to Tommy and Amy. "Are you two ready to see the dinosaurs?" Her voice was overly bright.

Tommy was actually reluctant to leave the emerald, but now the adults were in a rush to see the rest of the museum. Mrs. Sawyer grabbed Amy's hand while Tommy's mother herded him away from the emerald.

His father and Mr. Sawyer, however, remained behind.

"Why isn't Dad coming with us?" Tommy said.

"Dad and Mr. Sawyer need to do some guy things," Mom said. "They'll join us as soon as they're finished."

They spent the next hour touring the dinosaur exhibit, then visited the gift shop. Tommy bought a model of a T. Rex, while Amy selected a model of a pterodactyl. The women bought bandanas imprinted with the museum's logo: pink for Amy, red for Mom and Mrs. Sawyer, blue for Tommy and the two fathers. They admired the souvenir pocket watches adorned with images of the Empire State Building. But neither family could afford to purchase one.

The men joined the others for a late lunch in the museum cafeteria. Afterwards, they toured the city: Times Square, Rockefeller Center, Central Park, the Empire State Building.

By the time they returned to their hotel, both children were tired and cranky. Amy tramped into the adjoining room and crawled into bed. The adults, however, gathered around a small table.

"If you keep the volume low so you don't wake Amy, you can watch the television in her room," Tommy's father said.

Tommy hesitated. His family didn't own a television, so he'd been thrilled to hear their hotel offered "free television in all rooms!" But his father's happy voice sounded forced, like he was hiding something.

His father's next comment confirmed Tommy's suspicions. "Maybe Howdy Doody is playing."

"That's baby stuff," Tommy said.

He recognized a sneaky adult attempt to remove him from the room so he wouldn't hear their conversation.

His father raked fingers through his thinning hair.

"Well, how about The Lone Ranger? You like that, don't you?"

"Yeah."

"So go see if that's playing." Dad pointed at the door to the next room. "And close the door behind you."

Tommy reluctantly left the room. Amy lay on the bed, curled in fetal position.

Plopping onto the floor in front of the television, he began switching channels. But he wasn't in the mood for Uncle Miltie or Fireside Theater. And The Lone Ranger wouldn't be playing until tomorrow evening.

What he really wanted to do was find out why everyone was being so secretive.

He tuned the television to one of those dumb game shows then tiptoed to the closed door and cracked it open. Putting his eye to the crack, he spied the adults hunched over a table, their bodies stiff with tension. He strained to hear what they were saying.

But the combination of background television and adult whispering allowed him to hear only a few words: ". . . single guard . . . alarm broken . . . open window . . ."

"Whatcha doing?"

Startled by Amy's voice -- geez, she was standing right behind him -- Tommy jumped. He bumped the door and heard it slam shut. The sound was immediately followed by heavy footsteps.

Snatching Amy's arm, he dragged her onto the bed.

He laid down beside her and whispered, "Pretend you're asleep."

Amy glared at him, but obediently closed her eyes. Through his closed eyelids, Tommy sensed the room lightening and the air shift as someone opened the bedroom door. He feigned sleep for what seemed like days before the footsteps receded and the door closed.

Amy's eyes popped open.

"Why were you spying?" she demanded.

"I was trying to find out why everyone's acting weird, but you interrupted me." Tommy met her frown with one of his own.

Amy rolled her eyes. "Boys are so stupid. They're talking about stealing the emerald, okay?"

"What?"

"Shhh, you're gonna get us in trouble."

"But--"

"Mom says it's not really stealing 'cause it was ours to start with," Amy said. "The mining company stole it from our great-great, er, something grandfathers. We're just taking back what's rightfully ours."

"How do you know all this?"

Amy shrugged. "I'm better at spying than you."
She turned her back to him.

"Better get some sleep," she said over her
shoulder. "It's gonna be a long night."

Soon all he heard was her steady breathing.

Tommy lay in bed, fuming. He'd been out-
smarted by a girl. A girl! He needed to figure out a
better way to spy on his parents.

But it'd been a long, exciting day and the rhythm
of Amy's breaths soothed his ruffled ego. He drifted
off to sleep.

The sky was still dark, however, when his father
shook him awake.

"Get your things together," he whispered. "We're
leaving in fifteen minutes."

Since he'd fallen asleep in his clothes, Tommy
didn't have much to pack. Groggy with sleep,
Tommy stuffed his spare clothes, toothbrush,
pajamas, Lincoln Logs, Silly Putty and Slinky into
his small suitcase. After making sure no one was
looking, he checked an inside pocket to find his
Hubley pirate cap gun secure.

The hotel lobby was empty. The clock over the
sign-in desk read 3 a.m. Tommy yawned and
climbed into the Sawyers' Ford station wagon.
Mom and Mrs. Sawyer crowded in back with the
children while Mr. Sawyer drove and Dad rode
shotgun.

Fifteen minutes later, Mr. Sawyer turned the car

onto a side street next to the museum. Pulling to the curb between two street lights, he shoved the gear lever into park but left the car running.

For a few moments, no one said a word. The air crackled with tension. Then Dad slapped the dashboard.

"Let's do this," he said.

The two men exited the car.

Tommy peered out the window, noticing for the first time that both men were dressed head to toe in black. His father swung a dark-colored, padded satchel over one shoulder. The men disappeared into the shadows.

Mrs. Sawyer climbed into the driver's seat and began adjusting mirrors. Mom remained in the back with the children. She answered Tommy's questions with a sharp "Not now, Tommy."

Time slowed to a crawl. The dim streetlights cast gloomy shadows across the deserted street. Unseen critters scurried through bushes. The women hunched in their seats. Mrs. Sawyer clutched the steering wheel with white-knuckled hands.

A bang against the side door startled Tommy from a half doze. The door swung open and Dad pushed in beside Mom. Mr. Sawyer leaped into the front passenger seat.

"Go, go, go," he said, slamming his door shut.

The car tires screeched as Mrs. Sawyer pressed the gas pedal. Tommy was jerked left, then right as the car navigated the narrow streets. After a few moments, Mr. Sawyer touched his wife's arm.

"It's okay, you can slow down now," he said.

"So did you get it?" Mrs. Sawyer's voice sounded unnaturally high pitched.

Dad held up his satchel and started laughing. Mr. Sawyer joined in. Soon all the adults were laughing. The hysterical edge to their voices sent spiders crawling up Tommy's arms.

"So the window was open?" Mom said.

"Window open, alarm broken, guard asleep somewhere," Dad replied.

"Let me see it," Mom said.

Dad's eyes shifted to Tommy, who stared back.

"Let's wait till we get home," Dad said.

He set the satchel between his feet, leaned back and closed his eyes.

"Wake me when you want me to drive."

To Tommy's annoyance, everyone but Mrs. Sawyer -- still behind the wheel -- copied Dad's position. The rhythmic breathing soon lulled Tommy into closing his own eyes.

They drove through the night and the next day, stopping only for food and bathroom breaks or to change drivers. The two-lane paved roads might be an improvement on dirt or gravel, but even so, travel was slow. They arrived in Hiddenite well after dark.

To Tommy's surprise, the Sawyers didn't simply drop off their passengers and drive off. Instead, they helped carry in the luggage.

Dad placed his satchel in the middle of the kitchen table, then turned to Tommy and Amy.

"Time for bed," he said.

"But--"

"Don't argue. It's well after midnight and you look like you're about to drop."

Tommy looked from his father's stern face to the bag on the table. He crossed his arms and lifted his chin.

"I know what's in the bag."

His father scowled and pointed up the stairs. "Go to your room."

"Oh, for heaven's sake, Gary, let the children stay," Donalda Sawyer said. "They already know what we did. It's best to satisfy their curiosity."

"You have weird ideas about raising children," Gary Hicks grumbled.

But he said no more about sending the children away.

The adults perched in kitchen chairs while the children stood beside them.

Dad reached into his satchel and pulled out two pocket watches.

"Those are the ones from the gift store," Tommy said.

"Yes, and one day you and Amy will each inherit one." His father grinned. "These will become family heirlooms to remind us of this epic day."

He looked at Dominick Sawyer. "Shall we?"

Together, the two men reached into the satchel

and removed a nylon pouch. They opened it, then removed a long item wrapped in one of the blue museum bandanas.

Setting the bandana in the middle of the table, Dad slowly unfolded the fabric to reveal the North Carolina Emerald.

Tommy's breath caught. In the museum, the lighting and setting had given the emerald a brittle, harsh appearance. Under the kitchen light, the emerald shined with a warm glow. The three bolts of green jutted from a base, looking exactly like the towers of the Emerald City in the Wizard of Oz movie.

"I still think we should put this into a safety deposit box," Mom said.

"We've already discussed this," Dad said. "No way am I trusting the government with this."

"And don't forget," Mrs. Sawyer added, "if the police ever suspect us, they can freeze our accounts and force the bank to open our box."

She folded her arms. "Best if we hide it somewhere not associated with our names."

Mr. Sawyer lifted the emerald and pointed at the bottom where the crystals attached to a bit of rock. Someone had scratched numbers onto the rock.

"Why don't we just cut off the part with the museum's inscription?" Mr. Sawyer said. "Then they can't prove it came from the museum."

"No!" Tommy snatched the emerald from Mr. Sawyer's hand. "If you start chopping it up, you'll ruin it."

"Get real, boy. What did you think we were going to do with it? Use it as a paperweight? Can't make money unless we have it made into a bunch of gemstones."

He held out his hand. His eyes bored into Tommy's, challenging.

Tommy felt his face flush and the fist not holding the emerald clenched. Amy touched his forearm. When his eyes met hers, she shook her head in warning. Slowly, he relaxed his fingers.

He placed the emerald on Mr. Sawyer's palm.

"We can't do anything with the emerald until we're sure no one suspects us," Mom said. "So the problem remains: Where do we hide it until it's safe to sell?"

While the adults debated the merits of various hiding places, Tommy nursed his grudge. First his parents ordered him to bed. Then they remained silent while Mr. Sawyer humiliated him. They all treated him like a baby.

Well, he'd show them.

He lifted his chin and shouted over the adult voices. "Bury it."

All conversation stopped. Everyone stared at him.

He folded his arms. "Bury it beneath a tree just like the pirates did."

Amy broke the stunned silence.

"Great idea!" She punched him playfully in the

arm.

Tommy's father nodded.

"Tommy's right," he said. "If we bury it, we'll be the only ones who know where it is."

"Fine." Mr. Sawyer stood and reached for the emerald. "I'll bury it beneath one of our oaks."

Dad slapped his hand onto Mr. Sawyer's forearm. "Why don't we bury it on my property?" he said. "We're here now."

Mr. Sawyer pulled his hand away. "What's wrong, Hicks, don't you trust me?"

"Let's say I trust you about as much as you trust me," Dad said.

"So bury it between our properties," Mrs. Sawyer said.

"But that's Randy Benning's land," Dad said.

Mrs. Sawyer flipped a hand. "You think Benning knows what's on his property? He spends more time gambling than communing with nature.

"Besides, if the cops ever suspect us, they're going to want to search our property. That might include digging up our land. They'd never consider digging up someone else's land."

They argued for a few more minutes, the two men getting increasingly angry. Finally, the women called a halt to the discussion.

"Just bury it on Benning's land for tonight," Mrs. Sawyer said. "We can choose a better place tomorrow."

The men reluctantly agreed. Tommy's father

turned and ordered him to go to bed.

"But I wanna come!"

"It's past your bed time," Dad said.

"That's not fair," Tommy said. "Burying the emerald was my idea!"

"And a good idea it was." Dad reached for his coat. "Now off to bed with you."

"What about Amy?"

"She'll stay in the kitchen with her mother," Mr. Sawyer said.

"Actually, I'm kinda tired." Stretching arms over her head, Amy gave an exaggerated yawn.

Tommy's mother patted Amy's shoulder. "You can stretch out on our bed."

"Wait a minute," Dad said. "I need to get something from the room."

He trotted up the stairs and returned a few minutes carrying a black jacket.

He nodded to Mr. Sawyer. The two men hustled outside.

To Tommy's disgust, Mom accompanied the children upstairs and waited until both were tucked into their respective rooms.

As soon as she closed his door, Tommy leaped from bed, tiptoed to the door and pressed his ear against it. After a few moments, he heard Mom finally move away. Her footsteps sounded on the stairs, then headed in the direction of the kitchen.

Just to make sure this wasn't a trick, he waited a few minutes, then cracked open his door. The hallway was empty.

Perfect.

Crossing the room, he slid open the window and leaped onto a branch of the nearby apple tree. Climbing down, he paused to listen for the men's voices.

"It's about time," a voice hissed.

Tommy jumped and turned around. Amy stood by the tree trunk, arms crossed.

"How . . . how'd you--"

"My window had a tree too," Amy said. She tugged on his arm. "C'mon, they're getting away." She pointed to the right. "I think they went that way."

"You think? Didn't you see them?"

"Of course not. I couldn't leave until your mother stopped spying on us."

Tommy frowned and motioned for quiet. He listened for the men's voices, but heard nothing. Nor could he see the glow of their flashlight. They must have moved quicker than he'd expected.

With no other options, he set off to the right in the direction of Randy Benning's land. Though he set a fast pace, Amy stayed close behind him.

They trudged through the underbrush trying to make as little noise as possible. Periodically, Tommy halted to listen for sounds of the men. After ten or fifteen minutes, they finally heard their fathers' voices.

"You carry that gun all the way to New York and

back?" Dad's voice sounded strained.

"Did he say gun?" Amy whispered.

Tommy nodded. His heart raced.

"Of course," Mr. Sawyer said. "Never know when you need one."

"Well, now that you mention it--"

Fabric rustled.

"Hey!" Mr. Sawyer said.

"I have a gun, too, so we're even."

Dad sounded like he'd just run a race. What was going on?

"So what's it gonna be, Dominick?" Dad said. "Do we put our guns away and forget about this? We buried the emerald in a good spot; no one will find it. There's plenty of emerald for both of us."

Sawyer snorted. "Right now only two people know where that emerald is buried. And that's one too many."

A shot rang out, followed immediately by a second shot.

"Dad!"

Tommy ran toward the sound, Amy at his heels. He soon outpaced her. He burst into a clearing and tripped over something. Throwing his hands out, he fell into a thicket of blackberries. He rolled over and came face-to-face with Dominick Sawyer.

Sawyer's eyes were wide, staring and empty. Tommy scooted backward on his hands and knees.

"Daddy!" Amy threw herself to the ground beside her father. "Daddy? Daddy, wake up!"

Tommy didn't wait for Amy to realize the man was dead. He needed to find his own father.

He found him ten feet away.

Tommy dropped to his knees, a sob escaping his throat. Like Dominick Sawyer, his father's eyes stared at nothing. The gun he'd kept in the bedroom end table lay a few inches from his outstretched hand.

For a few moments, Tommy stared at his father, willing him to blink, to breathe, to scold him for not remaining in bed. Behind him, a coyote-like wail filled the air, pulling him from his trance. Amy.

Tommy pushed himself upright and trudged back to the girl. She held her father's head in her lap, tears streaming from her eyes.

"Amy? C'mon Amy; we can't stay here." He tugged on her shirt. "We . . . we've got to tell Mom."

Amy closed her mouth, wiped her nose on the back of her sleeve and stood. Tommy reached for her hand. They stumbled back through the dark to Tommy's home.

With tears streaming down their faces, they told their mothers what they'd seen.

"No!" Mrs. Sawyer leaped to her feet, her face drained of color. "No way!"

Turning, she charged through the front door.

"Mom!" Amy started to follow, but Tommy's mother pulled the two children close.

As Tommy inhaled his mother's familiar Ponds

cold cream smell, his sobbing became wails. His mother's arms tightened around them, her own tears making his hair damp.

The door slammed open and Mrs. Sawyer slunk in. Tears had tracked black mascara down her face, making her look like that sad clown in the circus.

"Damn fools shot one another."

Mom moaned. Tommy looked from Mom, to Mrs. Sawyer to Amy. He was now the only male in the room.

Crossing to the sink, he splashed cold water onto his face and used a paper towel to blow his nose. He carried the roll of paper towels to the table. Amy and the women tore off sheets to blow their own noses.

"Any . . . any sign of the emerald?" Mom said. "We're going to need money."

Mrs. Sawyer shook her head. "I did a quick search, but couldn't find any place where the dirt had been disturbed."

She looked at Tommy. "Are you sure you heard them say they buried the emerald?"

Tommy and Amy both nodded.

Mrs. Sawyer's mouth drew into a thin, determined line.

"We need a plan. While I was out . . . there . . . I erased evidence of the children's presence."

Her eyes met Amy's, then Tommy's. "No matter what happens tomorrow, you two must tell people you were sleeping. You heard and saw nothing.

Can you do that?"

Tommy glanced at Amy. Blood had formed on her lips from where she'd bitten down. He reached for her hand.

"We can do that," he answered for them.

Mrs. Sawyer turned to Mom.

"Tomorrow morning we'll call the police, tell them our husbands are missing. They'll want to interview all of us, but we'll insist on staying with the children.

"I don't know if they'll connect us to the emerald theft. Everyone in town knows we just returned from New York, so the sheriff might be suspicious. We need to act surprised when he mentions the emerald theft. Don't say anything more than required. If necessary, we'll hire a lawyer."

Mom nodded. Mrs. Sawyer turned to the children.

"Did either of you see where your dads buried the emerald?"

Tommy and Amy shook their heads.

"But ... but it's got to be near their ... their .. ." Tommy couldn't say the word "body."

Amy squeezed his hand.

Mrs. Sawyer nodded. "We'll find the emerald after the police lose interest in us."

The police investigation, however, lasted longer than anyone expected. The local sheriff did, indeed, connect the families' New York trip to the emerald theft. After finding the men's bodies, he used the double murder as an excuse to poke and prod and make a pest of himself.

He had no trouble convincing a judge to issue warrants for the Hickses' and Sawyer's houses, cars and land. The families' front and back yards soon looked like a prairie dog town. After two months, however, the sheriff finally closed the case.

Mrs. Sawyer waited another few weeks before bringing Tommy and Amy back into the forest. She urged them to remember the path they'd taken when following their fathers.

The events of that night were stamped permanently into the children's heads. Even though it'd been dark, they had no problem tracing their movements. But they found no evidence of newly dug soil.

Mrs. Sawyer suggested they expand their search. Days stretched into weeks.

At first, the women and children confined their hunt to times when Randy Benning, the owner of the land, wasn't home. After Donalda married Benning, however, she increased the intensity of the search. Every day, she'd meet the children at the school bus, then send them into the forest. Sometimes one of the mothers accompanied the children. Other times, the children hunted on their own.

But they never found the emerald.

Sixty some years later, Kim's standard poodle dug the emerald from beneath a tree.

"Now you know why Tommy was furious when he learned you'd found the emerald," Betty Hicks said.

"Those poor children," Kim said. "I can't imagine the horror of finding your father murdered."

"It was worse for Amy, of course. You heard that Randy Benning lost his land gambling, then killed his wife and himself?"

"Yeah, Drew McDonald told me," Kim said. "He also said Amy survived."

Betty nodded. "Amy was at a friend's house."

"Do you know what happened to Amy afterward?"

"She was placed in foster care," Betty said. "But she kept running away from home. Tommy said Amy would show up at his door, wanting to continue looking for the emerald. She said they owed it to their dead fathers to find it.

"Problem was the land now belonged to the Hamptons. They wouldn't allow outsiders to dig. For a while, they even hired guards with dogs to patrol the mine. Tommy warned Amy, said it was too dangerous. But she kept right on digging. Eventually, one of the dogs bit her."

"Oh, that poor child!"

Betty nodded. "The bite apparently left a scar on her upper arm. She stopped digging.

"But then someone let air out of the Hamptons' car tires, threw a rock through their window and sprayed their excavation equipment with graffiti.

Police nabbed Amy as she was setting fire to the underbrush surrounding the Hamptons' mine."

Kim shuddered. She could understand Amy's anger at the Hamptons. But fire setting took the girl's pranks to a whole new level.

"What happened after she was caught?"

"She was charged with arson, convicted and sentenced as a juvenile," Betty said. "They sent her to a reform school. When she turned 14, Amy ran away and no one has heard from her since."

Betty leaned forward.

"But I think she's back."

CHAPTER 19

"Boy, have I got a story to tell you." Kim slid into Scott's car, knocking a small package onto the floor.

"Tell me as we drive," Scott said. "The Hamptons expect us for cocktails in half an hour."

Kim glanced down at the jeans and t-shirt she'd donned early this morning.

"Er, do I have time to shower and change?"

"Afraid not," Scott said. "Everyone is waiting at the mansion."

"What about Al?"

They'd left the dachshund in Grandpa's care. Images of the mischievous chow hound running loose in Charlie's cabin swept through her mind.

"Max took him along," Scott said. "He promised

to keep the little scamp on leash until we get there."

Now Kim pictured the dachshund sneaking up to a coffee table loaded with hor d'oeuvres. If Grandpa wasn't watching him full time . . .

"Well, let's hope they aren't serving food that'll make him sick," she said.

Scott grinned, then nodded at the fallen package.

"I hope those will work for you."

Puzzled, Kim retrieved the package and opened it. Two navy blue bandanas slid out. She squealed and pecked Scott's cheek.

"Thank you! I can't wait to play Rory's scent game again."

She tucked both bandanas into her purse.

"So what did you learn at the newspaper?"

Scott snorted. "Not much, except that there's a lot of resentment toward the Hampton family. Apparently, Charlie's great-grandfather -- he's the guy who won the property from Randy Benning -- never associated with people he considered lower class."

"Unless he was playing a game of poker."

"Yep. Of course, after World War II, the U.S. economy flourished, so there were more people with extra cash to join in those poker games. But a lot of locals continued to struggle to put food on the table. They resented the lavish, always exclusive parties the Hamptons threw.

"Charlie's more recent ancestors were less kingly, but it wasn't until Deb married Mark that the family began inviting normal people to the mansion. Even so, the old-timers remember the earlier snubs and wouldn't mind seeing a Hampton arrested for murder."

"That is so unfair. Charlie is a decent guy."

"People will figure that out now that Charlie has moved home," Scott said. "Right now, however, he's still the outsider, which makes him easy to blame.

"Now it's your turn. Did Betty Hicks say anything interesting?"

Kim laughed. "Yeah, you could say that."

She paused to collect her thoughts. She wanted to jump right into Betty's revelation that the daughter of one of the emerald thieves might be prowling the area. But in order to understand the significance of that statement, Scott needed to hear the entire story.

So Kim started at the beginning with Hicks and Sawyer discovering the emerald, their dismissal from the emerald mine, the building resentment that became family lore. She detailed Tommy's and Amy's families traveling to New York to steal the emerald, the subsequent dispute and double murder, Mrs. Sawyer's re-marriage, the Benning murder/suicide and Amy Sawyer's emotional turmoil.

"No one has seen Amy since she ran away at age 14," she concluded.

She paused to give Scott a few minutes to digest everything she'd said. For a few beats, the only sound was the hum of the tires against the winding road.

"I take it," Scott said, "that there's a but to this story."

"Betty thinks Amy has come back to look for the emerald that her father buried 60 years ago."

Though Scott's mouth fell open, he kept his eyes focused on the road ahead.

"Amy's the same age as Tommy Hicks, right?" he said. "That'd make her . . ."

"Seventy-four. I didn't want to hurt Betty's feelings, but I share your doubt. Even if she's a spry 74-year-old, why would Amy Sawyer wait 60 years to return?"

Kim touched Scott's arm. "But what if Amy recently told a son, daughter or grandchild about the buried emerald?"

"A death-bed confession?" The humor in Scott's voice made Kim smile.

"I know it sounds hokey, but some people really do wait until they're dying to share family secrets."

"Okay, I'll give you the death-bed confession," Scott said. "You're thinking one of Amy Sawyer's children recently returned to Hiddenite? Why is that important?"

"You know those lights that Charlie has been seeing in the woods? Tommy has seen them, too."

Kim leaned toward Scott.

"But Tommy saw two distinct lights. The first glimmered near the area where we found Kirk's body. Tommy managed to creep up on those lights. He saw Kirk, along with his two friends, digging illegally.

"At the same time that Kirk and company were poaching, however, Tommy saw a single light twinkling farther away in the forest. He tried to locate the person shining that second light, but whoever it was must have good hearing because he was never able to sneak up on him."

"Sounds a little like Charlie's ghost lights," Scott said. "More likely, though, it was someone illegally hunting."

"That's what Tommy thought. Someone must be hunting or guarding a patch of marijuana or a still. Heaven knows all kinds of illegal undertakings occur in these woods. But in daylight, Tommy hasn't found evidence of those activities. No animal blood, no cleared patches, no booby traps.

"Instead, he found evidence of someone digging."

"Digging as in planting a marijuana bed or burying a body?"

"Digging as in go down a few feet, find nothing, fill the hole, move on," Kim said. "Betty thinks Amy Sawyer or one of her descendants has been looking for the Carolina Emerald."

Scott slowed the car to turn onto the Hamptons' driveway. "So there were two groups of people trespassing in the mine."

"I think so." Kim bit her lip. "But what would

happen if the two groups stumbled into one another? Maybe they argued or got into a fight and that's why Kirk died. His death might have been an accident."

"Framing Charlie for murder was deliberate." Scott parked the car beside Charlie's, then reached across the front seat to squeeze Kim's hand.

"I know how upset you are about losing the Carolina Emerald," he said. "But if Kirk was killed by someone looking for it, I'm glad it's no longer in our possession."

The curse! Rachael's voice whispered in Kim's mind. With a shiver, she opened her car door and stepped out.

Martha, the woman who worked as the Hamptons' housekeeper, cook and occasional food server, answered their knock.

"They're in the library," Martha said. "Do you mind finding your own way? I need to keep an eye on dinner."

Kim assured the over-worked woman that they didn't need an escort. With Rory trotting between them, they walked toward the rear of the house. As they approached an open door, they heard Charlie's voice.

"Are you nuts?" he yelled.

"Don't speak to your father that way," Deb said.

"But Dad's jeopardizing the family business."

"You have no idea what you're talking about," Mark said.

Charlie replied with a series of curses.

Kim froze, one foot pointed toward the library, the other back toward the door. With eight cousins, three aunts, three uncles and thirty-odd years of forced intimacy, she recognized a family squabble and had no desire to walk into the middle of it.

As she contemplated leaving, she heard her grandfather's placating voice.

Crap. No way would she abandon him to whatever was happening.

Straightening her shoulders, she marched toward the living room. She paused at the door and studied the tableau.

Charlie stood nose to nose with his father, the muscles in his neck and jaws tense. Both men's hands were clenched in fists.

Rachael stood to Charlie's left, gripping his forearm. Deb leaned forward in her wheelchair and used two hands to grip her husband's wrist.

Across the room, Grandpa stood with his hands spread, palms upward, in the traditional "let's calm down" stance. Aunt Ginny sat in a corner with both Al and Jack perched on her lap.

Time to interrupt.

"So," Kim said with false brightness, "anyone want to hear about our new suspect?"

Whether it was her question or the sound of a new voice in the room, the tension eased slightly.

Deb moved away from her husband and assumed her best hostess smile. While Charlie and Mark continued to scowl at each other, Deb summoned the tired cook to take drink orders.

Turning back to Kim, Deb said, "Rory doesn't need to be on leash. Jack's enjoying his new friends. He doesn't have many opportunities to act like a dog."

As soon as Kim unclipped him, Rory ran across the room to greet the two little dogs before leading them to the large window that overlooked the forest. All three dogs pressed their noses to the glass.

"Rory, get away from there," Kim said. "You're making a mess of the windows."

Rory turned to look at Kim.

"Oh, let him have fun," Deb said. "The windows all have Jack's nose prints. At least now when Mark complains, I can blame the dachshund. Their nose prints look the same."

Seeing an opportunity to lighten the mood, Kim said, "Actually, scientists have found that dogs' nose prints are as distinctive as human fingerprints."

Deb's eyes widened. "I've never heard that."

"We don't pay much attention to nose prints in this country. But the Canadian Kennel club accepts nose prints as a way of identifying dogs."

Kim grinned. "If I get tired of teaching, I may create a data base of dog nose prints just like the FBI's Automated Fingerprint Identification System. That way owners can figure out which of their dogs got into the trash or opened the refrigerator."

Deb laughed. The musical tinkle of her voice seemed to calm her husband and son. After the cook delivered everyone's drinks, Charlie turned back to his father.

"I still want to know," he said, "why you hired Donny Driver, Kirk Ballas and Rocky DiSoto to work in our mine. Everyone knows they're thieves."

"I didn't hire them for the mine," Mark said. "They worked the gravel quarry. You have no idea how hard it is to find people who can operate heavy machinery.

"Besides, I fired them months ago when I caught them poking around the mine."

Before Charlie could respond, Martha appeared at the library door.

"Sheriff Spits is here," she said.

As the sheriff strode into the room, the three dogs ran to greet him. Aunt Ginny stood and nervously patted the wrinkles from her skirt.

Kim frowned. Ginny never worried about wrinkled clothes. What was going on?

Deb held out both hands to the sheriff.

"Walt, how nice to see you! Please say you'll stay for dinner."

Sheriff Spits enveloped Deb's hands in his own and leaned over to peck her cheek.

"It's always good to see you, but I can't stay. I'm on duty."

"Well, at least let me introduce you to our friends."

She turned her wheelchair. "I believe you know Scott Wilson and Kimberley West. This is Max Hershey, Kim's grandfather, and Virginia Donaldson, Kim's aunt."

Everyone dutifully shook the sheriff's hand. When Aunt Ginny's turn came, however, Kim noticed a change in Sheriff Spits's posture. He stood a little straighter and his eyes widened and . . . Did he hold Ginny's hand just a tad too long?

For her part, Ginny offered a mischievous grin.

"Everyone calls me Ginny. Virginia sounds so formal, don't you think?"

The sheriff smiled and suggested she call him "Walt."

Hmmm . . .

Mark Hampton interrupted what promised to be an interesting exchange.

"So if you're on duty," Mark said, "what brings you here during dinner time?"

Sheriff Spits ignored the challenge in Mark's voice, smiling pleasantly at the group.

"Just needed to talk with this little lady here," he said, nodding toward Kim.

Ginny snickered; no one had ever referred to Kim as "little lady." Kim wrinkled her nose at her aunt. Ginny returned the gesture.

Mark looked annoyed, but Sheriff Spits chuckled. He opened his mouth, but was interrupted by Martha announcing that dinner was ready.

"Are you sure you won't stay?" Deb smiled at the

sheriff.

"Thank you, no."

"Why don't the rest of you go eat while the food is hot?" Kim said. "I'll join you when the sheriff and I finish."

"And I promise I won't keep her long," Sheriff Spits added.

Scott hung back with Al and Rory. Sheriff Spits waited until the others had left the room before turning to Kim.

"So, you wanted to talk to me?"

Kim nodded. "Uh, you know about the emerald that was stolen from the Hampton's cottage, right?"

Sheriff Spits gave a single nod.

"We think Donny Driver may have taken it."

She told the sheriff about Donny cruising the Gem Festival's lapidarists and asking questions about cutting an eight-inch emerald.

Sheriff Spits scowled.

"That sounds like something Driver would do. But I can't arrest him just because he asked someone about cutting an emerald. Large emeralds are mighty rare but not unheard of in this area."

"I can identify this one because it's so distinctive," Kim said. "There are three long bolts shooting from the same foundation. Also the museum's identifying marks should be etched onto the stone's bottom."

"Good enough."

He plopped his hat onto his head and turned

toward the door.

"I'll talk to Driver."

Kim fell into step beside him. "There's one other thing."

The big man turned and gazed down at her. Kim gulped. The sheriff's answer to this question would set the course of the next few days.

"Is Charlie still your main suspect for the murder?"

Please say no, please say no, please--

Distress flashed across the sheriff's face before he brought it under control. Without a word, he turned and trudged back to his car.

Kim followed Scott into the dining room. But her appetite was gone.

CHAPTER 20

Early the next morning, Kim tiptoed from the cabin and headed toward the emerald mine. Rory bounded ahead, his puffy tail wagging. His enthusiastic greeting of every new smell lifted her mood. Nothing like a dog to help put life into perspective.

Sipping from her travel cup, she considered the upcoming day. Rachael's and Charlie's engagement party would begin at 1 p.m. and last who knew how long. While she understood why the party would be held mid-day -- Deb's multiple sclerosis tended to worsen in the evenings -- Kim couldn't help but mourn the loss of time at the mine.

She'd considered rising at dawn to spend a few

hours digging before the party began. But last night Rachael announced her intention to spend the morning primping for the party. No way would Kim dig without her friend; the guilt would overwhelm any pleasure.

As she watched Rory loping along, she was pleased with her decision. The dogs weren't invited to the party, so this would be her only time to exercise the rambunctious young dog.

She fingered the new bandana she'd tucked into her jeans pocket. Poodles needed intellectual stimulation as well as physical exercise, so she planned to play some scenting games with Rory before returning to the pre-party madness.

Using a new bandana would make today's game challenging. To Rory, the old bandana smelled of Kim, Scott, Grandpa, Aunt Ginny, Grandpa's store, beach sand, Chesapeake Bay water and Rory himself. The new one probably smelled only of Rory, Kim and Scott. While true scent discrimination demanded a dog focus on a single scent, Kim wanted to build Rory's confidence by setting up games he could win.

She scowled. The emerald thief had probably unwrapped the gemstone then pitched Rory's dirty bandana into the nearest trashcan. What a waste.

They reached the clearing and Kim called Rory to her. Pulling out the new bandana, she spent a few minutes playing a tug game with him.

Satisfied that Rory was now interested in the

bandana, she cued him to release it and to sit. He immediately plunked his butt to the ground and threw her a doggie grin.

"Yeah, you know what's coming next, don't cha?" Kim held up a hand, traffic cop style. "Wait here. And no peeking."

She turned and walked away, stopping now and then to pretend she was hiding something.

Outside searches tended to be difficult; there were too many distracting smells. But Rory excelled at inside searches and needed a challenge to take the edge off his energy. If he didn't find the bandana, she'd make the next search easier so they could end on a positive note.

She tucked the bandana beneath a rock, then continued a few more steps and pretended to hide something.

She walked back to Rory and rewarded him for holding her "wait" cue. Then she told him to "find it."

Rory leaped to his feet, dropped his nose to the ground and followed the trail she'd made. Kim played out the long line attached to Rory's harness, marveling at the confident set to his tail. He paused at every fake hiding place, gave it a quick sniff, then moved on.

As he neared the spot where she'd hidden the bandana, she inhaled deeply, trying to relax. If Rory sensed any tension from her, he'd know the bandana was located nearby.

But before he reached the bandana, he suddenly slammed to a halt. Lifting his nose, he scented the air. With a doggie grin, he wheeled around and raced back the way they'd come.

Kim tightened her grip on the long line and turned in time to see her grandfather step into the clearing.

"Thought I'd find you here," Grandpa said as Rory reached him.

"Rory, sit," Kim called.

To her surprise, the young dog plunked his butt to the ground and grinned up at her grandfather. Grandpa rewarded him with praise and a dog biscuit.

Kim joined them and hugged her grandfather.

"What brings you out so early?" she said.

"I was afraid you might go down there alone."

He pointed toward the mine where they'd been working.

"Don't worry," Kim said, "I won't. I know the danger."

Grandpa fell into step as Kim headed back toward the hidden bandana, Rory bounding ahead.

"So how are things at the big house?" she said.

"Tense. After everyone went to bed, Deb and Mark fought about the way he'd treated the sheriff. I heard Mark storm out of the house shortly after midnight."

"Yikes. Would you and Aunt Ginny like to go to a hotel? I'm sure we can make up some excuse so we don't offend Deb or Mark."

"And miss all the drama?" Grandpa grinned. "No, we'll stay with the Hamptons. So tell me why you picked at your supper last night. It's not like you to turn down good food."

"I couldn't stop worrying about Charlie."

She briefly told her grandfather about her conversation with the sheriff.

"Sheriff Spits seems pretty competent," Grandpa said.

"Yeah. But right now most of the evidence points to Charlie."

Before her grandfather could reply, Rory leaped up and placed his feet on her shoulders. Startled, Kim stepped back, then spotted the new bandana hanging from his mouth.

"You found it!"

She mentally kicked herself for not paying attention. She should have watched Rory so she could reward him when he pulled the bandana from underneath the rock. Now she had to decide whether to reward him for bringing her the bandana or correct him for putting his paws on her shoulder.

As if reading her mind, Rory grinned, then dropped into a sit, still clutching the bandana.

She reached into a pocket and pulled out a dog treat.

"You're incorrigible," she told him as she exchanged the treat for the bandana.

"Sounds like someone else I know," Grandpa chuckled.

Rory suddenly shot to his feet and turned toward the trees on the far side of the clearing. Tail held high, every muscle tensed. Kim grabbed the handle on his harness.

"What's he see?" Grandpa peered into the trees' shadows.

"Probably a deer."

Rory emitted a low growl. Kim's own muscles tensed. Rory never growled at deer.

Kneeling beside him, she sighted along his muzzle. Something moved.

Donny Driver stepped from the shadows. He glared at her, his body as rigid as her dog's.

Rory barked. Donny raised his right hand.

"Grandpa, get down!"

Kim tugged her grandfather to the ground and rolled in front of him, trying to shield him. She stiffened, waiting to hear the sound of gunfire, to feel the burn of steel biting into flesh.

Harsh laughter drifted across the field.

Kim rolled onto her side and stared back at Donny. He raised both hands, palms toward her, to show he carried no weapon.

Then he curled the fingers of his right hand, leaving the index finger and thumb to form a gun shape. He pointed his hand at her and mouthed the word "Bang."

"I should have released Rory to bite him," Kim as they tromped back to the cabin.

"Then he'd press charges and both you and your dog would be in serious trouble."

Grandpa paused to remove a pebble that had lodged in his sneaker.

"Never let a bully bait you into acting rashly," he added.

Kim searched the shadows behind them. Even though Rory would alert her if Donny followed them, she couldn't shake the feeling that someone was watching.

Grandpa resumed walking and Kim fell into step.

"Given that you saw that man talking to gem cutters," Kim said, "I vote we move him to the top of the suspect list."

"We have a suspect list?" Grandpa grinned.

"We do now."

She used her thumb to point behind them.

"The motive for the murder could be as simple as a falling out among thieves."

Grandpa nodded. "But I think Detective Cummings is wise to look for a connection between the Carolina Emerald and the murder. To have a long-lost emerald surface just hours before a murder seems too coincidental."

He peered at her over the top of his glasses. "That means the Hickses must remain on the suspect list."

She sighed. She really didn't want to consider Betty or her husband as suspects. Unfortunately, Grandpa's logic made sense.

"I'll keep the Hickses in mind," she said. "But I'd also like to learn more about what happened to Amy Sawyer."

The cabin finally came into view.

Al greeted them at the door, then led Rory on a merry chase through the living room.

"Gentle!" Kim told Rory.

With a sigh, Rory dropped into a down and let his little buddy climb all over him.

"We're in the kitchen," Scott called.

She found Aunt Ginny and Scott at the table, bent over a laptop computer. Kim wrapped an arm around each of them and planted a kiss on their heads.

"Whatcha doing?"

"Trying to trace Amy Sawyer." Aunt Ginny flopped back in her chair. "Do you know how many Amy Sawyers live in the U.S.?"

"Did you try searching for the year she was born?"

"Yes, dear. And we searched for Amy Sawyers born in North Carolina. There are still too many."

"We need more information." Kim slumped into a chair.

"It'd help to know Amy's interests," Scott said. "I once helped a friend find a former classmate by searching vendors for the various Star Trek conventions. His classmate had been a rabid Trekkie."

"Well, Amy lived in Hiddenite for fourteen years," Kim said. "Maybe we can talk to former classmates. We can ask Deb--"

"Kiiiiiim!" Rachael's voice carried down the stairs and into the kitchen.

Kim jogged to the foot of the stairs. "Are you okay?"

Rachael appeared at the top. She was dressed in a terry cloth robe, her hair wrapped in a turban-style towel.

"I don't know what to doooooo."

"About what?" Kim started climbing the stairs.

Rachael swept a hand across her body.

"Me. My clothes, my hair, my makeup. Charlie wants to go to the big house an hour early so we can help with last-minute preparations. But how am I going to look presentable if I've spent an hour working?"

"So stay here and let Charlie go help."

Kim reached the top of the stairs. "You can ride to the house with us."

Rachael shook her head.

"No, if I'm going to be a part of this family, then I want to participate in what everyone's doing."

"Then take all of your stuff to the big house so you can change clothes after you finish working."

Rachael rolled her eyes.

"There's more to preparing for an event than

tossing on clothes. I have to do makeup and hair and nails and--"

"Okay, okay." Kim raised her hands in defeat. "What do you want from me? You know I can't apply makeup or fix your hair."

Kim had been a tomboy most of her life. While she'd experimented with makeup in college, she'd never worn it daily. She was probably the only 32-year-old woman who couldn't tell an eyeliner from an eyebrow pencil.

Before Rachael could answer, a bedroom door opened and Charlie stepped out. Unlike Rachael, he was fully dressed in jeans and cotton shirt.

Sensing Rachael's unease, he offered a sheepish grin.

"I'm going for coffee," he said. "Want me to bring you a cup of tea and some toast?"

"No, I'm too nervous to eat," Rachael said.

"Well, I'm not."

Kim turned around, but Rachael grabbed her sleeve.

"Kim, please," she said, "I'd just like your opinion on which dress to wear."

The hand on Kim's arm felt clammy. Startled, Kim studied Rachael's face. Her normal dewy complexion was pale, her undereyes puffy and dark. Sweat dotted her forehead.

This was more than worry about what to wear.

"What's wrong?"

"Not here. Get your food and meet me in my

room, okay?"

Rachael turned and scurried down the hall.

Kim frowned, then trotted down the stairs.

"I, er, need to help Rachael," she told the others. "Would you mind watching Rory?"

Though the calming effects of dogs had been well-document -- one scientific study claimed petting a dog lowered blood pressure -- Rory's idea of "helping" was to make people laugh. Kim suspected Rachael's room was too cluttered to be safe for a large dog to chase his tail. Crashing lamps and stolen undies would not soothe her friend.

She prepared a tray of toast and tea -- enough for two people -- and carried it to Rachael's room.

At the open door, she slammed to a halt.

Skirts, pants, shirts, sweaters and shoes covered the bed. Makeup and hair products cluttered a vanity table. A closet stood open, its contents holding only Charlie's shirts, jeans and sport coat.

Rachael gestured toward a bistro table and chairs sitting in front of a window overlooking the back forest. Kim skirted a pair of expensive looking, high heeled shoes. She had to brush two bras off of the table to make room for the food tray.

She turned to her friend.

"Okay, now I'm worried." She swept a hand to encompass the room. "Wanna tell me the name of the hurricane that tore through here?"

Unlike Kim, who never figured out how to tame paperwork clutter, Rachael had always maintained a pristine home.

Rachael sighed and plopped into a chair.

"I've been a bit nervous."

She leaned forward and pulled a taffy colored scarf from beneath her. With a shrug, she tossed it onto the floor.

Kim settled into the remaining chair and poured tea for each of them. She pushed a plate of toast toward Rachael, then sipped her tea. Her friend would explain when she was ready.

Rachael bit into her toast, wrinkled her nose, returned the toast to the plate and sampled her tea. Finally, she set the cup into the saucer.

"I don't know if I can do this," she said.

"Go to the party? Rachael, you're wonderful at parties. Much better than I am."

"No, not that. I'm not sure I can marry Charlie."

Kim felt her mouth drop open.

"But . . . but that's all you've talked about since you met him. You don't believe he killed that fellow, do you?"

"No! No, of course not. But look at this place. I've never lived anywhere so luxurious." She grimaced. "Well, it looked elegant until Hurricane Rachael hit."

"After digging in ruins and sleeping in tents," Kim said, "you're just not used to the way normal people live."

Instead of the smile Kim expected, her friend started to cry. Shocked, Kim leaped to her feet and pulled Rachael into her arms. After what seemed like days but was probably only a few minutes, Rachael pulled away.

Kim located a box of tissues, set it in front of Rachael and returned to her seat. She poured two more cups of tea, dumped extra sugar into Rachael's and urged her friend to drink.

Whether it was the sweet tea or the passage of time, Rachael's face grew less haunted.

Kim sipped her own tea and waited for Rachael to explain. She didn't have to wait long.

"When I met Charlie," Rachael said, "I had no idea his family was wealthy. I mean, he's a computer geek, right? He dresses in jeans and shirts with ink-stained chest pockets.

"But he was so much fun. And he seemed fascinated by my work."

She smiled. "Did I tell you about the time he came on a dig with me? He followed my instructions, never complained, put as much thought into what he was doing for me as he does when designing a software program. The poor man was burned to a crisp by the end of the day. But he never, ever complained."

Rachael paused, expecting a response.

Kim had heard the story of Charlie's helping on a dig many times. Even so, she nodded and said, "He's a good man."

"Yes! He's the best." Rachael frowned. "But Charlie waited a long time to tell me his family owned an emerald mine. He said he wanted to surprise me, but now I think it was more than that."

Rachael's eyes filled with tears.

"I think Charlie knew I'd never feel comfortable with his family's lifestyle. Did you know his parents' mansion has like six bathrooms? And there's a wine cellar and exercise room and media room and, of course, the lovely landscaping. It's like visiting Monticello."

"But you're not going to live there," Kim said. "I thought you and Charlie were staying in this house."

"Yeah, this is less pretentious. But I still have to deal with the Hamptons' business associates and friends. Charlie and I want a small wedding with just close friends and family. But he's the last son to marry and I think Deb favors him and she keeps showing me photos of these elaborate wedding dresses and describing how lovely they'd look when I descended their Gone With the Wind staircase. Charlie and I haven't had the heart to tell her we want to keep things small."

"Deb's a big girl. She loves Charlie and seems smitten with you. You need to tell her what you really want."

"How can I? They've invited 60 people to this engagement party. You know they're all going to expect a wedding invitation. If you and Ginny and Max hadn't agreed to come today, I'd have had to face a crowd of doctors and lawyers and judges and snooty gentry."

Ah, now we get to the crux of the matter. Rachael was terrified of stepping outside of her social class.

Both Rachael and Kim had grown up in solidly middle-class families. While they'd been aware that some of their classmates were wealthier than others, their stable home environments allowed them to ignore the differences and embrace the similarities.

That all changed when they went to college and needed to cope with people from all levels of society. They'd struggled against the chauvinism of a high-caste professor from India, watched in horror as the Dean's wife berated a grounds keeper for missing a weed, groused about the wealthy geology student who viewed cheating as his God-given right.

But class warfare wasn't a one-way street.

The boys in the school's wealthiest fraternity house routinely threw drunken bashes that ended with one of them punching a fist through the wall.

The custodian who maintained their building grew tired of repairing the walls. When he was called to perform yet another repair, he hid outward facing nails behind the plasterboard. The next time a boy punched the wall, he drew back a bloody fist and lost the use of his index finger.

Such incidents convinced Kim that despite the efforts to make the U.S. a meritocracy, people often viewed the world through the lens of their social class.

And yet, Kim firmly believed that love could, in fact, conquer all.

"Don't forget that Deb also grew up middle class," she said. "She couldn't have felt comfortable moving into Mark's house. Yet the two of them seem to have worked things out."

Rachael's mouth quirked. "Yeah, Deb does seem happy, doesn't she?"

"She also seems like a reasonable person," Kim added. "She'll understand if you tell her you really want a small wedding."

"It's not just the wedding."

Biting her lip, she stared at the floor. Several seconds passed. Finally, Rachael lifted her chin and met Kim's eyes.

"Don't you see? By marrying Charlie, I'm giving up the life I built. I love my old job, I love digging in the field, I love not having to worry about what some hot-shot stranger thinks of my dirty fingernails."

"But . . . but I thought you also loved the idea of working at the museum and living near the emerald mine."

"Living here is okay, I guess. It's a gorgeous area and I like the people I've met.

"But I didn't get a degree in paleontology so I could sit behind a desk. And please don't say I'm old enough to start thinking about leaving the field. Mary Anning was our age when she discovered that nearly complete plesiosaur and she was still hunting fossils in her '40s when she was diagnosed with cancer."

Mary Anning was the first female paleontologist. In the early 1800s, she uncovered Jurassic-age marine fossils in the cliffs along the English Chanel. Had she lived in the modern age, her cancer might have been controlled and she might have continued fossil hunting well beyond middle age.

"You know I'd never say you are too old to do something," Kim said. "But where does Charlie fit in all of this? I can't imagine he'd insist you do something you hated."

Rachael slumped back into her chair.

"That's just the problem," she said. "Charlie doesn't know how I feel."

She raised a hand to stay Kim's shocked protest. "And, yeah, I know I'm a liberated woman and I really shouldn't have let him think the museum job was a promotion. I mean, it is a promotion but not one that I want."

"Why haven't you told him?"

"Because he was so happy." Rachael sighed. "Mark has pooh-poohed Charlie's computer skills since, well, since forever. Charlie didn't even tell his father about the software he was developing until he was ready to try it out. And even then, the only reason he told Mark what he was doing was he couldn't hide the equipment he needed to rent.

"But now Mark treats Charlie like he walks on water. He practically demanded that Charlie return to Hiddenite to oversee new excavations. When Charlie asked for my opinion, I said something vague about lack of jobs here. But then the museum suddenly offered me the management position and it seemed like it was a sign that we should do this."

"But now you have your doubts," Kim said.

"I miss my job," Rachael said.

"What you miss is excavating. Surely the museum sponsors trips to dig for new specimens. You need to convince them to allow you time to participate in those."

Rachael brightened. "I hadn't thought of that. Maybe I really can have my cake and eat it, too."

"Right now, you'd better stick with toast."

They ate their toast in companionable silence. The conversation and food seemed to strengthen Rachael. Color returned to her cheeks and the self-confident woman that Kim knew reappeared.

"Okay if I change the subject?" Kim said.

"Please do."

"I told you that Betty Hicks thinks we should consider Amy Sawyer a suspect, right? Well, Scott and Aunt Ginny haven't had much luck tracking her on the internet.

"But surely Amy had friends here, classmates, people who'd remember her, might even know where she lives now. If the Hamptons invited long-time residents to your party--"

"Oh, believe me, they did."

Kim grinned. "So rather than worry about the

crowd, let's use the crowd to do some snooping."

CHAPTER 21

The prospect of using the engagement party as a cover to investigate Amy Sawyer cheered Rachael. Kim suggested they go to the mansion early to help Charlie's family. Afterwards, they would change clothes in one of the spare bedrooms and begin their sleuthing.

They joined the others in the kitchen and shared the plan. Aunt Ginny and Grandpa, of course, welcomed the chance to search for new suspects. Even Charlie expressed enthusiasm.

After a hurried breakfast, Aunt Ginny and Grandpa returned to the mansion to prepare for the party. Kim helped Rachael choose a simple, elegant outfit. She packed her own dress, then secured Rory and Al in Scott's room.

"Let's drive separate cars," she said as she joined the others. "If the party lasts more than a few hours, I'll need to return here to take the dogs outside."

Fifteen minutes later, they drove up the Hamptons' long drive.

The grounds were alive with activity. An enormous white canopy had been erected on the side lawn. Workers scurried around setting up tables and chairs. While several women tossed starched white tablecloths over the finished tables, a florist arranged baskets of autumn flowers. A second group of workers positioned warming trays on a long stretch of tables.

They parked the two cars near the catering van and found Deb in the kitchen directing activity.

Jack leaped off his mistress's lap to greet them, then took the opportunity to retrieve a fallen morsel of cheese from the floor.

"Jack, you're going to ruin your appetite for supper," Deb said.

"Ah, let him enjoy himself," Mark said as he joined them. "He can diet tomorrow with the rest of us."

"So what can we do to help?" Kim said. "I'm not much of a cook, but I can chop vegetables. Or, if you'd prefer, I can help set tables or something."

"Thank you for the offer, but, really, Connie has everything under control."

Deb introduced a slender brunette dressed in

jeans and a pink shirt embroidered with the words "Connie's Catering."

"Connie has lived in the area for less than a year," Deb said, "but I don't know what I'd do without her. Before she moved here, I had to hire people from Charlotte. They just didn't provide as thorough a service as Connie.

"And wait till you taste Connie's food. She is an amazing cook."

Connie's face flushed.

"Did you create the recipes yourself or are you using recipes from your family?" Kim said.

Connie bit her lip. "Oh, I use a bit of this and that. I'd better get back to work."

She turned away, leaving Kim wondering why the woman suddenly appeared uncomfortable.

"Ginny and Max are upstairs getting ready for the party," Deb said. "I'm going to do the same thing now. Why don't I show you to our spare bedrooms so you can put on your party clothes?"

"Are you sure, Mom?" Charlie gestured to his jeans and work shirt. "We came prepared to help. I don't want you overdoing."

Deb patted her son's hand. "I'm feeling fine. I want you and Rachael to just enjoy this special day."

Turning the wheelchair around, she led the way to a custom elevator.

Somehow they all managed to fit inside. As the elevator door closed, Kim realized this might be her only opportunity to speak to Deb before the guests arrived.

"Do you know if any of today's guests knew Amy Sawyer?" she said.

Deb frowned. "Amy Sawyer? You mean the little girl who survived that murder/suicide?"

Kim nodded. "She'd be in her early- to mid-70s now. Betty Hicks thinks Amy or one of Amy's relatives might have killed Kirk Ballas."

The elevator opened.

"One more suspect is good news." Deb wheeled into a long hall. "You must tell Walt."

"Well, we need more information before talking to the sheriff," Kim said. "Amy may have married and changed her name. I'm hoping someone attending the party knew Amy and will remember a detail that will help us find her."

"Dottie White is local and might have known Amy," Deb said. "And, let's see, maybe Rhonda Cruz and . . . Give me time to think about it. I'll make a list and be sure to introduce you to anyone who's here today."

She paused in front of an open bedroom.

"Let's put the fellows in here. You girls will need a bigger room."

Scott and Charlie said their goodbyes and disappeared into their designated room. Deb led the way to the last bedroom.

"There's a double sink and wall-sized mirror in the bathroom," Deb said, opening the door. "Clean towels are in the closet. If you need anything, please let me know."

As Deb headed to her own room, Kim gawked at the "spare" bedroom. Easily the size of most people's living rooms, it included a king-sized bed, dainty dressing table, recliner and reading lamp. A door to the right opened to reveal an empty walk-in closet equipped with shoe organizers, handbag hooks and pull-out pant hangers.

But the outer room paled in comparison to the bathroom. A frameless mirror topped by vanity lights stretched the length of one wall. Beneath it, a birch-colored vanity supported a marble counter top and double sinks. The shower completely covered the opposite wall. Through the clear doors, Kim spotted multiple body sprays and an overhead rain shower.

The toilet hid discreetly behind a second door.

"This is a spare bedroom?" Kim said.

"Yep. The room the guys are in is almost this size. It just lacks the separate dressing table."

Rachael folded her arms.

"You see why this place intimidates me. There are five guest suites like this. The master suite is on its own level and stretches the entire length of the house."

"And yet, everything feels clean, not ostentatious." Kim crossed back into the bedroom and draped her garment bag on the bed.

"That's Deb's doing," Rachael said. "Unlike

Mark, she didn't grow up with a silver spoon in her mouth. She goes out of her way to make people feel comfortable."

"She's probably the reason Charlie doesn't act like a spoiled rich kid," Kim said.

She pulled her hair into a tight ponytail.

"I'm going to shower first because you take too long."

Rachael snorted, but offered no comment. Kim ducked into the bathroom and closed the door.

The shower was as luxurious as it appeared. Kim could have stood under the rain shower all day.

But there wasn't time for that. Even though they'd arrived early, Kim wanted to be dressed and ready before the first guests arrived. Deb planned to use an informal receiving line to introduce Rachael and Charlie to their guests. Kim wanted to find a discreet spot to observe people's reactions.

Though none of her prime suspects had been invited to the party, she couldn't overlook the possibility that one of the Hamptons' friends or Mark's business associates was involved.

She quickly smoothed moisturizer over her body and face, applied mascara and lip gloss, and brushed her long hair until it shined. Unzipping the garment bag, she carefully removed a brightly colored blouse and the long, flowing skirt Aunt Ginny had helped her select.

Though the skirt was a basic black knit, a series of angled seams gave it character. Kim slipped it over her head and admired the way it skimmed her hips, then flared out into a flowing circle that ended at her ankles. She pulled on the light-weight blouse, then twirled in front of the mirror. The skirt made her feel like Ginger Rogers. Best of all, the long skirt looked great with flat shoes.

She made a mental note to once again thank Aunt Ginny for pushing her to try something beyond her comfort level.

She stepped into the hall and pulled the door closed behind her. Voices to her left drew her to the top of a majestic staircase.

Scott, Grandpa and a man dressed in a silver-gray suit stood at the bottom, chatting and laughing.

She paused to admire the plush, red carpet that covered the stairs. The balustrades were made of African mahogany. Kim reached out to stroke the highly polished handrail.

Resisting the urge to straddle the handrail and ride it to the end, she instead descended in Scarlett O'Hara fashion. Halfway down, the men sensed her presence and looked up at her.

Grandpa beamed in approval; for years, he'd urged her to try wearing something other than jeans. Scott, however, seemed to read her mind. He grinned as his eyes flicked from hers to the railing and back.

The man in the gray suit surprised her. Sheriff Spits had shed not only his uniform, but also his cop attitude. His blue eyes sparkled from a totally relaxed face.

As she neared the bottom, Scott stepped forward and offered a hand, palm turned upward. Kim lifted her chin and regally placed her hand in his. The giggle that escaped ruined the effect.

She turned to greet Sheriff Spits. Before she had a chance to quiz him about his investigation, she heard Aunt Ginny announce "I am here."

Her aunt posed at the top of the stairs, looking like a slightly overweight movie star. She'd tamed her graying curls and added mascara, blush and lipstick. She'd dressed in a long, peasant-style skirt and blouse. Kim knew that whatever earrings dangled from Ginny's lobes would be decorated with googly eyes.

Ginny lifted her chin and began descending while loudly humming the "Pomp and Circumstance" march.

Halfway down, however, she stopped, tossed Kim a mischievous grin and swung one leg over the stair rail.

"Aunt Ginny, that's going to be slick!"

"I've always wanted to do this." Ginny released her hold on the rail and began sliding down backwards. "Yippeee!"

But the slick polish caused her to quickly pick up speed. Her small body hurdled downward much too fast.

They all moved at once. Sheriff Spits reached the base of the stair rail first and easily plucked Ginny off before she fell. Somehow Ginny ended up cradled in the sheriff's arms like a baby.

"Whee, that was fun!" Ginny said. "I wanna do that again."

The sheriff, Grandpa and Scott laughed. Kim simply stared, wondering when Sheriff Spits would set Ginny down. As he looked down at Ginny, his face flushed and his eyes softened.

"What are you all doing in here?" Mark Hampton said as he stepped through the front door. "The guests are starting to arrive. Where are Charlie and Rachael?"

"We're here." Charlie and Rachael descended the stairs hand in hand.

Sheriff Spits used the distraction to discreetly set Ginny onto her feet. Now Ginny's face seemed flushed.

"Is Mom already outside?" Charlie said.

Mark folded his arms. "Everyone is outside but the guests of honor."

Charlie ignored his father's criticism. "Then I guess we'd best join them."

Without looking back, he opened the front door for Rachael.

As the others followed, Kim touched Ginny's arm to stop her. To her annoyance, the sheriff paused at the door.

"You ladies coming?"

"Er, I need Aunt Ginny's help with my, ah, hair," Kim said. "You go on; we'll catch up."

Aunt Ginny's eyebrows raised, but she remained silent until the others left and the door closed.

"What's going on?" Ginny said. "I know darn well you don't want help with your hair."

"The sheriff likes you," Kim said.

Ginny shrugged. "I like him too. So?"

"So he might reveal details of the investigation to you," Kim said.

Ginny had one of those open faces that people automatically trusted. Kim couldn't believe the number of times she'd watched people spill their inner secrets to her aunt.

"So you want me to use my feminine wiles on him?"

Ginny fluttered her eyes and puckered her lips. She looked like a guppy.

Kim laughed. "Just see what you can find out, okay?"

Ginny agreed. They walked outside and followed the tantalizing smell of cooked onions, meat and herbs to the huge canvas pavilion. Servers dressed in black and white now stood behind the food station. A few people dressed in garden party dresses or suits milled around the outside bar.

In front of the canopy, Deb, Mark, Rachael, Charlie and his brothers formed a reception line. Jack sat on Deb's lap, ears perked. As people shook Deb's hand, she introduced Rachael and added "you remember my third son Charlie."

Kim smiled as a woman wearing a hat worthy of

the Kentucky Derby solemnly shook Jack's paw, oblivious to the long line of people waiting behind her.

Scott stood off to the side where he could observe the faces of people shaking Charlie's hand. Grandpa and Sheriff Spits were nowhere in sight.

While Ginny continued walking into the tent, Kim sidled up to Scott.

"Anything interesting yet?"

He grinned. "No one's thrown themselves at Charlie's feet and confessed."

Kim gripped her shoulder bag by the straps and shook it under Scott's nose.

"Watch it, buster. This purse is a registered weapon."

Scott lifted her purse-wrapped hand and kissed it. He grinned at her surprised expression, then turned to watch the receiving line.

"It's getting kinda warm standing here in the sun. You think this is worth it?"

Kim swung her purse back onto her shoulder and shrugged.

"Probably not. It's just that I have a feeling someone close to the Hamptons is involved. Let's face it: Most of our current suspects are meaner than smart."

She scanned the faces of the people milling underneath the canopy.

"So we're looking for an organizing genius with a grudge against the Hamptons and the ability to control not one, not two, but three thugs."

"I know it sounds far-fetched, but . . ."

Kim's voice trailed away as she spotted Connie the caterer directing servers to add champagne glasses to the tables.

Hmmm . . . Connie seemed exceptional at organizing as well as controlling her employees' behavior. Though Donny Driver acted too chauvinistic to take orders from a woman, his over inflated ego made him the perfect sucker for a woman who knew how to manipulate.

"If you're thinking about the caterer," Scott said, "she's too young to be Amy Sawyer in disguise."

"Could be her daughter," Kim said. "Amy might have married and had children. If she took her husband's last name, we'd have difficulty finding her or identifying one of her children."

Scott folded his arms.

"You really think Amy Sawyer's daughter moved back to this small town simply to terrorize the Hamptons?"

"Of course not. But I could easily imagine Amy's daughter returning here to search for the stolen emerald. Remember, both Amy and Tommy believed the emerald belonged to their families. And Amy was more obsessive about finding it than Tommy. I could well imagine a daughter moving here and developing a business relationship with the Hamptons to cover her interest in the emerald."

She paused when she saw Deb motioning them

over. The reception line had ended. People now clustered around tables.

"I need to talk with Kim a minute," Deb said to her family, "so you all go in and eat. Sit at the reserved table. You'll find menus there so you can tell the server what you want."

She waited until the others were out of hearing range, then turned to Kim.

"I found someone who knew Amy Sawyer when they were children!"

Kim grinned. "That was fast work."

Deb's smile was sad. "I don't think we have much time. Walt won't give me details about the investigation, but he acts like he's preparing me for the worst."

Kim silently wished Aunt Ginny luck with the handsome sheriff. People sometimes confessed the most personal information to strangers. Aunt Ginny's sincere interest often triggered people into revealing more than they'd intended.

To Deb, Kim tried to convey confidence.

"Well, let's give the sheriff an alternative suspect."

Deb turned her electric wheelchair toward the pavilion.

"See the table in the back corner? The lady in the hat is Pat Wellington. She went to school with Amy Sawyer. I asked her to save two seats for you so you can talk."

While Deb joined her family, Kim and Scott

approached the back table. As they neared, she recognized the Kentucky Derby hat woman, the one who'd paused to shake Jack's paw. Good. Kim always felt at ease with dog lovers.

And, sure enough, two seats remained empty to the woman's right. On her left, however . . .

Aunt Ginny grinned up at her.

"Don't you just love Pat's hat?" Ginny said. "She designed it herself. I told her we should start a collection of designer hats and sell them on the internet."

Remembering the hat her aunt had worn to the Gem Festival, Kim grinned.

"Ms. Wellington's hat is gorgeous, but I don't think there's a market for your designs, Aunt Ginny."

"What's wrong with my designs?"

"Most people won't appreciate birds sitting on their hats," Kim said.

Pat Wellington came to Ginny's defense.

"Oh, but the Victorians used to perch stuffed birds on their hats. It was quite chic back then."

"Yeah, but I bet their birds weren't wearing googly eyes," Kim said.

It took a moment for Ginny's new friend to imagine a stuffed parrot sporting googly eyes peering down from a fancy hat. She guffawed.

Ginny folded her arms.

"Those googly eyes have become my signature. You only know it's a Ginny Donaldson original by the eyes."

Male laughter drew Kim's eyes to Ginny's left. Sheriff Spits sat next to Ginny with Grandpa on the sheriff's far side.

Kim settled into her seat. Sure enough, a monogrammed menu perched in the center of each table setting. Guests could choose an entree of chicken, beef or vegetarian. Side dishes included pasta, potato and vegetable salads. She was relieved to find iced tea on the menu.

A waitress appeared to take their orders. As soon as she left to collect their drinks, Kim turned to Pat Wellington.

"Did Deb tell you why I'm trying to locate Amy Sawyer?"

Pat nodded. "You do know I haven't seen Amy since she ran away, right?"

"That's okay. I'm just trying to learn everything I can about her. You never know what tidbit might help me find her."

Pat sipped her water before beginning.

"To understand Amy, you need to hear about her mother. Donalda Sawyer was one of those Rosie the Riveter types. You know who that was, right?"

"I've seen the posters," Kim said.

The cartoon-like drawing celebrated women who worked in factories and shipyards during World War II.

"Well, Donalda believed women could do anything men could and she conveyed that to her daughter. She even let Amy wear bib overalls to school."

Pat grinned at the what's-wrong-with-that expression on Kim's face.

"You have to understand, this was in the late 40s, early 50s, when girls wore gathered skirts, ruffled sweaters and frilled socks. We were being trained to be good little housewives who supported our some-day husbands.

"But Amy refused to play with the dolls and tea sets. During recess, she climbed the Monkey Bars. The boys weren't quite sure what to make of Amy, either, especially since she ran faster than most of them. So Amy didn't have many friends."

"Poor child."

"Don't worry," Pat said. "In third grade, everything changed when Amy punched George Dominion in the nose."

"I take it George wasn't well liked?"

"Oh, George was the class bully. He was bigger than the other boys and could intimidate all of us into giving him our favorite marble or our lunch or our last pencil. None of our families were wealthy, so losing school supplies was disastrous. But we were too afraid to say 'no' to George.

"Then one day, when the teachers weren't looking, George demanded Marty Stone's lunchbox. The Stone family was poorer than the rest of ours and Marty's lunchbox probably contained nothing more than an apple. The box itself was a hand-me-down from Marty's older brother and the picture of Hopalong Cassidy on the outside was dented and faded.

"But George wanted that lunchbox. And even though we knew George was wrong, we were all afraid to interfere because we didn't want him picking on us.

"Amy, however, marched over and punched George in the nose.

"George's nose started bleeding and he dropped his own lunchbox so he could use both hands to cover his nose. Amy opened George's lunchbox, removed his sandwich and gave it to Marty."

"That took a lot of nerve," Kim said.

"Amy had a strong sense of right and wrong. She always complained when she thought something wasn't fair or just. So punching George was an automatic response to his bullying."

"How did George react?" Kim knew from experience that bullies often backed down when challenged.

Despite the warm air, Pat shivered.

"He turned into a raging animal. The muscles on his neck corded and his nostrils flared and his lips pulled back to bare his teeth. And his eyes! People talk about seeing the whites of someone's eyes, but this was worse. When I looked into George's dark pupils, I saw evil.

"Before I could warn Amy, George threw himself at her. They fell to the ground with George on top and he started punching and kicking. I screamed for help. But the teachers were too far away.

"And then, from out of nowhere, Tommy Hicks appeared. He'd found a huge branch somewhere. He swung it hard enough to knock George off of Amy."

Pat paused as the waitress set drinks and salads in front of them. Before continuing, she reached for her iced tea. Her hand shook.

Kim touched Pat's arm.

"I'm sorry for asking you to relive this."

Pat brushed aside her apology.

"Oh, I'm just being overly sensitive. It all worked out for everyone except Tommy."

"But didn't you just say Tommy was the hero?"

"Yes, and that's what we told the principal. But she didn't believe us. Several of the other teachers had seen Tommy swing that branch and since he was a Hicks, they just assumed he'd instigated the whole thing. Amy told them what happened, but they didn't believe her, either."

Kim shook her head, disgusted. No wonder Tommy didn't trust outsiders.

"They were going to expel Tommy," Pat continued, "but Amy's mother put a stop to that. We were standing in the hallway when Donalda marched into the principal's office. Even with the door closed, we could hear her shouting."

"Did she win?"

"You betcha. Tommy remained in school and the

rest of us started including him and Amy in our games."

"What about George?"

Pat grinned. "He threatened to get even, of course. But then one day he came to school with a black eye and he never bothered any of us ever again."

"Who gave him the black eye? Tommy?"

"Doubt it. Tommy was about half George's weight. My guess is that one of Tommy's cousins took George aside and convinced him to leave Tommy alone."

The waitress arrived with their food. Kim had ordered the beef, asking that they not season it. To her delight, the meat was tender, juicy and plentiful enough for extras to use to train Rory. She cut off a chunk and set it aside.

"So the fight with George happened in third grade?" She did a quick calculation in her head. "This was a year or so before Amy's father died?"

Pat nodded. "It's such a shame because after her father's death, Amy just wasn't the same. Her grades plummeted. She angered easily. There were rumors that her foster parents sexually abused her."

Kim's stomach clenched and her skin suddenly felt too tight. She resisted the urge to bolt from the table.

Tales of abuse, whether physical, sexual or psychological, always sickened her. Even though whatever happened to Amy Sawyer occurred half a century ago, she still wanted to reach out and protect the girl.

Sensing Kim's discomfort, Pat laid a hand over hers.

"Don't worry," she said. "Tommy helped Amy run away."

CHAPTER 22

"I've heard that Amy Sawyer ran away," Kim said. "But no one said anything about Tommy Hicks helping her."

Pat shrugged. "I don't have proof that Tommy helped. But remember, teenage runaways weren't as common in the 1950s as they became in the 1960s. Amy didn't have the option of using a home computer to print a fake ID. Yet she managed to disappear without a trace. She couldn't have done that without help."

"And before you mention serial killers and sexual predators," Pat added, "you need to know that three months after Amy disappeared, Tommy told everyone that Amy was okay. Said he'd received a postcard from her."

"Did anyone see this postcard or confirm it was Amy's handwriting?"

"Tommy wouldn't show it to anyone. He said the postmark would give away Amy's location. When word spread, of course, police questioned Tommy. But he denied everything."

"Yet you still believed him," Kim said.

Pat ran a finger across the lip of her iced tea glass.

"I like to imagine that Amy met a nice man, married, had children and lived a normal life."

Kim bit her tongue. Most runaways lived on the streets, begging for food or money, seeking shelter beneath bridges or in doorways. They did not live happily ever after.

But she wasn't about to argue with her table mate. Why shatter her illusions?

The waitress appeared. Kim asked for a box for the meat she'd set aside for Rory. She leaned back to sip her tea and tuned in to the conversations around her.

Scott was discussing local ecology with a fish and game scientist. Aunt Ginny and Sheriff Spits had their heads together, the sheriff talking while Ginny listened with wide, attentive eyes. Grandpa had turned away from Ginny and the sheriff and was listening to a man lamenting the demise of old-fashioned pocket watches.

"A pocket watch said you were classy, know what I mean?" the man said. "When you wanted to impress someone, you whipped out your watch and paused just slightly so the fellow could see the gold decorations before flipping it open, know what I mean? And if you wanted to be really obnoxious, you glanced at the watch face, flipped it shut with a loud snap and announced you must depart, the implication being you had more important things to do than shoot the breeze with the people around you."

He turned around and slapped the back of a man seated at the next table.

"Like Mikey here. He's always showing off his pocket watch. Show Max your watch, Mikey."

Michael Dunning scowled.

"The name is Michael."

"Michael, Mikey, Mike, whatever, ya need to show Max your watch. He's a jeweler."

"I'm actually interested, Mr. Dunning," Grandpa said.

With a sigh, the red-headed lawyer reached into his jacket pocket and produced his pocket watch. Grandpa held the watch by the edges and gazed down.

"Hey, that's different from the one you usually carry," the pushy man said.

Michael bristled.

"I have more than one watch. This is my dress watch. It's solid gold."

"Actually, it's more likely gold-filled," Grandpa said. "Don't make that face. This beauty was handmade."

Kim leaned across the table. The center of the watch cover featured a majestic stag, his head held at a regal tilt. Small flowers, their petals colored blue, red and yellow with gemstones, circled the deer's head.

Grandpa pointed at the cover design.

"The early Victorians used natural images like flowers and animals in their jewelry designs."

He turned the watch over. A simpler flower motif adorned the back. Letters carved into the center appeared to be a monogram, but from a distance, Kim couldn't read the ornate letters.

"Gorgeous workmanship," Grandpa said.

"Did I get cheated?" Michael said. "The watch I inherited from my grandfather was one of those cheap, souvenir things. I wanted something classier for special occasions. The salesman said this watch was worth well over a thousand and I paid less than half that."

"You got yourself a bargain."

Grandpa returned the watch.

"The age of the piece -- that would be late 1800s, early 1900s -- coupled with the workmanship and the fact that it was handmade would bring a pretty penny from collectors."

Michael smiled, his whole face suddenly cheerful and attractive.

"It's a pleasure talking to someone who's knowledgeable about these things."

The pocket-watch aficionado slapped Michael's back.

"See? You didn't need to be so uppity, know what I mean?"

Kim bit her lip to keep from smiling and turned away. Across the room, she spotted the caterer talking with Deb. Jack, perched on Deb's lap, shifted his head from Deb to Connie and back as if he was watching a tennis match.

"Do you know anything about the caterer?" Kim asked Pat.

Pat glanced across the room and shrugged.

"Only that she's excellent. She's been in business here only a year or so. I'm not sure how Deb discovered her, but Deb's recommendation has made Connie the top caterer in the area."

"Does she remind you at all of Amy Sawyer?"

Pat's eyes widened. Turning, she studied the caterer. A third woman had joined them and said something to make Deb and Connie laugh. Still smiling, Connie waved her hands as she talked, clearly telling a story that Kim couldn't hear.

She glanced at Pat in time to see her shoulders slump.

"I just don't know," Pat said. "Her hair and eye color are similar. She's got Amy's confidence, but so do thousands of young women. Nothing particularly strikes me as 'this is Amy's daughter.'

"But it's been such a long time. If Amy had children, one of them could be sitting beside me and I wouldn't know unless he or she was the spitting image of their mother. And how likely is that?"

Kim admitted it was a longshot.

"Deb might know more," Pat said. "People seem to tell her things."

Kim frowned. People seem to tell her things. She'd heard that line recently. Where-- Oh.

"Someone told me Betty Hicks's mother has a reputation for eliciting confidences."

Pat nodded. "Amanda Corning teaches high school chemistry and the students love her. If we'd had teachers like her in my day, maybe Amy would have confided in someone and gotten help."

"Is Mrs. Corning here? I'd like to meet her."

Pat grinned. "She's standing with Connie and Deb."

Surprised, Kim looked closer at the woman who'd made the others laugh. Amanda Corning shared her daughter's blue eyes, button nose, full lips and infectious smile. The combination that made Betty Hicks cute, however, created a more sultry effect in the mother. Unlike Betty, Amanda had had her brown hair professionally highlighted to make the most of her light complexion.

Deb suddenly spun her wheelchair around and aimed it toward the canopy exit. Amanda Corning strolled beside her.

As the two women disappeared from sight, Kim laid her napkin on the table.

"Excuse me," she said, rising. "I'll be back in a few minutes."

She wove her way to the edge of the canopy and paused to search the grounds.

In this part of the estate, landscapers had pushed back the forest to plant rolling lawn dotted with small shrubs and flower beds. Though pretty, the stark contrast between cultivated and wild left Kim cold. She much preferred Deb's secret rose garden with its surrounding wall and welcoming smells and textures. Out here, she could easily imagine the forest marching in to reclaim its kingdom much as Malcolm had disguised his troops with branches to descend on Macbeth.

Reasoning that Deb's motorized wheelchair would require a solid base, Kim followed the only concrete path that stretched in the direction she'd seen the women disappear.

The path wound downhill toward the house. Kim passed a stand of evergreens before hearing voices. A final curve brought her to the rear of the house.

A fenced yard, maybe 30 by 40 feet, stretched from the house toward the woods. Inside Jack sniffed the fence edges, his plumy tail raised in the typical dog don't-bother-me-I'm-tracking fashion.

Deb and her guest had remained outside of the fence. Kim called a greeting and the two women smiled a warm welcome.

"I'm sorry to interrupt," Kim said, "but I've been wanting to meet Ms. Corning."

Betty Hicks's mother smile wavered.

"You look too young to be an unhappy parent . . ."

"This is Kimberley West," Deb said. "She's a friend of Charlie's fiancé and is trying to help us clear Charlie's name. Kim, this is Amanda Corning."

"Please call me Amanda," Betty's mother said, holding out her hand.

For a few minutes, the three women exchanged pleasantries, then Kim steered the conversation back to recent events.

"Everyone tells me people like to confide in you," Kim began.

Amanda interrupted with a laugh. "I hate to disappoint you, but no one's confessed to killing Kirk Ballas."

"Actually, I wanted to talk with you both about the caterer. Do you know anything about Connie?"

"Other than she's a great cook?" Amanda smiled.

"Well, for starters, what's her last name?"

"Taylor," Deb said. "She told me she was going to call her business 'Taylor Catering', but decided 'Connie's Catering' was more memorable."

"Is Taylor her married name?"

Deb's eyes widened. "You think she might be Amy Sawyer's daughter?"

"Amy Sawyer?" Amanda said. "Isn't she the girl who ran away after her family was killed?"

"Your daughter recommended I track her down,"

Kim said. "Amy Sawyer and Tommy Hicks both knew their fathers hid the museum emerald in the forest that now belongs to the Hamptons. If we assume Kirk Ballas was killed because someone stumbled on him while conducting their own illegal search, then Amy or one of her descendants could be suspects."

"You know," Deb said, "I have no idea if Connie Taylor is married, divorced or widowed. She never talks about herself."

"I've tried several times to draw her out," Amanda said. "But she always manages to change the subject. Now that I think about it, she's never even revealed her hometown to me."

"Maybe we need to confront her," Deb said.

Kim opened her mouth to disagree, but a change in the breeze carried a sooty odor. Frowning, she sniffed the air, turning slowly, trying to locate the source.

"Do you smell--"

She spotted gray smoke wafting above the roof.

Horrified, Kim ran toward what she hoped was the source of the smoke. She scanned the roof top, but saw no shooting flames. As she neared the corner of the house, she heard shouts. The smell of burning wood grew stronger.

She rounded the corner and slammed to a halt. At the edge of the forest -- only 30 or so feet from the house -- orange, red and yellow flames greedily devoured a bush and scattered brush.

To her left, people were leaving the canopy, pausing to gawk at the fire. Mark Hampton, his sons and Scott started running toward her. The whir of Deb's wheelchair alerted her to her hostess's arrival. Amanda Corning quickly joined them.

"I've called the fire department," Amanda said.

But even as she spoke, the fire made a popping sound and sparks flew onto the nearby dry grass. The grass ignited and began crawling toward the house.

The fire department would never arrive in time.

"Do you have an outside faucet and hose?" Kim asked Deb.

Deb nodded and pointed.

"It's on the other side of the house, about a third of the way back. You'll see the hose hanging above it."

As Kim ran past the front of the house, more sparks ignited dry lawn. Kim dodged a sudden flame, the smoke now burning her nostrils. She skidded around the corner and spotted the coiled hose hanging on the side of the house.

She ripped the hose from its holder. Fortunately, it was already hooked to the faucet. She turned the faucet as wide open as possible, then twisted the nozzle on the hose to stop the water flow. Praying the hose was long enough, she clutched the end and ran back toward the fire.

She found the men using their dinner jackets to beat out the small patches of burning grass. But the original fire continued to spew flaming debris into the air, igniting wherever it touched dry grass.

Kim opened the hose nozzle and aimed the water at the patches of fire closest to the house. The fire sizzled and hissed and emitted dark gray smoke. Kim coughed, but resisted the urge to turn away. After seconds that seemed like hours, the water reduced the most dangerous flames to smoldering ash.

She pointed the hose toward the original burning brush. Her eyes watered from the smoke and her throat felt raw and scratchy.

Finally, over the roar of the fire and shouts of the guests, a siren wailed.

Warm arms wrapped around her.

"I've got it," Scott said as he pulled the hose from her hands. "You might want to see if Deb needs any help."

Gratefully, Kim allowed Scott to take over the hose. As she hurried toward Deb, a fire engine raced up the driveway. Men poured from the truck and began unwinding professional hoses. Mark Hampton strode over to the tall man who was clearly in charge.

Grandpa and Aunt Ginny had joined Deb and Amanda. Grandpa stood behind Deb, a soothing hand laying on her shoulder.

Deb's face had drained of all color. Judging by the tension in her neck and shoulders, she was using every ounce of strength to remain upright.

"Is there anything I can do for you?" Kim said.

"Actually, yes," Deb said. "Could you find Jack for me? He was sniffing something near the fence and refused to come when I called him. So I left him in his potty area. He might have entered the house through his doggie door or he might still be in the fenced yard. He likes you so he'll probably come when you call."

Kim assured Deb that she'd find the little dog.

Reasoning that Jack would have smelled the smoke and remained outside, she headed toward the rear of the house. As she approached the fenced-in area, she called his name. But he didn't respond.

She scanned the small enclosure. Jack wasn't there. He must have gone inside.

Rather than trudge all the way around to the front door, Kim opened the gate and, after carefully closing it behind her, crossed to the side door. It was locked. Frustrated, she knocked on the door. No one responded. She waited a few minutes, then knocked again. Again no response.

She sighed. Everyone, including Deb's staff, were probably outside watching the fire department. Odd, though, that Jack hadn't responded to the knock. Papillons, despite their small size, were good watch dogs.

Maybe he'd respond if she called through his dog door. She kneeled and pushed on the papillon-sized flap that separated interior from exterior. It wouldn't move. She pushed harder. Still nothing. Like its larger counterpart, the dog door was locked.

She stood and once again scanned the yard. Had Jack, trapped here when the fire department arrived, dug his way out?

She walked the perimeter, scanning the bottom of the fence for signs of digging. Nothing.

Could he have squeezed through the gate? She pushed at it. No, with the gate locked, the gap wasn't wide enough for the little dog to slip through.

Once again, she studied the fence. Maybe four feet high, it would never contain a determined poodle. Rory would have cleared it with a single bound; smaller poodles would simply use the chain links to climb out.

Perhaps that's what Jack did.

She headed back toward the front of the house, periodically pausing to whistle and call Jack's name.

Relief washed over her when she saw the firemen rolling hoses, storing gear and preparing to leave. The Hamptons and a few of their friends had gathered in a loose group near the front steps. Amanda Corning and Mark Hampton flanked Deb's wheelchair like two sentinels prepared to battle anyone who approached. Rachael clung to Charlie, oblivious to the soot rubbing off on her designer dress. Charlie's two brothers huddled with

Michael Dunning.

Aunt Ginny, Grandpa and Scott stood a short distance away, their eyes focused not on the firemen but on the scorched trees at the edge of the forest where something moved.

Jack?

A low-hanging branch parted and Sheriff Spits appeared. In one hand, he carried something wrapped in a handkerchief. Noting his grim expression, Kim's breath caught.

She watched the sheriff trudge over to the fireman who'd been in charge. Extending his hand, he pulled back part of the handkerchief to reveal a scorched, rectangular-shaped can.

Kim breathed again.

She joined Scott and her family.

"Have any of you seen Jack? He wasn't in the back yard."

No one had seen the little dog. A knot formed in Kim's stomach.

"Have you tried the house?" Grandpa said. "Someone might have let him in and then locked up afterwards."

Okay. That made sense. All she had to do was trot up the front steps, open the door and whistle or call for Jack, right?

So why was she reluctant to take those few steps?

Before she moved, Sheriff Spits approached the Hamptons.

"Do you use charcoal lighter fluid?" he asked.

"Of course not," Mark said. "We've got a gas grill that works perfectly well."

Sheriff Spits nodded. "I was afraid of that."

He held out the can he'd been showing the fire chief. The scorched label read "premium lighter fluid."

"Someone intentionally started this fire," he said.

Deb moaned and Mark placed a protective hand on her shoulder.

"That makes no sense," Mark said. "If someone wanted to burn me out, why not just set fire to the house?"

"Maybe he was afraid to expose himself," Charlie said. "Setting the fire closer to the forest allowed him to hide behind a tree."

"Even so," Mark said, "the fire was too far from the house to do much, if any, damage."

"Maybe it was a warning," the sheriff said.

"Or a diversion," Kim said.

All eyes turned her way. Rachael asked the question on everyone's face.

"Why a diversion?"

Kim focused on her friend, afraid to even glance toward Deb.

"So someone could kidnap Jack."

She heard Deb's gasp and the sound of the wheelchair speeding toward the ramp. Charlie and his brothers ran up the front stairs and flung open the door. She could hear doors open and close, footsteps pounding, voices calling the papillon's name.

Though Kim longed to join the search, she didn't want to invade the Hamptons' privacy by poking through their house. So she remained outside with Grandpa, Aunt Ginny, Rachael and Scott.

"But I don't understand," Rachael said. "Why would someone kidnap Jack? Are service dogs worth that much?"

"Last time I talked to someone about it," Kim said, "service dogs cost upward of $20,000."

Everyone gasped.

"Trust me, the dogs are worth the cost. They're bred specifically for health and temperament. Then they have to be trained. Then the prospective owners have to be trained. All of that takes time and money."

"Jack might be worth a lot of money," Scott said, "but how many people would know the cost of a service dog?"

Kim shrugged. "An internet search would probably list prices. But if you've seen Deb with Jack, you'd know she'd pay a lot to bring him home. You can set a price for a well-bred, well-trained dog, but not on the bond that develops between dog and human."

She heard the front door open and turned to see Charlie step outside. He met their eyes and confirmed Kim's fear.

The little dog was gone.

CHAPTER 23

While guests began to leave, Kim escaped to the guest room to shower off the smoke smell. She changed back into her jeans and flannel shirt and joined the others in the library.

Grandpa and Aunt Ginny perched on the overstuffed sofa. Charlie, his two brothers and the red-headed lawyer stood nearby. Deb sat beside the fireplace, gripping a portable phone. Mark stood behind his wife's wheelchair, one hand stroking her shoulder, his expression alternating between rage and sorrow.

Charlie broke the tense silence.

"Donny Driver is the only person I can think of who's mean enough to steal Mom's dog," he said.

"Then let's go get the s.o.b." Diesel cracked his knuckles. "I'll convince him to give us Jack."

"You can't just go around beating up people," Michael Dunning said. "Or, if that's what you plan, don't tell me about it. You could get me disbarred."

"I've got no problem beating up whoever stole Jack," Jake said. "First, however, we have to find him."

"Didn't Donny inherit that trailer house from his uncle?" Diesel said. "We can start there."

"Donny may be careless," Michael said, "but I doubt he'd be stupid enough to hide Jack in his own house."

The four men continued to argue. Kim turned to Scott.

"I can't think of any way this is going to end well," she whispered. "If the thieves are smart, they'll insist Mark wire money into a foreign account. Why risk capture by staging a physical exchange?"

"I doubt whoever took Jack knows how to set up a foreign account," he said.

"Even so," she said, "the thieves have no reason to keep Jack alive. It's not like Deb can demand to speak to him before handing over the money."

She glanced at Deb, then quickly away. The pain etched on the woman's face brought tears to Kim's eyes.

Scott squeezed her hand.

"Jack's inability to talk may save his life. He can't

testify against the kidnappers, so they have no reason to kill him. After the thieves are paid, it'd be easy enough to drop Jack at a local shelter or beside a road."

Michael's raised voice drew Kim's attention.

"If you all would listen a moment," he said, "I think I have a possible solution."

When the room grew silent, the lawyer said "Why don't I drive to Donnie's trailer and talk to him?"

"And how is that different from us confronting him?" Diesel said.

Michael's mouth lifted into a wry smile.

"I don't pose a physical threat," he said, indicating his wiry frame. "But I can scare him with the legalities of what he's done. Dogs may not fall under kidnapping laws, but given Jack's value, Donny can be charged with a Class H Felony. Add in the arson and any prior convictions and he could face serious jail time.

"That's assuming, of course, that we can prove he has the dog."

"Look for nose prints on the inside of the windows," Kim said.

Michael snorted. "What good's that going to do? Donny will just claim they belong to a friend's dog."

"Sorry," Kim said. "I forgot you weren't here when we talked about dogs' noses. Their nose prints are as individual as human fingerprints.

"That means we can match the nose print on these windows--" Kim gestured toward the nose print studded windows -- "with prints found in Donny's home or truck."

"And if you actually find Jack," Deb said, "we can prove he's mine by scanning the microchip that we had inserted between his shoulders."

Michael nodded. "All good to know."

"You don't need to do this," Mark said. "We'll pay whatever he wants to return Jack."

"And give him the option of coming back for more? Better if I can stop this right now. I'll call when I know something."

Kim watched Michael leave, then pulled a chair close to Aunt Ginny and Grandpa. Scott joined them. The minutes ticked by in silence. The flames in the fireplace failed to offer solace.

Twenty minutes passed before Mark's cell phone rang. Everyone leaned forward. Mark's shoulders slumped.

"Thanks for trying," he said. "Yeah, we'll wait here."

Hanging up, he turned to the others.

"Michael said Donny's trailer was deserted. But Michael is going to drive around, see if he can spot Donny's pickup truck."

He squeezed his wife's hand. "Don't worry; we'll bring Jack home safe and sound."

Deb stared at the portable phone clenched in her hand. A maid served coffee and tea. Mark carried coffee to his wife. She ignored the proffered cup.

The phone in Deb's lap broke the silence.

"No caller ID," she said before punching the talk button.

"Hello?" Her brows furrowed. "You want me to put this on speaker? Oh, okay."

Pulling the phone from her ear, she punched a button and set the phone onto her lap. "You're now on speaker."

"Is the sheriff present?" The robotic voice had clearly been altered by some device. "Sheriff Spits, if you're there, speak up."

Kim shivered. The kidnapper sounded eerily like Darth Vader.

"Walt isn't here," Deb said. "It's just family and houseguests."

"Good. Keep it that way-- Shut that mutt up!"

The kidnapper must have moved the phone from his ear because now they could hear a small dog barking in the background.

"Jack!" Deb screeched into the phone. "Oh, Jack! Please don't hurt him."

Everyone leaned toward the phone. Kim could hear scrabbling, followed by a human yelp, followed by a slammed door and more barking.

"I hope that damned dog has all his shots," the Vader voice said.

"Did you hurt him?" Deb said.

"No. But that doesn't mean I won't. Now listen up. Here's how this is going to work.

"Mark Hampton, you will drive alone to the bank and withdraw $25,000 in fives, tens and twenties--"

"It's Sunday, asshole," Diesel said. "The banks are closed."

In the background, a male voice said, "I told you this isn't going to work!"

"If you return Jack now," Deb said, "we'll get your money when the banks open."

"You will get the money now!" Darth Vader boomed.

"Do you think I keep that kind of money laying around in petty cash?" Mark said.

"I don't care how you get it," the kidnapper said. "If you want this mutt back in one piece, you will put $25,000 into one of your fancy gym bags and wait for my call.

"You have one hour."

"There's no way I'm going to be able to collect that much cash in an hour," Mark protested.

"Well, I'm not keeping this mutt longer than another hour. Tell me now if you don't want it back. I can get a few bucks selling it to the owner of the local dog fight establishment. They always need new meat."

Deb screamed and burst into tears. Kim rushed to her side and pulled her into her arms.

"You're the only one who understands," Deb said.

Over the sobs, Kim heard Mark assuring the kidnapper that he'd do whatever was necessary to obtain the money.

"You have one hour," the mechanical voice said before clicking off.

Mark pushed Kim aside to hug his wife. As Kim stepped back, Deb's hand shot out and snagged Kim's hand, latching on in a death grip. Kim used her free hand to pat Deb's in what she hoped was a reassuring gesture and stared uncomfortably into space.

"It's okay," Mark said. "I might have enough money in the home and office safes to cover most of it. We can borrow any shortage from friends."

"Then . . . then why did you tell him you couldn't?"

"You should never accept the first offer when negotiating."

Deb released Kim's hand and whipped around in her chair to glare up at her husband.

"You're treating this as a negotiation? This is Jack's life!"

"Honey, I'm not going to let anyone hurt Jack--"

"Then why are you just standing here?" Deb clenched her fists. "You only have an hour! Go! Just go!"

Turning back around, she wheeled out of the room. Mark hesitated, then followed.

"Did you recognize the second voice on the phone?" Charlie said to his brothers. "That sounded like Rocky DiSoto."

"So Donny definitely has Jack." Diesel cracked

his knuckles. "Let's go find him."

"Find him where?" Jake said. "Michael is already out looking for him. We need to stay here and help Dad."

The three brothers started to argue. Kim tuned them out and gripped Scott's hand.

"There must be a way to figure out where Donny's hiding Jack," she said. "Do you know how to search property records? Maybe Donny or his buddy Rocky has a boat or a cabin or something."

"It's Sunday," Scott said. "Courthouse is closed."

"Won't that stuff be on the internet?"

When Scott nodded, Kim trotted toward the front door.

"C'mon. My computer is at the cabin."

CHAPTER 24

Kim flew into her room to retrieve her laptop. Donny had said he'd call back in an hour and they'd already wasted eight minutes extricating themselves from the chaos at the mansion and driving back to the cabin.

If they were going to find Jack, they needed to do so before Donny gave Mark instructions for the exchange.

With Rory and Al at her heels, she returned to the kitchen and set the computer on the table in front of Scott.

"You look while I deal with the dogs," she said.

Several minutes later, she brought the dogs inside and poured fresh water into their bowls.

"I'm not finding anything," Scott said. "Donny Driver owns his trailer and pickup truck, but no other property."

She leaned over Scott's shoulder and peered at the computer screen.

"What about his friend, Rocky DiSoto?"

"Is Rocky his real name?"

He returned to the public records search page and began typing.

"I'm not sure."

She pulled her cell phone from a pocket. "I can ask Charlie."

"Don't bother," he said. "I've got him."

Kim held her breath, conscious of the ticking clock.

Mark Hampton might have agreed to follow the kidnappers' orders, but she had learned the hard way that kidnappers were unpredictable.

A few months ago, one of Aunt Ginny's friends had been kidnapped. Kim would never forget walking that long, dark parking lot clutching the ransom to find a crazy man pointing a gun at her.

The life in danger then had been human, not canine. But Jack's kidnapper had sounded just as desperate.

And desperate people behaved irrationally.

"Doesn't look like Rocky owns any property," Scott said.

Kim frowned. If the kidnappers had been smart, they'd have stowed Jack in a crate in their car and parked somewhere isolated. But when the kidnappers had called and Jack started barking, she'd heard the distinct sound of a house door slamming shut.

"Maybe Donny brought Jack to a house owned by a relative," she said.

Scott agreed.

"But Driver is a common surname. And he could have relatives with a different last name altogether. We don't have time to trace a family tree, then cross-check with the public records."

"You must have run into this when you were a reporter working under deadline," she said. "What did you do then?"

"Talked to their friends, acquaintances, people they work with. But, other than Rocky DiSoto and the guy who was murdered, we don't know Donny's associates."

Kim reached for her phone.

"No. But I bet Betty's mother knows."

She called Betty Hicks to ask for her mother's phone number. When Betty heard what happened to Jack, she offered to alert her husband and his family.

"There are a lot of small, unoccupied cabins in these woods," Betty said. "People think they're going to come here to hunt, then lose interest or time. It'd be easy for Donny to break into one of those."

Kim's shoulder sank.

"If that's the case, we'll never find Jack. We don't have time to investigate every single cabin."

"Talk to Mom," Betty said. "She might have some ideas. In the meantime, Brian and his cousins can start looking. They know these woods better than anyone."

Kim thanked Betty, then dialed Amanda Corning.

"None of Donny's close relatives are alive," Amanda said. "When Donny was 16, his parents died in a car crash and he went to live with his uncle. But the uncle died a few years back and I don't think there's anyone else.

"Oh, this makes me so mad. Everyone knows Deb thinks the world of Jack. This is just the sort of nasty scheme Donny Driver would concoct."

"Why do you say that?"

Perhaps understanding Donny might help her figure out where he was hiding.

"Even as a child," Amanda said, "Donny went out of his way to hurt others. You know how children go through phases where they pull pranks? While the other children might let the air out of tires or smear soap on windows, Donny targeted people's valued possessions.

"When he was 11 or 12, he sprayed a slow-acting weed killer onto Bill McCarthy's prized rose bush. This was a week before those roses were to be entered into the rose society competition. Poor Mr. McCarthy went outside to cut his roses only to find the petals lying on the ground."

"That was his idea of a prank? I'm surprised he didn't end up in reform school."

"Well, he did settle down a bit in high school. The industrial arts teacher channeled some of Donny's aggression into car repair and welding. But after Donny's parents died, he reverted to his old ways. I don't know how his uncle tolerated living with Donny in that tiny trailer house."

"Is that the same trailer Donny owns now?"

"The very same. He inherited it when-- Oh, wait! I believe Donny's uncle also owned a hunting cabin. Donny should have inherited that, too."

Kim sat forward. "We didn't find a record of a cabin."

"Maybe Donny sold it."

"Or maybe he didn't transfer it into his own name. What was the uncle's name?"

"Samuel Bishop."

Kim repeated the name to Scott, who immediately began typing.

"Got it," he said.

She quickly thanked Amanda for her help, hung up and peered over Scott's shoulder.

"It's still in the uncle's name."

He typed the address into Google maps, then switched to satellite view.

The cabin was located deep in the woods. Other cabins dotted the area, but Donny's was the most isolated.

She pointed to the closest dwelling. While the

other buildings sported the peaked, brown roofs and square shape of classic cabins, this one appeared long, narrow and white.

"What's that?"

"Looks like a trailer--"

Scott's eyes widened. Opening a new screen, he typed in an address, switched to satellite, then compared the view to the one showing the cabin.

"We've got him," he said.

"This--" he pointed at the long dwelling -- "is the trailer Donny inherited from his uncle. And this is his hunting cabin."

"Is it close enough to walk from one to another?"

"Looks like it's two miles, so, yeah."

Kim leaped to her feet.

"Can you print a copy of that map? Let's check it out. You drive and I'll call Sheriff Spits and ask him to meet us there."

She tried to return the dogs to their room, but they refused to cooperate. Al ducked behind the sofa. Rory planted his feet and wouldn't move.

"Okay, you guys can come, but you need to be quiet."

She opened the car's back doors and secured the dogs in their seatbelts. As they drove, Kim called Sheriff Spits.

The sheriff, however, was still working with the fire marshal and couldn't be disturbed. Reluctant to deal with another officer, Kim left a message.

Hanging up, she checked the time. Donny would

be calling the Hamptons in 30 minutes.

Kim's fists clenched, wrinkling the map she held. She forced herself to breathe deeply and relax her hands. But the words "not enough time, not enough time" continued to drum through her mind.

The narrow road wound up the hill. In the dimming light, the trees that appeared colorful in the sun now looked stark and menacing. Up ahead, a break in the trees indicated a new road or driveway leading right.

She studied the map. "This should be it."

Scott stopped the car at the base of a gravel driveway and they peered up it. About fifty feet in, the road bent to the left. There was no sign of a cabin.

"We should probably approach on foot," Scott said.

Kim glanced into the backseat where Rory and Al were strapped into their respective seat belts. Bringing the dogs with them would prevent stealth. One of the dogs might bark and expose them.

The weather was cool enough to leave them in the car with the windows open. But she didn't want to leave them here, so close to the main road.

She looked at the map, searching for a place to hide the car with the dogs in it.

"The driveway is long and winding," she said. "Maybe we can find a place to back the car into the trees."

Scott nodded and drove slowly. The ping of

gravel against the car's underside sounded unnaturally loud. About half way up the hill, they found a mostly level shoulder where the trees had thinned. Scott backed the car in between two scraggly looking maples. Branches from a tall bush partially shielded the car from the driveway. With any luck, a casual glance from a passing car wouldn't expose them.

Scott opened the windows. Kim made sure the two dogs were securely strapped in.

"I think we're parked here." Scott pointed to the map. "If so, the cabin is almost directly across from us through these woods. It'd probably be easier to sneak up on the cabin if we cut through the woods, but we might get lost--"

Kim held up her compass. Scott grinned.

"You still carrying that around?"

"Laugh all you want, but this will keep us traveling north/northeast. Follow me."

She plunged into the underbrush.

Wild holly -- with its sharp, pointy leaves -- and thorny blackberries slowed their progress. Every time they veered off track to avoid a thicket of brambles, Kim whipped out her compass to point them in the correct direction. Despite their caution, fallen twigs and branches snapped underfoot.

After what seemed like hours but, in fact, was only five minutes, the cabin came into view.

Maybe 15 feet wide and twice as long, the house had been framed and sided with wood. Two steps led to a small porch. The central front door was flanked by double-hung windows. More windows dotted the side of the cabin. While the windows stood open, black screens and dark curtains shielded the interior from view. But light peeking through gaps in the curtains indicated someone was inside.

A single red pickup was parked in front.

Now that they were here, none of Kim's planned approaches seemed feasible. She'd hoped to watch from a safe distance, using the windows to track the people inside. The closed curtains ruined that plan.

The alternative plan was to sneak around the house, trying to find cracks in the curtains to peer in. But the movement might prompt Jack to bark and give her away.

The open windows offered a third option: Move close enough to eavesdrop. But would any movement trigger barking from Jack?

Before she could decide what to do, a loud pop sounded from inside the cabin. Scott threw Kim to the ground, then sprawled across her, shielding her from a second gunshot.

The screen on one of the side windows popped out. A man dived through.

Rocky DiSoto.

Rocky hit the ground hard, rolled to his feet and dashed toward the woods.

A hand holding a gun poked through the curtains. Rocky reached the woods and dodged behind a tree. Another pop-pop and bark flew from the tree trunk. Leaves crunched, footsteps pounded.

In the sudden silence, Al's baying pierced the air. Rory's deeper bark echoed off the trees.

The hand and gun disappeared.

Kim stared at the cabin door, frozen, heartbeat thrumming in her ears. They'd counted on the dim light, scattered trees and underbrush to hide them from the cabin. But none of that offered protection from a flashlight held by a gunman.

Seconds passed. A minute. No one charged through the front door.

"See that large tree to your left?" Scott murmured.

Kim shifted her eyes. A stately oak tree, maybe three feet in diameter, jutted skyward. Though it grew only six or seven feet from where they hid, the distance seemed impossibly far.

"Let's see if we can crawl behind it," he whispered.

"I can't move with you on top of me," she hissed.

While she appreciated Scott's protectiveness, she was starting to feel claustrophobic.

Scott shifted his weight and she wiggled out from under him.

As she inched toward the tree, her mind frivolously identified it as not just an oak, but a white oak. White oaks' exceptionally strong wood made them important timber trees. But would the trunk protect them from bullets?

After what seemed like years, they reached the tree and slid behind it.

Al and Rory continued to bark. From inside the cabin, the yipping of a smaller dog joined in.

"We need to protect Rory and Al," Kim whispered.

As much as she wanted to rescue Jack, she couldn't confront an armed dognapper. But now their own dogs were at risk. The barking would surely draw the gunman to the hidden car.

They needed to drive away and find a safe place to call for help.

"We should wait until--" Scott broke off and cursed.

Kim was already moving, slithering toward a tree deeper into the woods.

She heard Scott following.

Twigs and thorns scratched her hands as she crawled. She banged her knee against an exposed tree root. Biting her lip to keep from crying out, she used her good knee to lift her body up and behind the new tree.

Standing, she rubbed her knee. Scott joined her.

"Don't you think we should wait until whoever is inside leaves?" he whispered.

"No. When he leaves, he'll find Rory and Al."

She peered around the tree trunk. Seeing no movement at the cabin, she took a deep breath and dashed toward the car.

CHAPTER 25

The next 40 minutes passed in a blur. They reached Scott's car to find the dogs unharmed. Piling inside, they raced down the driveway, turned toward the highway and found a pull-out a safe distance from the cabin.

Kim called the sheriff's office and used the magic words: Shots fired.

Sheriff Spits himself came to the phone. She explained what they'd seen and heard. Spits ordered them to wait for him to arrive.

As soon as she disconnected from the sheriff, Kim called Betty Hicks and described what they'd seen at the cabin.

"You'd better warn Brian and his relatives that

there's a gun-toting madman roaming the forest," she said.

As Kim hung up, sirens pierced the night. Police cars zoomed past.

She considered calling Deb to tell her they'd found Jack, but decided to wait until they knew the little dog hadn't been injured.

Instead, she snuggled next to Scott to await the sheriff.

They waited. And waited. And waited.

Finally, the sheriff's car pulled in beside them.

Yes, he'd found Jack and yes, the dog appeared unharmed. The same might not be true of Jack's kidnappers. In the room with Jack, the officers found a torn, blood-stained piece of denim.

Spits refused to say more. He took their statements, then told them to return to the Hamptons' house and to keep themselves available for more questions.

As they drove back to the mansion, Kim finally called Deb.

"Jack is safe," she said when Deb answered the phone. "We'll tell you more when we reach your house."

They arrived at the Hamptons' mansion to find everyone -- including Mark's lawyer -- crowded into the living room.

As they entered, the others hurled questions at them: Did they catch them? What did the sheriff say? When can Jack come home? Did you see the killer?

The cacophony bombarded Kim's already tired mind. Al whimpered and Rory pressed against her leg. Kim resisted the urge to shrink against Scott.

She scanned the crowd, her eyes finally meeting Grandpa's. Though his face was pale with concern, he waggled his eyebrows at her -- a gesture that never failed to bring a smile to her face.

"Let the poor kids catch their breath." Aunt Ginny appeared at Kim's side. "They look exhausted."

Kim allowed her aunt to lead her to a sofa. Scott settled in next to Kim, throwing a protective arm over her shoulders. The dogs plopped onto their feet.

Deb switched into hostess mode and ordered pots of coffee and tea. Mark announced he needed something stronger and crossed to the bar. Rachael, Charlie, Charlie's brothers and Michael Dunning followed. Grandpa and Aunt Ginny drew up chairs near Kim, but recognizing her need to collect her thoughts, remained silent.

With Jack safe in the sheriff's custody, she focused on a question that had bothered her from the moment the little dog disappeared: Why?

Sure the dognappers had demanded $25,000 in exchange for Jack. But, when you considered the dangers, $25,000 wasn't a lot of money. Every step of the process -- from the snatch to the negotiations to the exchange -- exposed the kidnappers to discovery.

Stealing a dog created further complications. Dogs aren't intimidated by guns or threats. Even little dogs can do physical damage. An uncooperative dog magnified the risks at every step.

Yet Donny and Rocky not only accepted those risks, they'd snatched the dog in daylight with dozens of potential witnesses nearby.

Again, Kim had to ask: Why?

Why risk capture for a measly $25,000 when Donny already possessed a priceless museum emerald?

"Hey, you!"

Kim jerked back to her surroundings and turned to see Michael Dunning gaping at Rory. The big poodle stood over the lawyer's backpack. He'd managed to slide the main zipper half-way open. Rory bared his teeth in a grin.

"Rory, come."

As Rory trotted back to her, Kim apologized.

"Rory just learned to open zippers and I haven't had time to teach him it's rude."

"A poodle thief, huh?" Michael chuckled. "He probably smelled the power bars I keep in there. I don't always have time to eat."

Kim thanked Michael for his understanding, attached the leash to Rory's collar and shot a glance at Al.

"And you have no shame for teaching Rory that

rude behavior, do you?"

The little dachshund cocked his head. The "who me?" expression eased some of Kim's tension. Thank goodness for dogs and their perfectly timed comic relief.

The maid arrived with coffee, tea and leftover finger foods from the party. Kim gratefully accepted a steaming cup of tea and sweetened it heavily. She'd barely taken her first sip when Mark Hampton demanded a blow-by-blow of what transpired at the hunting cabin.

Kim gratefully allowed Scott to describe sneaking up on the cabin, the sound of gunshots, Rocky escaping through the window, the sight of the gunman's hand.

"Odd that the gunman didn't chase after Rocky," Grandpa said.

"We figured Al's baying warned him that people were coming," Kim said. "You know how far hounds' voices travel. And with Rory adding his two-cents, it probably sounded like a group of hunters approaching the cabin."

"So you never saw the shooter?" Michael Dunning said.

Kim shook her head.

"We were worried about the dogs, so we ran back to the car, drove until we had cell service and called Sheriff Spits and--" she nodded at Deb-- "you to let you know Jack was okay."

"Did Spits have anything interesting to say?"

Mark said.

"Wouldn't tell us a thing," Scott said. "Just made us wait around until he'd had time to get his team in there, look around and throw questions at us. We told him we'd be here if he has any more questions."

"But I don't understand," Deb said. "If Jack is all right, why didn't you bring him home with you?"

"I'm afraid that's my fault," Kim said. "The sheriff found a torn piece of jeans fabric in the room where Jack was kept. Said it looked like Jack had bitten one of the kidnappers. I suggested he swab Jack's mouth for the kidnapper's DNA. That way Donny or Rocky can't deny their involvement with Jack."

"Donny's not going to be denying anything," a new voice said.

They all turned to see Sheriff Spits stride into the room, Jack struggling in his arms. He set the little dog down and watched him race across the room and leap into Deb's open arms. After much kissing and cooing, Deb thanked the sheriff and offered coffee. He readily accepted.

"So," Mark said, "Did you find Donny Driver?"

The sheriff took two gulps of hot, black coffee before answering.

He stared toward the cluster of men standing near the bar.

"Found him in the cabin. Dead."

The collective gasps were followed by a

cacophony of questions. Spits sipped his coffee and let the voices roll over him.

Kim paid no attention to the others. Her mind flooded with questions.

When she'd seen Rocky DiSoto leaping from the cabin window, she'd assumed Donny was the one shooting at him. But if Donny was dead, then a third, unknown person was involved.

Amy Sawyer?

Leaning into Scott, she whispered, "Remember the hand holding the gun? Could it have been a woman's hand?"

"Don't know," Scott said. "I was too busy staring at the gun."

Kim closed her eyes and tried to re-create the scene. The gun had seemed so large. Did that mean the hand was small? Or had her fear magnified the gun?

She suddenly realized the room had grown silent. Opening her eyes, she watched Sheriff Spits set his now-empty cup onto an end table and pull a notebook and pen from his pocket.

"I can't answer your questions right now," he said. "But I need to know where you all were today between 5 and 8 p.m."

Mark Hampton's face flushed. "Are you accusing one of us of killing that slime bag?"

He stepped toward the sheriff, fists clenched.

Spits raised a hand, traffic-cop style.

"Don't come any closer," he said. "I don't want to

arrest you for assaulting an officer, but, believe me, I will."

Deb laid a hand on her husband's arm.

"Walt's just doing his job."

"By accusing innocent people?" Mark glared at the sheriff.

Sheriff Spits sighed. "I'm not accusing anyone of anything. I just need a timeline of everyone's movement. We can do this here or at the station."

"Fine." Mark folded his arms. "Since you know about Jack--" he nodded at the papillon perched on his wife's lap -- "you also know I needed to collect ransom money. I drove to the office to remove cash from the safe. And, before you ask, no one saw me. I don't make my employees work on Sunday."

Jake cleared his throat. "Actually, Dad, you have an alibi. Diesel and I followed you. I know you told us to wait here, but we thought it was dangerous to, you know, drive alone with all of that cash . . ."

Looking anything but grateful, Mark clamped one hand on each son's shoulder.

"Well, thank goodness you were there."

He glared at Spits.

Aunt Ginny broke the tension.

"I don't have an alibi," she said. "While we were waiting for Mark to return, I spent time reading in my room, alone."

Though her tone was sober, Kim recognized the mischievous glint in her aunt's eyes.

"Does that make me a suspect?"

Kim grinned. Oh, yeah, she could imagine Ginny regaling her friends with stories of being a suspect in a murder case.

The sheriff bit back a smile and nodded.

"Yes, ma'am. I'm gonna have to ask you to not leave town until this case is solved."

"Actually, I can vouch for Ginny," Deb said.

She nodded at Grandpa. "While we waited for Mark to return, Max and I stayed here, talking. As you can see--" she gestured toward the hallway -- "we'd have seen Ginny if she'd left the house."

"How do you know I didn't crawl out a window?" Ginny waggled her eyebrows.

Everyone, including Mark, laughed.

Rachael cleared her throat and said, "Charlie and I were together. We, er--" Her face turned red. "We needed some time alone."

Kim snickered. Rachael shot her a dirty look.

"I guess that leaves me," Michael Dunning said. "I was driving around looking for Donny Driver."

The sheriff frowned at Deb.

"Why look for Driver? Didn't you say the kidnapper used something to disguise his voice?"

Mark answered for her.

"Yes, he did. But we just assumed Donny was behind the theft. Very few people would hurt Deb by taking her dog."

"And I thought if I found him, I might convince him to return Jack by throwing legal jargon at him."

Michael grimaced. "Never occurred to me that an

unknown killer might be involved. Just as well I didn't find them."

"How long did you search?"

"Maybe an hour. The first time I swung by his trailer, no one was home and there were no cars parked outside. I called here to report, then drove around looking for his pickup."

Michael shrugged. "People probably saw me drive by, but I couldn't give you names.

"Anyway, after thirty or forty minutes, I returned to Donny's trailer. There was a pickup parked outside and the front door was open. I called out, but no one answered.

"I could see through the open door and it looked like a hurricane had hit the place. Someone had opened drawers, emptied cabinets, slashed cushions. I know I shouldn't have entered, but I was worried about Deb's dog and thought maybe I'd find Jack inside or, at a minimum, I'd find some clue as to where Donny might have gone."

He spread his hands wide. "When I found nothing, I returned here."

"What time did you arrive?"

"No idea. I didn't look at my watch."

The sheriff snorted. "You strut around with that fancy pocket watch and don't bother checking the time?"

"It's a pocket watch," Michael said. "That means it stays in my pocket which also means I can't get to it while driving."

Sheriff Spits gave an exaggerated sigh and turned to the others. But no one else knew what time Michael had returned.

"What about the Carolina Emerald?" Kim said. "Did you find it in Donny's cabin?"

"Not yet. We're still looking."

He directed another question at the group, but Kim didn't hear it.

She wanted to scream.

With Donny dead and Rocky on the run, she'd lost her last connection to the emerald. If the killer had found it, the Carolina Emerald would once again disappear, this time forever.

She needed to identify the shooter from the cabin. Fast.

The muffled sound of a cell phone interrupted the sheriff's questioning. Sheriff Spits pulled a phone out of his pocket, frowned at the caller I.D, then punched a button.

"Spits," he said.

He listened for a few minutes, then sighed.

"Sorry to hear that. No, no, you did good work. I just wish it'd been a different Hicks."

Kim leaned forward and stared at the sheriff. Seeing her interest, Spits turned his back and stepped away. She scooched forward on the sofa and strained to hear, but only caught snatches. Did he say the word "emerald"?

The sheriff pulled the phone from his ear.

Michael and Kim spoke at once.

"Did you find the emerald?" Michael said.

Kim's voice was louder. "Did you arrest one of the Hickses?"

"We haven't arrested anyone," Spits said.

"But you suspect a Hicks killed Donny, right?" Michael persisted.

"Let's just say we're questioning a person of interest," Sheriff Spits said.

Kim's stomach clenched. "Who?"

The sheriff didn't even glance at her.

"I'm not at liberty to say."

Spits turned to leave, but Kim leaped to her feet, blocking his path to the front door.

"Wait, please, if you're questioning one of the Hickses because he was wandering in the woods, you need to know that the Hicks family offered to help us find Jack. That's why they were near the area where Donny was killed."

"Sounds like a good way to set up an alibi," Michael said.

He pitched his voice high. "But, officer, I wasn't shooting no one; I was looking for a little dog."

Mark, Jake and Diesel laughed. Kim glared at the red-headed lawyer. Scott stood and touched her arm. Michael lifted his chin and smirked.

"It's not funny," Kim said. "The Hickses have been persecuted for generations. They--"

"Persecuted!" Mark shook his finger at her. "Young lady, you know nothing about our town, its history or its people. Ninety-nine percent of the crime in this area is committed by a Hicks."

"That can't possibly be true." Kim shot Mark a glare.

"Mark may exaggerate," Sheriff Spits said, "but the Hickses have never played by the rules."

He patted her shoulder. "Don't worry. I won't arrest an innocent person."

As he left, a wave of guilt washed over Kim. Betty Hicks had sent her family into the woods to look for Jack. Maybe no one would have been "brought in for questioning" if Kim hadn't asked for help.

She needed to do something to make this right. Maybe she could hire a lawyer -- a good lawyer like Charlie's friend Drew -- to help.

First, however, she needed to talk to Betty.

She pulled out her cell phone.

CHAPTER 26

"Still no answer."

Kim hung up her phone and stared gloomily out of the car window.

"Thanks for humoring me with this."

She'd spent half an hour repeatedly dialing Betty's phone. At first, she'd received a busy signal. Then the call went straight to voice mail. She'd finally decided to drive to Betty's house. Scott immediately offered to go with her.

"Maybe Betty isn't speaking to me," she said. "It's my fault her family was searching the woods when the police arrived."

"You don't know that."

Scott slowed the car to make the turn onto the

gravel driveway that led to Betty's and Brian's house.

"Tommy Hicks keeps a still in the woods," he said. "I suspect all of Brian's relatives patrol the area."

"Yeah, but it's my fault Brian was out there. If not for me, he'd have been home with his family. If he's the one they're questioning . . ."

She couldn't finish the thought.

The house came into view. Light glowed from the front window, revealing the kitchen beyond.

Kim fought a shiver as she remembered huddling in that kitchen, surrounded by Hickses, one of them pointing a long gun at the door.

Not wanting to startle anyone, she dialed Betty's number one more time.

It went immediately to voice mail.

"Betty, if you're home, I'm outside. I need to talk to you about getting a lawyer for whoever's been taken to the station."

Turning off the phone, she reached for the door handle.

"Maybe someone else is home."

Scott beat her to the porch. Kim knocked on the door, waited, then knocked again. She leaned toward the door, straining to hear movement inside.

Nothing.

"I guess we could go to the police sta--"

The snap of a shotgun cocking froze her in place.

"What are you doing here?"

She recognized Tommy Hicks's voice.

"Looking for Betty."

Raising her hands, she slowly turned around. Scott mimicked her. The shotgun looked huge in the old man's gnarled hands.

"We're here to help," she said.

Tommy snorted. "You've helped enough. Thanks to you, Brian's in jail."

Kim's chest tightened and she groaned.

"Not Brian," she whispered.

"If you'll let me pull out my cell phone," Scott said, "I can call a lawyer to help."

"Yeah, right," Tommy said. "And who's going to pay for that?"

"We're hoping Drew will defend Brian for free," Kim said. "If not, well, I have some money saved . . ."

"And I have savings as well," Scott added.

For a moment, Tommy Hicks stared at them. Then he lowered the gun.

"Yeah, call your lawyer."

His voice trembled. "Won't do any good."

As Scott pulled out his phone, Kim's knees gave way. She sank onto a porch step and stared up at Tommy's drawn face.

"What happened?"

Tommy's shoulders slumped.

"Cops found Brian in the woods with a bloody nose and scraped knuckles. Didn't believe him when he told them he'd tangled with that DiSoto character."

"Rocky DiSoto?"

Tommy nodded. "Brian said he was looking for Deb Hampton's dog when DiSoto came tearing through the woods. When Brian tried to stop him, DiSoto swung a fist. Brian got in a few licks, but said DiSoto fought like a mad man. Brian never was a fighter and, well, he wound up on the ground while DiSoto vanished."

Tommy shot Kim a glare.

"Instead of coming home like any sane man, Brian decided to play detective. Figured if he retraced DiSoto's trail, he'd find clues. 'course, that only led him to the police."

"Surely they didn't haul him into the station because he'd been walking in the woods."

Tommy shook his head.

"They give him a hard time, asked about the scrapes, then let 'im go. Showed up at the house an hour later, handcuffed him and marched him to their car.

"Betty begged them to tell her why they was draggin' her husband away. All they's say was they needed to question him."

Kim frowned. Between the time the officers found Brian in the woods and the move to detain him, something had changed. But what?

She pondered the phone call Sheriff Spits had received. Before turning away from her, he'd complimented the deputy for "good work" and mentioned the Hicks family. Then she'd heard only disconnected words: "gun," "search," "emerald."

Emerald?

"Surely," she mused aloud, "they don't think Brian was trying to recover the Carolina Emerald."

Tommy's eyes narrowed.

"You talking 'bout my emerald? What's that got to do with my grandson bein' suspected of shootin' some slime ball?"

She suddenly realized Tommy didn't know that she suspected Donny Driver of stealing the emerald from Charlie's cabin. Did he even know that she no longer had the emerald?

"You've heard that my dog dug up the Car-- er, your emerald, right? Did you know someone stole it from me?"

Tommy's eyes widened.

"You don't have my emerald? Then who does?"

"I think Donny Driver took it."

Kim told him about trying to disguise the emerald by wrapping it in Rory's handkerchief, the break-in and theft and Donny's suspicious behavior at the gem festival.

"With the ongoing murder investigation, the sheriff hasn't spent much time searching for the emerald," she concluded. "But he knows I suspect Donny stole it. Given your family's history with the emerald, the sheriff may think Brian confronted Donny and Rocky and, well, that things got out of hand."

"My grandson is not a killer."

Kim reached out and touched the old man's arm. "I believe you."

She felt a tremor run through Tommy's body. He straightened his shoulders and, with great dignity, said, "I thank you for that."

Before she could respond, Scott joined them.

"Drew's on his way to the station. Brian knows to stay silent until his lawyer is present, right?"

Tommy snorted. "All the Hickses learn that as toddlers."

He pulled out his pocket watch, glanced down and grunted.

"Boy's been there a long time," he said. "Hope this lawyer's as good as you say."

Kim stared at the pocket watch. It looked old, the image on the silver case rubbed smooth from loving hands.

"Is that the watch from your father?"

Tommy's smile was wistful. "Yeah."

"May I see it?"

She used both hands to hold the watch, handling it with the respect it deserved. It was a standard railroad watch, a simple style in which a clear crystal protected the face while making it easy to read the time. The numbers were large, the hour hand not only longer but also thicker than the minute hand.

She turned it over to study the fancy work on the back. The Statue of Liberty raised her torch beneath the words "Gateway to Freedom." The "G" and "F" appeared blurred, as if a thumb had loving caressed the words.

"Lovely."

She held the watch out to Tommy.

He accepted it and stared at the image on the back.

"I used to believe those words."

Color crept up his face and he turned away, tucking the watch safely into his pants pocket.

She quickly changed the subject.

"Did Betty go to the station with Brian? She's not answering her phone."

Tommy shook her head. "She took Cooper to her mom's."

Kim stood. "I'll call Betty's mom, let her know Brian now has a lawyer."

Tommy cleared his throat.

"Guess I'll be getting on home."

He tucked the shotgun under his arm, muzzle pointed toward the ground.

"I suppose the police now have my emerald."

"No, they couldn't find it. Apparently, Donny's trailer and cabin both looked like someone searched them."

"So who has my emerald?"

"I don't know. Donny might have hidden it. Rocky might have taken it or maybe the person who shot Donny has it."

She hesitated. She hated to open old wounds, but

there was a killer loose.

"Do you know where Amy Sawyer is?"

The surprise on Tommy's face was genuine.

"Amy? What's she got to do with all this?"

"Maybe nothing. But Betty told me Amy and her mother were obsessed with finding the emerald. Maybe Amy came home and . . ."

She trailed off, startled by the emotions racing across Tommy's face. After the initial surprise, his brows furrowed in confusion. Then his eyes narrowed, his lips pressed together, his jaw set.

"Where's Amy?" Kim said.

Tommy turned away and set off for the forest.

"Tommy, please! I'm trying to help."

Tommy halted. Without turning around, he said, "Amy's dead."

Amy Sawyer is dead.

As they drove back to the cabin, Tommy Hicks's words swirled through her mind.

She hadn't realized how much she'd hoped Amy Sawyer was the key to recent events. Like Tommy Hicks, Amy -- or her descendants -- knew for certain that the Carolina Emerald was buried somewhere on what was now Hampton land. Also like Tommy, Amy resented the Hamptons for winning the land in a poker game. Unlike Tommy, the teenaged Amy had expressed her anger by setting fires and vandalizing the Hamptons' mining equipment.

Kim could well imagine how Amy's childhood obsession might lead to murder.

And she really, really didn't want the killer to be one of the Hickses.

But now the police suspected Brian Hicks of shooting Donny Driver. Why?

Only one way to find out.

She pulled out her phone and scrolled through the list of outgoing calls until she found the one for Amanda Corning, Betty's mother. Mrs. Corning answered before the phone completed its first ring.

"Any word?"

Her anxious voice pierced Kim's heart.

"Mrs. Corning? This is Kim West, Betty's friend."

"Oh."

Kim pictured the woman's shoulders deflating.

"I, uh, actually have some good news," Kim said. "Drew McDonald, one of Charlie's friends, is on the way to the police station to represent Brian. Charlie swears Drew is a fantastic lawyer."

"Oh, thank God." The words came out in a breath.

Kim heard Betty's voice in the background. Amanda turned from the phone and related the conversation. The phone thumped, then Betty's voice talked into it.

"Is it true? Did you find a lawyer for Brian?"

"Yes. Drew should be with him soon."

"Thank you."

Betty choked back a sob.

"Dad's at the station, trying to get some answers. Mom and I have been going over budgets, trying to find money to pay a lawyer. There's not much equity in our house, but maybe--"

"Don't worry about the money," Kim said. "Drew does some pro-bono work and if, for some reason, Brian doesn't qualify, well, Scott and I have some money saved. We should be able to help."

"I . . . I . . ."

Whatever Betty was trying to say was lost in tears. The phone exchanged hands and Amanda Corning came back online.

Like her daughter, Amanda immediately gushed her thanks.

Embarrassed, Kim changed the subject.

"Did the police actually arrest Brian?"

"No. But they insisted he go to the station to answer questions. Betty said they made it sound like Brian didn't have a choice."

"Did anyone say why the police are interested in Brian?"

"The police wouldn't tell us, but an hour or so ago, one of Brian's co-workers called. He said an Officer Jennings questioned him about Brian's relationship with Donny. Apparently, one of the other workers told Jennings about the fight."

"What fight?"

Amanda sighed. "You know Brian works

construction while going to night school? Well, a few months ago he was promoted to foreman. Some of the guys, including Donny Driver, weren't happy."

Kim imagined big, tough Donny's reaction when told his new boss was a younger man who looked like a computer nerd.

"Is that why they fought?"

"Oh, no," Amanda said. "Donny couldn't risk losing his job. He'd been fired from several others and was running out of places that would hire him.

"But he wasn't capable of ignoring what he considered a snub. So he set out to undermine Brian's authority by initiating a series of practical jokes.

"At first the jokes were benign -- the construction worker equivalent of short-sheeting a bed. So Brian ignored them. But the jokes got nastier and, eventually, one of the other workers was injured.

"Brian called an ambulance for the injured man, then immediately fired Donny. Donny responded by swinging a two-by-four at the back of Brian's head."

Remembering the picket sign Donny had swung at Charlie, Kim shuddered.

"Someone yelled a warning and Brian ducked," Amanda said. "The board hit Brian in the shoulder and knocked him down. Donny raised the board to hit Brian again, but the other guys tackled him. If they hadn't grabbed Donny, I think he'd have killed

Brian."

"Why didn't the police arrest Donny?"

Amanda sighed. "Brian shares his family's distrust of the police. I tried to tell him the witnesses would support him, but he wouldn't listen to reason.

"But all of this happened months ago. I can't imagine why the police are now interest-- Hey, Cooper, why aren't you in bed?"

Kim heard the boy's sleepy voice in the background.

"Okay," Amanda told her grandson, "why don't we read for awhile? Kim? I need to run."

They said their goodbyes.

Kim clenched her phone and stared into the night. Donny Driver and his friend, Kirk Ballas, were dead. A third friend, Rocky DiSoto, was running from an unknown assailant. Brian Hicks was being questioned about Donny's murder. Charlie was still a suspect in Kirk's murder.

And while the police wasted time investigating people she considered unlikely suspects, the real killer either possessed the Carolina Emerald or knew where to find it.

"The murders and the stolen emerald must be connected," she said. "I know coincidences happen, but this is too much."

"Agreed. So where does that leave us?"

"Let's assume that obtaining the Carolina Emerald is the motive for everything that's happened."

"So we're looking at Tommy Hicks and Amy Sawyer," Scott said.

"They're the most likely, but don't forget people quickly learned that Rory had dug up the emerald. And I think we can remove the Hickses from our list of possible thieves. When I told Tommy that the emerald was stolen from my room, he seemed genuinely surprised. Surely he'd know if one of his relatives had taken it."

"So that leaves Amy Sawyer and her descendants or maybe even close friends."

Kim snorted. "You know, if this were a novel, Deb would be the culprit. She's the least likely suspect."

"That certainly wasn't Deb who knocked me down the stairs."

"No. But it could have been Diesel or Jake doing their mother's bidding."

"Okay, I'll play along," Scott said. "Why would Deb steal the Carolina Emerald?"

"Maybe she wanted to keep it instead of returning it to the museum."

"But Deb would never kill Kirk Ballas and implicate Charlie."

"I agree."

She sighed and dragged fingers through her hair.

"I keep thinking there must be a mastermind behind all of this, someone close to the Hamptons. Since they don't have a butler--"

Scott chuckled. "Even I know the-butler-did-it cliché."

She straightened.

"Wait a minute. The Hamptons don't have a butler, but they do have a housekeeper/cook. What do we know about her?"

"Ask your aunt. The other night, when you were talking with Sheriff Spits, I saw Ginny talking with the cook. You know how Ginny always discovers people's backgrounds."

"And their darkest secrets."

She grinned and dialed Aunt Ginny's cell phone.

"Please tell me you didn't find another body," Ginny said.

Ignoring her aunt's quip, Kim explained what they'd learned since leaving the Hampton mansion.

"Anyway," she concluded, "I was wondering if you know anything about the lady who cooks for the Hamptons."

"Well, I can tell you for sure that she's not Amy Sawyer's daughter," Ginny said. "Matty grew up in Hiddenite. Her father occasionally helps in the mine."

Kim sighed. "I don't suppose you met anyone at the luncheon who might be related to Amy?"

"Most of the people I met have lived near here their entire lives," Ginny said. "Although, Deb's caterer was an odd duck. She seemed friendly enough until I asked her where she grew up. She acted like she hadn't heard the question and suddenly found something she needed to do immediately.

"I did learn that she works out of a small pastry shop in Statesville. Maybe tomorrow Max and I will wander in there, see if we can learn more."

Kim agreed to Ginny's plan. As she hung up her phone, however, she couldn't push aside the feeling that tomorrow might be too late.

Scott turned onto the cabin's driveway.

"Is there an easy way to trace the caterer's background?" Kim said.

"Actually, I have an idea."

Scott parked the car.

"We now know that Amy Sawyer died. The death notices will list her surviving relatives."

"But you said earlier that when you searched, there were too many Amy Sawyers."

"We might be able to narrow the search by adding a possible married name. Do you remember the caterer's name?"

"Yeah. Connie Taylor."

"So let's see if we can find a death notice for Amy Sawyer Taylor."

Half an hour later, however, Scott pushed the computer aside and enveloped Kim in a hug.

"We'll find her," he said.

"Yeah. But we might be too late to save the Carolina Emerald from being destroyed."

The search for "Amy Sawyer Taylor" had, indeed, generated a shorter list than the earlier search. Even so, no one on the new list appeared to be the woman they sought.

"If Tommy Hicks knows that Amy Sawyer is dead," Scott said, "maybe he knows if she married and had children."

"Maybe. But I don't think he's going to tell us."

She pictured Tommy's expression when she'd asked him about Amy. After the initial surprise, his eyes had narrowed, his mouth had thinned, his shoulders had hunched and he'd drawn into himself -- all behaviors triggered by the subconscious mind when an individual tried to conceal his thoughts.

Of course, reading body language wasn't an exact science. As any police officer could tell you, deception was particularly difficult to identify.

Even so, Kim feared the old man was not only hiding something, but was also planning to help his grandson by doing something dangerous.

"You know," Scott said, "eventually the police are going to find Rocky DiSoto. He'll identify the killer."

"If Rocky has any sense, he packed his bags and kept on running. Besides, Rocky's been involved in this from the beginning. If the police catch him, he'll scream for a lawyer and we'll never know what happened. Rocky might even try to distance himself from everything by pointing the finger at Brian. People already believe the Hickses are involved."

She buried her face in Scott's shoulder.

"I still can't believe I held the Carolina Emerald in my own hands and then lost it."

Scott murmured reassurances, but she tuned them out. Yes, hiding the emerald in a bandana while attending the dinner party had seemed like the safest option. Yes, the Hamptons were the ones who'd endangered the gem by telling others about the discovery. Yes, it wasn't her fault that the stone was stolen.

She still felt responsible, not only for the loss of the emerald, but also for involving Betty and Brian Hicks.

She liked the young couple, liked the loving way they gazed into each other's eyes, liked the way Brian defended his son against that bully of a cop, liked the way they worked to pull themselves out of the lower economic class.

Heck, she'd even gained a grudging admiration for Tommy Hicks -- a feeling he seemed to share. Tonight she'd felt a real bond as they'd admired his "heirloom" pocket watch . . .

She straightened as a series of memories swirled through her mind. When describing the night of the museum burglary, Betty Hicks mentioned that Sawyer and Hicks had also stolen pocket watches. Tommy's father said the watches would become "heirlooms."

The watch Tommy had shown her tonight was just the sort of item sold in the American Museum of Natural History gift shop.

Was this one of the watches stolen at the same time as the Carolina Emerald?

If so, where was the second watch? Had Amy Sawyer given that watch to her heirs?

Another memory: When they'd attended the Gem Festival, Tommy had snatched a pocket watch from Michael Dunning and demanded to know its origins.

She hadn't been standing close enough to study the watch. But Michael had dismissed it as an inexpensive souvenir he carried only because it was a "family heirloom."

"Scott? Try searching for 'Amy Sawyer Dunning.'"

To his credit, Scott didn't question her request.

Kim held her breath as he typed in a new search. A list appeared on screen. Scott clicked on the first one.

And there she was: Amy Sawyer Dunning, born October 4, 1940 in Hiddenite, North Carolina.

She'd died a year ago in Atlanta, Georgia.

The simple obituary reported that her husband, Robert Dunning, pre-deceased her. She was survived by her only child.

Michael Dunning.

CHAPTER 27

"We have to tell the sheriff." Kim reached for her cell phone.

Scott laid his hand over hers.

"Tell him what?" he said. "That Michael Dunning is Amy Sawyer's son? How is that going to help the investigation?"

She waved her free hand at the computer screen containing Amy Sawyer's obituary.

"Isn't it obvious?" she said. "Michael moved to Hiddenite to look for the Carolina Emerald. He's the one who shot Kirk Ballas and tried to frame Charlie. He had motive, means and opportunity."

"Aren't you making some pretty big jumps in logic?" Scott said.

Kim folded her arms and lifted her chin. "Michael Dunning is the logical suspect."

"Maybe. But we don't have evidence of his guilt."

"Okay, let's look at the facts." She reached for a nearby tablet and pen. Drawing two columns, she labeled the first one "Fact" and the second "Theory."

"Fact number one," she said as she wrote. "Michael Dunning didn't move to Hiddenite until after his mother's death. That indicates that Amy didn't tell him about the Carolina Emerald until she was dying. What do you want to bet she urged him to return to Hiddenite to find the emerald, told him the best places to look?"

Scott nodded. "Okay, I'll play along. We know that Michael met Jake and Diesel at a rock hunters' meeting, then became Mark Hampton's lawyer."

"Michael's official position gave him access to the mine," Kim added. "That means he could identify potential hiding places for the emerald during the day, then return at night to dig.

"Oh! We also know Tommy Hicks saw two separate sets of lights at the Hampton mine. What do you want to bet that one set belonged to Kirk Ballas and his friends, who were illegally digging for emeralds? And the second light belonged to Michael."

As they talked, Kim jotted notes, separating fact from theory.

"You know, this is actually helpful."

She studied the list. Under "Fact," she wrote "Rory dug up emerald."

"Here's another fact for you." Scott's voice was grim. "Shortly before Charlie's engagement dinner, Michael called Jake. Jake told him about Rory's find."

"Giving Michael time to plot to steal the emerald." She snorted. "Do you remember when we met Michael at the dinner, he commented on my large bag and asked me to help him organize his backpack? I thought he was just making small talk. Now I wonder if he was hoping to look into my bag to see if I was carrying the emerald."

She bit her lip. And what would he have done if she'd had the emerald with her? Run them off the road, rob them at gunpoint?

Brushing the thought aside, she added another note to the "fact" column: Michael left the dinner party early.

"I wonder if Michael knew that Kirk and his buddies would be digging at the mine," Kim said. "Maybe he planned to blackmail them into breaking into Charlie's cottage."

"He must have been lurking nearby," Scott said. "He arrived quickly after we discovered Kirk's body."

Under "theory," Kim wrote: Michael hit Charlie, shot Kirk and set the scene to implicate Charlie. He used the cold-blooded murder to intimidate Donny and Rocky into breaking into Charlie's cabin. He circled back to the road, called the police, then ran into the woods to "help" Charlie.

"Why are you so certain Michael told Donny Driver to break into the cabin?" Scott said. "He doesn't strike me as the type to take orders."

"There's something I never told you," Kim said. "Right after we found the body, while the sheriff talked to Charlie, Michael accepted a phone call. He listened for a few minutes, then told the caller 'it's only a poodle.'"

"Rory."

Kim nodded. "Donny probably heard the two dogs barking and was afraid to break into the cabin. Al sounds like a small dog, but Rory's bark can be scary."

She jotted the overheard phone call under "fact," then wrote Rory's name under "theory."

For a moment, they studied the list in silence. Rory shifted position and laid his head on her foot. Al barked in his sleep, his paws twitching as if he was running. The refrigerator rumbled and the furnace thumped into action.

"It's all circumstantial, isn't it?" Kim said.

"Afraid so. The facts all fit together, but there's no evidence against Michael."

She tossed the pen onto the table. "I really hoped we'd have something to give the sheriff."

Scott straightened. "The sheriff might not be able to use this information, but Drew McDonald will find it valuable. Defense attorneys thrive on alternative theories."

"But in the meantime, Brian Hicks and Charlie remain suspects."

Scott reached for his phone. "Let's talk to Drew and see where we go from here."

Kim stared out her bedroom window at the brightening sky. After a sleepless night, her muscles ached, her stomach rolled and her mouth tasted sour. Her traitorous mind wouldn't stop rehashing the weekend's events.

Drew had responded to their late-night call by driving to the cabin. Over hot drinks, Kim and Scott had taken turns explaining why they suspected Michael Dunning of committing murder.

The lawyer had listened quietly, his handsome face showing no signs of skepticism. When they finished, Drew said he knew a good private investigator. If Michael was guilty, the PI would find evidence.

The conversation should have comforted Kim. After all, they'd placed the investigation into Drew's capable hands.

So why couldn't she shake the feeling that time was running out?

A scratching sound drew her attention to the far corner of the room. Rory stood over her backpack, pawing at the zipper that closed the main compartment. The zipper slid an inch, then held. As she gawked, Rory used his front teeth to grab the zipper pull. He tugged the zipper open, then plunged his head inside.

"Rory, no!"

Remembering the chocolate power bar she'd left in the pack, Kim leaped to her feet. Rory glanced over his shoulder, grinned, then tugged something free from the bag.

Kim slammed to a halt and stared at the bandana hanging from Rory's mouth. After a moment, she laughed.

"Well, if nothing else, you're perfect comic relief," she said.

Rory sat and waited for her to remove the bandana that dangled from his mouth. She accepted the proffered gift and scratched Rory's ear.

Perhaps it was time to distance herself from the horrible events of the last few days.

She smiled down at Rory. "Would you like to walk to the mine and do some scent work?"

At the word "walk," Rory leaped to his feet and trotted to the door. She reached for her clothes, then disappeared into the bathroom to wash.

Ten minutes later, they emerged into one of those glorious autumn days that make you want to find a pile of leaves to splash through. A light frost covered the grass beside the house. The air smelled of crushed leaves and wood-burning fireplaces. Rory gamboled through the woods, stopping only to sniff a special bush or to wait for Kim to catch up.

When they reached the clearing to the emerald mine, she dropped Rory's long line and let him zoom off excess energy.

The scenting game, however, was one of Rory's favorites so it wasn't long before he plopped at her feet and gazed up expectantly. Laughing, Kim removed the bandana from her backpack and instructed Rory to stay.

She turned and walked along the edge of the mine, stopping periodically to pretend to hide the bandana. After tucking the bandana beneath a rock, she continued walking and stooping.

She reversed direction and started back to Rory.

But the big poodle wasn't watching her. He was standing stiffly, staring into the forest.

"Rory, stay!"

Kim broke into a trot. She needed to snag Rory's long line before he chased after a deer or a squirrel or a--

A man stepped from the woods. The morning sun glinted off his red hair. Recognizing Michael Dunning, Kim stiffened.

Did he know she suspected him of murder? Had he followed her to the mine? Did he--

Wait a minute. Why was Michael holding his hands above his head?

Tommy Hicks appeared. He pointed a shotgun at the center of Michael Dunning's back.

"Mr. Hicks . . . Tommy, what's going on?"

Tommy nodded at Kim. "Don't you mind us. Amy's son and I've got business."

"You've got to help me."

Michael's eyes were wide, his pupils dilated.

"This crazy old man pulled me from bed and marched me here at gunpoint."

Gone was the suave, savvy lawyer. Michael's hair was mussed, his face sleep creased. His wrinkled shirt had been buttoned incorrectly; the tails hung crookedly outside of khaki trousers. Even the ever-present backpack seemed to droop from his left shoulder.

Despite knowing his role in stealing the emerald, Kim felt a rush of sympathy.

"Now, take off that purse nice and slow," Tommy said. "Good. Now drop it."

The backpack hit the ground. Without taking his eyes from Michael, Tommy kicked the pack away.

"So where's my emerald?" Tommy said.

Michael's eyes met Kim's.

"Why are you just standing there? Help me! This man's a cold-blooded killer."

Killer?

Kim studied the old man. In a few short days, she'd seen Tommy as the angry gnome, the doting grandfather, the proud bootlegger, the frightened family man and, last night, the dignified senior thanking her for believing in his grandson's innocence.

Tommy Hicks might kill to protect his family. But

Kim couldn't imagine him going on a killing spree.

She lifted her chin.

"I don't believe that."

Michael's eyes widened.

"Are you blind? I'm the one with the gun to my back."

"Enough!" Tommy nudged Michael's back with the gun. "Now where's my emerald?"

"Why don't you ask her?" Michael said. "We both saw her hiding stuff under rocks."

"I was playing a game with the dog!" Kim turned to Tommy. "Honestly, Tommy, I don't know where the emerald is. Donny Driver stole it but the police didn't find it at Donny's cabin."

Tommy nodded. "That's because Michael here got to Donny first."

"I told you, I don't know where he hid the emerald!" Michael said. "He said it's where I'd never think to look. I'm only assuming he hid it here. It could be anywhere."

Tommy prodded Michael's back.

"Then I guess it's time to start digging."

He marched Michael at gunpoint to the edge of the mine.

"Find my emerald."

"Can't search with my arms like this."

Tommy took a few steps back before allowing Michael to lower his arms. The lawyer shuffled along the edge of the mine, following the same path Kim had used when hiding Rory's bandana. He stopped every few steps to kick aside loose rocks. Tommy followed behind him.

Kim bit her lip, wondering what she should do. She didn't think Tommy would kill someone in cold blood. But what if she was wrong?

Falling into step with Tommy, she said "How long have you known Michael is Amy Sawyer's son?"

Michael stopped to glare at her, but a look from Tommy forced his eyes back to the ground.

Tommy answered without taking his eyes off of Michael.

"I knew Amy had a son. Didn't know he'd moved here till I saw him at the Gem Festival showing off his pocket watch. Our fathers stole matching watches when we were in New York."

"But the Gem Festival was days ago! Why haven't you said anything?"

"Warn't no reason to 'til you told me you didn't have my emerald."

"Stop calling it your emerald." Michael folded his arms. "It's as much mine as it is yours."

"You gave up your claim when you framed my grandson for murder."

"You have no proof of that," Michael said.

"Don't need none. I've got the gun."

The anger in Michael's eyes made Kim shiver. Tommy might have the gun, but Michael was younger, stronger and filled with hate.

If she didn't do something, this was going to end

badly.

"Stop stalling," Tommy said. "You wouldn't have shot Donny until he told you where he hid the emerald."

"Trust me, old man." Michael kicked a stone away. "I wouldn't have shot him at all if the idiot hadn't thrown a lamp at me."

Did Michael just confess to murder? Or claim self-defense?

"You can leave," Tommy said to Kim. "Don't need to stay to watch this."

She considered her options. Though Tommy thought he had Michael Dunning under control, the old man's arms trembled as if he was growing tired of holding the shotgun in position.

Yet what could she do? Her cell phone never had reception at the mine. To call the police, she'd have to run back to the cabin, a distance of half a mile. That would take too long.

But if she stayed, could she actually help?

She scanned the ground around her, searching for something she could use as a weapon. There were rocks a plenty, but those wouldn't be useful if Michael gained control of the gun. She'd feel more comfortable with something club like.

Michael suddenly dropped to his knees. Dirt flew into the air as he dug in the ground. Rising, he turned. He clutched Rory's bandana in his right hand.

With his fist clenched around the body of the

handkerchief, he held it out toward Tommy.

"Come get it, old man."

Kim protested.

"That's not--"

An excited yip from Rory drew everyone's attention. Rory stood over Michael Dunning's backpack. His tail wagged furiously as he pulled something out.

"Hey, that's my stuff!"

Kim ignored the irate lawyer. Rory was trotting toward her, a piece of dirty bandana dangling from his mouth.

She recognized that bandana.

She held out her hand. Rory laid the bandana and its fragile contents onto her hand.

Hands trembling, she opened the cloth to reveal the Carolina Emerald.

Tommy started laughing.

"Yep, Donny hid it where you'd never think to look."

"How . . ." Michael swallowed. "How did he . . ."

"You said yourself you have pockets in that thing that you never open," Kim said. "Donny must have believed you."

"Yeah, well . . ."

Kim registered Michael's tensing muscles a moment before he swung his right hand around. The bandana, now filled with something -- a rock? -- struck Tommy on the side of the head. Tommy fell back, his knees crumbling, the shotgun coming up and--

The blast roared in her ears. Rory yipped and ran away. Tommy landed on his back, still clutching the shotgun. Michael snatched the gun and raised it over his head like a club.

"Stop!" Kim yelled. "Stop or I'll destroy the emerald!"

Gun still raised, Michael froze and glared over at her.

Kim held the emerald over the mouth of the mine.

"Put the gun down."

She turned her hand so that the emerald caught the sunlight.

"If I drop this, it will shatter into a million pieces."

"You wouldn't."

"You wanna take that chance?"

Michael sneered. "What happened to your big ideas about the emerald's historical significance?"

"There have been larger emeralds discovered since this one disappeared," Kim said. "Now drop the gun."

The lawyer's eyes narrowed. He studied her, searching for what? Weakness? Determination?

Tommy groaned and pushed his elbows into the dirt, trying to sit up. Michael pushed him down with his foot. But the gun was still posed high above Tommy's body.

"Don't test me, Michael," she growled. "Tommy's

life is worth more than all the emeralds in the
world."

Michael started to lower the gun. For a moment,
she thought she'd won. Then the lawyer's teeth
clenched and his hands tightened and he swung the
gun toward her. The barrel rose, its deadly muzzle
taking aim at her stomach.

No time to run--

A black streak crashed into the lawyer's knees.
Michael howled in pain. The gun flew from his
hands. Arms pinwheeling, Michael lost his balance
and plummeted into the mine.

Rory gave a single bark, then ran to Kim and
threw his paws onto her rigid shoulders. She pulled
him closer, the warmth of his body easing her
tremors.

Rory leaned back and licked her face. She smiled
down at him.

"Yeah, you really are a hero, aren't you?"

The big poodle flashed a doggie grin. As he
dropped all four feet to the ground, Kim became
aware of something hard and sharp digging into
her right hand.

The corner of a blue bandana dangled from her
clenched fist.

The Carolina Emerald.

She sank to the ground. Laying the back of her
hand across her lap, she slowly peeled her fingers
from the gem. The bandana still covered most of the
emerald. Her fingers trembled as she opened the

cloth.

The Carolina Emerald glistened in the sun, its three crystals intact.

A groan to her right reminded her of Tommy. She tried to stand, but a wave of nausea swept over her. Setting the emerald on the ground, well away from the edge of the mine, she crawled to Tommy Hicks's side.

"Are you okay?"

The old man answered with another groan. Rory licked his face.

"Get this dang dog off of me," Tommy sputtered.

He struggled to rise.

"Rory, down."

Rory dropped into a down and watched Kim help Tommy into a sitting position.

"Does anything feel like it's broken?"

Tommy shook his head. "Just some aching bones."

He stared at the edge of the mine.

"Damn fool of a boy. I'm glad Amy's not alive to see this."

Kim had a million questions for Tommy Hicks. But right now, she needed to check on Michael Dunning and call for an ambulance.

She pushed to her feet, waited for the dizziness to subside, then crossed to the spot where she'd last seen Dunning.

Michael lay sprawled on a narrow shelf of land, 10 to 15 feet below. His left leg was bent at an unnatural angle. The shotgun lay at the very bottom of the mine.

"Michael?"

The lawyer groaned and moved his hands. The left hand gripped dirt. The right flopped over the shelf edge.

"Lay still!" she called. "If you move, you might fall."

Michael pulled his right hand next to his body. He groaned again, but didn't move.

"I'm going to get help."

He didn't respond.

She returned to Tommy. He'd pushed himself to his feet and was dusting off his pants. Though he moved stiffly, color had returned to his face.

"I need to find a place with cell phone reception," she told him. "Can you stay with Michael until I return?"

Tommy nodded, then pointed to the center of the clearing.

"See that mound of dirt there?"

Kim squinted. Sure enough, a pile of dirt, maybe three feet in diameter, rose a foot or two above the rest of the land.

"If you stand in the middle of that," Tommy said, "you should get one bar."

The suggestion seemed unlikely. But Tommy understood this forest the way she knew Osprey Beach.

She picked up the emerald and tucked it into an

inside pocket of her backpack. After replacing Rory's long line with a standard leash, she told him to heel and trudged up the hill. To her surprise, standing on the small rise did, indeed, allow her to make a phone call.

Rather than calling 9-1-1, however, she called Charlie. Unlike her, Charlie could tell the ambulance driver the best way to reach this part of the mine.

As she explained what happened, Charlie's sleepy voice grew more alert. He assured her he'd make the call and then join her at the mine. She asked him to wake Scott and bring him along.

Comfortable now that help was on the way, she returned to Tommy Hicks. She found him squatting at the edge of the mine, apparently talking to Michael Dunning.

"Don't tell me your mother would condone killing someone for that emerald!" Tommy said. "Amy was a good woman."

"You have no idea who she was," Michael snarled.

"I know she'd have given you a whumpin' for settin' up my grandson."

Kim reached Tommy and peered into the mine. Michael had dragged himself away from the edge of the shelf. Though he now lay only a few inches from the drop off, he was at less risk of falling should he lose consciousness.

Seeing her face, he scowled.

"If you help me out of here now," he said, "I won't press charges against you, the old man and your damn dog."

"Press charges? For what?"

"I was marched here at gunpoint," Michael said. "That's kidnapping. Then you and that curly-haired bear attacked me. That's assault."

"You know darn well there's more to the story then that."

"Really? Who do you think the police will believe, an esteemed lawyer or the local moonshiner and an out-of-town stranger?"

Tommy's shoulders slumped.

"Maybe you should give it to him," he said. "Durn thing's cursed, anyway."

Kim's fists clenched. Grandpa had told her to never back down from a bully. But how could she stop this sociopath from ruining more lives with his lies?

Sensing her doubt, Michael pressed his point.

"Help me out of here and give me the emerald. Otherwise, I'll have you and the old man arrested and your vicious dog destroyed."

Run! Take Rory and leave, just like Dorothy ran away with Toto in The Wizard of Oz.

But Dorothy's flight hadn't solved her problems.

Sensing her anxiety, Rory whimpered and leaned into her. She stroked his neck. Her mind whirred.

Michael Dunning's accusations were no more real than The Wizard of Oz. But the simplicity of his story made it more believable than reality.

She needed proof of Michael's duplicity. Something beyond the word of an outsider and the local pariah. The Carolina Emerald? No, Michael had never touched it and, in any event, she doubted the gemstone or the bandana that wrapped it would hold fingerprints.

Fingerprints. Something tugged at the back of her mind, but the feel of Rory moving away distracted her before the thought fully formed. She watched him trot along the mine's edge, his jaunty tail waving.

Too bad dogs couldn't testify. Their noses could more accurately identify people than the most reliable eye witnesses. The poodle probably knew of Michael's complicity long before she did.

Rory suddenly pounced on something, shook it, then turned and loped back to her. The bandana she'd hidden earlier dangled from his teeth.

The triumphant expression on his face made Kim smile. She extended her hand.

Rory, however, stopped a foot from her. Leaning over the edge of the mine, he released the bandana.

Startled, she watched the cloth unfold and float down, drifting lazily before landing on Michael's face. He snatched it away, grumbling "stupid poodle."

But Kim's attention wasn't focused on Michael. The movement of the bandana had drawn her eyes to the bottom of the mine.

"You know that story you plan to tell the police?" she said. "Nice try. But the evidence is on our side."

She pointed to the shotgun laying on the mine's floor.

"When the police recover the gun, they'll find your fingerprints overlaying Tommy's."

Michael scowled.

Kim smirked.

"Cheer up, you've just learned a valuable lesson: Never underestimate a girl and her poodle."

CHAPTER 28

Michael was still cursing when Scott burst through the trees. Kim leaped to her feet and ran into his arms. Rory danced around them while she clung to Scott and fought back tears.

Scott stroked her back.

"Since you insist on scaring me," he said, "I hope you like gray hair."

She smiled and caressed his unshaved cheek.

"How can a girl resist a man who runs to the rescue?"

He blushed and ran a hand across his scratchy chin.

"You really like this look?"

"Stop fishing for compliments."

He grinned. "Charlie and Rachael are waiting by the road so they can guide the paramedics and sheriff here."

The smile disappeared and his brow wrinkled. He brushed a lock of hair from her face.

"Wanna tell me what happened?"

His touch made her stomach flutter. She felt her face flush. And yet, just being near him made her feel safe.

Was she falling in love?

Brushing the thought aside, she closed her hand over his. With one hand clenching Scott's and the other gripping Rory's leash, she described Tommy marching Michael to the mine at gun point, Rory pulling the emerald from Michael's backpack, Michael striking Tommy with a rock, the sound of the shotgun blasting, Michael aiming the gun.

"If Rory hadn't acted so quickly . . ." Her voice trailed off.

Scott squeezed her hand.

"Maybe the sheriff will give him a medal."

She smiled. "Maybe when I return the emerald to the museum, they'll erect a statue of Rory. They can fit it between Lewis and Clark."

Rory's wagging tail announced the presence of someone behind her.

"Won't be any statues if Amy's son has his way," Tommy said.

Kim stepped to the side so she could see both Tommy and Scott.

"Michael can invent as many stories as he wants," she said, "but the evidence supports us."

Tommy shook his head. "Now he's claimin' his fingerprints are on top 'cause he took the gun away from me. But that he warn't gonna shoot us."

"It will be his word against ours."

Despite her confident words, the back of Kim's neck prickled. Would Michael convince the authorities that he was innocent? As a lawyer, he knew how to exploit the legal system. Even if the sheriff believed Kim's story, he couldn't stop a judge from releasing a well-respected lawyer on bail. Once free, Michael could systematically intimidate or even eliminate anyone who might testify against him.

She pulled her phone from her pocket.

"We need to talk to Drew."

"I'll do it," Scott said. "It'll take a few minutes for me to get a cell signal."

"You'll be able to call from there." Kim pointed to the small mound of dirt.

Scott raised an eyebrow, but followed her instructions.

"Maybe we'd better not talk to anyone until Drew arrives," Kim said.

Tommy snorted. "No problem. I never talk to cops."

Rory's bark announced the arrival of Charlie and Rachael. As Rachael enveloped Kim in a hug, paramedics, sheriff deputies and emergency workers emerged from the forest. Kim directed them to the edge of the mine.

"Michael Dunning fell in," she said, "but he landed on a ledge. His leg might be broken."

One worker pulled a radio from her belt and requested a rescue squad and stretcher. The second kneeled by the mine and tossed medical questions at Michael.

Detective Cummings, the hotshot investigator assigned to the Kirk Ballas murder, appeared and marched the mine's edge.

"I'll wait in the shade."

Tommy quickly shuffled away.

Remembering the detective's quick-to-blame reactions at Kirk's murder scene, Kim wished she could join him. Cummings was already arguing with the lead paramedic. What the heck was she doing, complaining about the workers contaminating the scene? And how would the woman react when she heard Michael Dunning's accusations?

"Sorry to see Detective Cummings here," Charlie said. "I called Uncle Walt directly, but I guess he sent the other officers ahead of him."

Two men bearing a stretcher pushed Cummings out of the way and lowered the stretcher into the mine.

Scott returned to Kim's side and wrapped an arm around her shoulders.

"Drew is on the way," he said. "He recommends

you not talk to the police until he arrives."

Kim gestured to the forest edge where Tommy now sat cross-legged. "Let's wait in the shade."

She led the way.

"Mind if we join you?" she asked Tommy.

"Cain't stop you. It's a free country."

Despite his words, the old man seemed pleased that she included him in the group.

"You know Scott and Charlie," she said, "but I don't think you've met Rachael."

To her surprise, Tommy pushed to his feet and nodded a greeting. He remained standing until Rachael joined Kim on the ground.

Rory settled in front of Kim, head resting on her feet, butt leaning against Tommy's legs. Tommy reached over and stroked the poodle's back.

"Cooper's been wanting a dog," he said. "Mebbe it's time."

Seeing an opportunity to draw him out, Kim said, "I'm surprised you all don't have a dog."

"Had a coonhound for 14 years," Tommy said. "Ol' Duke passed away six, seven months ago."

As if sensing the man's sudden sorrow, Rory rolled over and licked his hand.

Tommy grinned down at him.

"You're a good boy, but ain't no way we're bringing a poodle into the family," he said. "Got enough trouble without becoming a laughingstock."

She would have gladly chatted about dog breeds, but Rachael interrupted and demanded an accounting of this morning's events. As Kim once again described Michael's treachery, Charlie grew increasingly agitated.

"Michael was never my brothers' friend, was he?" Charlie said. "He's been looking for the emerald all along."

Before she could answer, Tommy said, "It's cursed, you know."

"See?" Rachael said. "Told you so."

Rather than argue, Kim said, "Sometimes beautiful gemstones bring out people's worse instincts. The Hope Diamond, the Black Prince's Ruby, the Black Orlov, Koh-I-Noor and Sancy diamonds were all said to be cursed."

"Good thing you're sending it back to the museum," Rachael said. "Let them deal with the curse."

Rachael's eyes suddenly widened.

"Hey, maybe the museum directors will be so grateful they'll name the emerald after you!"

Heat spread up Kim's cheeks. After Donny stole the emerald from the cabin, she hadn't had time to fantasize about returning the emerald to the museum. Was her childhood dream really going to come true?

Rachael linked her arm through Charlie's.

"So when are you going to find me an emerald?"

"Actually, I think Kim deserves the next one I find." Charlie tossed Kim an infectious smile. "Thanks for insisting Rachael share her fears about moving here. I was able to allay her concerns about being accepted in the community. As for her job, she's going to talk to the museum board about going on archeological digs."

He tossed Rachael a stern look. "But if the board refuses her request, she'll allow Dad to step in."

Kim's mouth dropped open. Rachael shrugged.

"Charlie told me I shouldn't let pride stand in the way of happiness," she said. "And in return for Mark's help, I'll quit whining about the wedding."

Kim laughed. "Sounds like a fair exchange."

Shouting drew their attention back to the mine. One of the workers now stood at the top, maneuvering the end of the stretcher. Michael's head appeared, then the rest of his body. The men lifted Michael, stretcher and all, onto a gurney.

Detective Cummings blocked the gurney. The paramedics argued and, for a moment, Kim wondered if the detective would arrest them. But Michael waved his hands and the rescue workers backed off.

Cummings leaned over the lawyer and appeared to be listening. Though her face remained expressionless, a slight stiffening of her body revealed excitement or anger or . . .

Cummings glared over at them. Her eyes raked over Kim, Rory and Tommy.

Kim's stomach clenched.

"He's telling his lies. Where the heck is Drew?"

"And Uncle Walt," Charlie said. "I can't imagine

what's taking him so long--"

He broke off as Sheriff Spits and Drew McDonald strode into view. The two men were laughing as if sharing a joke.

Kim leaped to her feet. "Can you take care of Rory while I talk with Drew?"

Scott accepted the leash. "Go get him, tiger."

As soon as Drew noticed her approach, he broke away from the sheriff and motioned her to a spot out of hearing distance of the others.

"I think I have some good news," he said, "but why don't you first tell me about this morning."

As she described the events for the third time, her emotions flatlined. She longed to crawl into a corner and withdraw from the world.

"Michael plans to tell the police that he never intended to shoot me, that he was only acting in self-defense," she concluded. "He's a respected local lawyer. I'm an outsider and Tommy is . . . well, he's not what people think, but no one is going to believe him."

Drew's smile chased away her exhaustion.

"Michael's reputation has become quite tarnished," Drew said. "A few hours ago, Rocky DiSoto turned himself in, saying he feared for his life. He called Michael a murderer and blackmailer. He babbled to anyone who'd listen and demanded police protection."

Rocky's story closely matched Kim's theory. Michael had, indeed, discovered the three friends illegally digging in the Hamptons' mine. Rather than call the police -- and face questions about his own night-time excursions -- he blackmailed Donny, Kirk and Rocky into sharing any gemstones they found.

On the night of the murder, Michael surprised the three men by demanding they break into Charlie's cabin to steal the Carolina Emerald. He told them he had a buyer and that he'd split the money with them.

"Only a fool would believe that," Kim said.

"That was Kirk's reaction. He advised the others against any more dealings with Michael. The four men were arguing when they heard someone crashing through the woods."

"Charlie."

Drew nodded. "Michael sneaked up behind Charlie, knocked him out and then shot Kirk. The others were so horrified that they agreed to do whatever Michael told them."

"Where did Michael get the gun?"

"He must have brought it with him to the mine. It was a throw-down gun with the serial numbers removed."

"I guess framing Charlie for the murder was Michael's revenge for the way the Hamptons treated his family." She frowned. "But Rocky's story doesn't prove anything. It's still his word against Michael's."

"That's where the good news comes in," Drew

said. "My investigator interviewed someone who, on the night of the murder, saw a car parked by the road. This was well before you heard the gun shots. The witness remembered the car because it looked like the driver had attempted to hide it."

He grinned. "But she could still see the license plate: LWYRUP. The plate, of course, belongs to Michael Dunning's car."

"But the witness's statement does nothing but place Michael at the mine before the rest of us. She didn't see him pull the trigger."

He patted her shoulder.

"Have patience. We build a case one brick at a time."

"Did Rocky admit to stealing the emerald?"

"Claims that Donny was the one who actually broke into the cabin. Donny planned to sell the emerald at the Gem Festival, saying they'd use the money to disappear far from Michael's influence. But the gem cutters and dealers dismissed his claims of finding an eight-inch emerald at a public digging place."

Kim snorted. "To find emeralds that size, you need to dig deep enough to reach rock that hasn't been eroded by the weather. That requires heavy equipment."

"Well, Donny's ignorance cost him his life," Drew said. "Michael was furious when he discovered Donny was trying to sell the emerald. He told Donny that if he returned the emerald, Michael would honor the original deal to split the sale price."

"More stories. Michael should have gone into politics."

"Well, this time he wasn't convincing. Both Rocky and Donny recognized that once they returned the emerald, Michael would kill them as the only witnesses to the murder of Kirk."

"So why hide the emerald in Michael's backpack?"

Drew rolled his eyes. "That was another one of Donny's schemes. He thought they could flee the area and, once out of Michael's grasp, place an anonymous call to the police. First, however, they needed money."

"Which is why they kidnapped Deb's dog."

Drew nodded. "Michael, of course, found the cabin where they were hiding. Rocky claims Michael shot Donny and tried to shoot him. The police will take another look at the cabin to see if any of the evidence supports Rocky's allegation."

"Too bad you can't legally use hearsay. Michael practically confess . . ." Her breath caught. She gripped Drew's arm.

"Michael told us he hadn't planned to shoot Donny, that the gun went off when Donny threw a lamp at him. Did the police find a broken lamp?"

"I'll have to ask Walt. Why is that important?"

"Scott and I never entered Donny's cabin. So how would I know about a broken lamp unless Michael told me? That makes it no longer hearsay, right?"

"It's not quite as simple as that, but you've given me some leverage."

They turned to study the cluster of people gathered around Michael Dunning's stretcher.

"I've never understood people who kill for money," Kim said. "Accidentally killing to protect yourself or a loved one makes a certain amount of sense. But Michael shows no remorse for what he's done."

Drew laid a hand on her shoulder.

"That's why I left the public defender's office," he said. "I never found an answer. Don't think about it. You'll just drive yourself nuts."

She sighed. "I'm a psychology professor. I get paid to drive myself nuts."

Drew chuckled.

She thanked Drew for his help, then trotted back to the others. Plunking onto the ground between Tommy and Scott, she pulled Rory into her arms and related her conversation to the others.

"Sounds like it's all going to work out." Rachael stood and dusted off her jeans.

"I don't know about you," she said, "but I need a shower and coffee, not necessarily in that order. After you called, we immediately threw on clothes and drove over here."

"Maybe pancakes are in order," Scott said. "Tommy, would you like to join us?"

Tommy's eyes widened.

"Uh, no, I'd best be getting back to the homestead."

Kim told the others to start walking without her. She wanted a few minutes alone with Tommy.

As soon as they were out of hearing range, Kim touched Tommy's arm.

"You know I have to return the Carolina Emerald to the museum, right?"

Tommy sighed. "Durn thing's caused nothing but problems. Best to take the curse away from here."

"Would you like to see it? With all that's been happening, you never had the opportunity to hold it."

She pulled the bandana-wrapped emerald from her backpack and carefully unwrapped it. A ray of sunlight struck the stone, illuminating the perfect green color.

She placed it in Tommy's work-roughened hands.

He cradled it, his eyes wide like a child's.

"Sure is purdy, ain't it?" he said. "I wish Amy--"

His voice caught and he shoved the emerald into Kim's hands. She wrapped the bandana around the stone, pretending to not notice the single tear that crawled down his cheek.

"You were the one who helped her run away, weren't you?"

Tommy dipped his chin.

"Why didn't you go with her?"

He stared at the ground. A minute passed.

Nearby, a mockingbird sang. Dry leaves rustled as a squirrel searched for the perfect spot to bury an acorn.

Just when she thought he wouldn't answer, he started talking.

"She wouldn't have me." He snorted. "Before she died, her mother filled Amy's mind with uppity thoughts. The Hickses weren't good enough. 'Course, Amy was too nice to put it like that. Just said she considered me a friend, nothin' more."

"I'm so sorry."

Tommy's shoulders straightened.

"Don't matter. I met me a wonderful woman, we had three fine boys and eight healthy grandchildren. The cancer took Susie afore she could hold her first great-grandson in her arms.

"But some day, I'm gonna take Cooper to that fancy museum, show him the statues of those explorers, teach him that he kin do whatever his mind sets about doin'."

Kim smiled, imagining Tommy and Cooper standing hand-in-hand in front of the American Museum of Natural History, gazing up at the words "Truth, Knowledge, Vision."

The powerful words had spoken to generations of people, young and old, lighting the way to a brighter future. Maybe Cooper's life would be happier than his grandfather's.

And maybe Kim could make at least part of Tommy's dream come true.

"I bet the museum offers a reward for the safe return the Carolina Emerald," she said.

Tommy brightened. "Enough to take Cooper and his folks to New York?"

"Certainly."

And, if the museum directors refused to reward Tommy, Kim would scrounge together the money for a family trip to New York.

"Just promise me that when you visit the museum, you'll show Cooper the display holding the Carolina Emerald," she said. "There will be a plaque attached to it. It will thank Tommy Hicks of Hiddenite, North Carolina for the safe return of the emerald."

"My name? Why would anyone thank me?"

"Because Amy Sawyer's mother was wrong. You're a good man, Tommy Hicks. Good enough for Amy and good enough to be recognized by a world-renowned museum."

She smiled.

"Maybe they'll even name the emerald after you."

Tommy gawked at her. Then he grinned and his eyes twinkled.

"Don't suppose you could git 'em to make a statue of me, could you?"

Kim laughed. "I'll see what I can do."

She kissed Tommy's cheek, then crossed the field to join Scott and the others.

Scott reached for her hand.

"You're going to ask the museum board to name the emerald after Tommy, aren't you?"

Kim's mouth fell open.

"How did you know?"

"Your empathy for others is one of the things I love about you."

"Love?"

Scott brought her hand to his lips and kissed it.

"Yeah, love."

DEAR READER

Thank you for reading *The Carolina Emerald*. If you enjoyed it, please tell a friend. Or tell many friends by writing a review on your favorite site. Sometimes it's hard to find a new author, so we must rely on each other for recommendations.

This book was such fun to write in part because I got to tour a real, honest-to-goodness North Carolina emerald mine. To read more about the stories behind the story, please visit my web site and join *The Diamond Digest*, my (mostly) monthly email to select readers. For more about *The Carolina Emerald*, please turn the page.

I've never been the greatest speller, so all of my books are extensively reviewed by professional editors and proofreaders. If, however, you do find an error, please email me at Lynn@LynnFranklin.com so I can fix it.

Actually, you can email me even if you don't find problems. I love to hear from my readers. You are the reason that I write.

LynnFranklin.com

Five Fun Facts About The Carolina Emerald

1. Dash, the current model for Rory, does, indeed, open zippers. He learned to do this as a puppy when Lynn unwittingly allowed him to play with Tucker, the long-haired dachshund model for Al. As an incorrigible food thief, Tucker perfected the find/open/grab skills when he discovered visitors often secreted goodies in their suitcases, purses and backpacks. Dash uses his nefarious talents to entertain families, friends and, unfortunately, total strangers.

2. Lynn's idea for *The Carolina Emerald* was triggered by an article recapping infamous jewel thief Murph the Surf's burglary of The American Museum of Natural History. The reporter mentioned in passing that Jack Murphy wasn't the first thief to break into the museum and abscond with jewels. Further research revealed that in 1950 unknown thieves entered through an open window and stole a small fortune in gems. Unlike Murphy, these thieves were never caught. Their haul included a 1,300-carat emerald from North Carolina. The Sawyer and Hicks families are fictional. But you can find a photo of the stolen emerald on Lynn's web site.

3. The first American Gold Rush did occur in

North Carolina. Rock hunters still occasionally find gold as well as emeralds, sapphires, rubies, amethyst, aquamarine, citrine and garnets. If you'd like to try your hand at gem hunting, you'll find a list of sites open to the public on Lynn's web site.

4. The Hamptons' emerald mine is fictional, but is based on a real U.S. mine. You can find photos of a North Carolina emerald mine on Lynn's web site.

5. People who enjoyed *The Carolina Emerald* also liked *The Blue Diamond* and *The Pirate's Ruby*. If you missed out on the first two in the series, don't worry; you can read them out of order. They are available on Amazon and Kobo. You can find more information on Lynn's web site. Or turn the page.

Other Books in the Series

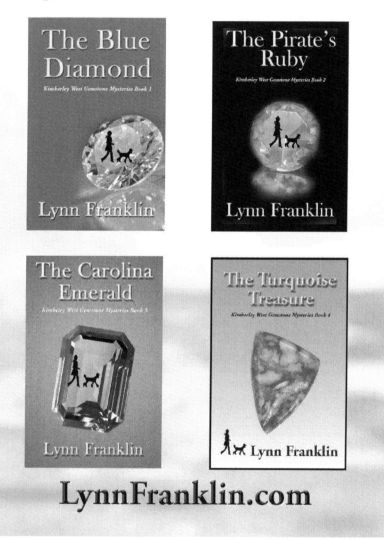

Seven Little-Known Facts about Lynn Franklin

1. Lynn's first-grade teacher predicted she would grow up to be a writer. We don't know if this was because of Lynn's proficiency with the English language or her propensity to scare the other children by telling ghost stories during recess.

2. Lynn's parents begged her to consider a more practical career, one that would actually earn money.

3. In response, Lynn created a list of alternative careers: circus trick rider, rodeo barrel chaser, treasure hunter, dog trainer and pirate. Her parents shot down each one. They also dissuaded her from becoming a paleontologist ("not enough jobs") or oceanographer (ditto).

4. Nancy Drew's adventures -- not to mention her spiffy red convertible -- inspired Lynn to create the perfect career. She would become a detective who

wrote mystery novels. This time she didn't share her aspirations with anyone.

5. To hone her detecting skills, Lynn used the cover of a forested park to spy on her neighbors.

One day, when she was ten years old, she followed the smell of burning paper to find a grizzly-bear-sized man ripping a manuscript and tossing the pages into a fire. The man's furtive head swivels convinced Lynn his actions were illegal.

Was he burning stolen FBI files, evidence of his criminal activities?

Peering from behind a tree, Lynn strained to read the mysterious document. But she was too far away.

She held her breath and creeped forward. Closer, closer . . .

A twig snapped.

The man's head whipped around. He pinned her with dark, evil eyes.

"What are you doing here?" he growled.

Lynn lifted her chin.

"Spying on you."

Her audacious answer distracted the man long enough for her to disappear into the woods before he could capture and hold her for ransom.

6. To this day, we're not sure Lynn's parents would have paid a ransom.

7. Lynn never became a detective.

Book Club Questions for The Carolina Emerald

1. Cooper accused Kim of harboring prejudices against his family. Have you ever had an experience where your thoughts or behavior were dictated by existing (known or unknown) prejudices? Were you surprised? How did you deal with it?

2. In the Prologue, Kim witnessed a class of children shun a boy dressed in old clothes. As a child, did you see discrimination based on income, race, social class? How did that influence your own behavior toward the child? How did the experience affect you as an adult?

3. What were your thoughts when Kim first visited the Hicks family? Did you fear for Kim's life? Why or why not?

4. Though we in the U.S. believe we don't have a socio-economic caste system like the one in India, Kim witnesses several episodes of upper class discrimination against the lower classes. What advice would you give to the Hicks family for overcoming this prejudice?

5. Do you think private land owners have a right to deny rock hounds and archeologists access to their land? Why or why not?

6. Who were your favorite characters in the book? What traits attracted you to those characters?

7. Were you surprised to learn that emeralds can be found in North Carolina? Have you hunted for gemstones in the United States?

8. What was your favorite gem legend in the story?

9. Cleopatra's favorite gem was emerald. Do you have a favorite gemstone? What draws you to it?

10. Even though Sheriff Spitz was a minor character in the story, the author chose to not depict him as a stereotypical redneck cop. What do you think of the author's decision? How did that decision affect the story?

11. Several characters in *The Carolina Emerald* have unusual hobbies. Kim goes rock hounding whenever she has time. Rita Thompson learned to do quilling. Jan Mayr dances with her dogs. Do you have an unusual hobby? What drew you to it? How does your hobby enrich your life?

12. Despite his diminutive size, Jack the papillon helps his wheelchair-bound mistress remain independent. There are also dogs who assist people who can't see or hear, veterans suffering from PTSD, children with diabetes or epilepsy. Discuss the role of service and support dogs in society. Why do you think dogs are so responsive to helping humans?

Acknowledgements

Thank you everyone who's written to me, posted reviews of my books or simply read and enjoyed the series. You are the reason I write.

A special thank you to everyone who entered the various "name the character" contests. For *The Carolina Emerald*, three contests resulted in three delightful winners.

Rita Thompson, winner of the drawing at Dickinson's Jewelers, is a world traveler who's dabbled in many craft activities. Rita's most recent craft -- quilling -- opened a new world to me. I hope you enjoyed reading about Rita and quilling.

Carol Malec won the DogRead drawing and the chance to name a dog character. The real Jack the papillon is not a service dog (though I've known papillons who performed all of the actions described here). But his appearance, "pappy feet" behavior and delight with standard poodles is real. Thank you, Carol, for introducing me to your wonderful papillon.

Jan Mayr won the contest held exclusively for members of *The Diamond Digest*. Her hobby of dancing with her border collies gave me the perfect opening act for the fictional Gem Festival entertainment. Anyone want to see Kim and Rory dance in a future book? If you do, send an email to Lynn@LynnFranklin.com.

The emerald mine owner who gave me a tour of

his mine asked that I not use his name. But I still want to thank him for showing me around a real, working mine.

Beta readers are invaluable to authors and I've got the most wonderful group. Special thanks to Charlene Dunlap, Jon Franklin, Adina Gewirtz, Doni Reisland and Joan Rose.

In addition to the beta readers, I'd like to thank the friends and family who encouraged me through the long process of producing this book. There are too many to name here, but I'd like to acknowledge Virginia Reinhart, Michelle Rockhill, Dolly, Phil, Karen and Cherish Scheidhauer, Kathy and Claude Dickinson and the members of the Poodle Support Group.

Finally, a special shout-out to Rhonda Pacchioli of Apacchi Standard Poodles. After my darling Sam died of old age, Rhonda introduced my husband and me to one of her fabulous litters. All nine puppies were gorgeous, but Apacchi Dashiell Hammett insisted he be the one to come home with us. Dash has been a pure joy and I daily bless Rhonda for her dedication to breeding healthy poodles with amazing temperaments.

Made in the USA
Middletown, DE
18 April 2021